MORE
COLLECTED
STORIES

MORE
COLLECTED
STORIES

V. S. Pritchett

VINTAGE BOOKS
A DIVISION OF RANDOM HOUSE
NEW YORK

First Vintage Books Edition, January 1985
Copyright © 1983 by V. S. Pritchett
All rights reserved under International and Pan-American
Copyright Conventions.
Published in the United States by Random House, Inc.,
New York. Originally published by Random House, Inc.
in 1983.

Most of the stories have been previously published in the
following Random House, Inc., or
Alfred A. Knopf, Inc., publications: *The Camberwell
Beauty, On the Edge of the Cliff, Blind
Love and Other Stories, When My Girl Comes Home,* and
*Sailor, Sense of Humor and
Other Stories.*
Four stories were previously published by Chatto &
Windus, Ltd., London.

The following stories originally appeared
in *The New Yorker:* "The Nest Builder,"
"The Liars," "The Rescue," "The Necklace,"
"Passing the Ball," "The Landlord," and
"The Ladder."

Library of Congress Cataloging in Publication Data

Pritchett, V. S. (Victor Sawdon), 1900–
More collected stories.

I. Title.
PR6031.R7A6   1985   823'.912   84-40018
ISBN 0-394-72584-0 (pbk.)

Manufactured in the United States of America

For my wife

Contents

CONTENTS

MORE
COLLECTED
STORIES

Our Oldest Friend

"Look out!" someone said. "Here comes Saxon."

It was too late. Moving off the dance floor and pausing at the door with the blatant long sight of the stalker, Saxon saw us all in our quiet corner of the lounge and came over. He stopped and stood with his hands on his hips and his legs apart, like a goalkeeper. Then he came forward.

"Ah! This *is* nice!" he crowed, in the cockerel voice that took us back to the Oxford years. He pulled up a chair and placed it so that none of us could easily get out. It passed through our heads that we had seen that dinner jacket of his before. He must have had it since the last term at school. It was short, eager and juvenile in the sleeves, and now his chest had bolstered it, he seemed to be bursting with buns and toffee. A piece of stiff fair hair stuck up boyishly at the back. He crossed his short legs and squeezed them with satisfaction as his sharp blue eyes looked around our circle over his strong glasses.

"How awfully nice." For niceness was everything for him. "Everyone is here," he said and nodded back to the people on the dance floor. "Jane Fawcett, Sanderson-Brown, Tony Jameson and Eileen—I missed them in Brussels, they'd just left for Munich—very nice catching them here. With the Williamsons!"

He ran off a list of names, looking over one lens of the glasses that were not quite straight on his young enthusiastic nose as he spoke them, and marking each name with a sly look of private knowledge. We were the accused—accused not so much of leaving him out of things, as of thinking, by so doing, that he *was* out of them. His short, trotting legs were infallible in old acquaintance. Names from the past, names that we had forgotten from school and then Oxford, came out, and made our wives look across at us at first with bewilderment and then set them to whispering and giggling.

"What are you doing, Saxon?" someone said. "Are you still on the Commission?"

"In principle, yes; in practice," said Saxon, uttering his favourite words, "I'm the liaison between Ways and Means and the Working Party."

"The liaison!" one of the wives said.

"Yes. It's awfully nice. It works very well. We have to keep in touch with the subcommittees. I saw the Dustman the other day. He's a trustee now, he came in from Arbitration."

"The Dustman?" Mrs. Selby said to her husband.

"Oxford," said Selby. "Lattersmith. Economist. Very old. He was called the Dustman because he was very dirty."

"Tessa's father," Saxon said. And as he shot the name of Tessa at us, he grinned at each one of us in turn to see what could be found in our faces. There are things in the past that become geological. Selby's face became as red as Aberdeen marble; some of us turned to sandstone; one or two to millstone grit or granite; that was how alarm and disclaimer took us.

"Your oldest friend," said Mrs. Selby to her husband, grinding out the phrase.

"In principle, yes, in practice, no," said Selby, bitterly mocking Saxon's well-known phrase.

"*My* oldest friend, if you please," said Thomas, always a rescuer.

"And mine!" two of us said together, backing him up.

"Is she yours?" said kind Jenny Fox to me.

"She is the 'oldest friend' of all of us."

We laughed together loudly, but not in unity of tone. Hargreaves was too loud, Fox was too frivolous, Selby was frightened and two or three laughs were groans. There was something haphazard, hollow, insincere and unlasting about our laughter, but Day saved us by saying in his deep grave voice to Saxon: "We ought to settle this. Who *is* Tessa's oldest friend? When did *you* meet Tessa, Saxon?"

"Selby and I were at school with her, at Asaph's."

"You didn't tell me that," said Selby's wife to her husband.

"I tried to get her to come tonight," said Saxon. "She's gone out with the Dustman. He said they might drop in later."

Our wives put on stiff faces: one or two picked up their handbags and looked at the door on to the dance floor, as if they were going to search it, and even the building. The incident was one of Saxon's always unanswerable successes, but once more Thomas saved us. He said to Saxon, "So *you're* her oldest friend."

And Selby said grimly, "Yes, you were at Asaph's a year before me."

"Saxon! You've been holding out on us," we said with false jollity.

One of the ladies nodded at us and said to her neighbour: "They seem to be a club."

The pious pretence on the part of our wives that they did not know Tessa Lattersmith was, in its way, brilliant in our embarrassed state. It brought out the hypocrisy in Harry James, who said in a light-headed way, "She's married now, I suppose?"

"Oh, no," said Saxon. "She's carrying on." And he meant carrying on, as it were, in the sense of working hard on the joint committee, himself informed because he was, after all, the liaison.

"You mean," said Mrs. Selby, "she hasn't found anyone's husband willing?"

"Shame!" said Saxon as at an annual general meeting. "Shame."

"Perhaps," said the kind young Jenny Fox, "she doesn't want to be married."

"She's very rich," said James.

"Very attractive," said Day.

"Big gobbling eyes."

"Lovely voice."

"I don't agree," said Fox. "It bodes. It comes creeping into you. It gets under your shirt. It seems to come up from the floor. Expensive clothes, though."

"Not like the Dustman's!" shouted Thomas, rescuing us again. "D'you remember? I used to see him at the station waiting for the Oxford train. He used to walk up to the very last bench on the platform, and flop down. I thought he was a tramp kipping down for the night, the first time. His clothes were creased as though he'd slept in them. He had that old suitcase, made of cardboard I should say, tied with string—and parcels of books tied up. Like Herbert Spencer. You know Herbert Spencer had to have everything tied to him? He sat there looking wretched and worn-out, with his mouth open, and his thick hair looked full of dust—a real layabout from the British Museum. He hardly got his feet off the ground when he walked, but sort of trudged, as if he was wading through sand. He must be well past seventy."

"No, he's barely sixty. Tessa's only thirty-two."

"Thirty-seven," said Mrs. Selby.

"He's sixty-two," said Saxon. "Tessa is a year younger than me."

"The Lattersmiths were rich," said James again. "I mean compared with the rest of us."

"The Dustman's wife had the money," said Thomas.

"She belonged to one of those big shipping families. Did you ever see her? She's like Tessa—oh, she comes after you with those big solemn eyes."

"We went to see her, didn't we?" Day said to his wife. "She saw Diana's necklace, her eyes were fixed on it . . ."

"*And* my rings!"

"She just wanted them. Greedy. She couldn't bear it that Diana had something that she hadn't got."

"She wanted you as well," said Diana.

"Oh," said Tom, the rescuer. "There's nothing in that. Old Ma Dustman wanted me too, in fact she wanted all of us. 'I am so worried about Tessa, I wish she'd settle down. I wish she'd find a nice husband —now *you*, you're fond of Tessa, I'm sure.' "

"Shame!" called Saxon again.

We had forgotten about him; he was sweating as he watched us with delight.

"No, it's true," I said to Saxon.

"And she couldn't have them, poor things," one of the wives said and the others joined in laughing at us.

James once more pushed us into trouble.

"Did you ever go on a picnic with them? I mean when they came down to school? No? Saxon, didn't you and Selby? Didn't you? None of your camp fires with damp sticks, thermos bottles and tea slopping over the tomato sandwiches. Oh, no! And it never rained: old Ma Dustman had ordered sun down from Fortnum and Mason's. They brought the Daimler and the butler came—how did they fit him in, I wonder? I bet he went ahead in the Rolls. He set tables and chairs. Silver teapot, the best Rockingham . . ."

"Not Rockingham, it can't have been."

"Well, old Spode. Something posh. The butler handed round the stuff. I only just knew Tessa then. I had brought a girl called Sadie and Tessa brought a girl called Adelaide with her and Tessa said, 'I want you to meet Harry James. He's my oldest friend.' Sadie looked sick."

"It had started then?" some of our wives cried out.

"Long before that," I said. "In the cradle."

"Exactly what she said just before we were married when you introduced me," said Mrs. Day to her husband.

"She said it to me at our wedding," said Mrs. Selby, and glaring at her husband, "I don't know *why.*"

"I don't get what her fascination for you all was!" said sly Mrs. James.

"Oh," we all said largely, in a variety of voices, "I don't know . . . She was about . . ."

"You know, I think it was sex," said Jenny Fox.

"Was it sex?" We looked at each other, putting as much impartiality as we could into the inquiry.

"Sex! Of course it was sex," said Mrs. Selby, putting her chin up and gripping her handbag on her knee.

"Not for me," said Harry James.

"Nor me." One wife squeezed her husband's hand.

"Why not?"

This dumbfounded us. We huddled together. Why had none of us made a pass? Were we frightened?

"You took her to picture galleries," said Mrs. Selby.

"Yes," said Selby. "She did nothing but talk about a man called Cézanne."

"That's it. A whole party of us went to Parma and she did nothing but talk of a man called Fabrice," said Tom.

"Fabrice?"

"Stendhal," said Saxon.

"I had Lawrence in Rome."

"There was always another man. Anyone have Picasso? Or Giacometti?" said James.

"Who did you have, Selby? Russell? Einstein?"

Selby had had enough. With the treachery of the desperate, he said, "She talked of nothing but you, James."

"No," said Tom the rescuer. "You can't have had. *I* had you, James."

"I had Tom."

"Day was my trouble."

"With me it was Bill."

"What a lovely daisy chain," one of the wives said. "The whole distinguished lot of you. Who's missing?"

"Saxon," Jenny Fox said.

We all stared accusingly at him. Saxon went on squeezing himself. He looked archly over his glasses.

"I had the Dustman," he said complacently.

We laughed, but Mrs. Selby silenced us and said to Saxon, "Go on. You're the only one who's telling the truth."

"She was always very worried about the Dustman," he said. "They're a wretched family. He scarcely ever goes home."

And at this, the band started again and Saxon got up and asked my wife to dance. We were left with Saxon's picture of that rich girl alone in the world. Before the evening was out he had danced with each one of our wives. We all grinned and said, "Look at old Saxon at the end-of-term dance."

If there was one non-dancer on the floor, it was he. His feet, rather like the Dustman's, trudged, in straight, fated lines, deep in sand, enthusiastically deep. He danced, as it were, in committee. Our wives found themselves in the grip of one who pushed them around, all the time looking askance from side to side as if they were sections or subsections for which he was trying to find a place in some majority report. They lost their power to dance. The matter had become desperately topographical to them; while he, as he toiled on, was running off the names of people.

"I saw him in Paris on the second day of the conference."
Or:

"They were in New York when Foreign Relations met the working party."
Or:

"They ran into one another in Piccadilly when the delegation met the trustees. Thompson, Johnson, Hobson, Timson, Richardson, Wilkinson—" Our wives returned to us like new editions of *Who's Who*.

Except Mrs. Selby. She was much taller than he and on the floor she had the prosecuting look of one who was going to wring what she wanted out of Saxon. She did not look down at him but over his head at the piece of fair hair that stuck up at the back of his head. He soon had to give up his committee style. She got a grip of him, got him into corners, carried him off to the middle, turned savagely near the band,

and in this spot she shouted to him, "What's all this stuff about Tessa and the Dustman?"

And as she said it, seeing him turn to the right, she swung him round to the left, and when the dancers were thinning on the floor she planted him in a quiet spot in the middle.

"Tessa's slept with all of you, hasn't she?" she said.

"Shame!" Saxon said, stopping dead. He took off his glasses and there was a sudden change in him. Often since, seeing that naked look on his face, I have thought: How he must have hated us. I remember at school how we stuffed sausage down his neck and how he just let us do it. Sausage after sausage went down. Then off came the glasses and he backed to an open window. Now, on the dance floor, with his glasses off, Saxon suddenly began to dance—if that is the word for it—as if he had been stung. Where had he learned these extraordinary steps? —that sudden flinging wide of his short legs and arms, that strange buckling and straightening of the body, the thrusting forward and back of his punchball head, those sudden wrenchings of Mrs. Selby back and forth, and spinning her round, that general air of looking for a knockout on the rebound off the ropes. Mrs. Selby's firm eyes were disordered as she tried to foresee his movements, and amid the disorder she was magnetized by the fiendish rhythm of his feet and by the austere look of his unforgiving face.

"Hasn't she?" called Mrs. Selby, in a last pitiable attempt.

The band stopped and she stood there getting her breath in the middle of the floor. Saxon, without music, dropped back into the goalkeeper stance we knew so well, with his hands on his hips and short legs apart. She was staring at Saxon, he was staring at her. It was a long stare. Selby and his partner passed them and he saw what Mrs. Selby saw: obstinate tears were forming in Saxon's naked eyes; water filled them; it dropped on his pink cheeks. He took out his glasses and pretended to wipe them with his handkerchief and put them on. He was sternly, silently, crying. Mrs. Selby put out her hand repentantly; no doubt he did not see her hand but walked with her off the floor. We were clapping in the silly way people do and someone called out: "Where did you learn that one, Saxon?"

He looked with bewilderment at us.

"I'll be back in a minute," he said and walked across the room to the outer hall of the hotel.

Mrs. Selby put herself with kind Jenny Fox and whispered to her for

a long time and Mrs. Fox said, "It's not your fault. How could you
know?"

"I only *said* it," Mrs. Selby said wretchedly, looking at the swing
door that let cold air in from the outer hall when it flashed round and
where Saxon had gone.

"What was the matter with Saxon?" Selby accused.

"He's upset—nothing," said Mrs. Fox, turning to Selby as she patted
Mrs. Selby's hand. And then, arguing for herself, Mrs. Selby told us.

Presently the swing door flashed and Saxon came back and three of
us got up to offer him a chair. We gave him the best one, beside a low
table which had a brilliant lamp on it. Instantly it threw his shadow
on the white wall—a shadow that caricatured his face—the long nose,
the chin that receded, the glasses tilted as he looked askance at us, the
sprig of schoolboy hair.

"They haven't turned up yet," he said.

We looked at our Saxon with awe. It was obvious he was in love with
that rich, beautiful woman. He must always have been in love with her.
We had pulled her to pieces in front of him. What he must have been
feeling as he pretended and as he submitted to our joke! And, after all
this, she had not come. Where was she? One or two of us wanted to
get up and find her. Where would she be? We could not guess. We
had to admit that Tessa merely slummed with us. She would never
think of coming to a second-rate hotel like this or to an old Asaphians'
reunion. She'd be at some smart dinner party, something very grand
—she certainly had "oldest friends" in very grand circles. One could
imagine her long neck creeping up close to the conscience of an
archbishop. Or disturbing the shirt of an ambassador, or her boding
voice creeping up the sleeve of a banker who would be saying: "Young
lady, what are all your hippie friends up to nowadays?" at one of old
Ma Dustman's dinner parties. *She* would be stripping the jewellery off
the women and telling Sir Somebody Something that one would be a
fool to sell one's Matisses yet. The Dustman would not be there. We
tried not to look at the unmarriageable silhouette of Saxon's head on
the wall.

"Where did you pick up that wonderful step, Saxon?" Mrs. Selby
said gaily, to make amends.

Saxon gave a forgiving glance. He had recovered.

"At the Cool It," he said.

"What's the Cool It?" Thomas said.

"A club," said Saxon.

"Never heard of it."

"In the docks," said Saxon.

"The docks?"

Saxon in the docks! The liaison committees in the docks! Saxon in low life! Saxon a libertine!

"What on earth takes you to the docks? Research? Come clean. Having fun?"

In our repentance, we made a hero of him. The old sly Saxon, pleased and pink, was with us again.

"In principle, yes," said Saxon. "I sometimes go with the Dustman."

We could not speak. Saxon and the Dustman in the docks!

"What is it—a cellar?"

"It's a sewer," said Saxon complacently. "Tessa goes there with her father."

"The Dustman takes his daughter to a place like that!"

"He says it will loosen her up," said Saxon, looking for hope in our eyes. "You see, he wants her to get married."

Saxon settled back, impudently, comfortably, in the chair. The brocade enriched him and he maliciously considered us one by one.

"To a stoker?" said Selby.

"No," said Saxon. "To me—in principle. That's why I go down there. You see, she's worried about him. We go down to see he doesn't get into trouble. I had to pull him out of a nasty fight last week. We got him out. We got him home. To her place. He hates going to his."

The notion of Saxon fighting was as startling as his dance.

"She must be very grateful to you," we said politely.

"Why do you say 'marry you, in principle'?" said Selby.

"He means," Mrs. Selby explained sharply to her husband, disliking the mockery, "the Dustman is her oldest friend, older even than Saxon is. Isn't that so, Saxon?"

"In practice, yes," said Saxon, entirely forgiving her. "I'll go and have another look for them. They promised to come. The Dustman said it would be awfully nice to see us all again. I'll just go and see."

And he got up and trotted across the yards of hotel carpet that had a pattern of enormous roses. It seemed that their petals were caressing him on his way to the door. The door spun round and Saxon vanished.

Our wives said, "What a sad story!" and "What a bitch that girl is." But we thought: Good old Saxon. And: He's suffering for us. Selby put it crudely, saying, "That lets us off the hook." And then our feelings changed. There was Saxon sitting like a committee on his own feelings, delegating them incurably to subcommittees, and sitting back doing nothing, relying on an amendment. He must have been doing this for the last eight years. But this led us to another feeling. *We* would never have behaved as Saxon behaved. Each of us saw that beautiful girl in our minds and thought we would have soon pulled her out of this ridiculous obsession with the Dustman and his low life. And how often we had heard of coquettes like Tessa settling down at last in their thirties with faithful bores like Saxon, men they had snubbed over and over again before that alarming age caught them out.

We kept our eyes on the main door of the hotel and were so fixed on it that we did not notice, at once, a figure crossing the dance floor at our side and looking in at us.

"Well!" we heard Tessa's slow, only too well-known voice, dwelling raffishly on the word, so that it meant "What are you up to? You didn't think you could keep me out of this." Her large solemn eyes, as forcefully shortsighted as Saxon's were, put their warning innuendo to each of us in turn and the mouth of a beautiful Persian cat possessed us one by one. The spell was on us. A comfortable mew to each of our wives indicated that she had known us years before they had.

We were nearly screaming for help. It was for Thomas, the rescuer, to save us.

"Saxon has just gone out looking for your father."

She was up from her chair at once and making for the main door. She had fine legs, a fast passionate step, and Mrs. Selby said of her dress:

"It's expensive, but pink is hopeless if you're putting on weight."

But Selby, overeager for any hope that could be got out of the situation, said, "Did you see her when she came in? It was exactly like Saxon. Hunting. You know—in principle, yes, but in practice—well. She's a liaison too. I think the Dustman's loosened her up and found the man for her."

But no one paid much attention to Selby, for the swing door flashed and across the hall came the Dustman, Saxon and Tessa together.

"Look, Daddy," she said to the old man. He had not, of course, changed into a dinner jacket and his tweed jacket was done up on the wrong button. His trudging step, I now thought, was not so much a trudge as a scraping caused by the probability that he was swinging by an invisible rope hooked to the seat of his learned trousers.

"Look," she said, "all my oldest friends!"

And Saxon stood apart with his hands on his hips, watching, his legs apart, keeping goal, wistful, admiring, triumphant.

"Who's dancing?" piped the old man. And soon all of us were on the floor, the Dustman shoving Mrs. Selby along as if to her doom, and Tessa following him with her eyes all the time, as Saxon leaped into his passionate, dreadful and unavailing antics all round her. Once in a while she would note where he was, open her mouth to say something pleasant, and then coldly change her mind.

1969

The Nest Builder

$$\text{⬦}$$

I have lost Ernest. We had been partners for a long time, but after a difficult year and the fiasco at Albine Rise, he went. Interior decoration is a hard, even a savage, trade; customers come to us not quite knowing what they want, but they know (and we know) that they want Perfection. That is very expensive. And there is a sad side to Perfection; there are losses, as you see around you in this shop now. They are Ernest's losses. The two cabinets in yellow lacquer, for example—Mrs. Cross, I call them. They were sent back by Mr. Cross, just when Ernest had finished the Chinese drawing room for her. Mr. Cross divorced her. There is Mrs. Raddock—the Empire sofa and the three chairs. She divorced Mr. Raddock, actually before we got the marble pillars into Mr. Raddock's study. The Hepplewhite four-poster, waiting to go into Cheyne Row while Ernest was still getting the Italian bathroom right —Mr. Fortescue died. A tragic business—but we get that, too, in the trade. The mirrors and consoles are Mrs. Hunstable, Mrs. Smith, and Lady Hatch, mirrors being a fate with Ernest. The moment he puts gilded mirrors with branches, cherubs, angels, scrolls, shells, or lions into a house, someone falls down the stairs, or there is a sarcastic scene between husband and wife or mother and daughter, and high talk of vanity, adultery, loss of looks or figure, even of camp or chichi; the next thing one hears is that the lease is for sale, then the accounts are disputed and the goods come back. The doctor or the lawyer, they say, sees deepest into the secrets of people's lives. I do not agree.

Yet it wasn't because of these losses that Ernest left us. They in fact stimulated his creative gift. When lacquer cabinets, Hepplewhite beds, mirrors, and so on, come back, he stands there stroking his small, soft beard, gazing at them at first as if personally affronted. Then one eyebrow goes up and he recognizes with admiration their extraordinary power to wreck human lives, and turns on me a gentle, conspiring, worldly young eye. "George, dear boy!" he says. "Mrs. Grant, I think —don't you? Or who was that woman who rang up yesterday?" And he would pay me a compliment, too. "George," he often said to me, "what a nose you have for booty!" He would be thinking of times when I came back from some place in the country with an Adam fireplace, a triptych, a gout stool, or a big chunk of Spanish choir stall, or had added to our collection of rare cattle pictures. My task was to go round to the auctions, to get into early Industrial Revolution houses in the North, to smell round rectories, look into the stabling of country houses, squint into the family detritus. That is, when I had the time, for I also had to deal with the trouble Ernest created for builders and painters, and his sneers at surly architects. It was Ernest—and this I gladly say—who brought the ideas to our business.

"My dear," I once said to him, "there are only two men in London who could turn a revolting Baptist chapel with Venetian excrescences into a Chinese pagoda. And you are both of them."

"You mean a Turkish bath, dear boy," he said. "Why two men?"

"One to think up the ghastly idea, the other to persuade the people to have it."

"D'you know, you've got very bald since Easter," he said. "Shall we have a little Mozart?"

Ernest at work was a frightening sight. Generally, he did not like me to come with him, but I've seen him at it more than once. He is a slender, shortish man, with carefully styled hair—neither fair nor grey, but in some subtle pastel shade, as soft as moleskin. It fits his head like an old-fashioned ink pad. His beard is itself one of those small objets d'art that women itch to touch. He has a voice as soft as cigarette smoke, an utterly insincere listening manner—the head a little inclined —and when, to take an example, Mrs. Raddock talked pell-mell about enlarging her dining-room bookcases, he nodded with the air of a dignified mourner who is not a close friend of the family. This habit of grieving distantly and respectfully (after a wild, wheeling look at the ceiling, walls, and windows of the room, and with one rather cruel roll of the eye at the door he had just come through) had the effect of inducing dismay in many women. They would give a touch to their hair and a glance at their clothes, in order to recover fortitude; they had not realized, until that moment, that their dining room, their drawing room, their whole house, was dead, the interment long overdue.

"Yes, I see exactly what you mean, Mrs. Raddock. The thing that worries me is the height of the folding doors." Mrs. Raddock, a confusing talker, foolish and flirtatious but a woman of will who until then had known what she wanted, was torpedoed at once by this shot. Ernest's words showed her her personal disaster: it was not that she had been three times married but that she had never noticed the height of her folding doors. And Ernest struck again. "It is a pity the original chimney piece has gone," he accused.

"My husband found this one down in Wiltshire," said Mrs. Raddock, desperately pushing whatever blame that might arise on to him. Already Ernest was dividing husband and wife.

"Houses like this, so purely Regency, are getting rarer and rarer," said Ernest sadly. "So many are let go. I have been doing a library in Gloucestershire, a rather nice Georgian house—a room with a cupola, a small domed ceiling, you know?"

Mrs. Raddock blushed at her lack of cupola.

"I'd better measure the height of the door," Ernest said. "The top moulding of your bookcase cannot possibly be below it. These houses put formality and balance first."

Ernest's steel ruler whizzed up the jamb of the door and lashed there for a second or two, then slipped back with a hiss into its holder. Mrs. Raddock stepped back. Formality and balance—how did you guess (her eager look seemed to say) that that is what I need in my life? She covered her defeat with a look of experienced irony at Ernest, but also of appeal. As I followed them around, I could hardly conceal my desire to protect the lady and Ernest from each other, and Ernest knew this. As we left the room to go upstairs to the drawing room, he gave me a glare. "Keep out of this," the look said, for I had the weakness of comforting suggestion to our customers. (At the shop, he once said to me crossly, "You are so tall, dear boy. It makes you look dispassionate.")

Now we were at the top of red-carpeted stairs outside Mrs. Raddock's drawing room. The door was open. We could just see in. Ernest paused and turned his back as if he had seen something dreadful, and nodded downstairs to the room we had just left. "Was it your idea or your husband's to have a black dining room?" said Ernest. He spoke of everything with the suggestion that it belonged to a past the customer was anxious to forget.

"Oh, mine," said Mrs. Raddock, making a guilty effort to take the blame herself this time. "Ten years ago," she said, breaking helplessly into autobiography, "when we moved up from the country."

"Ten." Ernest nodded. "That would be about the date." And Mrs. Raddock sank once more.

In two more visits, she was holding his arm, as he gazed up at the mouldings of the ceiling and she gazed at his little beard, trying to formalise herself. The case of Mrs. Raddock differs little from that of Mrs. Cross, Mrs. Hunstable, or, indeed, all the others. Ernest seized their flats and their houses with the ruthless hands of the artist, shook the interiors out of their own windows, and re-created them. He was really shaking his clients out of the windows, too. Dark rooms appeared as monkey-haunted jungles; light was dispensed from chaste or unchaste vases, dripped like expensive tears, or shot out at piercing, agony-creating angles. Ceilings went up or down, alcoves appeared on blank walls. He had once a line in Piranesi dining rooms and in hairy pagan bedrooms where furs and lewd hints of the goat's foot were tossed around. He did sickening things with shot birds, which made the ladies scream first; put down tigerish carpets, which gave them voluptuous shudders. He created impudent or intimate congeries of small furniture, and could make a large piece look like an Italian church. A pushing career woman like Mrs. Greatorex was given a satiny nest of such kittenishness that it suggested to the visitor that here lived some delicate hypochondriac with little bones and sad pink rims to her sensitive eyes, instead of—as she was—a brassy, hard-bloused lady bawling down the telephone. Ernest penetrated to the hidden self of his client, discerned her so-far frustrated dream of perfection. And then a sudden practicality sprang up in his apparently passive personality and he took rough charge. It was they who then watched him—startled at first, then attentively, then gravely, then longingly. Here was the nest builder, and without realizing it they grew irritable with their husbands, who came home—or what used to be home—to find the place half closed or in chaos. These moneyed brutes trod on paint. The wives screamed out, "Don't go in there! Be careful! Ernest has moved the banisters." "Ernest"—husbands wearied of the name. One or two coarse ones—Raddock and Cross were like this—threw out doubts about his sex. The ladies made a face, wriggled their shoulders, and

sighed that men like Ernest understood what most men forget—that
women are not merely female; they are feminine. The time came when
a flat or a house was finished. There was Mrs. Cross's Chinese boutique.
She stood entranced, hardly able to take a step, hardly able to see
because of the sparkle that came to her excited eyes, which themselves
looked jewel-like in this moment. She saw not only her house but
herself, perfected. But, as always in the face of perfection, a mysterious
sadness misted those eyes. There was the sense of loss that angels are
said to have when they look back from Heaven upon the earth. A
hunger made Mrs. Cross go limp, opened Mrs. Hunstable's uneasy
mouth, brought a shiver to Mrs. Raddock's nervous bosom. Their
houses were now perfect, but one thing was missing. What was it?

It was Ernest. They wanted him. For weeks he had been in and out,
caressing yet masterful. The creation was empty without the creator.
Mrs. Raddock rubbed herself against him; Mrs. Cross muttered in a
low voice, leading him to the bedroom, where she had a final question
to ask. Mrs. Greatorex frankly galloped at him. Our bad year began.
Mrs. Raddock left her third husband; a load of chandeliers came back.
Mr. and Mrs. Cross broke up, after years of bickering, in which the
Chinese drawing room had been a last emotional bid; the lacquer
cabinets were returned. Mrs. Greatorex went to Greece. Letters came
in from bank managers and lawyers. There were last longing looks of
farewell at Ernest. Some had wanted him socially, as a sparkler; others
had wished to be sisters to him; others had wanted him as confidant,
as an annoyance to their husbands. But why particularise? They wanted
him. The final blow in that year came from Mrs. Hunstable. This florid
and open-hearted lady, whose upper part suggested a box at the opera
in which she was somehow living and sitting, and who spoke in a jolly
mixture of aria and ravening recitative—this lady was caught, actually
caught, lying rather sideways on a Recamier couch, having her tears
wiped by Ernest while she stroked his neat pad of hair.

Mr. Hunstable caught them. She said she was comforting him.

"I was telling him," cried Mrs. Hunstable, jumping up and taking
her husband in her arms and wiping her tears at the same time, "I was
telling him he must not worry because he is different from other men.
Ernest's on the point of breakdown."

Mr. Hunstable looked operatically doubtful.

"They feel it, Harry, you know," she appealed. "Ernest feels it. They
all do."

Mrs. Hunstable was as near to telling the truth as a woman feels it necessary to be. The only correction needed here is that Ernest was comforting her. Ernest rarely spoke to me of his end-of-contract crises, but rumours are soon out. The telephone never stops in our trade, and more than half the calls are gossip. I often had to sweep up after Ernest emotionally. But Mrs. Hunstable was not easily put off. She came to the office when Ernest was out, her mouth wide open, her breasts in disorder, demanding to know more. She tried to ransack me. She was all out for confession. Naturally, I said nothing. "I see," she said to me with a cold smirk. "You hang together." She became the mortally insulted mother whose sons will not confide in her. She turned on us and sold the house, her husband landed the stuff back on us, and they went off violently to the Bahamas, leaving us to their lawyers.

The Hunstable episode was a shock to Ernest, and it worried me. As I say, it was the last one in a bad year. Until then I would have said that Ernest's successes with our clients depended on his skill in turning their desires into a ballet-like partnership from which he escaped by some beautifully timed leap, so to say, into the wings. But Mrs. Hunstable was no dancer. The world was no stage to her; it was property. It was to be owned. I confess that working with an artist like Ernest is apt to make a man at the business end, like myself, fall back on a vulgar tone in a crisis.

"It's a pity, dear boy . . . I mean—well, look, Ernest, let's not beat about the bush. Have another drink," I said. I stopped and gave a loud laugh.

"I mean," I said, "It's a pity you couldn't, just for once . . ."

"Be as other men?" Ernest said.

"I was only joking, dear boy."

"Not with Mrs. Hunstable," Ernest said. "Perhaps you, my dear—"

"Ernest," I said. "I'm sorry. I suppose we have to look at this in perspective. I've often wondered whether we realize what we are doing. I don't think you do—or perhaps you do?"

"Our mistake is that we deal with people," Ernest said.

"What a horrible thing to say," I said.

"People with inner lives," he said.

"You mean who send things back?" I said.

"Oh, all right!" he said angrily. "What d'you want me to do—the Flashback Bar, Nasty's Steak House? Or some self-service counter? Or the Svengali Room at the Metropole?"

"You cannot send a bar back. You can't return a restaurant," I said.

"What happened at the Sea Urchin?" It was six o'clock in the evening, December, a wet day. I had persuaded him to see what the manager of the Sea Urchin wanted, and he had just come back.

"They want fisherman's nets on the ceiling. That was *out* ten years ago. They're going to sit on capstans."

"Not sit, surely, Ernest," I said.

"I don't know—perhaps it was anchors," Ernest said, covering his face with his hands.

I went to the cupboard in our office and reached for the bottle of gin, and as I did so the telephone rang. Ernest picked it up. "My name is Richards. I wrote you a letter . . ." I could hear a jubilant voice, fermenting like a small vat.

"Men! I'm sick of them," Ernest said, handing the telephone to me.

"Richards, Gowing, and Cloud," the happy voice went on.

"Lawyers," I whispered to Ernest.

"You wrote us a letter? Oh, dear," I said.

I found the letter on my desk. It was one I had not had the heart to answer, and I passed it to Ernest—or, rather, I dangled it before him. I have, as Ernest says, a suicidal voice, and now I used it. "Mr. Richards," I said to Ernest, "is engaged to be married shortly to a divine girl called Miss Staples and has taken one of those little musical boxes on Albine Rise. It's all here in the letter."

Then I turned back to the telephone. "Why, of course, Mr. Richards," I said. "When would you like us to come?" And when he rang off I looked strictly at Ernest. "Eleven tomorrow morning," I said. "Ernest, it's this or the Sea Urchin."

You find little enclaves like Albine Rise all over London if you know where to look. It was a group of nine small early-Victorian houses, enclosed in a terrace of weeping elms on an expensive hill. "Musical box" is the term for any one of them. Only three hundred yards from a thundering and whining main road but set above it, the houses seem —to a London ear—to tinkle together in rural quiet. One glance must have told Ernest when we arrived that there was little for us here: the couple had bought Perfection already. I turned away from it to study them.

Mr. Richards, of the Queen's Bench voice, was a set piece: bowler hat, black coat, striped trousers, old Etonian tie. Miss Staples was the shock. She was a fat little thing with a ruddy face, dressed in hairy brown tweed—a girl with a decided look and a hard hand-grip. She said little except that she was in a hurry and must get to something she called the Dairy Show. We went into the house. "I just want it done in white!" she shouted.

"White?" said Ernest.

"All this chichi off. I want plain white," said Miss Staples.

Mr. Richards looked at Ernest with appeal. "Save me from plain white," the look said.

"White?" said Ernest. "Do you mean chalk or ivory or—"

"Just white. Any white. White!" shouted Miss Staples cheerfully.

"Like sheep—clean ones," said Mr. Richards with fruity sarcasm, but also with a glance at Ernest screaming in a gentlemanly way for help. Ernest took in the pretty sitting room and the pretty staircase outside, but he was looking with astonishment at the vigorous, golden, untidy hair of Miss Staples, at her cheeks as fresh as ham, her eyes as blue as blackbirds' eggs. He was astounded. Most women, however bold their faces, were put in the wrong by him, but he failed—no, he did not even try—to put Miss Staples in the wrong. She was, he must have seen at once, his opposite—not a decorator but a de-decorator. "White? Very chaste," Ernest said in a louder voice than usual.

"Isn't that rather personal?" she said archly. Ernest was taken aback. Miss Staples showed small white teeth. "Let me show you what the frightful people did—the people who had the place before," she said, leading him up the stairs and showing him the bathroom. "It may be O.K. for Cleopatra and her asp, but I keep dogs."

"In the bathroom?" said Ernest.

"They scratch at the door," said Miss Staples heartily. "All this," she said, pointing round the room, "will have to go."

"We have dogs," apologized Mr. Richards. Ernest looked at him. Mr. Richards was a stout, pale young man choking with legal deprecation. The sentence sounded like "M'lud, my information is that my client keeps dogs."

"That bloody traffic," said Miss Staples from the window. One could scarcely hear the traffic.

"Better than calving cows," said Mr. Richards.

"Jerseys have such pretty eyes," said Ernest. I was dumbfounded.

"Yes," said Miss Staples. "We've got fifty—two more coming this week. It's not the eyes, it's the yield! Isn't it, Robert? I want this place for Robert during the week. I hate London."

"This is where I shall be stabled," said Robert.

"We're keeping the oats in the country," Miss Staples snapped back offhand to her fiancé but gazing at Ernest. Ernest was entranced.

And so was Miss Staples.

Robert hated Ernest; Ernest despised Robert. Miss Staples looked Ernest over with open admiration, but with an occasional critical glance, her head on one side. "What a frightful tie you're wearing," she said. It struck me she was seeing what might, here and there, be altered. And Ernest was going over her in the same way, and was clearly finding, for the first time in his life, nothing that should be changed.

"The trees are very . . ." began Ernest, waving his hand at the weeping elms outside, but he was clearly indicating the waves of her hair.

"Give me twenty-five acres of kale any day," said Miss Staples.

"Me, too," said Ernest. I had never before heard Ernest lie.

"I'm afraid my wife—er, my future wife, it would be more correct to say—has rather drastic ideas. I hope Ernest will be able to exert an influence. In fact, that's why I asked . . ." Mr. Richards whispered to me.

"I've got to go. You'd better come down for the weekend," Miss Staples ordered. "There are the fox masks, the antlers, one or two prize cups—I don't see anywhere here to put a saddle."

"You're damn right there isn't," said Ernest, marvelling at her.

This interview took place on a Tuesday. The following weekend, Ernest went to stay with Miss Staples and Mr. Richards at her parents' house in the country. On Monday, he came back. He came into the shop about twelve. His usual quiet gravity had gone. He walked up and down and said, "Stuffy in here. No air. I'll open the door." It was a cold day.

"We shall die," I said as the wind blew four yards of brocade off a screen and took the screen with it to the floor. "What were they like, the older Stapleses?"

"Wonderful," said Ernest. "Like moulting owls. Perfect . . . Blast this stuff," said Ernest, and he did something terrible. He kicked the brocade out of the way as it lay crouching on the floor—kicked it with boots that had obviously been in some country lane. I could have screamed, brocade at the price it is. There were probably not another four yards of that quality and colour in London, and it takes months to get it from France.

"The order's off," Ernest said at last. "Albine Rise. We had a flaming row. Robert and Joanna—"

"Joanna?"

"Miss Staples. She's broken it off. He said he'd allow the hunting prints, if she insisted, but he bloody well wasn't going to have the heads of stinking dead animals and photographs of the Chester Cattle Show. And filthy white paint."

"Thank heaven, dear boy, it happened now, not later," I said.

"What d'you mean?" said Ernest curtly.

We moved into the inner office to get out of the wind while Ernest told me more. "Dear boy," I said, "what have you done to your eye?"

"Nothing," said Ernest. One eye was ringed in green and purple. "I was sawing a branch off a tree for her. She let go of the branch. It was too heavy for her. It sprang back and hit me in the eye. Wonderful girl. She didn't make a fuss."

"And I suppose she kissed it better and Robert saw you?" I said.

And then we heard a shout and dogs barking in the shop. We went to see what had happened. In at the open door came two dogs, fighting. One ran under the Chinese lacquer cabinet, and after them came Miss Staples with a leash and collars in her hand.

"Shut that bloody door! They've slipped their collars!" Miss Staples shouted at us. I shut the door, Ernest caught one dog by the neck. Miss Staples seized the other.

Reddened by the struggle, Ernest and Miss Staples stood excitedly looking at each other, with dogs' dribble on their clothes.

"Joanna and I are going out to lunch," Ernest said to me. "Do you mind if we shut Sydney and Morris in the office? Good fellow."

So our partnership ended. Ernest is farming now. Their house is terrible. It is the sort of house where dogs have their puppies on the sofa, where you can't see across the room for wood smoke, where the fake Jacobean furniture and brass trays are covered with old copies of the *Farmers Weekly*, where dogs' bones are found under rugs, where fox masks look down on you, where you can't see to read because the lamps are in the wrong place, and where Ernest sits in his gumboots reading the local paper and Joanna sits with a transistor mewing out the news in Welsh while she sews some awful cotton dresses.

"She's dead right here, isn't she? Exactly what a place like this needed," Ernest said to me, a flicker of the forgotten artist in him coming out—I flatter myself—at the sight of me. She had redecorated him.

The Liars

"We're all dressed up today," said the landlady, going downstairs to her husband in the kitchen from the old lady's room. "Diamond rings, emerald necklace—she's put the lot on. I said to her, 'You're all dressed up for company, I see.' 'Yes,' she said, 'Harry's coming.' I mean, it's childish. I don't trust that man. He'd stop at nothing and he tells lies. And do you know what she said?"

"What did she say?" said the landlady's husband.

" 'It's Thursday, Mrs. Lax,' she says. 'It's my day for telling lies.' "

It was a February afternoon. Under her black wig, the old lady upstairs was sitting up in bed reading her father's Baudelaire. She read greedily; her eyes, enlarged by her glasses, were rampaging over the lines; with her long nose and her long lips sliding back into her cheeks, she looked like a wolf grinning at the smell of the first snow and was on the hunt restlessly among the words.

> *"Vous que dans votre enfer mon âme a poursuivies*
> *Pauvres soeurs, je vous aime autant que je vous plains"*

she was murmuring avidly as she read. All over the bed were books, French and English, papers, detective novels that she had picked up and pushed away. On and off, in the long day, she had looked to see what was going on in the street; rain had emptied it. The only thing that still caught her eye was an old blackbird gripping the branch of the plane tree outside her window; its wings hanging down, alone.

"You're late," said the old lady, pulling her shawl violently round her arms, taking off her glasses and showing her strong, expectant teeth, when Harry came up to her room at four o'clock. The bold nose was naked and accusing. Harry put the library books he had brought for her on the table under the window by her bedside. He was a tall, red-faced man with the fixed look of moist astonishment at having somehow got a heavy body into his navy-blue suit and of continually hearing news.

"I had my hair cut," he said, moving a small cane-seated chair out of the muddle of furniture into the middle of the room. The old lady waited impatiently for him to sit down.

"No," he said. The old lady took a deep breath and gave a small hungry smile.

"No," he said. "A terrible thing happened when I came out of the barber's." The old lady let out her breath peacefully and let her head slip aside on her pillow in admiration.

"I saw my double," Harry said.

Two years ago she had been in hospital, but before that, Harry had the job of pushing her along the sea front in a bath chair on fine mornings. When she had been taken ill, he had started working in the bar and dining room of the Queens Hotel. Now that she was bedridden he brought her books. First of all, in the days when he used to wheel her out, it was "Yes, Miss Randall" or "Is that a fact, Miss Randall?" while she chattered about the town as it was when she was a child there, about her family—all dead now—and about her father, the famous journalist, and what he had done at Versailles after the 1914 war and his time in the Irish troubles, and her London life with him. And Harry told her about himself. "I was born in Enniskillen, ma'am." "Now that's a border town, isn't it, Harry?" "It's like living on a tightrope, ma'am. My father fought against the British." "Very foolish of him," said the old lady. "Oh, it was," said Harry. "He had us blown up." "The British *bombed* you, Harry?" "Not at all, it was one of father's bombs, home-made thing, it went off in the house." "Were you hurt, Harry?" "I was at my auntie's. So I went to sea." "So you did, you told me, and the ship blew up too." "No, ma'am, it was the boiler. It was a Liverpool ship, the *Grantham*." "Two explosions, I don't believe you, Harry." "It's God's truth, ma'am. It was in New York harbour. But I'd left her in Bueno...

went to that hacienda—no, you got a job in an hotel first of all—isn't that it?" "Yes, in two or three hotels, ma'am, until this American lady took me up to her hacienda." "To look after the horses?" "That is correct." "This was the lady who rode her horse up the steps into the dining room?" "No, ma'am," said Harry, "she rode it right inside and up the marble staircase into her bedroom." "She couldn't, Harry. A mule yes, but not a horse." "That part was easy for her, ma'am, it was getting the horse down that was the trouble. She called us, the Indian boy and myself, and we had to do that. Down twenty-five marble steps. She stood at the top shouting at us 'Mind the pictures.' " "I suppose there was an explosion there, too, Harry?" "No ma'am, but there were butterflies as large as plates flying through the air, enough to knock you down . . ."

"Harry," said the old lady one day, "you're as big a liar as my sister's husband used to be."

Harry looked at her warily, then around him to see if there was anyone he could call to for help if there was trouble.

"It's God's truth," said Harry rapidly and anxiously.

"There's truth and there's God's truth," said the old lady. It was after this that she had to be taken off to hospital.

"So you saw your double, Harry," the old lady said. "Stand up and let me look at you."

Harry stood up.

"They've cropped you at the back, you're nearly blue. I'll tell you whose double you are, Harry. My sister's husband. He was in the hotel business like you."

"Is that a fact?" said Harry. "Did your sister marry?"

"I've been thinking about it ever since you went to work at the Queens," said the old lady. "He was taller and broader than you and he had fair hair, not black like yours, and a very white face, a London night face—but the feet were the same, like yours, sticking out sideways. Sit down, Harry."

"I suppose," said Harry, who had heard versions of this story before. "I suppose he'd be the manager?"

"Manager!" shouted the old lady. "He wouldn't have considered it! Ambassador, archbishop, prime minister, more like it. That is what he sounded like and what he looked like—anyway what we *thought* he was. He was the headwaiter at a night club."

She stared herself into silence.

"No, it's God's truth," said Harry, taking his chance. "I was coming out of the barber's and I forgot your books and went back for them and when I came to cross the street, the lights changed. There was a crowd of us there on the curb and that was when I saw this fellow. He was standing on the other side of the street waiting to cross. I stared at him. He stared at me. We were the double of each other. I thought I was looking in a mirror."

The old lady let her head slip back peacefully on the pillow, a happy smile came on her face, and she took a biscuit from the tin.

"Same clothes?" said the old lady slyly.

"Except for the hat," said Harry. "Same height. He was staring at me. Same nose, eyes, everything. And then the lights changed and he stepped off the curb and I stepped off and we were still staring at each other. But when we got to the middle I couldn't look at him any longer and I looked away. We passed each other and I felt cold as ice all down one side of my body."

"Did he turn round? Did *he* recognize *you?*"

"He did not. But after we passed I looked back and he wasn't there. No sign of him at all. I got to the curb and I had a second look. He'd gone."

"He was lost in the crowd."

"He was not. There wasn't a crowd. He was the only one crossing from that side of the street. Except for the hat, it was me."

The pupils of Harry's eyes were upright brown ovals. He had been wronged, so wronged that he looked puffed out, full of wind.

"It was like passing an iceberg in the Atlantic. Or a ghost," Harry said.

"You could say Deb's husband was a ghost," said the old lady. "He was living upstairs in the flat above us for three years before we met him. We used to hear his taxi at four in the morning. He was out all night and we were out all day. Deb at her art school and I worked on the paper my father used to work on."

"You mightn't have met at all," Harry said. "I never saw the night porter at the Queens for a year."

"I wish we hadn't," said the old lady.

"It would be accidental if you did. Would there have been an accident?" Harry said, putting on an innocent look. "When I was working on that hacienda with the American lady, the one with the horse in her bedroom . . ."

"There *was* an accident!" said the old lady. "You know there was. I told you, Harry."

"He left the stopper in his basin," Harry said.

"With the tap dripping," the old lady said. "Deb got home one evening and heard the water dripping through the ceiling on to Father's desk. She put a bowl underneath it and it splashed all over Father's books—we had a very pleasant flat, not like this. Father left us some very beautiful things. When I got home I was angry with Deb. She was a very dreamy girl. 'Why didn't you get the housekeeper up instead of letting it ruin everything?' I said. *I* had to ring for him—stone-deaf, like your cook. Didn't you say the explosion on that ship, the *Cairngorm,* made your cook stone-deaf?"

"On the *Grantham,*" Harry said.

"You told me the *Cairngorm* before," said the old lady. "But never mind. The housekeeper got his keys and went upstairs to see what was going on. That flat, Harry. It was empty. When I say empty, just the lino on the floor . . ."

"I've got lino at the Queens," said Harry. "Brown with white flowers."

"Nothing—nothing but a table and a bed and a couple of chairs. It was like a cell. It was like a punishment hanging over us. Not a book. There was a parcel of shirts from the laundry on the bed—that would have told us something if we'd looked."

"It would," said Harry.

"Four o'clock in the morning," said the old lady, "he came home. The taxi ticking down below in the street! Like a ghost in the night. Of course he came down to apologize about the water. Harry, the moment he stood in the room, I knew I'd seen him before! I said to my sister, 'I've seen that man somewhere.' The way he stopped in the doorway, looking across the room at Deb and me and the chairs, nodding at them as if he were telling us where to sit, the way he held his hands together as he spoke, with his head bent. He had one of those kissing mouths—like a German. He looked at the books that had been splashed and said, 'Balzac and Baudelaire, very great men,' and looked fatter in the face after he said it. More important. We said they were Father's books and my sister said, 'Father was a special correspondent. Perhaps you've heard of him.' He said he'd heard people mention him at his club and it sounded as if he'd eaten Father." The old lady laughed out loud at this idea of hers and left her mouth open for a while after she had laughed. "I'll tell you who he was like," she said excitedly, "that statue of George the Second. Or do I mean the Duke of Bedford?

"I wanted to get rid of him: he was so large and serious and he sounded as if he was making a speech to Parliament about what some painter he knew had said about art and the public. He knew a lot of people—cabinet ministers, actors, judges. Well, I said, when he'd gone, I don't know who he is but he's a man 'in the know'! Deb did not like my saying this. 'He's a journalist, I expect.' Before he went Deb asked him to have a drink with us one day. 'Let me look at my diary. Thursday I'm free and Sundays, unless I go away to stay,' he said. 'Come on Sunday,' Deb said. He came. We had people there. The first thing he did was to start handing round the drinks. It was *his* party. He owned us. He'd eaten us too. I couldn't take my eyes off him. One or two people were as curious as I was. 'Who is he? The editor of the *Times?* What does he do?' He wasn't like any of our friends, we were all younger. You know what I think drew us to him—girls are such fools —his conceit! He was as conceited as a gravestone. I watched him moving about. There was his round white face, rather puffy, and his head bowing like the whole of the House of Hanover—the House of Hanover were very stiff, I know, Harry, but you know what I mean— and talking about the Prime Minister and politics in a pooh-poohing way; but down below were his feet sticking out sideways and scampering about beneath him—like messenger boys. 'Which paper do you work for?' I asked him. 'I'm not a journalist,' he said. 'Oh,' I said, 'the housekeeper said you were a journalist on night work. We hear your taxi every night.' And do you know what he said? 'I asked the housekeeper about *you* when I took my flat here. I wanted to be sure it was a quiet house. He said you were two ladies out all day.' Snubs to us, I said to my sister after he had gone, but she said, 'Fancy him asking about *us!*' and she danced round the room, singing up at the ceiling, 'I'm a lady out all day.' We could hear him upstairs walking about."

"Yes, but that's what I can't make out about this man," said Harry. "I was thinking about it yesterday. Why wouldn't he tell you what his job was?"

"He thought we were a pair of snobs," said the old lady. "I expect we were."

"Out all night, he could have been a printer," said Harry.

"Or the post office! Or the police! Night watchman. Actor. We thought of that," the old lady raced along. "It was clever of him: you see what he did. He didn't tell a single lie but he started us imagining things and telling lies to ourselves. Deb couldn't leave it alone. Every time he dodged our questions, she made something up."

The old lady pulled her arms out of the shawl and spread her arms wide.

"Burglar came into *my* head," she shouted. "I came home from the office one evening and there they were, both of them, sitting on the sofa and he was saying he had heard on the 'highest authority'—the highest authority, he actually used those words, I always called him the highest authority after that to annoy Deb—that the Cabinet had decided to legalize street betting. When he left I said to Deb, 'Deb, that man is not in politics: he is in crime.' 'I can tell you he is *not* in crime,' Deb said, 'I asked him straight out.' "

Harry leaned forward and began to rub his hands up and down his sleeves, making a sound like breath.

" 'I asked him straight out what he did,' Deb said, 'and he said he was very sorry but it was secret work, something he couldn't talk about, but not crime.' He made her promise not to ask or try to find out, but he said he would tell her when he was free to say."

"If you'd looked at those shirts on his bed you'd have known the answer," Harry said. "Dress shirts."

"The headwaiter at a smart night club," the old lady said.

"And earning good money, I suppose," said Harry. "That is where he picked up his talk."

"I've told you all this before, Harry," said the old lady.

"Things come back," said Harry.

"The chief steward on the *Grantham*," said Harry, "used to pass himself off as the captain when he went ashore. That was to girls too."

"Oh, he talked very well and took us in. You can call him a waiter if you like but you know what I call him? Bluebeard."

"Bluebeard?" said Harry, very startled. "Was he married?"

"No, but he had Bluebeard in him," said the old lady. "A girl will do anything to find out a secret."

"That's true," said Harry.

The old lady stared at Harry, weighing him up. Then she said, in a lower voice: "I can talk to you, Harry. You're a married man. I mean you've been a married man. Show me your wife's picture again."

Harry opened his wallet and took out an old snapshot of a young girl with smooth dark hair drawn in an old-fashioned style round an oval face.

"She was pretty, Harry. Deb was fair and a bit plump."

She looked at the photograph a long time and then gave it back to Harry, who put it in his wallet again.

"You miss her, Harry."

"I do that."

"You would have had a home," said the old lady. "I haven't got a home. You haven't got a home—and yet, years ago, before we moved to London, my family had a large house in this town."

The old lady suddenly changed her mood and her voice became sarcastically merry. "Bluebeard! Oh, we were all mystery! Secret service, Russian spies. When Deb went to bed at night, she started drawing back the curtains, turning out the lights and undressing by the light of the street lamp down below. And she would open the window wide—in the winter! The fog blowing in! She would stand in her nightdress and say, 'Can't you feel the mystery of London? I want to feel I am everywhere in London, seeing what everyone is doing this minute. Listen to it.' 'You'll get pneumonia,' I said. But it was love. He came down to see us very often now. One day he was saying something about the French ambassador and French foreign policy, it sounded boastful and I said (I remember this), 'Father was one of Clemenceau's very few English friends'—which wasn't true. I told you he made us tell lies. That impressed him because before he went he asked us both out to dinner—at the Ritz! The Ritz! And that was where something funny happened—only a small thing. A party at another table started staring at him and I was sure I heard someone mention his name. I'm sure I heard one of the men say, 'There's Charles,' and I said to him: 'Someone knows you over there.' 'No,' he said. 'They were talking about you. They were saying it was unfair a man taking out two pretty sisters.' Deb was very pleased. 'He's very well known,' she said. 'In that case, he can't be secret, can he?' I said. He never took us out again."

The old lady scowled. "After that it was champagne, caviar, lobster. Up in his flat and Deb took her gramophone—I never went. 'He must be a cook,' I said, and she said, 'No, he sends out for it,' and wouldn't speak to me for a week afterwards. She was clean gone. She gave up her classes because she couldn't see him during the day except on Thursdays and Sundays. She was mad about him. And she got very secretive, hiding things, not like her at all. I told her she'd have a bigger secret than she bargained for."

The old lady sniggered.

"I was jealous," said the old lady in a moping voice.

"Ah, you would be, I expect," Harry agreed.

"Yes," moped the old lady.

"And then," said Harry, giving a loud slap to his knee. "There was this ring at the bell . . ."

The old lady looked suspiciously at him.

"The same as the time I told you about, when we docked at Marseilles—with that Algerian. Short black socks he had on and . . ."

The old lady woke up out of her moping, offended.

"Algerian! He was not an Algerian. It was a Cypriot. I was very surprised to hear a ring at that time of the evening. I thought it must have been one of those Jehovah's Witnesses. I went to the door and there he was, this little dark Cypriot with a bottle sticking out of his pocket—I thought he was drunk. He asked for Mr. Charles. 'There is no Mr. Charles here,' I said. 'What number do you want?' 'Six,' he said."

"And you were four!" said Harry.

" 'This is four,' I said, pointing to the number on the door. Well, you'd think people could read. 'Number six is upstairs.' And I shut the door quickly, I was frightened."

"You can mark a man with a bottle," said Harry. "I've seen that too."

"I heard him ring the bell upstairs. I heard talking. And then it was all quiet. Then suddenly I heard a shout and I thought the ceiling was coming down, like furniture being thrown about."

"An argument," said Harry.

"An argument?" said the old lady. She tightened her shawl round her and leaned back as if she were warding off blows.

"Screams, Harry! Lobster, Harry. Glass! And Deb rushing out to the landing, making a horrible squeal like a dog being run over. I rushed out of our flat and up the stairs and there was Deb in her petticoat shrieking and just as I got to her the Cypriot rushed out with ketchup or blood, I don't know which, on his boots and ran downstairs. I pulled Deb out of the way. Her scream had stopped in her wide-open mouth and she was pointing into the lobby of the flat. There was Charles getting up from the floor, in his shirt-sleeves with blood all over his face. You couldn't walk for glass."

The old lady stared at Harry, and picking up Baudelaire's poems, contemptuously threw them to the end of the bed. Then slowly she smiled and Harry smiled. They smiled at each other with admiration.

"Yes," said Harry with a nod. "It's feasible."

The old lady nodded back.

"It's feasible, all right," Harry said. "The same as I was saying happened in Marseilles when I was in the *Grantham*—Egyptian onions from Alexandria—you could smell us all over the port. I went ashore with the second mate and we were having a drink in one of those cafés with tables on the street—only there five minutes and this Algerian comes in, a young fellow. He walks straight between the tables to the headwaiter who was flicking flies off the fruit and shoots him dead. Not a word spoken. Same idea. The headwaiter had been fiddling chicken and brandy, selling it on the side and when the boss tumbled to it, the waiter said this Algerian kitchen boy—that is what he was—had done it and the boss fired him. Same story. They're very hot-blooded down there. It was all in the papers."

"The Cypriot was kitchen boy at the club. Champagne, lobster, caviar, it all came from there! Week after week," said the old lady.

"Yes," said Harry.

"We kept it out of the papers, of course," said the old lady loftily.

"You don't want a thing like that in the papers," Harry agreed. "Just sweep up and say nothing, like that time at the Queens when Mr. Armitage . . ."

"We had a reason," said the old lady. "I'll tell you something I never told you before. When Deb came screaming to the door, I didn't tell you—she had a broken bottle in her hand."

"Is that so!" said Harry, very startled.

"It's true. That is what happened. It was Deb that did the fighting, not the Cypriot. It was Deb."

"God Almighty," said Harry. "And she married him after that!"

"She didn't marry him," said the old lady. "I know I said she did, but she didn't. 'I wouldn't marry a man who cheated like that,' she said. She wouldn't speak to him. Or look at him. She wouldn't get a doctor to look after him. He had a terrible cut on his forehead. I had to clean it and bandage it and get him to the hospital and nurse him. She wouldn't go near him. But it wasn't because he'd cheated. Now she knew about him, the secret, she didn't want him. She was a girl like that. It was a pity. He did well for himself. I showed you the postcard of his hotel—it must be one of the biggest in Cannes. When you sit like that with your feet turned out, you remind me of him. He could tell the tale too," she suddenly laughed. "You're the double."

And then the landlady came in with tea and put the tray across the old lady's lap.

"There," she said. "Tea for two, as the saying is. And don't you tire her out, Mr. O'Hara. Another quarter of an hour."

The old lady frowned at the closed door when the landlady went, and listened for her steps going down the stairs.

"I *could* have married him," the old lady said.

"Now, this woman, Harry," she said quickly. "With the horse. She was after you, wasn't she? Why did she make you come up and get that horse down? Why couldn't she ride it down, she rode it up. You're trying to throw dust in my eyes . . ."

"No, it was a fine horse and Irish bred," said Harry, "she bought it off a man who had lost his leg . . ."

The afternoon had darkened. The bird that had been sitting on the tree all day had gone. Harry said goodbye to the old lady. "See you next Thursday," he said.

"And don't be late. Don't let that woman at the Queens keep you. It's your day off," she called as he stood by the open door at the top of the stairs.

He went back along the front, listening to the laughter of the sea in the dark, and then into the bar of the Queens Hotel. But because it was his half day off, on the other side of it, as a customer, drinking a small whisky and listening to what people had to say.

1966

The Rescue

After the bad spring, the first two or three weeks of that summer turned on a sudden blaze and the pain went out of Mother's shoulder, and she let me buy the shortest mini-skirt in town. My tall brother and his taller friend George came down from Cambridge with beards like barley, and when I went out with them my golden hair seemed to flow from shop window to shop window as we walked by. The sunlight spanked like the cymbals and trumpets of a regimental band in the park, celebrating a triumph. And it *was* a time of victory in our family, especially for Mother. Why had we got a Socialist mayor at last? Why had the Council given in, after years of speeches, committee meetings, votes and letters to the papers, and agreed to turn the lake in the park into a lido? Who was behind all this but Mother? On top of this, there was the annual pageant; she ran that, too.

"You ought to take a rest," people said to her. There was always someone at the door—people rushed in to see her while she sat at the typewriter, made her lists, jumped to the telephone.

"Get on!" she would call to us. "Get on with it. Don't stop." She was short, stout and bouncing—born to rule.

This year she was putting on King Arthur and the Knights of the Round Table—nothing to do with the history of the town, but pageants were an annual holiday for Mother. Instead of bossing the Coun-

cil, she would take a breath for a day or two, then start organizing the
past. I was to be one of Guinevere's ladies. Every day, new bundles of
plastic shields, helmets, spears, swords and dresses were dumped in the
house, so that there was hardly room to sit down. And when my brother
and George came, they added Africa to it; thump, boom and howls
came off the records, and they larked about, dressing up in robes and
swinging swords at each other.

Get on? We would have done that much faster but for the people
she brought in to help. She rarely came home without some new
adherent; her strong glasses picked them out as she raced down the
street on her short legs or looked out of the car window. She caught
people suddenly, as a frog catches flies, and digested them without a
blink. Just at our busiest time she brought home the slowest young man
in the town, a real plague called Ellis, a boy of twenty. He worked in
the library; I had often seen him there when she sent me for books on
the costumes of King Arthur's time.

"We want him for advice," Mother said. Ellis was Advice in person.
Once he was in the house we could not get rid of him; he sat among
the helmets on one of the sofas, gazing at Mother, worshipping her,
and, between long silences, uttering deep opinions that came up from
his boots. In this hot weather he wore a thick suit, a waistcoat, and
woollen socks. Having got him for advice, Mother never listened to
him. The only thing I ever remember her saying to him was, "Why
don't you take your jacket off?" We said she'd brought him home to
get him to undress.

"Your boyfriend is in there," we'd say when she came in with a new
pile of costumes for the procession.

"Tell Ellis to count these," she'd say.

I would go up to him, shake my long hair from one shoulder to the
other and say, "For you. To count."

One evening I accidentally let out our secret joke about him: "Count
these, Lancelot."

Ellis ignored this. He lived for opinion, not for action.

The Lancelot joke had started because soon after Ellis had adopted
us, Mother lost the man who was going to take the part of Lancelot
in the pageant. "Every year an accident," Mother said. "That is life."
This year's Lancelot had been knocked off his bicycle by a dog and had
broken his ankle.

"Don't worry," George said. "You've got a Lancelot here. Promote
Ellis."

Mother ignored this but kept on worrying about her difficulty for days.

"Ellis for Lancelot," we kept on at her.

"Don't be malicious," Mother said, at her typewriter. "He lives alone in lodgings."

What was the real Lancelot like? Tall, I thought, with a fair beard and cool blue Cambridge eyes, like George's. But George said, "Don't be a nit. Arthur's knights were dwarfs. Bad food in the Middle Ages made everyone short."

Perhaps he was right. Our Lancelot was a stump, not more than five feet two inches high, with a low forehead and heavy arms. His habit of uttering opinions was a way of making himself seem taller. He hauled up his views from some deep mine inside him, and as they came up he stood on tiptoe and his chest swelled, and ignoring us, he unloaded them like coals for Mother alone.

Our joke did not make Ellis wince or laugh. Rather, it made him grow in importance and gaze even more profoundly at Mother, labouring at something he would sooner or later bring out, and when Mother came in and said she had found someone exactly fitted for the part, we saw Ellis looking scornfully at us and even more admiringly at Mother.

"I'm glad," he said. "If you had asked me, I would have had to refuse."

Refuse Mother! We were amazed.

"On principle," he said.

We were putting the helmets into boxes and we stopped.

"He was an adulterer," Ellis said.

We all laughed, except Mother.

"It happens to be a fact," Ellis said.

"But—" we all shouted together. We were soon at it, shouting about history, art and life, love and sex.

"Let him speak," said Mother, getting on with her work.

"It has nothing to do with history," he said. "If I had my way, I would pass a law making adultery illegal. If a man or woman committed it, they would be brought to the courts, tried, fined two hundred pounds, and imprisoned for two years."

"Why two hundred?" my brother said.

"Back to the Middle Ages," said George. "You said you're not influenced by history!"

"And when they came out of jail, I would have them branded on the back of the hand."

"With the letter A like in Nathaniel Hawthorne," I said. I had read him that term at school.

Ellis looked at me and for the first time smiled, congratulating me for having read the book.

"That's right," he said.

"You mean you'd make Lancelot march in the pageant wearing a letter A on his hand?" George said.

"Yes," said Ellis.

"You'd make it fashionable," said my brother.

"Anyone like to join the club?" said George, dancing about and waving his hands. "I've got my A. I see you've got yours. What about it?"

Because George did this and to show I was on his side and to make him take notice of me instead of going off with my brother all the time, I went to the desk by the window and drew a large A on the back of my hand.

"Look," I said, showing my hand to all of them. "A."

"You won't get that off in a hurry, my girl—it's marking ink," said Mother. George looked coldly at me.

The strange thing was that having uttered his thoughts and seeing us make fun of them, Ellis went flat and bewildered. He looked at Mother in appeal. He sat back on the sofa, astonished at the ruin of his ideas.

"Do you think it would make it popular?" he asked Mother simply.

Mother was holding up a red robe against George. "Is this too long for Kate Mason?" she said. "I haven't been listening." And to be kind to Ellis she changed the subject and said to him, "The mayor's opening the lido tomorrow, three o'clock. Bring your trunks."

It is strange to see adoration harden into fear. Ellis seemed to step back to the shadows of his lodgings suddenly, away from us.

"I can't get off from the library tomorrow," he said.

A simple statement, of course, but a contradiction of Mother's order. She was not used to being refused anything. She put the robe down. "I will speak to Mrs. Lowkes," Mother said. Mrs. Lowkes was the librarian, and when Mother said "speak" she meant she would require Mrs. Lowkes to do as she was told.

One shock leads to another. Ellis stood up and looked fiercely at me and obstinately at Mother. "I haven't got a suit," he said.

"There are plenty here," said Mother.

"I can't swim," said Ellis, drawing on hidden capital.

"That doesn't matter," said Mother. "We'll teach you."

Ellis moved back towards the door of the room.

"No one can teach me," he said, heaving up a load of pride into his chest. "I hate water. My father was a sailor. *He* couldn't swim. He drowned."

"How awful," I said.

He turned to me and said, "He left my mother. She died."

Until now we had never thought of Ellis as a member of a family. We hadn't even thought of him as being human, except in a general way. Seeing he had silenced us, he added information that built up the tragic distinction of his family. "Very few sailors can swim," he said. "They are fatalists."

Ellis, our fatalist!

Mother saved us. "Don't worry," she said. "There'll be a crowd there tomorrow."

But having made his stand, Ellis got even bolder with Mother. "I don't like crowds," he said. "They'll ruin the lake."

Her adorer was telling her that she was wrong—she who had fought for eight years to get the lido for the town! He was defying her and was appealing to me.

Mother was at her sewing machine. "You mustn't hate so many things, Ellis," she said.

After he left I said, "He looked as though he was going to cry."

"No. His eyes just swell up when he looks at you," my brother said.

"I'll say!" said George.

I knew that. Ellis had very large eyes and they did swell whenever he saw me come into the library. I used to make up questions about books until I made him leave his desk and say, "I'll get that book for you."

I used to have a special look that said, "You can do better than that," or "Why do you do what you are told?" And I had another, very long look that said, "I know that when you are saying things to Mother you are really saying them to me. You are frightened of me." And I would run my forefinger slowly down the edge of his desk as we talked. At sixteen, a girl likes to see what a young man will do. I hung about while other people came to the desk because I could see I was embarrassing him. Then I went off. Once when I turned round as I got to the door and caught him looking at me, he dropped five books he had in his hands. There was a noise that made everyone stare. A thrilling noise, like a tyre blow-out.

Mother got her way with the librarian, of course. Ellis was forced to come with us to the lake. As Socialists, she said, it was our duty to see that all mankind was happy. We drove to the park gate, left the car, and walked the last two hundred yards across the grass. George and my brother ran on fast to get into the water. I raced with them, for I liked giving Ellis a distant view of myself, and left him and Mother dawdling behind. Ellis had the bathing trunks under his arm; the bundle looked like a book he was going to read. Presently Mother broke into a trot to make up for lost time, talking as she ran. Ellis trotted, too.

"I can't run in these shoes. I've ricked my shoulder," said Mother as she puffed up to me. She sat on a stone bench on the stretch of concrete where the diving board and the newly built changing rooms were. She shook her shoulder to get her breath back, and as she gazed at the lido she said, "Have you ever seen anything so wonderful?"

I went off and got changed. The lake was a sight! I don't exaggerate. There were thousands of people—well, no, hundreds—some in the water already, others queuing up at the gate, and others lined up two deep to get at the diving board. A flag was flying over one of the buildings. For years the lake, which is large and with willows hanging over the far bank, was simply ornamental and empty except for a few ducks quacking on it. Now it was striped with bodies near the water's edge, and farther out there were hundreds of what looked like coconuts —the heads of the swimmers. Half the town was there.

Ellis's first words were: "They've smashed it up." A good description. Usually still or rippling, the water was now like a splintered mirror and there was scarcely a yard between any of the people—at any rate, not near the shore.

"A mob," Ellis said, opining.

Mother said, "Ellis, you mustn't be a snob."

Ellis heaved up a thought. "I prefer nature," he said.

"But people are nature, Ellis," Mother said.

Ellis was taken aback. He frowned. One more opinion had been ruined. His love for Mother had gone.

"Come on," said Mother to Ellis, taking off her glasses and greedy for the water. "Get your things off." And she went off to change. I had already changed, as I have said, and was made to stand guard over Ellis, who did not move. I saw he was plotting to slip away when we had gone in.

"I took a walk here last night. I often go for a walk," he said quietly to me. "It was still light. No one was about—only a dog. You could see every branch, every leaf of the trees reflected in the water, going down and down and down."

"It's only ten feet deep in the middle," I said.

"Ten feet!" he said and stepped back, wiping his forehead with the back of his hand.

He was disappointed with me when I laughed.

There were shouts from the diving board, where a very thin man with his trunks flapping on his bones was bouncing up and down; then up went his heels. George and my brother followed him. I was longing to go. At last Mother came out, bulging in her old-fashioned black suit —an embarrassing sight. "Please get into the water quick," I wanted to say to her. But she waited to say to Ellis, "Why haven't you changed?"

Ellis gave her a lover's last pleading look and then went off miserably.

"He is scared," I said. "He thinks he'll sink through to Australia."

"Look after him and see he goes in," said Mother, who was off at once to the diving board. She went in with a thump and a man said, "Wait for the tidal wave on the other side."

I was tired of waiting, but when Ellis came out, changed, I cheated. "Good," I said and left him.

I was soon in the water. George and my brother were swimming out beyond the thick crowd along the shore. Mother was following them and I raced after them.

"Where's Ellis?" shouted Mother when I caught up.

"He's back there."

"You oughtn't to leave him like that. It's selfish."

"He can't swim."

"Teach him," Mother said. "I'll be along in a minute."

Mother was always on at me about my selfishness. So after a while I swam back and waded through the crowd.

"Good!" I shouted.

Ellis was in, all right. He was standing scarcely waist-deep in the brown water. It was strange to see only half of Ellis; it made him seem more human. People bumped into him and every time this half-Ellis was bumped he turned his head as if to say a few words. He was standing lost, as puzzled as a bust by what was going on around him. Then his arm moved; he scooped up some water in his hand and had a look at it, as if to say something about water to anyone near. But since everyone was tumbling and splashing about him, he glumly tipped the handful of water back. When he saw me, he waded back three yards

to the rocky bank, with the sudden vainglory of one baptized late in
life, and got out. He stood with the water pouring off his thick white
body and making a pool around him. He had the furtive look of one
who has done half his duty. I had done mine. I left him and went off
to the diving board.

The crowd was still pouring in at the gate. The queues for the
high-diving platform and the diving board were long and busy. I joined
one of them and looked out for Mother, and after a long wait I saw
her. She was coming in. You couldn't miss her black suit in the crowd,
and when she got to the shallow water she stood up, looking for Ellis.
Then she ducked under, somersaulted and tumbled about like a kid.
She was enjoying herself. Someone turned round and saw her bottom
and gave it a slap. I wished she wouldn't make an exhibition of herself,
but no one in the water noticed her much. They were all packed
together, splashing.

I went for the high-diving platform. On my way up the crowded
ladder, where people were so slow, I looked again for Mother and Ellis.
I didn't see her at first, but I saw him. He was still standing on the bank,
dripping, with three or four youths nearby. He was touching one or two
of them on their arms, to make them listen to him. They nodded and
turned away. Then he pulled at them again and started pointing. I got
slowly higher up the ladder. Ellis had not got the attention of the group
and his opinions were increasing. He was still pointing. Presently his
shoulders straightened and his chest filled out; an enormous opinion
was coming out of him—one that made them draw away, gaping
shiftily at one another. And then I saw Mother. I saw her face as she
rolled over on her back in the water. Her mouth was open and her face
was dirty at the lips and both her legs came up in the air. Her eyes were
closed. A girl next to me on the ladder said, "Look—that woman down
there is in trouble. She's drowning."

Although there were several people only a yard or so away from her
—two of them were actually throwing a ball over her—no one paid any
attention. I pushed my way back down the ladder and then I saw Ellis
turn and shout to the group that had moved back to consider her. I
saw him step down in the water and wade toward her. He was alongside
her, trying to get his arms round her body. She rolled out of them and
then I saw mud on her feet. He was wrestling with her and calling to
a man to hold her, but the man's hand slithered. Then Ellis at last got
her by the slippery waist, blew out his chest, and in a struggling lunge
lifted her, heaved her, blundered with her, dragging her to the bank.

I was down from the ladder and was rushing to the spot where a policeman was saying, "Put her over there," and there was Ellis alone, carrying Mother—the whole of her!—to a bench against the wall, with a trail of water following him and, after the water, a cortege of respectful people. I pushed my way among them and bumped into Ellis, who, being short, was shoved away by the crowd from the bench where Mother lay.

"She's all right," he said importantly.

Then George and my brother ran up and pushed their way into the scrum.

I can't give a clear account of what happened. I got to Mother. She looked so slimy and wet and swollen in the face. A lot of people were saying what a scandal it was—a woman drowning a few feet from the shore in a crowd like that and no one taking any notice of her; and arguments about what is nearest to the eye is hardest to see, and strong swimmers are always the weakest, and the same thing happened to a child at the town swimming bath last year, there ought to be a law, and an argument about who pulled her out. Mother came back to life quickly and the crowd thinned away, moralizing. When we got her wrapped up and sitting up, she was soon herself and very angry. I took her to the changing room and got her dressed.

"Horrible little man with his arms round me," she said. "Quite unnecessary."

"It was Ellis."

"No, it wasn't," Mother said. She'd been pulled out by some brute who tore the shoulder strap of her suit, she said. We got the car round and put her into it. Ellis was alone and stood ashamed, at a distance. He conveyed that he had not intended to intrude in a family matter.

"Come on, Ellis," my brother called.

Ellis did not answer; he looked crushed. What he wanted to do was to stand there and give a full account of what had passed while he stood arguing with the youths at the water's edge. We pushed him into the car, and Mother said irritably as we drove off, "Ellis, why don't you take off your waistcoat?"

She glowered, and when we got home and gave her a drink she went on glowering. She hated anyone to take charge of her and she hated our few cautious jokes. "My shoulder went and I lost my balance," she said. She was firm that whoever the brute was who brought her in was not Ellis. He had the tact to say nothing and we were obliged to thank him with our glances.

But slowly, as we began to think back on the incident we came round, as always, in self-defence, to Mother's point of view. We stopped murmuring thanks to Ellis; it was not quite right that an outsider should rescue Mother. And there was a change in him. He had lost his habit of gazing at Mother and all desire to have an opinion seemed to have gone out of him. Before long, we were relieved to hear him say he must go. We didn't want him there all night. I went with him to the door.

"See you soon," I said, putting out my hand.

He took my hand and held it hard. His hand was not like George's or my brother's.

"Three feet of water," he said. "Three feet of water. Muddy at the bottom." Not in self-disparagement, not an opinion, though perhaps a criticism of something.

Whatever it was, we both gave a shout of laughter and shut the door, and I walked to the gate with him laughing, and the laughter so shook me from head to toe that I suddenly kissed him in a "Now-what-do-you-think-of-that?" way. All he said was, "Come out."

"I'll walk with you to the corner."

We marched down the street, silent as soldiers. We said nothing and we could hear only the sound of our shoes. It was as if our feet were talking. At the corner, where the main road begins, cars were rushing by.

"Come on," he said. And again his hand gripped mine and all the houses I knew in that street began to look different. We walked on and suddenly Ellis gave a peculiar jump, like a frog, and we laughed to the next turning and the next, from street to street, bumping together.

"Where are we going?"

"To the park."

"It's closed."

"I know a place where you can get in."

And so we did get in. The everyday smell of the pavements went and we stood in the night glow of the grass, under the trees, which were as black as men against the town lights. The sky was like pink water above us and we were sinking, sinking, sinking. My heart thumping for breath, at the bottom of the world, until somewhere near the trees Ellis stopped his little jumps and I sat down exhausted. I was clutching at him, pulling him under with me and struggling with the kisses that came out of him and throwing my hair back to get more. He looked wicked in the dark.

The next day, to the *bang, bang, bang* of the band, we marched in the pageant. It banged the way my heart banged in the park. I wore a high conical hat with a veil hanging from it. Ellis had a green jerkin and carried a pikestaff. I could hardly bear to look at him for fear of laughing, but when we got near the town hall and the band stopped, I said, "Well, Lancelot, show me the back of your hand."

"It's not the same thing," said Ellis and started to explain, but I stopped him.

I taught him to swim that summer.

1968

Our Wife

I agree that my wife is a noise and a nuisance, especially in a seaport and sailing place like Southampton. Even her little eyes long for trouble. People come down to sail on the weekend, clumping about in gum boots and sweaters, and they hear Molly's voice and ridicule by the quay: "Stupid yachting people! Look at *him*. He's missed the mooring twice. They can't even sail."

In the restaurant—it is called The Ship—it is ten to one she will be shouting, and then she'll suddenly stop dead. "Why does everyone stare?" she says.

"I expect it is because your conversation is more interesting than theirs," I say.

And Trevor, who is with us, of course, and who always repeats her last phrase or mine, slaps his eager knee and says, "Yes, more interesting."

"After all, you *were* talking about my first wife," I say.

Another slap from Trevor, who grins and says, "Your first wife!"

Molly is as noisy as a guttersnipe. Or as Jack (I remember) once said, "As noisy as a blow-lamp, but pretty." Jack was her first husband.

The noise is what has attracted us all to her. We have loved it. She has opinions about everything. She loves an argument. Anything will do. In the old days, I remember, she started a row about whether Jack and I were the same height. He was, in fact, exactly the same height as myself—six feet one and a half inches. She wouldn't have it. About height she is a fanatic. She is under five feet high, and one of her boasts is that her father was the shortest captain in the Royal Navy. I can see her getting up on a chair in the sitting room to peer at the pencil marks we had made on the wall. Standing on the chair, she was the same height as ourselves. This wonder silenced her, but when I helped her down she was arguing again. Our ruler was wrong and so was the tape measure—the taunts shot up at us like a boy's pellets. Jack and I stood looking like a pair of fools who had overgrown our strength, while she went on to say that most of the weights and measures used in shops were fraudulent.

"They probably are," Jack said.

"There you are," she jeered at me.

"Jack's right," I said.

She gaped at us. "I see," she said. "You've fixed it between you."

Those were happy days.

That memory of Jack and me standing against the wall ten years ago takes me to something else—what he said in a pub in the little place on the Kent coast where they then lived. She was sitting on a bar stool between two men who were arguing with her about sailing—her father, the Captain, had been a tartar about boat behaviour when she was a child, and she hated sailing more than anything—and Jack and I heard her say to one of them, "You want cooling down," and she put her hand out for the ice bucket. If she had been tall enough, she would have reached it and emptied it over their heads.

Jack was ill, as he often was in those days. In the lazy, detached, speculative voice of the very sick, he said, "See that? Two of them. Molly is a girl who needs two husbands at a time."

He had seen something I had never noticed, and he said this with a little malice. He was either warning or defining me—or even arranging for the succession.

I am a construction engineer and I was working near their village on a new dock for tankers that was being built in this marsh country. I was a widower living in lodgings, without much to do in my spare time except play about with my boat. All those attacks on people who sailed were really attacks on me. It was one of the bonds between us—her hatred of my boat. She and Jack lived in an old house in the village that had become a hell of trucks and bulldozers on the way to the dock. I got to know Jack and Molly when a big tree was blown down in a gale

in their garden and made a large gash in a brick wall. I talked to them
and very soon I was offering to clear up the mess. Molly's husband was
not strong enough. He was hacking at the tree with a weak man's fury,
and was soon exhausted. I got a machine from the dock, and soon they
were watching me work. I am a practical man. I'm good at things like
that. The noise of the machine drowned her opinion of what I was
doing. All she could do was to shake her brown hair.

In the following evenings, I rebuilt the wall and she stood arguing
that it was "only a theory" that plumb lines hang straight. After that
job was done I was captured. It was an old house, and soon I was
mending doors, unstopping drains, relagging pipes, putting in washers,
repairing their car. I even painted a door bright blue after she and Jack
quarrelled about the colours. And all the time she was arguing about
how our dock would pollute the river, destroy the countryside, and
drive away the bird life.

"Think of the tankers bringing oil for your car," I'd say.

Then she would turn on Jack's doctors, on hospitals, and then on
Jack and me. Men were always up to something. "You can't deny it,"
she would say. "Look at Jack. Look at you. It's guilt."

I don't know what she meant by "guilt" and I don't think Jack did,
either, but it made us feel more interesting. She'd get on to "guilt" and
say Jack was oversexed, or turn about and say he was undersexed. Or
that he threw money away. Or never spent a penny. Or was shut up
in himself. Or perpetually running after other women. She wore her
hair short and had the habit of giving a nervous sniff in the middle of
her sentences—an original and wistful sound in the general clatter
which attracted me—and her face would go very red while her mouth
went sputtering gaily away like a little motorbike. Jack listened to her,
blinking busily as if he were taking notes. After a tirade, he'd get up,
give a nod, and say quietly. "She's an old character." And he would go
off, leaving me with her. I would often get up to go with him, but she
would stop me. "Stay here. He's going to sit on the sea wall. Leave him
alone. It may be a poem."

For Jack was a poet; here was the fascination for me. In my trade
I'd never run across a poet. Goodness knows how they lived—he read
for publishers, I think—but every so often he would go up to his room
or sit on the sea wall, and as if he were some industrious hen, he would
(as I once said) lay a poem. Molly was angry with me when I said that.
She allowed no one to make jokes about his poems except herself.

I wish I had not made this joke, for in a few months his health got
very bad. He collapsed. It was I who took him to hospital. I thought

he simply had an ulcer. He sat up in bed with a tube in his mouth and I tried to cheer him up.

"You must not make me laugh," he said. "It will tear the stitches."

In a few days he came home, walked down the village street, and took a glass of whisky when he got back, and that night he died.

The first thing Molly said to me was indignant. "He borrowed five pounds from me this morning," she said.

Then she became exalted and tender. "It was wonderful that he left the hospital the day before that nurse who was so good to him was leaving. She couldn't bear the matron. No one could."

Then her grief overcame her. "I can't bear it," she wept. "I can't believe he isn't upstairs now."

"Neither can I," I said. "I've never felt like this before."

I loved Jack. I loved her. I had, I felt, been married to both of them.

"The lock on the wardrobe door has gone again," she suddenly said, angrily weeping and accusing me.

I put my arm round her shoulders. She had become motionless and heavy as lead with grief, and she shook my arm off.

"I'll go and look at it," I said. "Leave it to me."

For a poor man, Jack had occasional reckless fits. He hankered after expensive antiques. This wardrobe I knew well, for I had three or four times tried to repair the lock for them. Owing to the weight of the doors, it was often going wrong. The wardrobe was an oaken piece brought over from France by Huguenots—so Molly swore—in the seventeenth century, and it stood in their bedroom. It was the first of Jack's purchases, and she and he had a monumental row about it. She had been going to send it back to the shop, but Jack saved it in a very clever way: he wrote a poem about it. This made it sacred in her eyes. After this, he became a secret furniture buyer and had to store the stuff out of her sight, and once or twice I collected it for him.

"So that is what you and Jack were up to," she said after he died. She admired our shadiness. To punish me—and Jack, too—she sold the lot, but not the wardrobe.

The furniture episode became another bond between us, especially because of the to-ings and fro-ings of the sale, during the time of her grief. Her grief recalled mine when my wife had died, and we often talked about it. She would gaze and nod and talk quietly. She became, except for the tiny sniff, a soundless person. Slowly her grief passed. After a year, my job at the dock came to an end. I was to be moved to the London office and I started packing.

Molly's character suddenly returned to her when she saw my clothes stacked on the table in my lodgings. "It's a good thing!" she said. "It will get you away from that idiotic boat."

My transfer to London was a victory for her opinion. She glittered with victory.

"I'll take you out in it," I said, "for a last sail."

I was astonished, even moved, by her reply. "All right!" she said defiantly, but I could see that, despite her victory, her lip was trembling. I could see that she did not want me to leave, and I didn't want to leave her. I knew that when we were out on the water and I was, perhaps, coming about and making her duck the boom, I would be able to say what I could not say to her on land. We set off, but soon it began to blow, the sails rapped out, and the wind carried away everything she said. She was indignant and frightened. When we got ashore she said, "You're a masochist, like Jack. It is all guilt."

"I'm going to sell her," I said, looking down at the boat from the quay wall. While we were out and I was putting in a reef, I had asked her to marry me.

"When you sell it," she said.

I sold it.

Unluckily for her, we hadn't been married for three months when the firm moved me from London back to Southampton. There was the sea again! There were those detested lovely white tents dotted over the water.

"All yachtsmen are liars," she said when she saw them, accusing me of arranging my transfer. I paid no attention to her; in fact, the trouble we had moving the furniture to our house took her mind off it.

Our house at Southampton was small. I wanted to put the wardrobe —she called it the "armoire"—on the ground floor, but she said it must go into the bedroom. To get it up there I had to take out a tall window and put a hoist in from an attic. The thing weighed a ton. It took two days and three men to get it into the bedroom. It had been Jack's first extravagance, and Molly was very proud of the difficulty it caused. She stood in the garden shouting at the men and came peering at it, to see they did not damage it. In fact, the lock did scrape the brickwork when the thing was halfway in.

The scrape on the brickwork must have weakened the lock, or perhaps the damp summer affected the doors in some way, for they did not easily close. In the winter, there would be a sudden click and one door would swing forward. I put it right, and then, after a malicious lull, the wardrobe—the armoire, I should say—would come open again.

Sometimes I worked on the lock; sometimes I wedged and re-wedged the feet, blaming the slope of the floor.

In the end, I succeeded, and for a long time the thing was quiet. But one night when I was making love to Molly a door came groaning open like a hound.

"What's that?" said Molly, pushing me away.

I paused in my efforts. "It's only Jack," I said. "It's haunted."

Now, why on earth I should have said such an appalling thing, and at such a moment, I cannot think. If there is one thing we all know, it is that you should never make a joke—if you call that a joke—when you are making love. I would have given anything to take the words back. Perhaps it was a sign that I was beginning to want help, as Jack had done. Hadn't he said she was a woman who needed two husbands?

The effect on Molly was surprising. She sat up, put on the light, and looking excitedly at the doors, she laughed. " 'Haunted'—that's very perceptive of you," she said, admiring me.

I was shocked by her laugh and pushed her down again. (But to be frank, love was a fitful thing with Molly. Now that we were married, she said I bullied her into it.) She got free of my arms, put on the light once more, gave herself a little shake like a dog, and gazed in a rapture of importance. "It's weird," she said. "It *could* be haunted. Jack always said nothing is forgotten."

Molly loved to sit up arguing in the middle of the night when I was exhausted. She said that all things were permeated by the people who had touched them. Now I made my second mistake: I said the armoire was probably alive with the hands of Huguenots. This idea annoyed her.

"It's very funny about you," she said. "I didn't know you were a jealous man. Or are you trying to change the subject?"

Jack! Huguenots! All of you! Listen to this! I want help! I cried to myself.

We were still arguing at three o'clock, when she changed round and said, "I'm glad you're not a jealous man. That means a lot to me."

I was carried away by this compliment and the softness of her voice. Only exhaustion could have put me off my guard.

Working in Southampton, I could see from my office window the sloping funnels of liners, the cranes dipping toward them and, beyond that, the water. As I have said, there was always a sail or two in sight, and on weekends there were scores of them. I had sometimes to go to the boatyards and there I would look with longing at some craft with beautiful lines on the stocks outside the sheds. The wings of the angry gulls and their quarrelling voices made me think of Molly with love, and it was while I was gazing in this weak mood at a beautiful, dark-blue thirty-foot sloop one afternoon that a man climbed out of her. He was a tall, lazy-voiced fellow, with a tired face, very slim and fair.

"She's lovely," I said.

"Lovely," he said.

"Cigarette?" I said.

"Cigarette? Thanks," he said. "I am selling her."

"Selling her?" I said.

He nodded. I nodded. An interesting fellow—quiet, a listener. We walked round the boat and had a look inside.

"Frankly," he said, "I can't afford her. I've got to give her up. I've just bought an Aston-Martin. I can't run both."

Speed was what he liked, he said. He liked to *move.* He gave a lick to his lip; he was a man like myself, a man giving up one thing for another. I sighed at our singular unity.

"We might do a deal—if I can persuade my wife," I said.

"Ah," he said, "your wife."

His name was Trevor. I asked him to come up to the house later and have a drink. "But not a word," I said.

Trevor was an understanding man.

"Who is this man you're bringing up here?" my wife said when I told her. "One of your sailing friends—I know! What are you and he up to?"

"No," I said. "He's given up sailing. He can't afford it."

One more victory was in my wife's small eyes. And when Trevor arrived, wearing a white pullover under his dandyish long jacket, and very narrow trousers, she looked from one to the other of us to see who was the taller. I saw her immediate interest. Without realizing it, I was at the beginning of a master stroke. I had brought to the house a tall man who had given up boats. She was excited by the arrival of an ally.

"My husband's mad about them, quite out of his mind," she said to Trevor. "He's thinking of them all the time. He's always up to something, hanging around boatyards—don't think I don't know. He pretends he's at the engineer's, but it's always a boat."

"A boat," said Trevor. There was a gentle, weary note in his voice, and it conveyed to her that mine was one of those infantile and tedious vices that afflict so many men and from which he was now free.

"Better than chasing women," I said.

"Women!" she said. "It's a substitute! Don't tell me."

Trevor listened to us with appreciation as we wrangled. He lived alone, and he looked with pleasure at the excitements of home life. My wife, walking up and down and clattering on, with a glass in her hand, was adding to her victories, and Trevor occasionally glanced at me with private congratulation.

"I'll tell you what happened the other night!" she cried. "We've got an old French armoire in our bedroom and the lock keeps going wrong. He makes out he's repaired it, but I don't know—it's weird! It opens every time we get into bed. Do you know what Tom said? He said, 'I bet that's my first wife again.' " She gave a loud laugh. "Look at his face. Guilt."

"Guilt it must be," I said.

"You've been married before?" said Trevor—his first original sentence. I felt gratitude to him for saying this; it created an intimacy.

"Of course he has," said my wife. "He keeps quiet about it. That's what is infuriating about him. He keeps so quiet."

"Jack was quiet," I said.

"No need to bring up Jack," she said in her sacred voice.

"Who was Jack?" said Trevor.

"He was my husband," she said, stopping with dignity. And then she turned on me. "Tell him about your wife's iron boot," she jeered.

"Iron boot!" said Trevor. He was overjoyed by her.

But she saw she had gone too far and calmed a little. "Not actually an iron boot," she said, and when she laughed her eyebrows were like a pair of wings. "Her skates. He took her roller-skating—roller-skating, my dear!—and one came off and she fell over and he got engaged. Poor Tom."

Then Trevor uttered his next original sentence to me: "Why can't you mend the lock?"

"He's always mending it—or says he is," she said. "He's useless with his hands."

"It's a French thing, very heavy, eighteenth-century," I said.

"Seventeenth," she said. "The Huguenots brought it over."

"Full of Huguenots," I said.

Trevor heard out this dispute, and then he uttered three original sentences. "My mother has got one," he said. "We had a lot of trouble with it. I got it right in the end."

I gazed at Trevor's hands. Like his voice, they were limp and tired. They were long and thin.

"I wish you'd mend ours," Molly said to him in a business-like way. "And then we'd get some sleep." She gave me a sharp look.

"It's probably like my mother's," Trevor said. "They're all alike. I don't mind having a go. Tomorrow?"

I saw that I had found a treasure. The boat was as good as mine, if Trevor and I worked together on it. And there was more to it than the boat.

"There you are!" said Molly, sneering gaily at me at having an order obeyed as simply as that.

The following evening I found Trevor on the sofa in our sitting room with a large broken-veined bruise on his forehead. He had mended the lock, but he had moved my wedges, and just as he was testing it the door swung open and hit him on the head. Molly was mopping the wound.

I elected him at once as Molly's additional husband.

Our life—or, rather, my life—is more peaceful now. I don't mean less noisy or less of a wrangle, but simply that Trevor now bears some of the burden. He comes round most evenings and if he misses a few days she is out after him to find out what he is up to.

"He has girls in his flat," she says angrily when she comes back. "I know! Making out he stays in and listens to records. He never listens to ours!"

"He likes noise," I tell her. "He said so last time when he was here. It's company."

Trevor turns up again, and he and I say nothing about our transaction. She has been out with him in his racing car, which terrifies her, and to me she says, "It's nothing but sex. A substitute. You defend him, of course."

It is true that when he runs her up to London for the day I go sailing. When he brings her back she says, "Racing drivers are a lot of impotent morons."

I say to Trevor, "She's an old character."

"Character," says Trevor, slapping his knee at the word. Then with a sly look at me—for he likes danger as much as I do—he perhaps says, "Let's go and eat at The Ship." (It is near the mooring where I keep my secret boat.)

We drive down, and at the first sight of a sail she starts about "the stinking yachtsmen." At dinner, she says, in a voice that makes everyone in the restaurant stop eating and stare at us, "Guilt, that is what it is! There is something going on between you two. Men!"

And when her voice drops for a second, she entrances both of us with that other noise, the little dog-like sniff.

1969

The Last
Throw

The new week began for Karvo. For him weeks were always new. Cheered by the doorman, receptionists, secretaries, he went impatiently into purdah in the lift: on the silent top floor he came out, all animal, onto the stretches of green carpet which seemed to grow like the lawns of the country-house life he had just left. He raced to his enormous desk, on which lay an elephant's foot mounted on silver presented to him by an African ruler after his latest film, and he pressed a button. The call was answered by the fit of dry coughing that contained Chatterton.

"Chatty," Karvo began vigorously—then reproachfully, "I thought you had given up smoking?"

"I have," said Chatty. "That was nostalgia. I live in the past."

"Can you spare a minute?"

It always took Chatty longer to get to Karvo than Karvo could bear. Passing the open doors of offices, meeting people in the corridors, anywhere in the building, Chatty paused and, with the cough and the ravaged smile of dandyish human wreckage, asked people how they were. How far downhill on the way to dilapidation are you, when shall we all be human souls together? his large eyes seemed to ask. One or two hypochondriacs would tell him in detail. Why does this preposterous organization run so well, Chatty sometimes asked himself—for he had the vanity of casualties—and replied, "I am the oil in the wheels, the perambulating clinic, the ambulance, the Salvation Army, the conscience—if it has one—kept alive by a sun lamp, an expensive tailor and dozens of teeny-weeny little pills." And with the air of one saying goodbye to himself, Chatty walked on.

Also, he added honestly, kept alive by Karvo, King of Kings, the Elephant's Foot, the Life Force. Now for the Monday morning shot! At board meetings Chatty often doodled pictures of Karvo as an elephant sitting in the studio with a crown on his head, a cigar in his mouth and a sceptre in his hand, while a naked cast of well-known actors and actresses and teams of cameramen the size of ants crawled before him. Now Chatty slipped into Karvo's room like a well-dressed fever and saw Karvo in clothes that Karvo supposed were the right thing for high life in the English countryside. He was sitting in front of a very fat book that looked like the family Bible, and there was an uncommon expression of piety or, at any rate, of elevation on his large, unmanageable face.

"When did you go to the doctor last?" said Karvo kindly, but passed immediately to what he loved to talk about on Mondays: his weekend.

Karvo was at that period in his life when the tide of democracy and cinema had floated him into the private boscage where peers, millionaires and merchant bankers spent their lives. Chatty sat down on a sofa and waited to be carried into Karvo's dreamland. At once Karvo was on to the Hamilton-Spruces for a second, advanced to the Hollinsheds and then, after a long detour among the connexions of the Esterhazys, the Radziwills, the Hohenzollerns, the Hotspurs, Talbots, Buckinghams, the Shakespearean cast of the English counties, finally swerved to France to meet the Albigenses.

"Aren't they cousins of the Radziwills?" Karvo wanted to know.

"No," said Chatty. "The Albigenses were a persecuted race. They are extinct."

Karvo turned to the title page of the book before him. It was not the Bible: it was not the *Almanach de Gotha*. It was a bound typescript.

"They were massacred," said Chatty. "In the South of France. About the twelfth century. Because of their religion."

"The South of France," said Karvo. His eyes switched on a sharp commercial light. "How many were massacred?"

He was thinking of a crowd scene.

"I don't know—a million; no, perhaps only a few hundred thousand," said Chatty.

"The French ambassador gave this manuscript to me at the Hamilton-Spruces. His wife wrote it," said Karvo. "Will you have a look at it?" Chatty had one more of his coughing fits as he took the manuscript.

"You *haven't* given up," Karvo accused him. "Cheating never pays."

"It's your cigar," said Chatty.

Chatty went to his office, opened the bottom drawer of the desk where he kept his dozens of bottles of pills, and rested his feet on the open drawer as he sat down to read. First he looked up the name of the ambassador. Then he studied the name on the title page. As he expected, the author could not possibly be the wife of the French ambassador. In the hothouse of Society, Karvo usually misnamed the blooms. The name of that lady was not even in the long list of acknowledgments which began with a few eminences, went on to the Bibliothèque Nationale, the British Museum, combed the universities, and ended with inexhaustible gratitude to a dearest husband without whose constant advice and patient etc., etc. The dedication read, "To Doggie from Pussy."

Chatty studied the index and appendices and then, rearranging his feet on the drawer, was unable to prevent himself from memorizing six hundred pages of historical research. On Friday he went in to see Karvo.

"I'm just off to the country," he said. "I've read that thing. The author is Christine Johnson, a learned woman, first-class historian—no doubt about that. If you're interested in the Albigenses, this is the last word. You'll be glad to hear about the Cathari heresy. You know, of course, that the Cathari were dualists. Early dieters too: fast Monday, Wednesday and Friday every week. This annoyed the Pope. I think she'll have trouble all the same in Chapters Nine and Ten. Speaking as an historian . . ."

Karvo looked up from the script he was reading.

"Thank you," said Chatty. "Speaking as an historian I would say she is entirely speculative in Chapter Ten. Mad, I'd say. Massacres, of course. Several. The Albigenses were exterminated. There's nothing in it for us."

"Massacres?" said Karvo again. "What's the story?"

"Page 337. Incest," said Chatty. "Brother and sister, separated at birth by religious fanatics, meet again, don't know each other, get married—not knowing that after she's been raped in Toulouse and as

they escape over the Pyrenees a woman called Clothilde de San
Severino has betrayed them to the Inquisition, which tortures both.
Roughly that."

"Torture," said Karvo looking up. "What kind? Incest? Have you
marked the pages I'd like to see?" He softened. "My sister would never
have let you get into the state you're in, Chatty. Would you mind
seeing this woman—just politeness—tact, you know."

"All right," said Chatty.

Karvo's face blurred into one of his occasional looks of shame.

"Do you know her?" Chatty said.

Karvo shrugged.

The woman, Christine Johnson, had gone to her house in Paris but
came to Chatty's office a fortnight later. Chatty spent an hour and a
half with her. Late in the afternoon he went to Karvo's office, opening
the door wide instead of sliding in, and shutting it with careful cere-
mony. He sat down on Karvo's distant sofa, put his feet up and said
nothing.

"You're quiet," said Karvo.

"Have you ever experienced a miracle?" said Chatty.

"Many," said Karvo.

"Yes, I know. So have I. I'll put it another way. Have you ever met
again or accidentally passed in the street, your first girl friend whom
you haven't seen or heard of for fifteen or twenty years?"

"Mine was in my pram," said Karvo. "I don't remember."

"I'm not talking of childish vice. I mean your first adult girl friend.
Have you seen her since, even at a distance?"

"That's a miracle I've avoided."

"Why?" said Chatty. "I can see her: short, very fat, strong glasses,
a touch of something on the skin, spots perhaps, dirty raincoat, sullen
with congested virtue, round-shouldered. (There's nothing against that.
A lot of girls go in for being round-shouldered: they are trying out ways
of being important or graceful, learning the job.) But wearing a seaman's heavy black jersey, no breasts or, rather, creased woollen bumps.
The jersey is too large. Walking as if still marching into the classroom.
'Girls! Forward, march! Follow Diana.' Another thing—you could
never see her alone. She was always with some other girl—very pretty,
but for some insane reason the pretty one didn't appeal to you."

"Come to the point," said Karvo.

"And I don't suppose you've ever seen her years later with the man she married eventually. You imagined he was a weed who kept a small electrical shop or something like that and they lived out at—well, you know those places—with four children who have kicked the garden to pieces. Informative, rebuking, that's what she was. Always ticking you off—'No, Karvo. Stop it, Karvo.' "

"I remember that," said Karvo, putting on his martyred face. "Stop wasting my time. Kitchen sink is finished in pictures—you know that, Chatty."

"I've just met mine," said Chatty. "Can I have a drink? No, don't ring for it. I'll get it myself."

Chatty went to Karvo's drink cabinet. It was large and designed to look like the west front of a Gothic cathedral but without the saints.

"I can see why you shy off the subject," said Chatty. "I would have done so two hours ago, until Christine walked into my office. Except for the electrician and the four children, she used to be exactly as I have told you—but, my God! A butterfly has risen from that awful chrysalis. If it had been her pretty friend Ann I would not have been surprised —but Christine! The miracle has happened. As a matter of fact, I must have changed too. Down at reception she told the girl she had an appointment with Sir Arthur Chatterton. She is not the wife of the French ambassador."

"Who said she was?" said Karvo.

"Sweet Jesus—but let it pass.

"She's not only exquisite. She has brains." Chatty's voice became sad. "More than brains. Considering what she's got—what a waste."

"How d'you mean?" said Karvo. "Many women have first-class minds."

"I wasn't thinking of her mind," said Chatty. "I was thinking of her money. She's rich. I was thinking of her clothes. How many distinguished lady historians do you know with emeralds on their fingers, who have sacked Paris for their clothes, whose hats seem to have blown over from the Place Vendôme and who, besides owning houses in London and Paris, spend their winters on their dear, dear brother's estate in Toulouse?

"She was wearing a hat like a birthday cake made of air and a very short dress. I suppose it was a dress? She seemed to be getting out of it rather than wearing it—pretty well succeeded on the left thigh and the right shoulder. A hothouse flower with large glasses like windows. All the fat gone. A butterfly—but what am I talking about? A dragonfly," he said. He coughed.

"You oughtn't to talk so much," said Karvo.

"I knew her by her teeth," Chatty said sadly. "And her voice. It used to come out frosted out of the heart's deep freeze. It still does. Oh dear, it brought it all back. Christine and then her pretty friend Ann and me all sitting in Lipps," said Chatty.

"Is she married?" said Karvo.

"To a man in the Foreign Office, an adviser, whatever that is. Ronnie," said Chatty.

"So," said Karvo. "You've missed the boat."

"Oh no," said Chatty, "they've asked me to dinner the week after next when they come back from Scotland. They're staying with the Loch Lomonds."

Karvo raised both his chins.

"I've stayed with the Loch Lomonds," he said.

"So what was it like?" Karvo sneered. "Bollinger, Mouton Rothschild . . ."

Chatty was lying once more on the sofa in Karvo's room.

"You remember the husband of your first girl friend," said Chatty. "The man with the small electrical shop or television rentals, if you like —the man who replaced you in the loving heart you broke . . ."

"I never broke any girl's heart," said Karvo, looking up from his letters. "Accountants break mine."

"Imagine you are back in Paris. Now here's a girl, Cambridge, double first, ruins her poor pink-rimmed eyes in the Bibliothèque Nationale, borrows the occasional ten or twenty francs from you because she's hungry—you see her, this Miss Sorbonne in her chrysalis days, your friend, suddenly avoiding you in the Boulevard Saint Germain, walking by night, in silence, except that she scrapes a foot. She is with a tall young man who keeps bumping his dirty raincoat into hers because he walks aslant and bends to talk down into the top of her head, as if he were trying to graze there—not that there was much to graze on, her hair was very thin. He edges her towards the gutter or into those walls saying *Défense d'afficher*, as the case may be, talking about the Guermantes, say . . . And you say bitterly to yourself, 'Two pairs of strong glasses, two sets of rabbit teeth have felt an irresistible attraction.'"

One of Karvo's telephones rang.

"Karvo," said Karvo, heaving half of his body over the desk and in a voice suddenly plaintive said, "No, my darling. Yes, my darling. You'd better not, my darling. In that case you must, my darling."

And then put down the telephone and got his body back onto the chair, breathless, his eyelids blinking, paler than his face. He had his crucifixion look and he said to Chatty, "What were you saying? That was Dolly."

"I was saying," said Chatty, sitting up and raising his voice, "they now live in a bloody mansion! Cézannes, Picassos, Soutines, Renoirs, up the stairs, everywhere. From the drawing-room window you can see all the most expensive flowering shrubs and trees in bloom in the Crescent. A manservant brings in the champagne and in comes the adviser to the Foreign Office."

"Who is that?"

"I've told you," said Chatty. "Ronnie.

"There he is," said Chatty. "And he leans down and starts grazing on *your* hair now. He is young but has gone bald early—very confidential and nods at every word you say. Congratulating himself. As she floats into the room he says, 'It's a winner, isn't it?'

"She is wearing a dress made of two sheets of flame. One of the flames appears to be looped between her legs, but, of course, that can't be true, and for the rest of the evening you keep trying to work out how she got it on. And she says, as she comes in, 'Doggie!' And he looks at her and says 'Pussy!' They've come back from Scotland via Vienna and Paris."

"Who else was at the party?" said Karvo thirstily.

"No party," said Chatty. "Just his sister Rhoda. Up from the country for a couple of days' shopping. A nice pensive woman, older than her brother, looking like an engraving of George Eliot, heavy dark hair peacefully parted in the middle, Victorian brooch, a long romantic poem. A woman you see talking to gardeners, walking on lawns, driving off in a little car to local education committees. A botanist too, in a religious way. We talked about a bowl of white peonies in the drawing room. 'Paeonia,' she said. She was very reserved and shy. She said the plant had been introduced into Cornwall by the Brethren of Saint Michael. In the thirteenth century. She wouldn't interest you, Karvo, she's a good woman."

"She doesn't," said Karvo.

"Quite a medieval evening up till then," said Chatty. "Suddenly Ronnie, the husband, says, 'Pussy, you must *show* them!' As he says this he gives a lick of glee to his lips and his hands jump about in his trouser pockets. 'Oh, Doggie,' she says. 'Shall I be naughty? It's dreadful, dearest Chatty. Hats, Chatty! I've robbed the Place Vendôme. Bring your champagne.' "

And Chatty told how her weak thin hand took his—he could feel all the bones in it—attached to an arm of steel. He was nearly dead, he said, by the time they all got up the long curving staircase, not from the climb so much as from sinking almost to the ankles in the hush of a deep yellow stair carpet. The four of them arrived in a large bedroom that had three high wide windows, the bay swelling over the lawn of the Crescent. But Chatty imagined from what was going on on the walls of the room that he was in the Burmese jungle. He wouldn't have been surprised, he said, to see the violet bottoms of mandrills sitting in the branches. Furry animals, like animal royalty, were spread on the floor. There was a golden bed, a Cleopatra's barge. Ronnie's sister stood apart. She had obviously seen it all before, and as beauties often do, looked unwell. Ronnie's face had stopped nodding. His mouth opened and he looked like a man congratulating himself on being about to be turned into a tiger, for Christine took a little run, almost a flight, to a wardrobe—

"Don't bother about the wardrobe," said Karvo.

"—she pulled the doors open and out fell an enormous heap of hats, like a cloud of petals on the floor. About eighty of them. I spilled my champagne down my tie," said Chatty. "It was the least I could do. Let me go on. 'She'll wear them all,' Ronnie says. 'Pussy, is your back tired? She has to rest her back.' 'Doggie,' she says and pouts. Rhoda, the sister, is still standing apart. She is not drinking. She is a healthy woman who likes country walks, but when the hats come tumbling out she swells up and goes red in the face as if she is struggling against a pain in the chest. The stairs, of course. Heart, I suppose—all those stairs."

So, Chatty said, he tried to calm her by asking where she lived in the country, and she said she lived this side of Bath and he told her his aunt had a farm on the far side of the city and how he went down there for weekends. "It's your part of the country too," he said to Christine. "How nice, how strange.

"Always be careful when you talk to girls, Karvo," said Chatty. "Profit by my experience. She said I was mixing her up with Ann. Ann came from Bath. *She* came from Yorkshire."

"What of it?" said Karvo.

"Didn't your first girl friend ever slice you in half with a look?" said Chatty.

Karvo had stopped listening, so Chatty got down to business.

"We went downstairs to the Albigenses."

Ronnie edged him into a wall against a small Soutine as if about to give him extremely private information about a foreign government.

" 'The return to the twelfth century,' Ronnie says, 'it's absolutely *the* modern subject. It's the world today. Religious wars, mass murder, the crushing of small cultures. The Inquisition. It went on for a century. They appealed to the Pope, of course.' 'Dear dreadful Pope Innocent,' Christine called across. 'The Stalin of the time,' says Ronnie, bearing down closer. 'Tortures. The Provençal nobility appear in crowds on the scene.' "

Chatty gathered there was a sort of liberal called the Duc d'Aquitaine trying to keep the peace, but the murder of Peter of Castelnau brought Pope Innocent's storm troops down from the north.

"Castelnau, weren't they cousins?" says Christine to her husband. And to Chatty: "The Johnsons came originally from Toulouse."

The sister interrupts. "Putney," she says.

"You'll find it in the Cistercian records," says Christine. "Or you can look it up in Schmidt or in Vaissete."

It was a piquant moment, Chatty said. There you had on the one hand a scholarly genealogist who could slip back to the thirteenth century as easy as pie but who, to be frank, was a *belle laide,* especially when she showed her teeth, being challenged by a peaceful botanist who had a corner in monkish gardening.

"I enjoyed it," said Chatty to Karvo. "It took me back to the old days in Paris. I'm afraid the two ladies don't get on."

Karvo put on his martyred look.

"It was all right," said Chatty. "Ronnie saved the situation. A born diplomat. He started telling me about the children of light and the children of darkness and finished up talking about the Perfecti."

Karvo looked up.

"It's not a cigar," said Chatty.

The Johnsons asked Karvo to dinner.

"That woman's electric. You're wrong about her book," said Karvo to Chatty when he came back. "I read the passages you marked. Wow! There's a story. She's going places."

When the mid-Atlantic slick flooded into Karvo's English, Chatty knew that one of what he called Karvo's Seasons was about to begin.

"I think," said Karvo, "you offended her. Did you say something?"

"Something rude about the thirteenth century, I expect," said Chatty.

"No, something's bugging her," said Karvo.

"I left with Rhoda that evening. We walked down the side of the park under the trees," said Chatty. "Perhaps it was that. Now Rhoda, there's a woman. She knows the names of flowers. Too plump for you, Karvo. And forty. She's the complete English lady. So beautifully conventional and uncandid, quiet but deep, you know—when they talk about their neighbours you aren't sure whether they are people or rhododendrons; whether the Winstanleys, say, are a breed of cattle or the county education committee or an asparagus bed. A good green-fingered woman—knows what is ranunculaceous and what is not. In human life, I mean. The only trouble is that they are always doing something for others. Lovely summer night and all she can do is to ask me the name of Christine's professor in Paris. One of her neighbours wants to send her daughter there."

"What are you talking about?" said Karvo.

"I'm talking about love," said Chatty. "Not as you know it. I could love a woman like that."

"I want a treatment for this story," said Karvo. And with that, Karvo's Albigensian period began. The word "massacre" had caught him. So had "torture." So had "incest." So had Christine. His head filled up with crime, sex and churches, Romanesque towers, medieval obscenities, antiques. After a month he bought a Van Gogh—and wouldn't say what he gave for it—one of the painter's swirling cornfields, done in the asylum. It matched his mood. He galloped over the Pyrenees with the incestuous rebel couple. Everywhere he went—to expensive restaurants, embassies and house parties—Christine and her husband were there. They gave enormous parties.

"They never ask me," said Chatty.

"You know, of course," Karvo said, "she's a Castelnau. That's why she wrote the book."

"No," said Chatty. "That's her husband."

"I don't take to him," said Karvo. "You've got it wrong."

"I think," said Chatty, "they're both Castelnaus. There's a Castelnau Road in Putney."

"That's not surprising," said Karvo, briefly a historian. "The survivors and descendants of the Albigenses split up, half joined up with the Huguenots and went to Bordeaux and the other half to England. They made a fortune in cotton. That's where she gets her money. She told me her brother's still got the place in Toulouse."

"Incidentally, the Castelnaus were on the wrong side—in the pay of the Pope. Did she mention it?" said Chatty. "Of course, I know one should never trust one's ancestors. Does Dolly get on with her?" Chatty asked, speaking of Karvo's latest wife.

"You know what women are about clothes. I'm taking Dolly to Paris," said Karvo.

"My aunt is not well. I'm off to the country," Chatty said.

There were long seasons in Karvo's life; there were short ones when he was between pictures. Seasons were apt to turn into cycles. The summer passed. The winds of early September were bashing the country gardens. "The hollyhocks are flat on their backs," Rhoda wrote in a note to Chatty. She added a postscript saying, "I discovered the professor's name—it was Ducros." Grit was blowing into Chatty's office window as he read the treatment.

"The story has no shape or end," he said to Karvo. "What does it mean, what is the message?"

Karvo spread his arms wide and held them in the air. Seeing nothing in them he began to reach for a button on his desk.

"I'll tell you what it means, what we have got to bring out," Chatty said. He stood up and recited, "The massacre of the Albigensians meant the final disappearance of the great medieval culture of Provence. It was lost forever to European civilization."

Karvo was suspicious, then appalled. He changed physically before Chatty's eyes. The word "culture" piled up like a wall that got larger every day. He stared at all that masonry, and boredom settled on him.

"Funny," he said, "those are the very words Christine used."

"They're in the script," said Chatty.

"It is true," he went on, looking at a pill on the palm of his hand and then swallowing it, "nothing lasts."

The learned Christine had cooked her goose, so Chatty said, with a phrase. In the following weeks she and the Albigensian heresy were done for.

"Write her a note," said Karvo. "There's a good fellow."

"No," said Chatty. "She's your baby. She dropped me. I burn with resentment. I still can't think what I did."

"It's personally embarrassing," said Karvo, lifting his blotter and pretending to look for something.

"Much more for me—old time's sake, you know," said Chatty. "Get Phillips to do it." Phillips managed Karvo's company. "Dear Mrs. Johnson, we have now had a full breakdown of the costs, etc., etc. . . . He is a master of the commercial lament."

The letter was sent and Chatty returned the manuscript.

"My office seems empty without it—modern almost," said Chatty. "Sad. You meet your childhood sweetheart again and then—nothing."

He waited for the inevitable aftermath of Karvo's dreams: he would hear Christine's syllables freezing the man who ignorantly rejected Provençal culture and the birthplace of the Castelnaus.

But there was no reply. After a few weeks the manuscript was returned by the post office.

"Unknown" was written across it in pencil by an enthusiastic hand.

Chatty telephoned to the house. No manservant answered. He heard the voice of the cook. She had come in, she said, to collect her things before the removal men got them. You could trust no one today. The Johnsons had gone to their house in Paris and Mrs. Johnson had gone to Toulouse—her brother had died—such difficulties about the estate! The cook did not know the address. The London house had been sold. She was damping the telephone wires with her tears.

"Such troubles," she said.

An inexplicable hole had opened in London social life. It was as if whole streets, indeed the Crescent itself, had been removed, as if the map had been changed, without consultation, overnight, and nonentity had supervened.

"Anyone could see there was trouble there," Karvo said. "Ronnie Johnson was an adventurer. He came in, stripped her of every cent she had. I heard him talking to a Greek banker at the Hollinsheds about the trouble she was having about getting money out of France."

"I'll find out where she is from Rhoda," said Chatty.

"Forget it," said Karvo.

"I don't want to talk about it on the telephone. May I come and see you?" Chatty heard Rhoda's clear harvesting voice gathering sheaves of moral beauty as it came across the hills, the fields and the woods, the gardens and the village churches from the borders of Somerset. Partridge shooting had begun.

When Chatty was clearing up after Karvo's passages through people's lives he usually took the grander casualties to The Hundred and Five, but it was closed for redecoration, and Chatty was obliged to ask Rhoda to The Spangle. This little club was hardly the place for a lady from the country and one who could never be a casualty. The Spangle would be packed with people whose cheques bounced and whom "one had never met." By nine in the evening, couples were hunched and whispering nose to nose across the gingham cloth of their tables, listening not to each other but for erotic news from the table behind them. It was a place for other people's confessions. There was the hope of being refreshed by scenes breaking out now and then. Les, the proprietor, who wore a cowboyish shirt, was a big-bellied, soft man with heavy spongy arms, white as suet pudding. He was in his sixties and was damp and swollen with the public secrets of his customers. Most people came in asking for someone else.

"Was John in last night?"

Les would perhaps reply, "Sarah was asking for him," or "I had a card from Flo. She's in Spain," or "Phil can't leave his dog," or, flatly, "Ada's barred."

Rhoda was wearing a cardigan, a green blouse, a tweed skirt and good walking shoes, but Chatty saw her face had changed. The sad George Eliot gaze had gone. The thick smooth black hair had been cropped into a variety of lengths so that she looked as if she had been pulled, not unwillingly, through a hedge—that is to say, younger. Victory, even giddiness, was in her beautiful brown eyes. Les stared with suspicion and offence at any new woman guest brought into the club and scarcely nodded to her when Chatty introduced her, but Rhoda did not mind. She sat down, and, after an efficient look around her, said, "What a killing place." The word "killing" made Chatty happy; it was so lyrically out of date.

"Tell me who everyone is," she said.

"Les is in a bit of a mood tonight," Chatty began by apologizing for Les. "He's on the watch for people who forgot to bring him a present for his birthday. He used to be an actor."

So Chatty and Rhoda fell to whispering and looking around like everyone else. He thought he was in for a restful evening and started talking about his farm. He looked at her and saw starlings flocking, avenues of elms. Rhoda allowed this, then abruptly she said, "So you turned down Christine's film?"

Chatty's face twitched. Experienced in consoling discarded actresses and mistresses, he had little experience in consoling authors. He certainly did not know how to begin with an author's relatives.

"The sad fact is," he said, "that the best films are made out of bad books, not out of good ones."

He saw the formidable Rhoda appear.

"That is not true," she said with the quiet authority of a thoughtful life. He now saw himself in for an ethical evening. But he was wrong again. She was too firm or too gentle to argue. He ordered their meal and he saw her pursuing truth placidly on her own through a large plateful of whitebait, a fish that would have given him gout within an hour.

"It is always embarrassing turning down the work of a friend," he said. "One always does it at the wrong moment. Family crisis, brother dying—actually dead, I believe. I hear Christine's in Toulouse. For the funeral, I suppose."

Rhoda, a frugal woman, scrupulously ate the last small fish and then drank a glass of white wine straight off. He noted the care of the first operation, the abandon of the second.

"That is what I want to talk to you about," she said.

Les was calling to a young woman: "Hullo, darling. Where's Stephen? Andrew was asking for him."

"Stephen," whispered Chatty, "has forgotten Leslie's birthday."

But Rhoda had lost interest in the killing aspect of the club.

"They are not in Toulouse," she said.

"Perhaps it was Paris, I forget," said Chatty.

"Christine's brother is not dead. She hasn't got a brother."

"But surely!" Chatty said. If there was one thing he remembered about the Christine of so many years ago, it was Christine telling him of her brother, retired from the Navy, living in the South of France, growing his own wine—"the head of the family," with its old-fashioned overtones of solid money, family councils, trusts, wills, marriages, crests on the silver and so on, and the weary care of her voice as she threw away her brother's distinctions; the phrase had stuck with him. He had read it in novels. To hear it spoken had been one of those instances of a forgotten piece of social history flying out of the past into the present like a stone coming through a window.

"Paul, the head of the family," said Chatty.

Seeing Rhoda's eyes studying him, he lost his confidence.

"Perhaps it was Ann's brother. One of them had a brother. It's a long time ago," he said.

"I've never met Ann," said Rhoda. "But I am quite certain Christine hasn't got a brother."

Chatty backed out, for he saw the truth seeker in Rhoda's eyes.

"Or I may be mixing it up with the book," he said. "The girl who went off with her brother."

"I haven't read the book," said Rhoda with a flick of the whip in her voice.

Chatty started telling the story, but she interrupted.

"There is *no* family," she said.

"But she comes from the north," Chatty said. "Yorkshire or some-where. She said so at dinner. Her mother died, the father was killed in an air raid. There was just this brother."

"Her mother died," said Rhoda, "but her father and her stepmother are still alive. Not in the north of England. They've never been near it. They live less than twenty miles from you, the other side of Bath. They run a small public house."

Chatty saw that pile of pink, white and lacy hats come tumbling out of her wardrobe like butterflies and heard Christine's voice saying, "No, I am a Yorkshire woman. You're thinking of Ann."

"I have been to see them," said Rhoda. "They haven't seen or heard of Christine for sixteen years. Her father used to be a seed salesman. They haven't heard a thing about her since she was a student in Paris. They didn't even know she was married. Their name is Till. She has a sister who runs the place, a nice girl, but it's an awful pub. The father retired there to drink the profits. He said, 'Tell that girl if she comes near here I'll get my belt out.' "

The waitress brought *boeuf bourgignon* for Rhoda and, for Chatty, a sole. What an appetite she had! Rhoda continued at once her pursuit of the truth in silence through the food. Chatty gaped at his fish.

"This is good," she said at last. "You're letting yours get cold. I found them through the headmistress of her school. I am on the Education Committee. She said Christine was the cleverest girl they had ever had."

It was a principle of Chatty's to believe everything he was told, but now the very fish on his plate seemed opposed to him. It had been served on the bone and he hesitated to put his knife to it for fear of what he would find inside. He moved his mind to Paris. He saw a heavy black sweater, a pair of twisted stockings, a student's notebook on a café table.

"I can't believe it," said Chatty. "Hundreds of girls leave home, I know . . . They turn up in this place . . ."

"The London house is sold, the bailiffs have the pictures. Ronnie is at home with us. He has left her—thank God."

"Oh dear," said Chatty.

"The film," said Rhoda, "was her last throw. In the last ten years she has run through more than a hundred thousand pounds of Ronnie's money," said Rhoda. "One hundred thousand."

Rhoda changed before Chatty's eyes. The twined leafy branches that had seemed to frame the pensive face of the rural botanist dissolved. He saw instead the representative of a huge family trust.

"Where is she now?" he said.

"In a nursing home," she snapped at him. "I know where I'd put her!"

Chatty put down his knife and fork. He could not bear the sad colour of the fish.

"Poor Christine," he said, looking at it.

"Poor Christine!" said Rhoda loudly, indeed addressing the club. The quiet oval face became square and the country skin flushed to a dark red. "Poor Ronnie, you mean. She has ruined him."

"They were rather going it, of course," said Chatty. "I suppose Ronnie knew what he was doing. What does he say?"

"He knew nothing until ten days ago. Nothing at all about her. Lies from the beginning to the end."

And when she said "Lies," Rhoda shouted.

The customers of The Spangle looked up and glanced at one another with joy. A row! That shout was in the genuine tradition of the club. Everyone was at home. At such moments the quarrelling parties usually called for more drink. Les stepped behind the bar ready to get it. Rhoda corrected herself.

"Lies," she said quietly. "Pure invention."

"Ronnie *must* have known," Chatty said. "How did he find out?"

"He didn't. I did. Ronnie knew nothing, absolutely nothing. I had had my suspicions when he brought her down to stay before they were married; I couldn't stand her delivery."

Chatty raised the bottle to Rhoda's glass and he filled his own.

"It took time," said Rhoda. "You've known her longer than any of us," she said, "did she ever say or do . . ."

She stopped. She saw Chatty's face, so rakishly marked by the lines of his illnesses, smooth out and another face set very hard upon it. She was going to accuse him next. The pursuit of truth was going too far. Rhoda's voice had lost its note of moral beauty. He was thinking of the postscript to her note: "The name of the professor is Ducros." She had been hunting then.

"Mr. Chatterton," she said. "I love my brother. He is everything to me. He always will be. We have always been close all our lives since we were children. He is something very rare—a good man. I would die for him. I knew I was right about that girl. He is easily deceived. It isn't the money. I hate what she has done to him. I love my brother more than anything in the world."

How many times Chatty had heard the word "love" spoken at The Spangle by girls with globes of tears hanging in their eyes, by girls with their teeth set, by girls with their mouths twisted by rage. He patted their hands, told their fortunes, made up love affairs of his own—generally the most successful way of soothing them. He had the sad story of the girl who was in a Swiss sanatorium with him; they had both lost a lung. Such affectionate creatures all these girls were! They forgot their rages when they heard this, and looking at him with contented superstition, as if he were a talisman, their eyes cleared, glanced around the room and began their eternal quest once more.

But Rhoda was not in their case. She gazed at him not asking for help, but with the self-possession of one born for a single passion. In twenty years' time that look would be unalterably there. She not only loved, she was avenged. She had not given up until she had got her brother back. Chatty wished that victory in love would look more becoming.

"It is extraordinary, I agree, and I am sure if you say so, it is true," said Chatty.

"Every word," said Chatty.

"And a hundred thousand pounds is a lot of money."

"It's not only the money," she said.

"Well, I don't see really, if you think about it, what harm has been done. Ronnie was having the time of his life. He obviously adored her—"

"He was tricked."

"—buying her houses, taking her round, enjoying a splash, showering her with Renoirs and hats. With a brain like hers she might still be sitting on the steps of the British Museum eating a sandwich out of a paper bag. He must have liked it. Quite frankly, she isn't a beauty. Ronnie created her."

"She deceived him."

"I think he knew," said Chatty. "I expect he'd been bored up to then. Boredom makes you close your eyes and take the plunge."

"She's such a snob. That accent!" said Rhoda.

"Pedantic," he said. "Scholars often are. Anyway, one gets used to accents in the theatre."

He saw he was annoying her.

"It's really a fairy tale, isn't it?" he said. "Ronnie waved a wand."

For a moment he thought she was going to lean across the table and hit him. He sat back and recited:

> " 'The Owl and the Pussy-Cat went to sea
>   In a beautiful sea-green boat.
>   They took some honey, and plenty of money,
>   Wrapped up in a five-pound note.' "

The poem was too much for her. A tear dropped down her cheek.

"You've got the line wrong," she said, struggling against the pain. "It was a *pea*-green boat.

"It was all those scholarships that gave her away. I traced them back," she said bitterly.

The situation became too clear for Chatty. He did not wish to see, too distinctly, the good woman who in a passion of jealousy had hunted her sister-in-law down. He was disturbed by a wish that Christine and not Rhoda were sitting before him. He gave a number of dry coughs, but he could not cough the wish away.

"Diana," Chatty called the waitress, an overworked girl who had the habit of keeping a cigarette burning on a saucer by the kitchen hatch, "if you'll bring me a packet of cigarettes I'll marry you."

"You, Mr. Chatterton!" said the girl. "That'll be the day."

"It's desperate."

The girl saw Rhoda's tears and pulled a face. The Spangle liked tears. She fetched the cigarettes. Chatty stood the packet on end, considering it, not with passion but with lust. Rhoda saw the packet through her tears.

"You can't! You mustn't," she said strictly. Chatty picked up the packet and held it to his nose.

"Lovely temptation," he said, touching the packet with his lips and putting it down again. Rhoda's tears had stopped. In none of Chatty's experiences at The Spangle had he ever known that a packet of cigarettes could bring tears to a sudden end.

"Did they have any children?" Chatty asked.

"No—that is one blessing."

"Perhaps that was the trouble?" said Chatty.

The expression on the good woman's face was one of horror so deep that she was silent.

And now Les came to their table, ignoring Rhoda.

"How's Karvo?" he asked. "Maggy was asking for him."

"Oh God!" said Chatty.

"Who is Maggy?" asked Rhoda when Les walked off.

"It's a long story. Too personal. Some other time. I'm thinking about Christine. What a performance—one has to admit."

"I don't think that remark is appropriate," said Rhoda. "There's a time when sympathy stops. I think of her sometimes. What a hell she must have lived in knowing every day for years that she might be found out."

The satisfaction in Rhoda's voice shocked Chatty. He gave up trying to charm her.

"Oh, I don't think conscience troubled her at all," he said gaily. "I don't think she was in hell. That is what I mean by performance. She knew her part in every detail. It must have thrilled her to act it, adding a little touch every day. Only an academic could do that! It's a pretty commonplace everyday story really, but to her—what a triumph! What documentation! Imagine her memory! And making Ronnie love it."

"Not now," said Rhoda. "She has lost him for good."

"That is true," said Chatty. "The really sad thing is that she has lost Paul."

"You are infuriating," said Rhoda. "He *never existed,* I tell you."

"I know. She invented him. That is what makes it worse. She has lost her only real friend."

Chatty was glad to see that the perfect Rhoda looked troubled.

"What you are saying is that I did wrong," she said.

"I think you did what you *wanted* to do," said Chatty.

"I can see," she said, "that you don't like me. Hasn't anyone any moral sense nowadays? You knew her. I thought it was my duty to tell you. That was my only motive."

Rhoda picked up her handbag.

"Diana, my sweetheart," Chatty called to the waitress. "I seem to want my bill."

They sat silently until the bill came and then Rhoda said, "Thank you for a lovely evening. You must drive over and see us sometime. Ronnie would like that."

Karvo said to Chatty, "A hundred thousand pounds? Who told you?"

"Clothilde," said Chatty. "She was on the Pope's side. You remember the Albigensians . . ."

"We didn't make it," said Karvo.

"I know," said Chatty. "I mean the escape of the lovers over the Pyrenees, but Clothilde is with them. She has tracked down the incest story and she betrays them to the Inquisition out of jealousy. Rhoda Johnson. Another tragedy in my life. I've seen into the heart of a good woman. Never do that."

Karvo ignored this.

"It was a Swedish story really," said Karvo furtively. "The Swedes could do it."

"No, not Swedish, not even Albigensian—very English, west country. The brother's name was Paul, purely imaginary. Still, his estate was useful naturally as capital security, especially when he died."

"Who are we talking about?" said Karvo.

"Christine's brother, Paul," said Chatty.

"But he's dead."

"You don't listen," Chatty said. "Think of what he was going to leave her. Did she ever mention it to you?"

"Yes," said Karvo, surprised. "She did. Why?"

"Historians go mad. All that research and detail work gets them down. They crack up. Get delusions of grandeur, and in two minutes, they are popping in their personal story. They're badly paid, too. She needed the money. You can't blame them," said Chatty.

"When did the Johnsons leave?" said Karvo.

"They didn't leave. She's had a breakdown. She is in a nursing home."

"Yes, you told me—when was that?"

"Weeks and weeks ago." Chatty took out his diary. "October fourth."

Then Chatty saw Karvo do an extraordinary thing. The man who couldn't remember his wife's birthday, the martyr who was always in trouble because he could not remember the dates of his several wedding anniversaries, the man for whom everything was done by secretaries, the man who was entirely public, surprised Chatty by the secretive way in which he now performed a private action. He took out a pocket diary. Chatty had seen Karvo do this only once before when he was ill; indeed Karvo had shown him a page with an X and a figure written against it. The first Tuesday in every month he recorded his weight. He opened the diary now and said, "October fourth—that's what *I've* got. Why did you make a note of it?"

"A sense of loss," said Chatty. "She'd gone."

"I didn't know she meant anything to you," said Karvo bashfully.

"There it is," said Chatty. "Nor did I. One thinks of it at night."

"Chatty . . ." Karvo began. "Well, no—I don't want to pry into your private affairs."

"Oh no, there was nothing like that in it. I liked her best when she was dirty and fat. I asked them both down to the farm but she wouldn't come. It rather hurt at the time, but I see it now. It might have saved them, even both of them."

Karvo pressed the button and asked for his chauffeur to be sent round.

"A hundred thousand pounds," said Karvo, but in the fond, impersonal, admiring manner of one who sees yet one more piece of financial history pass down the Thames, under the bridges and out to sea.

"Tell the chauffeur to wait," said Chatty. "Karvo, I don't want to pry into *your* private affairs. I want to ask you about ours—yours and mine."

Karvo saw no escape from Chatty when the lines of his face smoothed out.

"All right, if that is what you want to know, she's as frigid as stone," said Karvo. "I tried—well, not actually tried—at the Hollinsheds'."

"Oh I know *that,*" said Chatty. "I discovered that in Paris years ago. I was just finding out when Ronnie Johnson knocked at my door. A very innocent fellow—he didn't realize what was going on. Or perhaps he did. I remember he nodded. Don't let's talk about it. What I want to know is how much she touched you for on October fourth? She got fifty pounds out of me. I made a note of it."

"You fool," boasted Karvo. "She got seven hundred and fifty out of me, guaranteed by the estate."

"Paul's," said Chatty.

Karvo had a special way of falling into speechlessness. He would lean back in his chair, then would seem to be making a quick inventory of everything in the office, then close his eyes. It was as if he was under an anaesthetic at the dentist's. His inner life would become brilliant with ridiculous dramas, and when he came round, panting, he would see what he must do. He came round now.

"I can get it off expenses," he said. "Why did you do it, Chatty?"

"Oh, you know—the pathos of the rich."

Karvo grunted and got up.

"Can I drop you anywhere?"

"No," said Chatty. "I'm going to try and see Christine."

"Don't be a fool," said Karvo. "You'll never get it back."

"That is not what I'm going for," said Chatty. "She's alone."

1970

The Worshippers

Eeles worshipped Lavender, Lavender worshipped Eeles but worshipped Gibbs absolutely—but what is worship? It is not love. To worship is to be put in a trance by an image. There is not much time for this commodity in the rag trade in that district of London that lies infested by anxiety between the north side of Oxford Street and the Middlesex Hospital.

At eight-fifteen every morning Lavender is sulking like a middle-aged schoolboy, head down, under his bowler hat, as he walks towards his office building. He affects a hump to his shoulders, but when he gets there, or rather, when he "comes alongside" or smartly "up to moorings"—as he still says after his time in the Navy years and years ago—he lowers his shoulders and gives a sway as he turns, feeling the roll of *Ripper*, the destroyer he was in, mostly in the Channel, or the French gunboat in which he served on the Yangtze. He is wearing an expensive suit and carrying a correctly rolled umbrella. Five seconds later Eeles, who has been standing in another doorway reading a newspaper and on the lookout for his boss, slips the paper in his pocket and follows Lavender up five flights of dirty stone stairs and joins him just as he is putting his key in a door lettered LAVENDER & COOK in black on the frosted glass, and follows him into the inner office. There Gibbs, Lavender's great-uncle, is waiting for them. Gibbs has been there all night, hanging on the wall, done in oils and heavily encrusted in a gold frame, three foot three by two foot nine, first shown publicly at the Royal Academy in 1882.

Eeles, short, going bald, and getting plump, but much younger than Lavender and nothing like as well-dressed, stands at attention as at an inspection of armoured cars in which he served in the war, while Lavender glances at Gibbs to see whether he is hanging straight. Then both men go to their desks.

"He's much better in this room than he was when we were in the front of the building," Lavender has said more than once.

Once or twice Eeles has said, "Much better now he's been cleaned up."

Gibbs, in his eighties perhaps, is sitting with the difficulty of very stout men, at a desk. His white hair sticks up short like pig's bristles; his cheeks, chins, and the roll of fat around his neck are as pink as a baby's; his little blue eyes are bright and gluttonous. Below the neck the body rests like three balloons at bursting point, the last one resting on his legs. A watch chain travels across his waistcoat like a caravan of annual profits. The whole figure has the modesty and the anonymity of pork, for—as Lavender has many times told Eeles and others—Great-Uncle Gibbs had made a quarter of a million in the bacon trade and contained, even consumed, the firm of Drake, Feldström, Gibbs, and Schmidt (London, Colchester, Hamburg, and Copenhagen, Ltd.), and was the best judge of claret south of the Wash.

Eeles's worship of Lavender had begun when he first saw the portrait. The picture might be terrible, old Gibbs might be vulgar, but in him Lavender had an ancestor. Lavender was, therefore, a gentleman. Eeles decently agreed that to be a gentleman was an asset, though as one who could offer nothing like it in return, he privately thought the condition might not be worth the candle and could even be tragic. What was good for bacon was not necessarily good for the rag trade.

As for the credit side of the account, Eeles would never forget Lavender's handling of Cook. The title of the firm had become a commercial fantasy. Cook had been a non-worshipping man—a *haben Sie?* fellow, hand outstretched, as Lavender said, drawing on the three or four words of German he had picked up in the firm's connexions with Frankfurt—who had suddenly cleared out two years ago, taking customers with him and starting up in competition. Lavender's manner during this row reminded Eeles of Lavender's version of what happened to the officer commanding *Ripper* who, having scraped the hull

of that destroyer against the wall of a Dutch harbour as a stick of bombs
fell on it while getting a Royal person out safe and sound, received an
engraved document from the Admiralty expressing "Their Lordships'
displeasure." Lavender was a master of being as displeased as a lord, if
the occasion arose.

Eeles said, "I wanted to kick the bugger downstairs."

This so pleased Lavender that his worship of Eeles began.

"S-s-so," said Lavender, who stammered a little but mastered it by
pulling a face and giving an attractive twist to his neck, "s-so did I."

After Cook saw the red light and cut his losses, money was tight for
Lavender and Eeles, and the firm moved into two smaller and cheaper
office rooms at the back of the building. They looked over an alley
where the light was dimmer but one could at any rate open a window
and let what passed for air into the place. The two men cleaned up the
rooms one Sunday. "Operation Removal" began. Lavender stripped to
his underpants, as he had often had to do when he was Ordinary
Seaman 0267etc. before he got a ring of gold braid and his commission.
The dandy was surprisingly strong, hairless, and in good condition, no
sign of fat on him except in the jowl; with his long lashes and thick
dark hair he looked like a youth. He had been a pretty child. Eeles, who
was much younger but was putting on weight, took off only his shirt
and jacket and was sandy-haired and very pink—as pink as Gibbs,
Lavender noticed. They swept down the dirty cream walls of the two
rooms with brooms, Lavender being finicky about dust, then washed
them. It was Lavender who, saying he had of course scrubbed decks
and cleaned grease off propeller shafts, went down on his knees and
scrubbed the lino left by the previous tenant, calling out that it was
"coming up" green as grass. Eeles protested at the sight of an older man
like Lavender getting down on his knees—an officer too—but he
remembered his major in the war who screamed like bloody hell if there
was a speck of dirt on a tank. Lavender got up with his pail of filthy
water from time to time and looked out of the window. He said it was
a pity the street below was not the English Channel or the Yangtze.
Eeles was nervous about this but controlled himself.

Then they moved the furniture. This Sunday was the most enjoyable
day in the history of the firm: they talked often about it afterwards.

"Back a bit," said Eeles as they heaved the two desks from the front
of the building to the back.

"Mind the bloody door handles," said Lavender, not concerned with
Eeles's knuckles but with possible scratches on the wood. He was

touchy about scratches. While they were lifting the metal filing cabinet two of the drawers slid open, letters and invoices showered on the floor. The two men put the thing down and picked up the papers.

"Good God, here's one from dear old Hauser," said Lavender, picking it up. In more prosperous days they had had the Hauser agency for Swiss lace but had lost it when Hauser died. The letter was written in French, and Lavender started reading it aloud. Lavender had spent two years in a French silk factory, learning the trade, when he was young. Eeles did not understand French, had never met Hauser, but stood more or less at attention respectfully because Lavender's eyes were glistening with worship.

"After he died I stood outside Le Coq au Vin where we had dinner every time I was in Lausanne and I cried like a child," he said. He had worshipped Hauser, Hauser's wife, Hauser's daughters and their husbands.

Eeles nodded his head and said to break the emotional moment, "Now we come to the big stuff."

There were heavy rolls of lace, brocades, and so on, eight feet long. To heave this dead weight down the corridor from the old office was like lifting dead bodies. There was nothing to grip. One had to cuddle the damn things. Lavender put his hand to his back. When he was a boy a Gibbs cousin of his, he said, had pushed him off a tree and he had nearly broken his back: he often got twinges there even now. Still, he did his part. After four in the afternoon the job was done except for the most important thing: hanging the picture of Great-Uncle Gibbs.

It was disturbing when you thought about it, Lavender said, that an old man who must have weighed two hundred and fifty pounds in life should weigh so little in a portrait, even allowing for the frame. A relief —as Eeles said. But to get at the right height on the wall above Lavender's desk called for ruler and pencil marking, arguments about the exact spot, Eeles holding the picture up for Lavender to consider and Lavender holding it up for Eeles, who said eventually, as his arms ached, that the old man had come to life and was making his weight felt. An hour passed before the wall was plugged and the picture was hung.

When they had washed and dressed they came back to the room and considered the picture again.

"It gives the room a glow," Lavender said. "Lights up the place." It sometimes irritated him in the old office when the lights came on in the afternoon in the shops opposite, especially the neon lights, that they made the old man jumpy as if he were on the razzle. "It made him look tired," he added.

"He'll be quieter in here," said Eeles.

Lavender smiled defensively. If a client came to the place and cracked a joke, such as "It must have been years since the old boy saw his fly," Lavender would close his eyes, offended. A man, Eeles understood, could call his ancestors bastards if he liked, but strangers ought to keep their mouths shut; but he did venture a small joke. "Pity he can't answer the phone."

He and Lavender were usually out on their calls half the day.

"Yes," said Lavender with a short laugh, "it would save me quite a bit on the answering service." Then he became serious and intimate. When he got back from Brussels, Frankfurt, or Belfast, he said, "I always drop in here to look at him before I go on to the club. I don't know why."

"Well," said Eeles at last, "I suppose I'd better get home to the wife and kids."

"Yes," said Lavender. "Thanks for coming. You won't have a quick one round the corner?"

Eeles excused himself and Lavender said, looking doggish, "D'you really mean that?"

"Yes," said Eeles.

"Pity," said Lavender. "Oh well—gin and women, always my trouble, as the fellow said."

Two months after the move, Lavender went on business to Hamburg and when he got back Eeles said, "There's a letter from the bank."

"Damn impudence," said Lavender when he read it. "They're all the same, afraid of Head Office. I'll go round in the morning. I'll tell him where he gets off."

Eeles gaped. "He's rung up three times. What are you going to say?" Eeles asked.

"Chop, chop, move the account," said Lavender.

That is what Eeles admired: Lavender's nerve.

"Anything else?"

"Mrs. Baum rang," said Eeles.

After Eeles left that evening and when Lavender was unpacking his samples, a soft but mannish voice called from the door of the outer room. Lavender was raking up an old row he had had with his father and for the moment thought it must be he, although he had died years before. Then he recognized the voice of Mrs. Baum (Prunella Gowns. Wholesale Only). He had been as nervous of a visit from her as he used to be of his father when he was a boy. She was an old business friend and he had not told her that he had moved the office.

"B," she said—he hated to be called Bertrand: hell at school, "effing B-B-Burlington Bertie" when he was in the Navy. Bloody sissy name, weak.

"Those stairs, B! Eeles told me you'd moved."

She opened her fur coat to get her breath back. Her face looked wolfish in a good-natured way and made her look older than she was, but her eyes were dark and alive and sparkled like her rings.

"Sit down, sit down, I'll take your coat," said Lavender.

"I'll keep it," she said.

She was very much a woman, but her voice brought the pleasant chords of men's voices to Lavender's head—Eeles, for example, old Hauser, Alfie, her husband—a long procession going back to "displeasure" Stamford of *Ripper;* and Law who "opened his heart" to him when they were in the hospital in Bombay; Monnier in Saigon; Jack Gibbs; Porter the racing driver who had lost a leg and who had secretly taught him to drive when he was sixteen, which had led to that god-awful row with his father—all worshipped and worshipping. So that when Alfie Baum turned out to be a swine and left Jess Baum for a model at a trade show in Manchester and "broke Jess's heart," she took Alfie's place in the male procession. Lavender felt like marrying her himself in a kind of way; the difficulty was that by that time he was already married to Phyllis, whom Alfie and Jess, as worshippers, had warned him against.

"How is Eeles getting on?" said Mrs. Baum.

"Hard-working. Loyal. Straight as a die," said Lavender.

"What did I tell you?" she said possessively. "If you had listened to me, you would have got rid of Cook years ago."

"*Mauvais type,*" said Lavender. Mrs. Baum made him feel Continental.

She ignored this and looked shrewdly at the bleak office. "Who on earth's that?" she said, pointing to the picture.

"You've seen it before," he said.

"Never."

"Never? That's funny. It was in the old office. G-Great-Uncle Gibbs," said Lavender.

"What's it doing here?"

"Phyllis won't have it in the house; her sister doesn't like it."

Lavender gave the twist to his neck. For him the picture was the great test: by their response to it one knew who saw life as one saw it oneself. Neither Phyllis nor her sister did.

Mrs. Baum sighed. Alfie had told the young Lavender, "Never marry a girl from the same office; as bad as the girl next door."

Then her eyes looked greedy and her face softened. "You'd have to pay a fortune for a frame like that, B. It's Victorian. They don't even make them now. All that goldwork in it," she said. "You can see," she added, "it's a likeness. You told me about him, I know, but I never *pictured* him."

A whole group of fat commercial men, bursting at the waist, came into her suddenly affectionate mind—Alfie, of course; then a cousin of his who was a theatrical agent; and on her side of the family, men whose knees she had sat on when she was a child. Her feelings were for the comforts and the sadness of the flesh. She was on the stout side herself.

"I don't see any of you in him," she said. "Not your figure, not your eyes. Not your father's side of the family. I don't see any Lavender in him, B."

"Best judge of claret south of the Wash," said Lavender. "Left his money to the Lords' Day Observance Society." And added, "Gin and women, always my trouble. Negative father."

Mrs. Baum nodded. Baffled by this word the first time she had heard Lavender use it, she was proud now of knowing the code. Alfie had told her that it came from the days when ships used flag signals and ran up a flag with a X on it to signal: "Cancel last message."

"Not your father's side. Your mother's, I suppose."

"N-no, no, no, no," said Lavender softly as if conjuring up spirits. "Frankly," he said. "Sort of. Let me see, grandmother's, sister's husband—what have you?"

Mrs. Baum was a hard-headed woman but she loved his "No. No. No. No's"; they enveloped him in a mist. The vagueness of Lavender had always attracted her—she seemed to glide with him towards the unknowable. A wave of comforting madness washed over her; her rings sparkled with sentiments and her lips loosened with appetite. She remembered large foggy photographs (but cocoa-coloured) in her home as a girl, and people looking silly in coloured snaps, but there was nothing as bold, bright, "as large as life and twice as natural," as her mother used to say, like a portrait framed in gold. Her heart—as she grew up—worshipped the sight of old men, pink as babies. They made her feel younger.

"You shouldn't keep a valuable picture like that here," she said restlessly. "Any burglar would lift it for the frame alone."

"Phyllis hates it," he said.

"How is Phyllis?" she asked, without interest.

"*Comme ci, comme ça,*" said Lavender. "*Plus ça change . . .*"

She liked his bits of French. They made her think she had just come back from Paris. As Alfie used to say, he ought to have been on the stage.

"No," added Lavender, and to get off the subject of his wife he changed his face and manner. He became "One"—she always admired that. Not only he, but his truly beautiful suits, seemed to be speaking. "One gets off the boat train late at night, after a couple of double gins, drops the luggage in at the office. There he is, waiting," he said. He waved a hand towards the picture. "The longer one lives, the more one values someone to come back to."

Mrs. Baum felt a short ugly stab in the heart. She knew what he felt. Often she would leave her flat, she said, and go back to the showroom in the evening when the girls had gone and it was closed. "And yet, B, you never *knew* him. I mean, he was dead before you were born. Life is funny the way it takes you . . ." She gazed at the portrait.

"There is more in life than one thinks," said Lavender.

"You're right, B," said Mrs. Baum. "A picture like that can take you back."

"Frankly," he said. "Yes and no."

But Mrs. Baum understood this. In her business-like way she thought that her life had begun when she was a very young woman and she really did look lovely: you knew it wouldn't last and you packed all you could into it—but men were different. A man like B—like Alfie, too —never got beyond the time when they were boys and, damn them, it kept them young. It came to her as a revelation. B did not see Gibbs when he looked at the picture: he was seeing his childhood.

This was the boring side of men and the damn thing was that they played on your feelings; she could feel this happening to her now. She kept quiet about this and changed the subject.

"How's business?" said Mrs. Baum. "I'll tell you what I came about. My niece, Zita, is getting married, and of all things, she wants to get married in Irish lace . . . I thought I'd pop round to see if you had any."

"Foolish virgin," said Lavender: "Come in here." And she followed him into the outer room. "There you are." And he pointed to the long rolls packed in oiled paper stacked against the walls. "Take your pick. As the American said, 'Brother, you want lace, we've got it.'" And he dropped into his Irish turn as he looked at the labels and tried to lift the top parcel off. "We're on strike, God help us, don't mind the broken windows but t'anks to the Blessed Virgin there's a darling piece for the dear child, me brother won't put a bomb under the place till after the wedding."

Lavender tried to lift one more of the parcels.

Mrs. Baum looked about the room. It was small, and stacks of samples rose halfway up to the window, so that there was scarcely any light. Against one wall there was a small typing desk and a chair.

"Look at that," she said sentimentally, "I had one like that when Alfie and I started up."

The table, he said, was for a German secretary he sometimes had, one of the *haben Sie?*'s.

"Don't bother now," she said.

"There's yards of it here, I know," said Lavender, looking at the dust on his hands. "Eeles has been in Belfast. I'll get him to find some."

"Yes," she said. "Don't spoil that beautiful suit. Look at your hands. Let's go and have a drink."

"Will do," he said, relieved. "This stuff weighs a ton, it gets you in the back. I'll wash this off."

She liked the distress he showed when he looked at his blackened hands. He went to wash them in an alcove in his own office, and while she waited she went up to the portrait of Great-Uncle Gibbs and put a finger out and touched it. Lavender returned, and seeing her near the picture, straightened it and then put his blotter straight on his desk, saw that the telephone books were in the right order on Eeles's table. Then he got his coat from the coat stand, remarking that Eeles had only one bad habit: he often used Lavender's peg by mistake.

"Small things," he said, "irritate."

Mrs. Baum liked a man who fussed about small things. Alfie had fussed about his shirts.

Lavender gave one last look at the picture before they left. "You can call it sentimental or what you like, but if I was down to my last penny, I wouldn't sell Great-Uncle Gibbs."

"What's wrong with sentiment?" she said, taking his arm. He looked up and they walked to the stairs of the silent, empty building.

"Let's go to Giuseppe's."

Giuseppe's was a bar in a large hotel a hundred yards around the corner, and still holding his arm, Mrs. Baum felt what she always liked about Lavender. Cook had called him a snob and a fool, Alfie had told him to grow up, but Lavender was a gentleman who took your mind off things: he was like a whole crowd of men, yet blessed with a loneliness like her own. The street outside was empty at this time of the evening except for an occasional couple like themselves. Their footsteps echoed off the walls of the closed offices and the windows of closed sandwich bars, and were suddenly silent as they passed an empty, grave-like doorway.

They found themselves on the huge carpet of the hotel on which thousands of pairs of shoes without people in them might be treading. The place was empty now but notable for packed trade shows where she and Alfie and B had often met. The lounge immediately inside was remarkable for a row of tall bronze dancers standing on marble pillars and each holding a tray or a brass tambourine over her head, presumably to cheer the models who arrived. Mrs. Baum remembered sitting at a table there and Alfie telling her to give up her job in Birmingham and start up in his business with him; she had often mentioned this to Lavender. They went past this now empty hall, done in what Alfie had said was the Moorish style, into the enormous panelled bar, also empty, where the barman was reading a paper.

"*Il ne marche pas,*" said Lavender.

"It's dead," she said. "No trade since Giuseppe left."

"Negative Giuseppe," said Lavender, swinging her back to the doors.

"Let's go round to the flat," she said scornfully to the empty bar.

"Hard to starboard," he said, leading her out.

They arrived at her block of flats, built in white tiles suited to plumbing on a vast scale. He knew the place well.

There was always something wrong in his cottage in the country when he got home on Saturday mornings. "Poor Phyllis," he said, always would put his piles of *Punch* in the wrong order, and never learned to draw a pair of curtains properly, and never put things away in the kitchen. After the Navy it drove him mad. She had a peculiar habit of standing behind him when he was reading which he could not cure her of, and it brought on the pain in his back because it reminded him of the time when Flo Gibbs, the sister of the superb Jack—much older than himself—whom he had worshipped, had pushed him off the tree. He ought to have married Flo but she was much too rich, or one of dear old Hauser's Swiss daughters, any one of them. They could run a house and old Hauser would have been in and out. He would have had a son whom he could have put into the Navy. A man's life, not like the rag trade.

Mrs. Baum's three rooms, kitchen, and bathroom were spotless and would have passed an admiral's inspection. He liked the white curtains with their large tomato-like spots, the spongy leather sofa that slumped like the perfect substitute for Alfie in the room, suggesting that Mrs. Baum had no intention, indeed no need of marrying again. He liked that: an ideal. He liked its rival, the blue, yellow, and white Chinese carpet, although the glass-topped dining table upset him. Sitting at it, one could see other people's feet. The place was so much fresher than it had been in Alfie's cigar-smoking time.

How often he and Mrs. Baum had sat there talking of this and that! The sofa was made for going over the past.

"You go and get the drinks, B," called Mrs. Baum from her bedroom. "You know where they are."

"Gin and women . . ." Lavender began. And when she came back and as they raised their glasses, he said, "Happy nights." "And no regrets," she said.

"So you're flying to Frankfurt again," she said.

"Negative aircraft," he said. "By sea."

She knew that, of course.

"No," he said and told her what he had told her a dozen times before. She liked her flat to have someone else's voice saying the same things again and again.

"No," he said, holding up his hand and closing his eyes for a second or two, so that his blank eyelids made him look as if he were going into a trance and that he was telling her not to interrupt him in a sacred matter. "When Jack Gibbs retired he took a house in France for the winter and he always got a cabin on one of the *Queens* as far as Cherbourg. 'Only way to travel: see the Channel.' Jack was right. I always go via Cherbourg.

"Last time I went an American said to me," Lavender went on, " 'Brother, if you're heading for Frankfurt, you're on the wrong ship.' 'Saves time,' I said and told him. 'Well, I'll be darned,' he said.

"No," said Lavender, defying reason in a way that gave Mrs. Baum one more twinge of worship. "One picks up the *Queen* at Southampton. Go straight to old Frank at the bar, pink gin, double of course. 'Nice to see you again, sir. Blowy tonight.' 'Glad to hear it.' 'Bad for the bar, sir.' 'Only thing I miss, she doesn't roll. *Ripper* bucked like

a horse. One misses that.' 'Not me, sir, I was in minesweepers.' A few
more double gins and in six hours one is at Cherbourg, wakey, wakey,
Paris train waiting for you, cut across Paris in time for a bottle of
Chablis at the Café de la Paix. *'La sole meunière comme toujours,
Monsieur Lavandaire,'* to the Gare de l'Est and you're in Frankfurt
eleven o'clock. *Haben Sie?*'s all round you. It's the only way. One can
argue that it takes longer and costs more . . ."

"Well, B, it does," said Mrs. Baum. "It only takes an hour by air."

"But people *know* one," said Lavender, shutting his eyes again. "You
know where you are. Dear old Hauser, he wouldn't fly either. I was
thinking of him. Swiss have no navy. Had to take the train from Zürich,
but crossed Dover-Calais. Kept him young. And . . ."

"Help yourself to another," said Mrs. Baum. "Nothing for me."

"Great-Uncle Gibbs always took the boat to Copenhagen or the
Hook even when he was turned eighty," said Lavender, pouring himself
a drink.

"Flying hadn't been invented. Alfie was never near a boat in his life,"
said Mrs. Baum.

"That's what was wrong with him," said Lavender.

Mrs. Baum switched on the television. "Oh dear," she said. "Look
at that. Another bomb in Belfast. I hope Eeles is all right."

She switched it off. "I can't stand it," she said. "You get your shop
burned down—what for?"

"Eeles?" said Lavender, looking at his watch. "He's on his way back
by now. Nothing can touch Eeles anyway.

"No," he went on. "Up and down the Channel, bringing in a convoy
at night with the fireworks going—Alfie would have enjoyed it. I think
of it when I go to Cherbourg. One goes on deck and a flash of summer
lightning brings it back, the sea lit up like an ice rink and some silly
sod says 'Where's the cat?' when the stuff comes over. Cat hated
gunfire. Sunrise, all quiet, and the cat comes back and the signal comes
through: 'Thank you, *Ripper*, rather a nice party, I think.' Stamford
was always sloshed to the eyeballs when he went up to the bridge at
Dover, stone sober when he got outside."

Mrs. Baum had heard this story very often and said pleasantly, "Alfie
always took our accounts down to the shelter in the war if anything
happened. We moved the office to Bury St. Edmunds. Wasn't that
near your uncle's place?"

"Bury . . ." Lavender began, but stopped because the telephone rang.

Mrs. Baum answered it. "Who?" said Mrs. Baum. "No. I can't. I have people here." And banged down the telephone in a sudden temper.

"What's that?" said Lavender.

"That's the trouble with this place, B," she said. "It's not what it was. They've let a different class of people in, you don't know who they are. When you're on your own you feel nervous. I never used to feel like that. It is a man called Williams on the tenth floor. He keeps pestering me. He knocked on the door three nights ago. I keep the chain on now."

Lavender tried to rise from the sofa. "What's his number? I'll tell him where to get off," he said and knocked his glass over.

"Stay where you are," said Mrs. Baum. "Don't move till I get a cloth."

"On your carpet," said Lavender, getting up at last and following her, and when she came out of the kitchen he tried to pull the cloth from her.

"I'll do it," she said. And got down on her knees and rubbed.

Lavender admired this. She was stout but looked very neat on her knees and her hair kept its shape. When she stood up, Lavender took the cloth from her and went down on his knees too and continued to rub. He even moved the sofa in case any of the drink had gone under it. "Careful of your back," Mrs. Baum said. "Don't spoil your suit."

"Negative suit," he said.

She fetched a clothes brush. She was impressed by his brushing: a fastidious man.

"Give yourself another drink," she said.

Lavender got himself another large one and stood it carefully on the table, but did not drink. It stood there, still as an idol.

Her friendly voice suddenly had a note of accusation. "I rang the club the other day and they said you weren't living there any more."

Lavender's talking face became still and he stared at her a long time and then his voice took on the general, indignant noise of men grumbling at a bar. "The food's gone off. Usual story. New chef. They put the prices up."

"You resigned?" she said, shocked and insinuating.

"Yes and no. Sort of."

He looked ashamed.

He had taken her to dinner there more than once on Ladies' Night. He must be doing well to belong to a club like this, she thought. Paintings of inhumanly tall field marshals, admirals, viceroys in splendid frames and with killing eyes, hung in the vast Dining Room. The effect of all this glorious manliness was girlish. It was like a dress show for men, a sunrise of hermaphrodites—it excited her. She admired especially the sapphire sash which one of those eminences was wearing across his breast—not this season's colour for women, too pale—but she found herself thinking more than once that a sash like that would have suited Lavender and that she could easily get one of the girls in the workroom to make him one. Blue, she had daydreamed, was the colour of Uncle Gibbs's eyes—*Great-*Uncle Gibbs, why did she always make that mistake and call him Uncle?

She always put on something fashionable, not in the shops yet, but in spite of the imperial splash on the walls, most of the tables were empty—only a few old people were there and the women looked proud of being dowdy in their biscuit-coloured cardigans. The room was cold and the waiters were negligent; all foreigners, she supposed, who couldn't understand Lavender's English. They fetched one who was baffled by his French. "All *haben Sie?*'s," he said. The good thing was the sight of Lavender blinking at the wine list as if it were sacred and then hearing him say, "Châteauneuf-du-Pape—old Hauser drank nothing else." But Gibbs was a claret man. So was Jack.

Now as they sat on the sofa in her flat, she said, "They want to put my rent up. I haven't made up my mind. What were we talking about when that prowler Williams rang?"

For it struck her that Lavender was not touching his drink: giving up his room at the club, moving into a pokey office at the back of the building. Something wrong?

"Drink up," she said gently. He drank.

"Bury, that was it," he said. "You mentioned Bury."

"When Alfie and I were in Bury we drove out to a posh hotel in the country, with long crinkly chimneys. On a hill," she said.

"Nor'west of Bury?" Lavender asked.

"I never know which is south, east or west," she said, laughing. "The name will come to me . . ."

Lavender ran off a list of small towns and villages: Flaxton, Pyke Market, Market Plympton, Bush Vale, Lord Beverley's place with the long grey wall which Lavender had climbed over to see the deer when he was a boy.

"Something Manor," she said. "Littlestone?" she said.

"Lytestone," he corrected her.

He slipped into his tragic Saint Bernard look: his youthfulness vanished and he put his hand over his forehead.

"Don't go on," he said. "The Gibbs place."

"That's what Alfie said. We had a lovely room," she said, leading him on. (With all that Gibbs money behind him, why did he resign from the club?) "With a balcony. The car park was packed. People coming and going all night. They couldn't complain of business. Fancy that belonging to your uncle. We wondered which room you had when you lived there. We were talking about you."

Lavender watched the red spots on Mrs. Baum's curtains arrange themselves in vertical lines and begin to move upwards, reach the rail and descend in a shower and then slowly move up again.

"*Great-*uncle," Lavender corrected her. "What room?"

"When you stayed; when you visited."

He stared at her. The red tomato-like spots on the curtain began to rise faster like a reel unwinding.

"When you were a boy," she said.

Lavender stared at Mrs. Baum and his reddened face turned as pale as veined stone. His stare was concentrated, and if a minute before he was drunkish, he was now sober. He was accusing her, examining her, suspecting her, searching her with an intensity that made her uncomfortable. He waved a hand, waving her away, but she was still there. She wished she had not spoken.

"My room?" he said.

"Yes," she teased. "I bet they put you next door to your cousin Jack."

"Flo," he said sharply.

"Flo," she said. "I knew it. The one who pushed you off the tree. I can see it all. You've been a lucky devil, B. Fancy being brought up in that lovely place. The staircase! There was an old gardener who had been there when the family had it. You'd know him. He showed us round the garden. Have you ever been back? You ought to do that. It's interesting."

Lavender looked away from her, but he put out his hand and gripped her by the wrist. His hand was large and strong and hurt her.

"What was the gardener's name?" he said.

"I don't remember—but he said he remembered you."

"He's a bloody liar," he said.

"You're hurting me, B. That's what he said. You ought to go and see it—you ought to see where I was brought up, Stepney! Alfie and I had to laugh. Well, the servants they must have had to run a place like that! We asked which room you had."

He let go of her hand and turned to face her. He said in a jeering voice, hurrying over the words, "Over the stables at the back. Sixteen months, Mother's cousin was cook there. I was ten."

"You never told me that, B," said Mrs. Baum, who loved exciting news. "Alfie and I thought you were brought up there."

"A fellow called Law, the best friend a man ever had, when we were in hospital in Bombay, he opened his heart to me. He came from Stepney. I told him. His mother was a cook. We used to go for walks and talk of this and that, private things," he said, shutting his eyes.

"Well," said Mrs. Baum taking a big breath. "We've come a long way, B. I wasn't prying into your private affairs."

He got up and got himself another drink.

"You know your trouble, B. You've got a soft heart," she said.

"No, no, no, no, no," he said, cheering up as he created what she called his mist. And suddenly he said loudly, "Lytestone taught me something. I made a vow . . ."

But the red tomato-like spots of the curtains started once more to stream upwards and he lost what he was going to say. He had a confused feeling that she might be Law. He wanted to tell her things he had told Law, but all he could remember was Jack Gibbs's playroom with a whole fleet of little lead models of ships set out on the floor. Not to be moved unless Jack said so, and he was older. Battle of Jutland. Then Jack letting him move one ship, then two, shouting to his sister Flo to clear out. That was why she pushed him off the tree, bang on his back, afterwards. Unconscious. Doctor. That's why they had to let him stay all that time.

He struggled to explain this to Mrs. Baum (or was she Law?), that he worshipped Jack, as he tried to stop them becoming spots on the curtains. Only one thing was certain: "Chop, chop," he said. "All gone. House sold. Auction."

"B," she said. "Sit down. I'll get us some coffee."

"Wait," he commanded. "I bought the picture. Fifty pence. Damn shame. No one left in the family would touch it," he said.

She was hurrying to the kitchen.

"Negative coffee," he shouted to her. "I made a vow . . ."

She looked back. "I can hear, B," she said.

"To look after the poor old bastard," he muttered to himself. He got up and made a wild swing towards the bottles and then wheeled back and flopped onto the sofa, astonished. She turned off the stove, but by the time she got to him he had passed out.

For a while she considered him. Once he seemed to speak.

"Gin and women. Chop. Chop," he said.

She waited anxiously, but he said nothing else. She cautiously got a chair and put it near his feet and she lifted them on it. She opened the door to the bathroom and was in and out of the kitchen, eating a bun, watching him. His breathing became louder. There was a kind of happiness in seeing him there. It was like having Alfie back. After two hours she understood he was there for the night. She took off his shoes and got a rug to put over him. She turned down all lights except one, went to her own room and left her door ajar in case he stirred. For the first time since Alfie left her she felt safe for the night and slept deeply.

In the morning she heard him in the bathroom. She put on one of her gaudier dressing gowns and came in when he was dressed. He looked heavy in the face and flinched at the brilliant red-and-yellow garment, but said, "Very sorry about last night. Something went wrong with the steering. Did I say anything?"

"That's all right—you never stopped," she said, laughing.

He had folded the blanket neatly, straightened the sofa.

"Feeling better?"

She brought him a cup of coffee.

"Now," she said firmly, "when did you give up the club?"

"Two months ago," he said.

"I don't mean that," she said. "Where have you been staying? At the cottage?"

"No, no, no, no, no," he said quickly. "Fares have gone up. Negative cottage."

"Where, B? With your sister?"

"Yes and no," he said. "At the office."

"What!" she shouted.

"I've got a sleeping bag. By the way, don't tell Eeles. I put it away every morning before he comes. I walk up the street. Turn round. He's always there on time."

"On the floor—with your back? What is wrong?" she said. "Is it Eeles?"

Mrs. Baum was perplexed by him and by herself: there was an expression of disaster concealed in Lavender's face which made her feel masterly and grand. She was prosperous: energy had flowed out of her after Alfie had left her, but she missed the sense of gamble that always seemed to hang about Alfie. It struck her as being rather fine that B had rescued the picture of that ugly old man who was no connexion of his—it was silly but it showed a sort of decency—and that his mother's cousin had been a cook in that house.

"You haven't sacked Eeles, have you?" she said suspiciously.

"No," said Lavender. "He's been in Ireland settling the strike."

Well, she thought, that's not what's on his mind. "Has he settled it?"

"Yes and no. It settled itself. Depends which way you look at it. They pinched the looms out of the factory and two of the machines and put a bomb in it. Negative workshop. Bloody funny really. They're all on social security—except Eeles and me."

"Why didn't you tell me last night?" she said to him. "Was Eeles all right?"

"Oh yes," said Lavender. "Sergeant, ex-armoured cars. Straight as a die. You're all right there. You walk down the middle of the street with a bottle of whisky sticking out of your coat pocket. Like going up the Yangtze in the war—we always kept to the middle of the river. By the way, he'll have got the lace. He probably went round to the fellow who pinched it."

"Well, thank you, but I can't spend the morning talking about the Yangtze," Mrs. Baum said. "I've got to get to the showroom. When are you coming back from Frankfurt? None of this Cherbourg nonsense: take the plane. Cook left you holding the baby with that Irish business. You've lost a lot of money. Stick to Frankfurt. When are you coming back? Wednesday? Are you going home?"

"No, no, no, no, no," said Lavender. "Negative home."

That "negative" shocked her, but she shook off her pain.

"I sometimes feel sorry for your wife, B," she said. "But you can't sleep on the floor in that office. I won't have it. You'd better come here. That will keep Williams quiet. And we've got to have a talk. You've got to cut down your expenses."

They left the flats. The commissionaire gave a sort of salute and Mrs. Baum held her chin up and looked very grand and very respectable. They parted at the street corner.

"What did you pay at the club?" she asked.

"One way and another, if you reckon it up—" he began.

"Tell me on Wednesday," she said. "You could bring Great-Uncle Gibbs." And at that afterthought she sighed. It was the wrong thing to say.

"I don't think Eeles would like that," he said sternly.

"Anyway . . ." she said and went away, saying to herself, "I'm a fool."

Outside the office Eeles was reading his paper, and though surprised to see Lavender coming up the street instead of coming down it, he followed him up the stairs into the office.

The Vice-Consul

Under the blades of the wide fan turning slowly in its Yes-No tropical way, the vice-consul sloped in his office, a soft and fat man, pink as a ham, the only pink man in the town, and pimpled by sweat. He was waiting for the sun to go down into the clouds over the far bank of the estuary, ten miles wide here, and to put an end to a bad week. He had been plagued by the officers and crew of a Liverpool ship, the *Ivanhoe*, smoking below in the harbour. There was trouble about shipping a puma.

His Indian clerk put his head in at the door and said in the whisper of the tropics, "Mr. McDowell's here."

Years at this post on the river had reduced the vice-consul's voice also to the same sort of whisper, but he had a hoarseness that gave it rank. He believed in flying off the handle and showing authority by using allusions which his clerk could not understand.

"Not the bloody Twenty-third Psalm from that blasted tramp again," he said and was glad McDowell heard it as he pushed in earnestly after the clerk. McDowell was a long-legged man with an unreasonable chin and emotional knees.

"I've brought Felden's licence," he said.

"I ought to have had it a week ago," said the vice-consul. "Have you got the animal aboard yet? It was on the dock moaning away all day. You could hear it up here."

"We've got it on deck," said McDowell.

"Typical hunter," said the vice-consul, "thinking he could ship it without a licence. They've no feeling for animals and they're liars too."

"No hearts," said McDowell.

At this low hour at the end of the day, the vice-consul did not care to have a ship's officer trump his own feelings.

It was part of the vice-consul's martyrdom during his eight years at the port that he was, so to say, the human terminus on whom hunters, traders, oilmen, television crews, sailors whose minds had been inflated by dealing with too much geography, dumped their boasts. Nature in the shape of thousands of miles of jungle, flat as kale, thousands of miles of river, tributaries, drifting islands of forest rubbish, not to mention millions of animals, snakes, bloodsucking fish, swarms of migrating birds, butterflies and biting insects, had scared them and brought them down to the river to unload their fantasies.

"Take your boa constrictor . . ." they began. "Take your alligator . . . Take your marching ant . . ."

Now he had to "take" a man called Felden who had tried to stuff him up with the tale that his fourteen-year-old son had caught the beast on his fishing line in a backwater above Manaos.

The vice-consul was a sedentary man and longed to hear a fact. "When do you sail?" he said when McDowell sat down on an upright chair which was too small for him.

"The day after tomorrow," said McDowell.

"I can't say I'll be sorry to see you lot go," said the vice-consul, making his usual speech to departing sailors. "I'd like to know where the hell your company gets its crews."

"I'm from Belfast," said McDowell, placing his hands on those knees.

"Oh, nothing personal," said the vice-consul. He stamped the licence, pushed it across his desk and stood up, but McDowell did not move. He leaned forward and said, "Would you do me a favour?"

"What favour?" said the vice-consul, offended.

McDowell started to caress his knees as if to get their help. "Would you be able to recommend a dentist in the town?" he said.

The vice-consul sat down, made a space on his desk and said, "Well, that's a change. I thought you were going to tell me you had got yourself clapped like the rest of your crew and wanted a doctor. Dentist? Afraid not. There isn't a dentist in the place, not one I'd recommend, anyway. You've been here three weeks and can see for yourself. Half the population have no teeth at all. None of the women, anyway.

Go down the street, and if you're not careful, you can walk straight down their throats."

McDowell nodded. The vice-consul wanted more than a nod.

"It stands to reason," he said, expanding. "What do they get to eat? Dried meat and manioc covered in bird droppings, fish that tastes of newspaper from the bloody river. No fresh milk, no fresh meat, no fresh vegetables—everything has to be flown in and they can't afford it. It would kill them if they could."

McDowell shook his head and kept his knees still. "Catholic country," he said.

"No topsoil," said the vice-consul, putting on a swagger. "If you've got a pain in the jaw, I'm sorry. Take my advice and do what I do. Get on the next plane to Miami. Or Puerto Rico if you like. It'll cost you a penny or two but it's the only way. Sorry for you. Painful."

"Oh," said McDowell, sitting back like an idol. "My teeth are all right," he said.

"Then what do you want a dentist for?"

"It's my dentures," McDowell said, gleaming as he made the distinction.

"All right—dentures," said the vice-consul.

"They've gone. Stolen."

The vice-consul looked at McDowell for a long time. The jaws did not move, so he turned sideways and now studied McDowell, screwing up one annoyed eye. The man swallowed.

"Mr. McDowell," he said, taking the syllables one by one. "Are you feeling the heat? Just give your mouth a tap. If I'm not mistaken, you're wearing them."

McDowell let his arms fall to his sides and parted his lips: a set of teeth gleamed as white and righteous as a conjuring trick. "I never sail without me spares," he said.

The vice-consul wasn't going to stand funny business from British subjects. He had an air for this.

"Very wise," he said. "You fellows are always getting your teeth knocked out by your pals. Makes you careful, I suppose. What do you want *me* to do? You've got a captain, haven't you?" He became suspicious. "I suppose you're not thinking of Filing an Official Complaint," he said, pulling a form out of his drawer, waving it at McDowell and putting it back, "because I can tell you, officially, that who pinches what from whom on the bloody *Ivanhoe* is no concern of mine, unless it's connected with mutiny, wounding, murder or running guns."

The vice-consul knew this kind of speech by heart.

The sun had floundered down into the clouds; he shouted to his clerk to put on the light but switched it on himself. He decided to match McDowell on the meaning of words.

"You said 'stole,' McDowell. You must have some prize thieves in your crew. But will you tell me how you get a set of dentures out of a man's head against his will, even when he's asleep, unless he's drugged or tied up. Were you drunk?"

"I've never touched a drop in my life," said McDowell.

"I suppose not," said the vice-consul coldly.

"I took them out myself. I always put my dentures in a glass."

"So I should hope," said the vice-consul. "Filthy leaving them in. Dangerous too. What else did they take? Watch? Wallet? Glasses?"

McDowell spoke carefully, picking over the peculiarity of an austere and personal case. "Only my dentures," he said. "It wasn't the crew. I don't mix with them. They read magazines. They never think. I wasn't aboard," he said softly, adding to his mystery. "It wasn't at night. I was ashore. In the afternoon. Off duty."

The Indian clerk put his head in at the door and looked anxiously from McDowell to the vice-consul.

"What do you want now? Can't you see I'm busy?" said the vice-consul.

The man's head disappeared and he shut the door.

McDowell stretched his long arms and placed his hands on his knees and his fingers began to drag at his trousers. "I saw it with my own eyes," he said. "I saw this girl with them. When the rain started."

"What girl?" the vice-consul said, lighting a cigar and putting a haze of smoke between himself and his torment. "The rainy season started six weeks ago," he swaggered. "You get your thunderstorm every afternoon. They come in from the west and build up over the river at two o'clock to the minute and last till ten past three. You can set your watch by them."

The vice-consul owned the climate.

"Tropical rain," he said grandly, "not the drizzle you get in Belfast. The rain comes down hot, straight out of the kettle, floods the streets and dries up in ten minutes, not a sign of it except the damn trees grow a foot higher. The trouble is that it doesn't clear the air: the heat is worse afterwards. You feel you're breathing—I don't know—boiled stair carpet my wife says, but that's by the way." He waved at the smoke. "You'll tear the knees of those trousers of yours if you don't leave them alone."

A dressy man, he pointed his cigar at them. McDowell's knees stuck out so far that the vice-consul, who was a suspicious man, felt that they were making a displeasing personal claim on him. They indeed gave a jump when McDowell shouted in a voice that had the excitement of sudden fever, "I can stand thunder. But I can't stand lightning, sheet or forked. It brings my dinner up. It gets under your armpits. A gasometer went up in Liverpool when I was a boy and was blown blazing across the Mersey—"

"I thought you said you came from Belfast," said the vice-consul. "Lightning never bothers me."

"There was this thunderbolt," said McDowell, ignoring him, and his voice went to a whisper. "I'm in the entrance of this hotel, looking at the alligator handbags to take one home for my wife and I've just picked one up and down comes this bolt, screaming behind my back, with a horrible violet flame, and sends me flying headfirst up the passage. There's a girl there, polishing the floor, and all the lights go out. The next thing, I'm in an open doorway, I'm pitching headfirst on to a bed in the room and I get my head under the clothes. It's like the end of the world and I'm praying into the pillow. I think I am dead, don't I?"

"I don't know," said the vice-consul coldly. "But what do you do at sea? And where was this place?"

"It's natural at sea," said McDowell, calming down. "The Columbus. Yes, it would be the Columbus."

"Never heard of it," said the vice-consul.

"I don't know how long I am there, but when it gets quieter I look up, the lightning is going on and off in the window and that's when I see this girl standing by the mirror—"

"The one who was polishing the floor, I suppose," said the vice-consul with contentment.

"No," said McDowell, "this one was in the bed when I fell on it, on top of her, I told you."

"You didn't. You pulled her in," said the vice-consul.

McDowell stopped, astonished, but went on, "Standing by the mirror, without a stitch of clothing on her. Terrible. She takes my dentures out of the glass, and the next thing, she opens her mouth wide and she's trying to fit them, this way and that, to her poor empty gums."

"You couldn't see all that in a flash of lightning. You must have switched the light on," said the vice-consul.

McDowell slapped his knee and sat back in a trance of relief. "You're right," he said gratefully. "Thank God you reminded me. I wouldn't want to tell a lie. The sight of her with her poor empty mouth destroyed me. I'll never forget it. It'd break a man's heart."

"Not mine," said the vice-consul. "It's disgusting. Shows ignorance too. No two human jawbones are alike."

"The pitiful ignorance, you're right!" said McDowell. "I called out to her, 'Careful what you're doing! You might swallow them. Put them back in the glass and come back to bed.' "

The tropical hoarseness left the vice-consul's voice. "Ah," he shouted and put his cigar down. "I thought we'd come to it. In plain English, you had come ashore to commit fornication."

"I did not," said McDowell, shocked. "Her sister works for the airline."

"Oh, it's no business of mine. I don't care what you do, but you were in bed with that girl. You said so yourself. But why in God's name did you take your dentures out? In the middle of the afternoon?"

McDowell was even more shocked. He sat back sternly in his chair. "It would have looked hardly decent," he said, "I mean on an *occasion* like that, for any man to keep his teeth in when a poor girl had none of her own. It was politeness. You'd want to show respect. I've got my principles."

He became confident and said, "My dentures have gold clips. Metal attracts lightning—I mean, if you had your mouth open, you might be struck dead. That's another reason why I took them out. You never know who the Lord will strike."

"Both of you, I expect," said the vice-consul.

"Yes," said McDowell, "but you've got to think of others."

The vice-consul got out his handkerchief and wiped his face and his head.

"You'd never get away with this twaddle in a court of law," said the vice-consul. "None of this proves she stole your dentures."

"She had gone when I woke up, and they had gone. The rain was pouring down outside or I would have gone after her," said McDowell.

"And you wouldn't have caught her if you had," said the vice-consul with deep pleasure. "She sold them before she got to the end of the street. You can say goodbye to that lot. You're wasting my time. I've got two other British ships docking in an hour. I've told you what to do. Keep clear of the police. They'll probably arrest you. And if you want a new set of dentures, go to Miami as I said."

"But they're not for *me*," exclaimed McDowell. "I want them for

this girl. I've got the money. It's wrong to steal. Her sister knows it and
so does she. If you see a soul in danger, you've got to try and save them."

"God help me," said the vice-consul. "I've got enough trouble in this
port as it is, but as a matter of interest, who told you to go to this place
—the Columbus—to buy handbags? You can get them at every shop
in the town. The river's crawling with alligators."

McDowell nodded to the outer office where the Indian clerk sat.
"That gentleman."

"He did, did he?" said the vice-consul, laughing for the first time and
achieving a louder shout to his clerk.

The Indian clerk came in. He loved to be called in when the vice-
consul was talking business. He gleamed with the prestige of an only
assistant. The vice-consul spoke to him in Portuguese with the intimacy
of one who sketches his way through a language not his own. The clerk
nodded and nodded and talked eagerly.

"My clerk says," said the vice-consul, in his large way, "that you
came in at midday the day before yesterday and asked where you could
get a girl. He says he knows the airline girl and her sister. He knows
the whole family. The father has the barbershop opposite the church
and he is a dentist too. He buys up teeth, mostly after funerals."

The clerk nodded and added a few words.

"He says he fixed him up. He says this man's got the biggest collection of teeth in the town."

The clerk's neck was thin; he was like wood. He opened his mouth
wide with pride for McDowell to see. There were five sharp steel teeth
and two with gold in them.

The vice-consul went on, "He says he often sells them to missionar-
ies. The Dominicans have a mission here. The poor devils come back
from far up in the Indian settlements looking like skeletons after three
years and with their teeth dropping out. I told you: no calcium. No
fresh vegetables. No milk. The climate . . ."

The Indian said no more.

McDowell got up and moved towards the clerk suspiciously, setting
his chin. "What's he say about the Dominicans?" said McDowell in
a threatening way.

The vice-consul said, "He says you could go down to this man, this
barber chap, and you might find your teeth."

The Indian nodded.

"If you don't—well, they've been snapped up and are being flown
up the river. Sorry, McDowell, that's all we can do. Take my advice

and get back double-quick to your ship. Good day."

The vice-consul picked up some papers and called to McDowell as he left the room, "They'll be up there, preaching The Word."

The following day the vice-consul went out to the *Ivanhoe* to have a last drink with the captain and to have a look at the puma, and grinned when it opened its mouth and snarled at him. The captain said McDowell would be all right once he got to sea, and went on to some tale about a man who claimed to have a cat that backed horses.

It's the bloody great river that does it, the vice-consul thought as he was put ashore afterwards and as he walked home in the dark and saw all the people whispering in their white cotton clothes, looking like ghosts. He was thinking it was only another year before his leave and that he was the only human being in the town.

1977

The Evils
of Spain

We took our seats at the table. There were seven of us. It was at one of those taverns in Madrid. The moment we sat down Juliano, the little, hen-headed, red-lipped consumptive who was paying for the dinner and who laughed not with his mouth but by crinkling the skin round his eyes into scores of scratchy lines and showing his bony teeth —Juliano got up and said: "We are all badly placed." Fernando and Felix said: "No, we are not badly placed." And this started another argument shouting between the lot of us. We had been arguing all the way to the restaurant. The proprietor then offered a new table in a different way. Unanimously we said: "No," to settle the row; and when he brought the table and put it into place and laid a red and white check tablecloth on it, we sat down, stretched our legs, and said: "Yes. This table is much better."

Before this we had called for Angel at his hotel. We shook his hand or slapped him on the back or embraced him and two hung on his arm as we walked down the street. "Ah, Angel, the rogue!" we said, giving him a squeeze. Our smooth Mediterranean Angel! "The uncle!" we said. "The old scoundrel." Angel smiled, lowering his black lashes in appreciation. Juliano gave him a prod in the ribs and asked him if he remembered, after all these years, that summer at Biarritz. When we had all been together? The only time we had all been together before?

Juliano laughed by making his eyes wicked and expectant, like one Andalusian reminding another of the great joke they had the day poor So-and-So fell down the stairs and broke his neck.

"The day you were nearly drowned," Juliano said.

Angel's complexion was the colour of white coffee; his hair, crinkled like a black fern, was parted in the middle, he was rich, soft-palmed, and patient. He was the only well-dressed man among us, the suavest shouter. Now he sat next door but one to Juliano. Fernando was between them, Juan next to me, and at the end Felix. They had put Cæsar at the head of the table, because he was the oldest and the largest. Indeed, at his age he found his weight tiring to the feet.

Cæsar did not speak much. He gave his silent weight to the dinner, letting his head drop like someone falling asleep, and listening. To the noise we made, his silence was a balance and he nodded all the time slowly, making everything true. Sometimes someone told some story about him and he listened to that, nodding and not disputing it.

But we were talking chiefly of that summer, the one when Angel (the old uncle!) had nearly been drowned. Then Juan, the stout, swarthy one, banged the table with his hairy hands and put on his horn-rimmed glasses. He was the smallest and most vehement of us, the one with the thickest neck and the deepest voice, his words like barrels rumbling in a cellar.

"Come on! Come on! Let's make up our minds! What are we going to eat? Eat! Eat!" he roared.

"Yes," we cried. "Drink! What are we going to drink?"

The proprietor, who was in his shirt-sleeves and braces, said it was for us to decide. We could have anything we wanted. This started another argument. He stepped back a pace and put himself in an attitude of self-defence.

"Soup! Soup? Make up your minds about soup! Who wants soup?" bawled Juan.

"Red wine," some of us answered. And others: "Not red, white."

"Soup I said," shouted Juan. "Yes," we all shouted. "Soup."

"Ah," said Juan, shaking his head, in his slow miserable disappointed voice. "Nobody have any soup. I want some soup. Nobody soup," he said sadly to the proprietor.

Juliano was bouncing in his chair and saying, God, he would never forget that summer when Angel was nearly drowned! When we had all been together. But Juan said Felix had not been there and we had to straighten that matter out.

Juliano said: "They carried him on to the beach, our little Angel on to the beach. And the beach superintendent came through the crowd and said: 'What's happening?' 'Nothing,' we said. 'A man knocked out.' 'Knocked out?' said the beach superintendent. 'Nothing,' we said. 'Drowned!' A lot of people left the crowd and ran about over the beach saying: 'A man has been drowned.' 'Drowned,' said the beach superintendent. Angel was lying in the middle of them all, unconscious, with water pouring out of his mouth."

"No! No!" shouted Fernando. "No. It wasn't like that."

"How do you mean, it wasn't like that?" cried Juliano. "I was there." He appealed to us: "I was there."

"Yes, you were there," we said.

"I *was* there. I was there bringing him in. You say it wasn't like that, but it was like that. We were all there." Juliano jumped protesting to his feet, flung back his coat from his defying chest. His waistcoat was very loose over his stomach, draughty.

"What happened was better than that," Fernando said.

"Ah," said Juliano, suddenly sitting down and grinning with his eyes at everyone, very pleased at his show.

"It was better," he said.

"How better?" said Juliano.

Fernando was a man who waited for silence and his hour. Once getting possession of the conversation he never let it go, but held it in the long, soothing ecstasy of a pliable embrace. All day long he lay in bed in his room in Fuencarral with the shutters closed, recovering from the bout of the day before. He was preparing himself to appear in the evening, spruce, grey-haired, and meaty under the deep black crescents of his eyebrows, his cheeks ripening like plums as the evening advanced, his blue eyes, which got bloodshot early, becoming mistier. He was a man who ripened and moistened. He talked his way through dinner into the night, his voice loosening, his eyes misting, his walk becoming slower and stealthier, acting every sentence, as if he were swaying through the exalted phase of inebriation. But it was an inebriation purely verbal; an exaltation of dramatic moments, refinements upon situations; and hour after hour passed until the dawn found him sodden in his own anecdotes, like a fruit in rum.

"What happened was," Fernando said, "that I was in the sea. And after a while I discovered Angel was in the sea. As you know, there is nothing more perilous than the sea, but with Angel in it the peril is tripled; and when I saw him I was preparing to get as far away as possible. But he was making faces in the water and soon he made such a face, so inhuman, so unnatural, I saw he was drowning. This did not surprise me, for Angel is one of those men who, when he is in the sea, he drowns. There is some psychological antipathy. Now, when I see a man drowning my instinct is to get away quickly. A man drowning is not a man. He is a lunatic. But a lunatic like Angel! But unfortunately he got me before I could get away. There he was," Fernando stood up and raised his arm, confronting the proprietor of the restaurant, but staring right through that defensive man, "beating the water, diving, spluttering, choking, spitting, and, seeing he was drowning, for the man *was* drowning, caught hold of me, and we both went under. Angel was like a beast. He clung to me like seaweed. I, seeing this, awarded him a knock-out—zum—but as the tenacity of man increases with unconsciousness, Angel stuck to me like a limpet, and in saving myself there was no escape from saving him."

"That's true," said Angel, admiring his fingernails. And Cæsar nodded his head up and down twice, which made it true.

Juan then swung round and called out: "Eat! Food! Let us order. Let us eat. We haven't ordered. We do nothing but talk, not eat. I want to eat."

"Yes, come on," said Felix. "Eat. What's the fish?"

"The fish," said the proprietor, "is bacalao."

"Yes," everyone cried. "Bacalao, a good bacalao, a very good one. No, it must be good. No. I can't eat it unless it's good, very good *and* very good."

"No," we said. "Not fish. We don't want it."

"Seven bacalaos, then?" said the proprietor.

But Fernando was still on his feet.

"And the beach inspector said: 'What's his name and address and has he any identity papers?' 'Man,' I said, 'he's in his bathing dress. Where could he keep his papers?' And Juan said: 'Get a doctor. Don't stand there asking questions. Get a doctor.' "

"That's true," said Juan gloomily. "He wasn't dead."

"Get a doctor, that was it," Angel said.

"And they got a doctor and brought him round and got half the Bay of Biscay out of him, gallons of it. It astonished me that so much water could come out of a man."

"And then in the evening"—Juliano leaped up and clipped the story out of Fernando's mouth. "Angel says to the proprietor of the hotel—"

Juan's head had sunk to his chest. His hands were over his ears.

"Eat," he bawled in a voice of despair so final that we all stopped talking and gazed at him with astonishment for a few moments. Then in sadness he turned to me, appealing. "Can't we eat? I am empty."

". . . said to the proprietor of the hotel," Fernando grabbed the tale back from Juliano, "who was rushing down the corridor with a face like a fish. 'I am the man who was drowned this morning.' And the proprietor who looked at Angel like a prawn, the proprietor said: 'M'sieu, whether you were drowned or not drowned this morning, you are about to be roast. The hotel is on fire.' "

"That's right," we said. "The hotel was on fire."

"I remember," said Felix. "It began in the kitchen."

"How in the kitchen?"

This then became the argument.

"The first time ever I heard it was in the kitchen."

"But no," said Angel, softly rising to claim his life story for himself. Juliano clapped his hands and bounced with joy. "It was not like that."

"But we were all there, Angel," Fernando said; but Angel, who spoke very rapidly, said:

"No and no! And the proof of it is. What was I wearing?" He challenged all of us. We paused.

"Tripe," said Juan to me, hopelessly wagging his head. "You like tripe? They do it well. Here! Phist!" he called the proprietor through the din. "Have you tripe, a good Basque tripe? No? What a pity! Can you get me some? Here! Listen," he shouted to the rest of the table. "Tripe," he shouted, but they were engrossed in Angel.

"Pyjamas," Fernando said. "When you are in bed you wear your pyjamas."

"Exactly, and they were not my pyjamas."

"You say the fire was not in the kitchen," shouted Fernando, "because the pyjamas you were wearing were not yours!" And we shouted back at Angel.

"They belonged to the Italian Ambassador," said Angel, "the one who was with that beautiful Mexican girl."

Then Cæsar, who, as I have said, was the oldest of us and sat at the head of the table, Cæsar leaned his old big pale face forward and said in a hushed voice, putting out his hands like a blind man remembering:

"My God—but what a very beautiful woman she was," he said. "I remember her. I have never in my life," he said speaking all his words slowly and with grave concern, "seen such a beautiful woman."

Fernando and Angel, who had been standing, sat down. We all looked in awe at the huge, old-shouldered Cæsar with his big pale face and the pockets under his little grey eyes, who was speaking of the most beautiful woman he had ever seen.

"She was there all that summer," Cæsar said. "She was no longer young." He leaned forward with his hands on the table. "What must she have been when she was young?"

A beach, the green sea dancing down white upon it, that Mexican woman walking over the floor of a restaurant, the warm white houses, the night glossy black like the toe of a patent shoe, her hair black. We tried to think how many years ago this was. Brought by his voice to silence us, she was already fading.

The proprietor took his opportunity in our silence. "The bacalao is done in the Basque fashions with peppers and potatoes. Bring a bacalao," he snapped to a youth in the kitchen.

Suddenly Juan brought his fists on the table, pushed back his chair, and beat his chest with one fist and then the other. He swore in his enormous voice by his private parts.

"It's eleven o'clock. Eat! For God's sake. Fernando stands there talking and talking and no one listens to anybody. It is one of the evils of Spain. Someone stop him. Eat."

We all woke up and glared with the defiance of the bewildered, rejecting everything he said. Then what he said to us penetrated. A wave roared over us and we were with him. We agreed with what he said. We all stood up and, by our private parts, swore that he was right. It was one of the evils of Spain.

The soup arrived. White wine arrived.

"I didn't order soup," some shouted.

"I said 'Red wine,'" others said.

"It is a mistake," the proprietor said. "I'll take it away." An argument started about this.

"No," we said. "Leave it. We want it." And then we said the soup was bad, and the wine was bad and everything he brought was bad, but the proprietor said the soup was good and the wine was good and we said in the end it was good. We told the proprietor the restaurant was good, but he said not very good—indeed, bad. And then we asked Angel to explain about the pyjamas.

The Two Brothers

The two brothers went to Ballady to look at the house. It was ruinous but cheap, there were miles of bog and mountain alive with birds, there was the sea and not a soul living within two miles of it. As had always happened in their childhood and as had repeatedly happened since the war when "the Yank" had returned to the Old Country to look after his sick brother, "the Yank," with his voracious health, had his way.

"Sure it's ideal," yelled the Yank.

The time was the spring.

"We'll take it for six months," he exclaimed.

"And after that?" asked Charlie, watching him like a woman for plans and motives he had not got.

"Och, we'll see. We'll see. Sure what's the use of worrying about the future?" said the Yank.

He knew and Charlie knew the question hung over them; the future watching them like an eagle on a rock, waiting to shadow them with its wing. In six months he would be left alone. He knew how the Yank, his brother, dealt with time. Out came his gun and he took a pot-shot at it, went after it, destroyed it and then laughed at his own skill and forgot.

In the sky and land at Ballady there was the rugged wildness of farewell. This was the end of the land, prostrating itself in rags before the Atlantic. The wind stripped the soil so that there was no full-grown tree upon it, and rocks stood out like gravestones in the bigoted little fields. A few black cattle grazed, a few fields of oats were grown, the rest was mountain and the wide empty pans of bog broken into eyes of water. The house lay in a hollow out of sight of the sea, which was only half a mile away. It was a grey, rambling place of two stories with outhouses and stables all going to pieces. It was damp, leaky and neglected and barely furnished. There were fuchsia bushes growing right up to the windows, beating against them and blinding them in the gales, pressed close as people in the night. The garden was feet deep in grasses, the gravel drive had become two grass ruts, and for a gate there was an iron hurdle propped against a gap in the stone wall. From the hill above Ballady Charlie and Micky had made out its slate roof silvery in the light, the ribs of the roofless stable like a shining skeleton.

"The way it is," the Yank explained when he went in to Ballady alone for a drink now and then. "The poor bloody brother he's after having a breakdown." The Yank was a wild, tall, lean, muscular fellow, straight and springy as a whip, with eyes like dark pools, with bold brows, lips loose and thin, and large ears protruding from his bony skull. His black hair stood up straight and was cropped close like a convict's, so that the skin could be seen through it; his nose was straight and his face was reddened by the wind. He went about with a cigarette in the corner of lips askew in a conquering grin, and carried a gun all day. A breezy, sporting chap. He wandered up and down the bog and the fields or lay in the dunes waiting; then, bang went his gun, the seabirds screamed over the sand and up he got from his knees to pick up a rabbit or a bird. The sun burned him, the wind cut him, the squalls pitted him like shot. He had no secrets from anyone. Fifteen years of Canada, he told them, four years of war, and now for a good time while his money lasted. Then, he said publicly to all, he would go back. All he wanted now was a bit of rough country, a couple of drinks and a gun; and he had got them. It was what he had always wanted. He was out for the time of his life.

How different Charlie was, slight and wiry, nervous and private as a silvery fish. His hair was fair, almost white, and his eyes were a keen dark blue in the pupils and a fairer blue was ringed round them. His features were sharp and he kept his lips together and his head down as he walked, glancing nervously about him. He looked like a man walking in his thoughts. If, when he returned from the sea, he saw someone in his path, he dodged away and made a long detour back to the house. If taken by surprise and obliged to talk to a stranger, he edged away murmuring something. His voice was quiet, his look shrill, pleading and shy. He was absorbed in the most private of all pieties, the piety of fear to which his imagination devoted a rich and vivid ritual.

He did not badger his brother with speech. He followed him about the house, standing near him, asking with his eyes for the virtue of his brother's strength, courage, company, and protection. He asked no more than his physical presence and to watch. In the mornings at first, after they had established themselves in the house, there was always this situation: Micky restless, burning to be out with his gun, and Charlie's eyes silently asking him not to go. Micky bursting to be free, Charlie worrying to hold him. Sometimes Micky would be melted by an unguarded glance at his brother. For a moment he would forget his own strength and find himself moved by an awed tenderness for this clever man who had passed examinations, stayed in the Old Country, worked his way up in a bank and then, when the guns had started to popple, and "the troubles" began, had collapsed.

Micky was kind and humoured him. They would sit for hours together in the house, with the spring growing in the world outside, while Charlie cajoled him with memories of their boyhood together, or listened to Micky's naïve and boasting tales of travel. In those hours Charlie forgot the awful years, or he would have the illusion of forgetting. For the two surrounded themselves with walls of talk, and Charlie, crouching round the little camp-fire of his heart, used every means to keep the talk going, to preserve this picture of life standing as still as a dreamy ship in haven and himself again a child.

But soon the sun would strike through the window and the fairness of the sky would make Micky restless. He would lead his brother, by a pretext, into the garden and slyly get him to work there, planting lettuces or digging, and when he had got him to work he would slip away, pick up his gun, and be off to the dunes.

Shortly after moving into the house, Micky went into Dill, got drunk as was his habit, and returned with a dog, a young black retriever, very strong, affectionate and lively. He did not know why he had bought it and could hardly remember what he had paid for it. But when he got home he said on the impulse to Charlie:

"Here, Charlie boy. I've bought you a dog. One of the priest's pups."

Charlie smiled slightly and looked in wonder.

"There y'are, man," Micky cried. "Your dog."

"Hup! Go to your master," said Micky, giving the dog a push, and sent it over to Charlie, who still incredulously gazed.

"Now that's kind of you," he murmured, flushing slightly. He was speechless with pleasure. Micky, who had given the animal to his brother on the spur of the moment, was now delighted with himself, sunned in his generosity.

"Sure, now ye've got yer dog," Micky kept saying, "ye'll be all right. Ye'll be all right now ye've got the dog."

Charlie gazed at Micky and the animal, and slyly he smiled to himself; Micky had done this because he had a bad conscience. But Charlie put these thoughts aside.

Both brothers devoted themselves to the retriever, Micky going out and shooting rabbits for it, and Charlie cooking them and taking out the bones. But when Micky got up and took his gun and the retriever jumped up to go out with him, Charlie would whistle the dog back and say:

"Here! Stay here. Lie down. Ye're going out with me in a minute."

It was his dog.

At last Charlie went out and the watchful creature leaped out with him. Charlie drew courage from it as it loped along before him, sniffing at walls and standing stiff with ears cocked to see the sudden rise of a bird. Charlie talked to it in a low running murmur hardly made of words but easing to the mind. When it stopped, he would pass his clever hands over its velvety nose and glossy head, feeling the strange life ripple under the hair and obtaining a curious strength from the tumult. Then he would press on and whistle the creature after him and make across the fields to the long finger-bone of rock that ran down to the sea; but as the retriever ran it paused often, as Charlie began to note with bewilderment and then with dread, to listen for Micky's voice or the sound of his gun.

When he saw this, Charlie redoubled his efforts to win the whole allegiance of the dog. Power was renewing itself in him. And so he taught the dog a trick. He called it over the rocks, slipping and yelping, to the sea's edge. Here the sand was white, and as the worlds of clouds bowled over the sky to the mountains where the light brimmed like golden bees, the sea would change into deep jade halls, purple where the weeds lay and royal blue under the sparkling sun, and the air was sinewy and strong. Charlie took off his clothes and, shivering at the sight of his own thin pale body, his loose queasy stomach and the fair sickly hairs now picking up gold from the light, and with a desire to

cleanse himself of sickness and fear, lowered himself cautiously into the
green water, and wading out with beating heart, called to the dog. It
stood up whining and barking for a while, running up and down the
rock, and at last plunged in pursuit. Then the man caught hold of its
tail and let himself be towed out to sea, and for minutes they would
travel out and out until, at a word, the dog returned, snorting, heart
pumping, shoulders working and eyes gazing upwards and the green
water swilling off its back until it had pulled Charlie back into his
depth.

Then Charlie would sit drying himself and listening to the scream
of the birds while the black retriever yelped and shivered at his side.
And if Micky were late for his meal when he returned, through drinking with the schoolmaster or going away for a day to the races, Charlie
would say nothing. He would build up a big turf fire in the empty room
and wait with the dog at his side, murmuring to it.

But it took Charlie hours to make up his mind to these expeditions,
and as time went on they became irregular. There were days when the
absences of his brother left him alone with his fears, and on these days
he would helplessly see the dog run after Micky and go off with him.
Soon it would hardly obey Charlie's call.

"You're taking the dog from me," Charlie complained,

"Sure if ye'd go out the dog'd follow you," said Micky. "Dammit,
what's the use of staying inside? I don't want the dog, but the poor
bloody creature needs a run an't follows me. It's only natural."

Natural. That's it, Charlie reflected. From him that hath not shall
be taken even that which he hath. But he cried out sharply:

"Sure you have it trained away from me."

Then they quarrelled, and Micky, thinking his head was getting too
hot for his tongue, went out to the dunes and stood in the wind staring
at the sea. Why was he tied to this weak and fretful man? For three
years since the end of the war he had looked after Charlie, getting him
out of hospital and into a nursing-home, then to houses in the country,
sacrificing a lot of his own desire to have a good time before he returned
to Canada, in order to get his brother back to health. Micky's money
would not last for ever; soon he would have to go, and then what would
happen?

But when he returned with cooler head, the problem carelessly
thrown off, he was kind to his brother. They sat in eased silence
before the fire, the dog dreaming at their feet, and to Charlie there
returned the calm of the world. His jealousies, his suspicions, his re-

proaches, all the spies sent out by his reconnoitring fears, were called in, and with Micky he was at peace and no shadow of the future was on him.

Yet as the months climbed higher out of July into August and swung there awhile, enchanted by their own halcyon weather, before declining into the cooler days, the question had to be faced. Micky knew and Charlie knew, but each wished the other to speak.

It was Micky who, without warning, became impatient and spoke out.

"Lookut here, Charlie," he said one evening as he washed blood off his hands in the kitchen—he had been skinning and cleaning a couple of rabbits—"are you coming back to Canada with me in September?"

"To Canada is it?" said the brother, putting his thin fingers on the table and speaking in a gasping whisper. He stood incredulous. Yet he had expected this.

"And leave me here alone!"

"Not at all," said Micky. "I said 'You're coming with me.' You heard me. Will ye come with me to Canada?"

Charlie drew in his lips, and his eyes were restless with agony.

"Sure, Micky, ye know I can't do that," he said.

"But what's to stop ye? Ye're all right. Ye're well. Ye've got your bit of pension and ye'll be as comfortable as in your own home. Get out of this damn country, that's what ye want. Sure 'tis no good at all except for old people and children," cried Micky.

But Charlie was looking out of the window towards the mountains. To go out into the world, to sit in trains with men, to sleep in houses with them, to stand bewildered, elbowed and shouldered by men in a new country! Or, as the alternative, to stay alone without Micky, left to his memories.

"You'll not leave me, Micky boy?" he stammered in panic.

Micky was bewildered by the high febrile voice, the thin body shivering like a featherless bird. Then Charlie changed. He hunched his shoulders, narrowing himself and cowering round his heart, hardening himself against the world, and his eyes shot out suspicions, jealousies, reproaches, the weapons of a sharp mind.

" 'Tis the schoolmaster has been putting you against me," he said.

Micky ridiculed the idea.

"Ye knew as well as I did, dammit, when we took the place, that I'd be going now," he said. Yes, this was true, Charlie had known it.

Micky took the matter to his friend the schoolmaster. He was a stout, hard-drinking old man with a shock of curly grey hair. His manner was theatrical and abrupt.

" 'Tis the poor bloody brother," Micky said. "What am I to do with him at all?"

"Ye've no more money," said the schoolmaster.

"Ye've been with him for years," he went on. He paused again.

"Ye can't live on him.

"And he must live with you."

He glowered at Micky and then his fierce look died away.

"Sure there's nothing you can do. Nothing at all," said the schoolmaster.

Micky filled their glasses again.

He continued his life. The summer glided down like a beautiful bird scooping the light. The peasants stood in their long shadows in the fields and fishermen left their boats for the harvest. Micky was sad to be leaving this beautiful isolation.

But he had to return to the question. He and Charlie began to argue it continually day and night. Sometimes Charlie was almost acquiescent, but at last always retired within himself. Since he could not sit in the safety of the old talk, his cleverness found what comfort it could for him in the new. Soon it was clear to Micky that Charlie encouraged the discussion, cunningly played with it, tortured him with vacillations, cunningly played on his conscience. But to Charlie it seemed that he was struggling to make his brother aware of him fully; deep in the piety of his fear he saw in Micky a man who had never worshipped at its icy altars. He must be made to know. So the struggle wavered until one night it came out loudly into the open.

"God Almighty," cried out Micky as they sat in the lamplight. "If you'd been in France you'd have had something to cry about. That's what's wrong with this bloody country. All a pack of damn cowards, and ye can see it in their faces when they stare at you like a lot of bleating sheep."

"Oh, is that it?" said Charlie, gripping the arms of his chair. "Is that what you're thinking all these years? You're saying I'm afraid, is it? You're saying I'm a coward. Is that what you were thinking when you came home like a red lord out of hell in your uniform, pretending to be glad to see me and the home? But thinking in your own heart I'm a coward not to be in the British Army. Oh, is that it?"

His voice was quiet, high and monotonous in calculated contrast to Micky's shouting anger. But his body shook. A wound had been opened. He *was* a coward. He *was* afraid. He was terrified. But his clever mind quickly closed the wound. He was a man of peace. He desired to kill no one. He worshipped the great peace of God. This was why he had avoided factions, agreed with all sides, kept out of politics and withdrawn closer and closer into himself. At times it had seemed to him that the only place left in the world for the peace of God was in his own small heart.

And what had Micky done? In the middle of the war he had come home, the Destroyer. In five minutes by a few reckless words in the drink shop and streets of the town he had ruined the equilibrium Charlie had tended for years and had at last attained. In five minutes Charlie had become committed. He was no longer "Mr Lough the manager," a man of peace. No, he was the brother of "that bloody pro-British Yank." Men were boycotted for having brothers in the British Army, they were threatened, they were even shot. In an hour a village as innocent-looking as a green-and-white place in a postcard had become a place of windows hollow-eyed with evil vigils. Within a month he had received the first note threatening his life.

" 'Twas yourself," said Charlie—discovering at last his enemy. " 'Twas yourself, Micky, that brought all this upon me. Would I be sick and destroyed if you hadn't come back?"

"Cripes," said Micky, hearing the argument for the first time and pained by this madness in his brother. "Cripes, man, an' what was the rest of ye up to? Serving God Almighty like a lot of choir boys, shooting up some poor lonely policeman from a hedge and driving old women out of their homes."

"Stop it," shouted Charlie as the memories broke upon him, and he put his fingers to his ears.

Micky threw his cigarette into the fire and took his brother by the shoulder in compassion. He was sorry for having spoken so; but Charlie ignored him. He spoke, armouring himself.

"So it's a coward I am, is it!" he said. "Well, I stayed when they threatened me and I'll stay again. You're thinking I'm a coward." He was resolute. But behind the shrubs brushing against the window, in the spaces between the cool September stars, were the fears.

There was nothing else for it. Charlie watched Micky preparing to go, indifferent and resigned, feeding his courage on this new picture of his brother. He turned to it as to a secret revelation. Micky was no longer his brother. He was the Destroyer, the Prince of this World, the man of darkness. Micky, surprised that his good intentions were foiled,

gave notice to the landlord, to force Charlie. Charlie renewed the
agreement. He spoke little; he took no notice of the dog, which had
now completely deserted him. When Micky had gone it would be his.
Charlie kicked it once or twice as if to remind it. He gave up swimming
in the sea. He was staying here. He had all the years of his life to swim
in the sea.

Micky countered this by open neglect of his brother. He entered
upon a life of wilder enjoyment. He gave every act the quality of a
reckless farewell. He was out all day and half the night. In Ballady he
drank the schoolmaster weeping under the table and came staggering
home, roaring like an opera, and was up at dawn, no worse for it, after
the duck.

"This is a rotten old wall," Micky said in the garden one day, and
started pushing the stones off the top of it. A sign it was his wall no
longer. He chopped a chair up for firewood. He ceased to make his
bed. He took a dozen empty whisky-bottles and, standing them at the
end of the kitchen garden, used them as shooting targets. He shot
three rabbits and threw two of them into the sea. He burned some
old clothes, tore up his letters and gave away a haversack to the
fisherman and a second gun to the schoolmaster. A careless enjoyment of destruction seized him. Charlie watched it, saying nothing.
The Destroyer.

One evening as the yellow sun flared in the pools left by the tide on
the sand, Micky came upon Charlie.

"Not a damn thing," Micky said, tapping his gun.

But as they stood there, some gulls which had been flying over the
rocks came inland and one fine fellow flew out and circled over their
heads, its taut wings deep blue in the shadow as it swung round. Micky
suddenly raised his gun and fired and, before the echoes had broken
in the rocks, the wings collapsed and the bird dropped warm and dead.

"God Almighty, man," cried Charlie, turning away with nausea, "is
nothing sacred to ye?"

"It's no damned good," grinned Micky, picking up the bird by the
wing, which squeaked open like a fan. "Let the fish have it." And he
flung it into the sea. This was what he thought of wings.

Then, with a week to go, without thinking he struck a bad blow. He
went off to Dill to say goodbye to the boys, and the retriever followed
him although Charlie called it back. The races were on at Dill, but
Micky spent most of the time in the pubs telling everyone he was going
back to Canada. A man hearing this said he'd change dogs with him.

His dog, he said, was a spaniel. He hadn't it with him but he'd bring it down next fair. Micky was enthusiastic.

"I know ye will," said Micky. "Sure ye'll bring it."

"Ah, well now," said the man. "I will bring it."

" 'Tis a great country the west," said Micky. "Will ye have another?"

"I will," said the man, and as he drank: "In the three countries there is not a place like this."

Micky returned the next day without the dog.

"Where's the dog?" said Charlie suspiciously.

"Och sure," began Micky evasively, realizing for the first time what he had done. "D'you see the way it is, there is a man in Dill . . ."

"Ye've sold it. Ye've sold my dog," Charlie shouted out, rushing at his brother. His shout was the more unnerving because he had spoken so little for days. Micky drew back.

"Ah now, Charlie, be reasonable now. Sure you never did anything for the dog. You never took it out. You didn't care for it . . ."

Charlie gripped a chair and painfully sat down, laying his head in his hands on the table.

"You brought the war on me, you smash me up, you take the only things I have and leave me stripped and alone," he moaned. "Oh, God in heaven," he half sobbed in pleading voice, "will ye give me gentleness and peace!"

Now the dog was gone, Charlie sat still. He would not move from the house, nor even from the sitting-room except to go to bed. He would scarcely speak. Sulking, Micky repeated to his uneasy conscience, sulking, sulking. He's either mad or he's sulking. What could he do? They sat estranged, already far apart, impatient for the act of departure.

When the eve of his departure came, Micky was relieved to see that Charlie accepted it, and was even making it easy: and so touched was Micky by this that he found no difficulty in promising to spend that last night with Charlie alone. He remained in the house all day, and when the night came a misted moonlight gleamed on the cold roof and the sea was as quiet as the licking of a cat's tongue. Charlie drew the curtains, made up the fire and there they sat silently listening to the clock. They were almost happy: Charlie pleased to have this final brief authority over Micky; Micky relieved by the calm, both disinterested. Charlie spoke of his plans, the work he would do in the garden, the furniture he would buy, the girl he would get in to cook and clean.

" 'Twould be a fine place to bring a bride to," said Micky, giving Charlie a wink, and Charlie smiled.

But presently they heard footsteps on the drive.

"What's that?" exclaimed Charlie sharply, sitting up. The mild mask of peace left his face like a light, and his face set hard.

Without knocking at the door, in walked the schoolmaster. He was in the room before Charlie could get out. He stood up and retreated to the corner.

"Good evening to ye," said the schoolmaster, pulling a bottle out of his pocket, and spreading himself on to a seat. "I came to see your brother on his last night."

Charlie drew in his lips and gazed at the schoolmaster.

"Will ye have a drink?" said Micky nervously.

That began it. Gradually Micky forgot his promise. He paid no attention to Charlie's signs. They sat drinking and telling stories. The world span round. The alarm clock on the little bamboo table, the only table in the bare room, ticked on. Charlie waited in misery, his eyes craving his brother's, whose bloodshot eyes were merry with drinking and laughter at the schoolmaster's tales. The man's vehement voice shook the house. He told of the priest at Dill who squared the jockeys and long thick stories about some Archbishop and his so-called niece. The air to Charlie became profane.

"Isn't your wife afraid to be up and alone this time of night?" Charlie ventured once.

"Och, man, she's in bed long ago," shouted the schoolmaster. "She is that."

And Micky roared with laughter.

At two o'clock Charlie went to bed and left him to it. But he was awake at five when Micky stumbled into his room.

"Before God, man," Micky said, "I'm bloody sorry, Charlie man. Couldn't turn out a friend."

"It's too late now," said Charlie.

Micky left at seven to catch a man who would give him a lift to the eight o'clock train.

The autumn gales broke loose upon the land a month after Micky's departure and the nights streamed black and loud. The days were cold and fog came over the sea. The fuchsias were blown back and the under leaves blew up like silver hands. The rain lashed on the windows like gravel. There were days of calm and then the low week-long mist covered the earth, obliterating the mountains, melting all shapes. All day long the moisture dripped from the sheds and windows and glistened on the stone walls.

At first Charlie did not change. Forced to go to the village for groceries, he would appear there two or three times a week, saying little and walking away quickly. A fisherman would call and the post-boy lingered. Letters came from Micky. Charlie took little heed of all this. But as the weather became wilder he hung curtains over the windows day and night and brought his bed down to the sitting-room. He locked the doors upstairs, those that had still keys to them. He cooked on the sitting-room fire. He was narrowing his world, making a smaller and closer circle to live in. And as it grew smaller, the stranger the places beyond its boundaries seemed. He was startled to go into the empty kitchen, and looked with apprehension up the carpetless stairs to the empty landing where water dripped through the fanlight and was already staining the ceiling below. He lay awake in the night as the fire glowed in the room.

One morning when he found the noises of his isolation supportable no more, he put on his hat and coat and packed his things and walked out of the house. He would stay no longer. But with his fear his brain had, as always, developed a covering cunning. He went up the lane to see if anyone was coming first. He wanted to be away from people, yet among them; with them, yet alone. And on this morning the Ballady sailor was reloading a load of turf that had fallen off his cart. Charlie returned into the house. He took off his hat and coat. He had not been out for a week because of this dread.

There was still food in tin for a few days. It was the thought that he could last if he liked, that he could keep the world off, that made him satisfied. No letters came now. Micky no longer wrote; effusive in the first weeks, his letters had become rare. Now there had been no news for a month. Charlie scarcely thought of him.

But when late in December the mists held the country finally, the twigs creaked on the drive like footsteps and the dark bushes divided in the wind as if they had been parted by hidden hands, he cowered into his beating heart, eating little, and the memories began to move and creep in his head. A letter threatened him with death. He drove alone with the bank's money. At Carragh-cross road the signpost stood emptily gesticulating like some frightened speaker with the wind driving back the words into his mouth, and the two roads dangling from its foot. He knew what had happened at Carragh-cross road. He knew what had been found there lying with one leg out of the ditch. He saw it. And Micky, the Destroyer, with his convict's head and his big red ears, shooting down the Holy Ghost like a beautiful bird, grinned there blowing smoke down his nose.

These memories came and went. When they came they beat into his head like wings, and though he fought them off with prayers, they beat down and down on him and he cried out fast to the unanswering house:

"God give me peace," he prayed. "Holy Mother of God, give me peace for the sake of thy sweet Son. . . ."

When the beating wings went, his cleverness took possession of him again. He prepared a little food, and once or twice walked around the garden within the shelter of the walls. The ground was frozen, the air still and a lace of snow was on the paths. But if the days passed in peace, his heart quickened at the early darkness, and when the turf smoke blew back down the chimney it was as if someone had blown down a signal. One night he had a terrible dream. He was dead, he had been caught at last on the road at Carragh-cross. "Here's the man with the pro-British brother," they cried and threw him into a bog pool, sinking deeper and deeper into soft and sucking fires that drew him down and down. He was in hell. And there in the flames calling to him was a woman with dark hair and with pale insects walking over her skin. It was the schoolmaster's wife. "And he thinking you were in bed," said Charlie, amazed by the justice of revenge. He woke up gasping in the glow of the sitting-room fire, and feeling that a load was still pressing down on his chest.

In the morning the dream was still in his mind; mingling with some obscure sense of triumph, it ceased to be a dream and became reality. It became like a new landscape imposed upon the world. The voice of the woman was more real to his ear than his own breathing.

He felt free, was protected and cleansed, and his dream seemed to him like an impervious world within a world, a mirage in which he musically walked. In the afternoon he was exalted. He walked out of the house, and taking the long way round by the lanes went to the schoolmaster's. The frost still held and the air was windless, the land fixed and without colour. As it happened, the schoolmaster had taken it into his head to go as far as his gate.

"Man, I'm glad to see ye about," cried the schoolmaster at the sight of Charlie. "I meant to see ye. Come in now. Come in. 'Tis terrible lonely for you in that place."

Charlie stood still and looked icily through him.

"Ye thought she was in bed," he said. "But I'm after seeing her in the flames of hell fire."

Without another word he walked away. The schoolmaster made a rush for him. But Charlie had climbed the stone wall and had dropped into the field opposite.

"Come here. Come back. What's that you say?" called the schoolmaster. But Charlie walked on, gathering speed as he dropped behind the hill out of sight going to his house. Then he ran for his life.

The schoolmaster did not wait. He went in for his coat, bicycled into Ballady Post Office and rang up the Guards at Dill.

"There's a poor feller here might do harm to himself," he said. "Will you send someone down?"

But on the way back to the house Charlie's accompanying dream and its hazed exaltation left him. Speaking had dissolved it. It lifted like a haze and suddenly he was left alone, exposed, vulnerable in the middle of the fields. He began to run, shying at every corner, and when he got to the house he clawed at the door and ran in gasping to throw himself on the bed. He lay there on his face, his eyes closed. There had been brief excitement in the run, but as he recovered his breath the place resumed its normal aspect and its horror became real as slowly he turned over and opened his eyes to it. And now they were open he could not close them again. They stared and stared. Slowly it came to him there was nothing in life left for him but emptiness. Career gone, peace gone, God gone, Micky gone, dog—all he had ever had, trooped with bleak salute of valediction through his mind. He was left standing in the emptiness of himself. And then a shadow was cast upon the emptiness; looking up he saw the cold wing of a great and hovering bird. So well he knew it that in this last moment his mind cleared and he had no fear. " 'Tis yourself, Micky, has me destroyed," he said. He took out a razor and became absorbed in the difficulty of cutting his throat. He was not quite dead when the Guards broke in and found him.

1932

Pocock Passes

The cities fall, but what survives? It is the common, patient, indigenous grass. After Mr. Pocock's death this thought lay in a muddle in Rogers's mind; if Rogers had a mind. He was enormously fat; a jellyfish which is washed and rocked by sensations and not by thought. The Wilcoxes, the Stockses and Rogerses, the three ordinary, far-back tribes who made the village, alone had history; and this plain corporate history, like the eternal grass, choked out the singular blooms. The death of a Rogers is something. A card is shuffled into another pack and he joins the great phalanx of village Rogerses beyond the grave, formidable in their anonymity. But the death of a stranger like Pocock, who had been in the place only a few months, was like a motor smash. Vivid but trivial, it sank out of village memory to the bottom of time.

Rogers admitted to himself that he had had a fright. Mr. Pocock had been a man of fifty like himself, as fat as Rogers was, too—they had compared waist measurements once—and he drank heavily: that came home rather close. So close that although Rogers was Mr. Pocock's only friend in the last months of his life, Rogers could not bring himself to go to the funeral. He put on his black to show willingness, but at the hour of the funeral slipped on the doorstep and twisted his knee and had to be kept in his house. With a sort of penitence or hoping for a last order, Askew, the village publican, went—he followed all his customers to the end—and came back saying:

"Mr. Pocock, he drank too much. I often tried to stop him."

Then it was that Rogers, who had gone down to the pub once the funeral was over and Pocock was set in his grave—then it was that Rogers saw a profound truth:

"You're wrong there," he said.

"He didn't drink too much," he said. "The trouble with Mr. Pocock was that he didn't drink enough."

One thing the death of Mr. Pocock did for Rogers was to make him stay at home. There was nothing to go out for. Outside was the road, the village, the four-eyed faces of the villas called Heart's Desire Estate, which Rogers had built on the flat fields and had sold before anyone had discovered that the site was a water meadow. There was his wooden hut too, where he slept over the typewriter sometimes, with its estate-agent's plate on the door. His wife ran his business now—such as it was. Above all this was the sky. He was inclined to see a hole in things like the street or sky after Pocock's death, a hole with simply nothing beyond it. Staying at home with his family kept Rogers from seeing the hole. Hearing his wife use the typewriter or telephone in the office, drinking a cup of tea, listening to his two girls, torpidly watching them, his slow mind lay down like a dog in the domestic basket. "Wife and family—you're lucky, ol' boy," Mr. Pocock had said many times in his husky, half-rapacious voice. Rogers brooded. Perhaps he, surviving, was the better man.

Yet with all his heart and with some plain builder's shrewdness and village vanity, Rogers had wanted to believe in the singularity of Mr. Pocock. People came down from London and took a house in old age, and when they died, these strangers always turned out to be less than they had at first seemed to be. He was used to that. A handful of dust —often scandalous dust—was all they were against the great tribal burial mound of the village Wilcoxes, Stockses, and Rogerses. Pocock not only had looked different but had sounded different and behaved accordingly. Yet the death of Pocock had left in Rogers's mind some suspicion of fraud—indeterminate yet disturbing, like waking in the night and thinking you smell a carpet smouldering, and yet no coal on it when you get out to look.

Pocock was a painter. Not only that, he was a well-known painter from London; he knew other painters. Not only other painters, but studios and actresses. He knew the stage. Yet after the ambulance went like a soft clap of low white wings between the hedges of the main road, taking Pocock to the hospital and his end, Rogers said to people who had come to look at property: "We had Pocock here." They merely said blankly: "What's that? Never heard of him." No one at all had heard of Mr. Pocock, the famous painter.

Rogers and Mr. Pocock had come together not because of their minds or tastes, but because of their bodies. They were drawn will-lessly together by the magnetic force of their phenomenal obesities. There is a loneliness in fat. Atlas met Atlas, astonished to find each saddened by the burden of a world. Rogers was short and had that douce, pleading melancholy of the enormous. His little blue eyes, above the bumps of fat on his cheek-bones, looked like sinking lights at sea; and he had the gentle and bewildered air of a man who watches himself daily getting uncontrollably and hopelessly fatter. His outsize navy-blue jacket hung on him like another man's overcoat. The coarseness and grossness of his appearance, the spread of his nostrils, the crease of his neck, gave him a pathos: there is an inherent delicacy, a dignity and spirituality in pork. He lived in a quiet sedentary fever in which, as his own bounds daily grew, the world seemed farther away to him. His gentleness was like that of the blind, indicating how far he was from other people. There was no one like him in the village. Rogers was a show-piece. His visits to the public-house were a hopeless try for gregariousness, but there were no seats broad enough in the tap, it didn't "do" for him to go to the bar where his workmen were, and, anyway, there were no seats in it. He went instead to the small parlour and was usually there alone, like a human exhibit, with an aspidistra and a picture of Edward VII.

Rogers's first impression, as he came into the parlour one night, was that an enormous bull terrier in a black-and-white chessboard jacket had got up on a chair in the darker corner. Rogers's perceptions were slow; but at last he saw the figure was a man and not a dog. Between the check suit and check cloth hat was a face, a raw-meat face which had grown a grey moustache, and under that was a small, furiously proud and querulous mouth. An old dog who would fly out at you if spoken to. The check coat went on to check knicker-bockers. There was a rose in Pocock's buttonhole—the smell of the rose and of Turkish cigarettes in the room—and he had a spotted bow to his collar. But what surprised Rogers, after he had said "Good evening" and was leaning forward with the usual difficulty to tap the bell on the table, was the stranger's voice. Husky, swaggering, full-tempered, it said, daring you to contradict and yet somehow weary: "What are you having, old boy?"

Deep called unto deep: Rogers saw to his astonishment, not a stranger, but a brother. Not his blood brother, of course, but something closer—a brother in obesity.

Mr. Pocock's was a different kind of fatness, tight where Rogers's was loose, dynamic where Rogers's was passive and poetic, aggressive where Rogers's was silkily receptive. Mr. Pocock's pathos was fiery and bitter. A pair of stiffly inflated balloons seemed to have been placed, one under and one above Mr. Pocock's waist-line, and the load forced his short legs apart on either side of the chair, like the splayed speckled legs of a frog. And there was another bond. Mr. Pocock, it was evident, was a drinker. A gentleman, too (Rogers observed), as the evening went on, arrogantly free with money. A sportsman also. There were a couple of illustrated papers on the table and one had a photograph of tropical game. A peeress had taken these photographs. One showed a hippopotamus rising like a sofa out of a lake.

"Damn cruel, old boy," said Mr. Pocock in a grating gasp, having an imaginary row with the aristocracy and Rogers about it. "All these bloody white women following poor defenceless animals around with cameras, old boy. Bloody hippopotamus can't even drink in peace. Animals much sooner be shot, old boy—what?"

Yes, Mr. Pocock was a sportsman, a blaspheming sportsman of some elegance, for now Rogers noticed a couple of rings on one hand.

Yet not a sportsman, after all, for he looked bored when Rogers spoke of the duck and snipe and the teal which float like commas on the meres at the back of the village.

"Can't eat it, old boy," replied Pocock. "Game's poison to me. Bloody waste of time following birds, if you ask me. Need every ounce of daylight for my work."

The bell on the table was tapped again and again. In and out went Askew, the publican. Even he straightened up under the snapping orders of Mr. Pocock.

And there was no reserve in Mr. Pocock. His talk was free and self-explanatory. "I've come down here to see if there is anything," said Pocock. "If there is, well and good. If not, all right. There may be something."

("What?" wondered Rogers.)

"I've got to, old boy," said Mr. Pocock. "I've got to cut down the overheads. Have another, old boy? With this bloody crisis," he said with an angry and frightened look in his eyes. "I had my own studio in London and a housekeeper, but with this crisis, and the critics in league against you, the bottom's gone out of things. There may be something here—I don't know. Two rooms, a bed, a table, do my own cleaning up and cooking—that's all I want and no women about. No," said Mr. Pocock, "no more women.

"You married, old boy?" asked Mr. Pocock.

"Yes," said Rogers.

"You're lucky, old boy," said Mr. Pocock. "Bloody lucky. Excuse my language, old boy, but woman's a b—"

"Oh, fifty-fifty," said Rogers, not clear whether he meant only half lucky or wholly lucky to have a wife he could share everything with, she doing the office work and looking after his house while he built up his figure and did the drinking. For Rogers had reached the point of saturation in his own life when drinking was work. It never stopped.

Rogers's slow mind wanted to explain, but Pocock interrupted.

"I know, old boy. You can't tell me anything about women. They're a bloody question-mark, old boy. There's two answers to it, one's right and one's wrong. When I want what I want, I don't ask anyone's opinion, I go and get it.

"What?" added Mr. Pocock.

"You're right," said Rogers in his slow, groping voice. "You know the story of the couple who . . ."

They didn't laugh out loud at the story. Rogers shook and shook and his eyes sank out of sight. Mr. Pocock strained in his chair and seemed to fizz with austere pleasure like a bottle of soda-water.

"It's nature," said Mr. Pocock when his head stopped fizzing.

Rogers was out of his depth here. His head was lolling forward. He had reached the stage when Mr. Pocock had a tendency to rise to the ceiling and then to drift away sideways towards the door in great numbers.

"Take salmon," said Rogers heavily, this coming into his mind at the moment.

"Salmon, old boy? Why bloody salmon?" said Mr. Pocock.

"They go—" said Rogers. "They go—up fresh water."

"Salmon?" said Mr. Pocock. "Salmon? They come from the sea."

"They don't breed in it," said Rogers uncertainly. He was beginning to forget why he had mentioned them.

"I know," said Mr. Pocock peremptorily. "They live in the sea and go up the river when they feel like it."

"Feel like it," repeated Rogers. Somewhere near here was the reason for raising the matter.

". . . I've seen 'em, old boy," continued Mr. Pocock, putting down his glass with a bang.

"Out of the sea," insisted Rogers.

"Don't be bloody funny, old boy," said Mr. Pocock, banging his glass again. "We know they do."

The landlord called: "Time."

Rogers and Mr. Pocock got up with common difficulty, exchanging a look of sympathy. Foot by foot, after they had unbent, stopping between paragraphs, they talked and stopped their way out of the public-house and outside its door. Facing the night, surprised by it, they halted again. The moon arrested them. It was a white full moon, the most obese of planets, with its little mouth open in the sad face.

"Just made for an artist, I should say," said Rogers, slapped across the face by the cold wind, but warm within in his linings. Yet as a villager he had an obscure feeling that for a London stranger to paint the place insulted it. His feeling was primitive; he did not want the magic of an alien eye upon his home.

"It *used* to be pretty, old boy," said Mr. Pocock. "Till some bastard ran up those bloody villas."

"I put them up ten years ago," said Rogers dispassionately; and he meant that time justified and forgave all things.

"Good God, old boy. Bloody ugly," fizzed Mr. Pocock.

They stared at the villas and grinned, almost sniggered, like boys peeping through a fence at something shocking. It gave Rogers and Mr. Pocock pleasure, they being human, to know the worst about each other. And as they gazed with tenderness upon the raped virgin, the sight started Pocock's mind on his own affairs and prompted him to the words which were the final thing to bind Rogers to him.

"I don't mind telling you, old boy, I've been hurt," Mr. Pocock said. "I've had a jerk. I haven't told a bloody soul so far, but I'll tell you. *Last year I started living on my capital.*"

Rogers turned his back on Mr. Pocock and affected to look up the road for traffic. It was empty. All lights in the village houses were out. He felt a stirring of the bowels. His wife did not know, he hardly let himself know—but he, too, had passed the crest of his life, he, too, was beginning the first harassed footsteps downhill, crumbling away to pieces like a town in a fog; and no one, hitherto, to watch or share the process. Rogers also had started living on his capital.

After this, day by day, they sought each other out like two dogs. First of all they were halting and suspicious. Rogers said: "Have you been painting, Mr. Pocock?" but this was not, he discovered, a welcome question. Mr. Pocock replied that he was sizing up the situation. Midday, Mr. Pocock could always be found sizing things up at The Grapes or The Waggoner. He was sizing up and settling in. And, anyway, he hadn't been feeling too well lately.

"Been having trouble with my foot," said Mr. Pocock defiantly at Rogers.

"It's the weight you carry," said Rogers. "I get it myself."

Mr. Pocock, as one heavy drinker to another, appreciated the tact of that lie.

"I keep clear of doctors, old boy," said Mr. Pocock. "Always have."

"They cut you down," said Rogers, emptying his glass.

"All wrong, old boy," said Mr. Pocock. "Want to kill you."

At night they met like lovers. They were religious drinkers. Whisky was Mr. Pocock's religion, beer was the faith of Rogers. An active faith ranges widely. After the public-houses of the village there were two or three on the main road. The headlights of cars howling through the dark to the coast picked out two balloons in coats and trousers, bouncing and blowing down the road. Dramas halted them.

"What's that, old boy?"

"Rabbit."

"No, old boy, not a rabbit. It was a fox. I know a fox."

"I reckon it was a stoat."

The point became intricate under the stars.

"Bring Mr. Pocock in to supper one evening," Mrs. Rogers said. She was a plump, practical woman, with hair set like a teacake. She was a one-time nurse, abnormally good-tempered, pleasantly unimaginative. She ate well and enjoyed the anxiety of being the business management of an exhibit like her husband. Incapable herself of his deterioration, hers was the craving, so strong in the orderly and new, for its opposite, the romantic ruin. Rogers, like many men, and especially drinking men, who neglect their wives and are slowly ruining their families, had an ideal picture of his family in his mind, a picture to which his fancy was always putting more delicate touches of reminiscence. For, like all the world beyond his hazy corpulence, his family became remote, a little farther away each day, like a memory of an old master.

"Bloody funny thing, old boy," Mr. Pocock said. "When I paint a picture, I get the feeling I have for a woman."

It was Rogers's feeling about his own picture, of his family, that private masterpiece of his. Rogers wasn't interested in any other pictures; Mr. Pocock wasn't interested in domestic life. And The Crown was placed strategically between their homes.

About once every couple of months, Mr. Pocock hinted, he "broke out." He always had. He always would. There was a large manufacturing town with a river, pleasure-boats and a Hippodrome twenty miles away, where life, said Rogers, abounded. He and Mr. Pocock put roses in their buttonholes, cigars in their mouths, and went. Rogers explained that he hadn't seen quite so much life since he was married, but when he was a youngster . . . Oh, dear. This stirred up memories in Mr. Pocock. They arrived and, to make a start, went to the station buffet. After this the past was vivid. They went to the Hippodrome for the second act of a play about divorce. The seats were narrow and Mr. Pocock said he couldn't breathe. They left. Mr. Pocock said all this modern stuff was dirty. Nothing but sex. (What's yours, old boy?) Dirt, like Epstein and Cézanne.

The last train back was the twelve-seventeen. It brought the Hippodrome people. For a long time the station with its hoardings and iron and glass façade seemed unattainable, but at last, after a long time on the curb opposite, they rushed it. The train was crowded. Rogers had been sorry to leave the Hippodrome. He smiled, wagging his head, thinking about it, then he began to laugh and nudge his neighbours. They were soon entertained by Rogers. It was like the old days.

"I've been divorced today," Rogers suddenly said; "and he's my co-respondent." Mr. Pocock at once offered him a cigarette. Rogers refused.

"Why do you refuse my cigarettes, old boy?" Mr. Pocock asked abruptly. He was out for a quarrel.

"Do you think I want your wife?" exclaimed Mr. Pocock angrily. Rogers laughed idiotically.

"Because you're a swine if you do," said Mr. Pocock.

But they didn't fight. They got out at their station, helped out by the passengers, and the guard, while the engine-driver watched from the cab. They passed Rogers's villas.

"Damned awful, old boy," said Mr. Pocock.

"Come in," said Rogers when they got to his house.

A look of sobered terror came into Mr. Pocock's face.

"Your wife in?" he said.

"She's in bed," Rogers said.

"Thank God," said Mr. Pocock. "I'm drunk."

"Come in," said Rogers.

"She'd hear my language," said Mr. Pocock. Rogers opened the door and led the way into the sitting-room.

Mr. Pocock sat down while Rogers went to the whisky bottle.

"It's empty, old man," Rogers said, looking blankly at Mr. Pocock.

"Thank God, old boy." Mr. Pocock stood appalled, like a man who had never been in an inhabited house before. He looked shocked. He saw with horror the cretonne-covered sofa, the photographs, the slim silver vases with maidenhair fern in them.

"She's taken the other one away and put this one here."

"Women," said Mr. Pocock.

They stared at each other.

"Come round to my place," said Mr. Pocock.

Still talking, they went out, leaving the door open. A woman's head appeared at the window.

"Alfred!" the voice called.

Rogers stopped and stared at Mr. Pocock. Mr. Pocock stared back like a fierce dog at Rogers.

"Better answer, old boy," said Mr. Pocock, banging his stick on the ground.

"Yes," called Rogers.

"Had a good time?" said the woman's voice. They could not see her in the darkness, but Mr. Pocock raised his hat.

"Better go," he whispered.

He went off alone. Rogers followed him at last. Mr. Pocock's house was the last of a row of labourers' cottages, one room and the scullery downstairs and two little rooms up. Now Rogers was shocked by what he saw. In the downstairs room was an old bit of carpet laid to the edge of a cooking range, and the carpet was stained with grease. Tins and the remains of a meal were on the table. Mr. Pocock used only one of the rooms upstairs. They went up. Its boards were bare. There was a suitcase on the floor and there was an iron bed and a chair. The place smelled of mice and also of the smoking candle stuck on the mantelpiece. They sat down.

"That's what I ought to have done—got married," said Mr. Pocock. His face looked greenish in the candlelight. "Bloody lonely without a woman, old boy."

"There's a woman," Mr. Pocock exclaimed violently. There were canvases stacked against the dirty wall. He turned one round. He filled his glass. What Rogers saw shocked him. It was the picture of a thin, dark-haired woman sitting on a bed, naked. Not lascivious, not beautiful, not enticing, just naked and seeming to say: "It don't feel natural, I mean having nothing on."

"Oh dear, oh dear," was all Rogers could say. He went hot. It was the painting of the bed that shocked him. Mr. Pocock seemed to him a monster.

Mr. Pocock began to boast and Rogers hardly listened. There was a bottle of whisky. Rogers's eye kept going with astonishment to the picture. A dancer, Mr. Pocock said. He knew all the stage crowd, he said. Could have had her, he said. Words and words came out of Mr. Pocock, gobbling and strutting like a blown-out turkey in the room, words making an ever-softening roar in the set, cold silence of the cottage where no clock ticked.

Suddenly Rogers had a shock. It was daylight. He had been asleep on the floor and the sun was shining on him. He gaped. There was Mr. Pocock on the bed. Still holding his cane, the rings shining on his podgy fingers, which had grey hair at the knuckles, Mr. Pocock lay. He was snoring. His body heaved up and down in the loud suit, like a marquee with the wind loose in it. Remote in sleep with his picture above him, Mr. Pocock looked sacred and innocent, in the bare room.

The spring came with its glassy winds, its air going warm and cold and the lengthening light becoming frail in the evenings. Rogers and Mr. Pocock were both ill. Rogers received illness as part of his burden; he was more aware of his wife and of his children when he was ill. But Mr. Pocock was an aggressive invalid. He saw conspiracy. He was terrified and he blustered to conceal this and made war on the doctor. He would not stay in bed.

"Kimble thinks he's got me, old boy. Knocked off my beer and cut me down to two whiskies a day. It isn't right! It isn't human! He's got to be fair."

When Rogers got up they met in the pub.

"I've had seven, old boy," Mr. Pocock said. "But if Kimble says anything to you about what I drink—it's two. I've treated him fairly. I've been reasonable. That man wants to kill me. But not a word to him! You've got to deal with these doctors."

First of all when he had come to the village Mr. Pocock had a charwoman to clean and wash up for him, but he was hardly ever in his cottage and he ate at any time. He had got rid of the charwoman and looked after himself. He had brought his bed downstairs when he

was first ill because he had been frightened in the upstairs room. One
night he felt tired and low. A bus-ride had upset him. He went to bed
early. In the middle of the night he woke up in black terror. He felt
sick and he was fainting, and he was sure he was in London. He reached
for his stick and knocked on the floor to make the woman come up to
him, the woman whose portrait Rogers had seen and who lived downstairs. All the night sleeping and waking he dreamed he was knocking
to make himself heard on the floor. For the model, then for Mrs.
Rogers, then for his mother.

In the morning he could hardly move. Then he remembered he was
on the ground floor and had been knocking on the carpet which
covered the flags, which covered the earth. He had been knocking on
the hard crust of the earth. All he could do was to crawl from his bed
to the cupboard where the whisky bottle was and then crawl back. But
he called no one; he stiffened with anger if there were any signs of
anyone coming to the door. He was not going to be caught like this.
He was not going to admit anything. He cursed the doctor.

It was two days before Mr. Pocock's illness was discovered.

"Mr. Pocock's ill," Rogers's wife brought the news. She knew all the
illnesses of the village.

Rogers sat up, alert. He was at once frightened for himself. He did
not want to see Mr. Pocock before the doctor had been. Rogers sat in
his chair, unable to move. He wanted to do something for Mr. Pocock,
but he was paralysed. He sat in a stupor of inertia and incompetence.
He looked appealingly at his wife. She got a car and had Mr. Pocock
brought to the house.

"It's the bloody sugar, old boy," murmured Mr. Pocock with a regal
weariness as three men carried him upstairs.

Mrs. Rogers was glad when the ambulance came that, for once in
his life, Mr. Pocock had had a real home with a woman to look after
him.

That was the last of him.

A dealer came down to look at the pictures after the funeral, but he
would not take them. One or two others came hoping for frames. But
the twenty-odd canvases there had no frames on them. A brother came
down to clear up Mr. Pocock's affairs.

"We never corresponded," said the brother. Of all things he was a
clergyman.

Two fair and tall young men in suède shoes and pullovers, so alike
they looked like a pair of tap-dancers, turned up at the same time. They
were tap-dancers.

"Terrible," they said. They were looking at the pictures; but Rogers supposed they referred to the death, the poverty of the house—or perhaps the clergyman. Rogers had been told by Mr. Pocock that in reward for his kindness he might have one of the pictures, but he did not know which to choose. The only picture he felt anything about was the picture on the bedroom wall, the nude. He detested it.

"Women," he thought, "that must have been Mr. Pocock's trouble. Not drink. Oh dear, not drink, women." So when everyone had gone, he took the small picture, wrapped it in newspaper, and put it in a shed in his garden. That picture, and a corkscrew, which he stuffed in his pocket, because a corkscrew was useful. He took the picture because, without knowing it, he felt it symbolized the incomprehensibility of the existence of other people. The corkscrew was the man he knew, the picture the man he did not know at all. He thought that one day he had better destroy the picture—in case a bad impression of his friend was formed.

And so, slipping out of the funeral, keeping in the background afterwards, staying in his own house, Rogers eluded the memory of Mr. Pocock. Rogers was forgetting everything as he grew larger. He forgot yesterday, last week, last year—he dreamed through time like an idle whale, with its mouth open, letting what would come into it. He contemplated through a haze his own work of art—his family. He watched his wife's second chin when she gave her practical laugh. His two girls swam up to him like fish. They were an extra pair of eyes and ears for him. They saw things quickly. They laughed at things long before he heard them. On Saturdays he took them to the cinema. Every Saturday. A year passed, and then two years. He never said now: "We had Mr. Pocock, the painter, here." He had learned his lesson.

And then came the most extraordinary fortnight of Rogers's life. He was with his daughters in the cinema. They were watching a gangster film. A film four years old: they only got the old films in these country towns. Two men were going quietly up the stairs of a hotel and then along a corridor. It was at night. They were making for the room where a Mexican, behind closed doors, was covering a girl with a gun. But they were not sure of the room. They hesitated at doors. It was trying for Rogers, because his mind was still in the pillared lounge below, re-minded by it that he was living on his capital. How had the Mexican got the girl in the room? Then the two men stopped. One said: "O.K.," and they pushed open a door marked 13 and switched on the light. Rogers's daughters jumped in their seats and a shout of laughter came from the audience. A large, round-faced man with a huge stomach was lying on a bed in check suit and knickerbockers, asleep and snoring, with a bottle, rolled on its side, near by.

"Mr. Pocock!" the girls shouted.

It was. Rogers's heart went small in his chest and seemed to shoot like a stone in his throat. The gangsters rolled their eyes ironically. The audience laughed. One of the gangsters picked up the bottle and made to prod Mr. Pocock with it. The audience sent up blast after blast of laughter; especially shrill laughter went up first from the children in front. The other gangster touched his friend's arm, raised his eyes to the ceiling, and said: "R.I.P." Wave after wave of laughter passed by as the snores stopped and then began again like a car toiling and missing uphill.

"It's Mr. Pocock, Mr. Pocock, Dad," Rogers's daughters cried, jumping on their seats. And the laughter went on. For the achievement of Mr. Pocock was that he did nothing, nothing at all. He just lay and snored, the human balloon.

Rogers couldn't believe it.

It became urgent for him after this to decide the matter. Films in the town moved down the road, ten or twenty miles to the next place in the week. Four times he followed that film in a fortnight. Four times he saw that scene. It was unmistakably Pocock. And each place the audience roared until one night at the Hippodrome, where it was the big picture, he heard a packed house shout out with enthusiasm at Pocock's sublime unconsciousness. He had three minutes of the film, but those three minutes brought the house down.

It terrified Rogers. Pocock was lying exactly as Rogers had seen him that morning after the binge when he had waked up in Pocock's cottage. He dreaded that the eyes would open, the voice speak. And then, after the sixth time of seeing the film, as he walked home down the village street, he longed to meet that preposterous figure, to slap him on the back and tell him. He longed for him to wake up on the screen and hear that helpless applause, to see those wide-open laughing mouths. "He kept it quiet," thought Rogers. And the drowning soul saw no irony in it all; but rather felt that life was incomprehensible no more. Something had been settled.

When he took the picture from his garden shed and burned it on the rubbish heap soon after, Rogers heard in the husky roar of the flame the sound of a soul set free, all stain removed.

1938

The Œdipus
Complex

"Good morning, Mr. P.," said Mr. Pollfax, rinsing and drying his hands after the last patient. "How's Mr. P.?" I was always Mr. P. until I sat in the chair and he switched the lamp on and had my mouth open. Then I got a peerage.

"That's fine, my lord," said Mr. Pollfax, having a look inside.

Dogged, with its slight suggestion of doggish, was the word for Mr. Pollfax. He was a short man, jaunty, hair going thin, with jaunty buttocks and a sway to his walk. He had two lines, from habitual grinning, cut deep from the nostrils, and scores of lesser lines like the fine hair of a bird's nest round his egg-blue eyes. There was something innocent, heroic, and determined about Mr. Pollfax, something of the English Tommy in tin hat and full pack going up the line. He suggested in a quiet way—war.

He was the best dentist I ever had. He got you into the chair, turned on the light, tapped around a bit with a thing like a spoon and then, dropping his white-coated arm to his side, told you a story. Several more stories followed in his flat Somerset voice when he had your mouth jacked up. And then removing the towel and with a final "Rinse that lot out," he finished with the strangest story of all and let you go. A month or so later the bill came in. Mr. Pollfax presents his compliments and across the bottom of it, in his hand: "Be good."

I have never known a dentist like Mr. Pollfax.

"Open, my lord," said Mr. Pollfax. "Let's see what sort of life his lordship has been leading. Still smoking that filthy pipe, I see. I shall have to do some cleaning up."

He tapped around and then dropped his arm. A look of anxiety came on his face. "Did I tell you that one about the girl who went to the Punch and Judy show? No? Nor the one about the engine-driver who was put on sentry duty in Syria? You're sure? When did I see you last? What was the last one I told you? That sounds like last April? Lord, you *have* been letting things go. Well," said Mr. Pollfax, tipping back my head and squirting something on to a tooth, "we'll have a go at that root at the back. It's not doing you any good. It was like this. There was a girl sitting on the beach at Barmouth with her young man watching a Punch and Judy show . . ." (Closer and closer came Mr. Pollfax's head, lower and lower went his voice.)

He took an instrument and began chipping his way through the tooth and the tale.

"Not bad, eh?" he said, stepping back with a sudden shout of laughter.

"Ah," I mouthed.

"All right, my lord," said Mr. Pollfax, withdrawing the instrument and relapsing into his dead professional manner. "Spit that lot out."

He began again.

There was just that root, Mr. Pollfax was saying. It was no good there. There was nothing else wrong; he'd have it out in a couple of shakes.

"Though, my lord," he said, "you did grow it about as far back in your throat as you could, didn't you, trying to make it as difficult as you could for Mr. Pollfax? What we'll do first of all is to give it a dose of something."

He swivelled the dish of instruments towards me and gave a tilt to the lamp. I remembered that lamp because once the bulb had exploded, sending glass all over the room. It was fortunate, Mr. Pollfax said at the time, that it had blown the other way and none of it had hit me, for someone might have brought a case for damages against someone—which reminded him of the story of the honeymoon couple who went to a small hotel in Aberdeen. . . .

"Now," said Mr. Pollfax, dipping things in little pots and coming to me with an injection needle; "open wide, keep dead still. I was reading

Freud the other day. There's a man. Œdipus complex? Ever read about that? Don't move, don't breathe, you'll feel a prick, but for God's sake don't jump. I don't want it to break in your gum. I've never had one break yet, touch wood, but they're thin, and if it broke off you'd be in a nursing home three weeks and Mr. Pollfax would be down your throat looking for it. The trouble about these little bits of wire is they move a bit farther into the system every time you swallow.

"There now," said Mr. Pollfax. "Feel anything? Feel it prick?" he said. "Fine."

He went to a cupboard and picked out the instrument of extraction and then stood, working it up and down like a gardener's secateurs in his hand. He studied my face. He was a clean-shaven man and looked like a priest in his white coat.

"Some of the stories you hear!" exclaimed Mr. Pollfax. "And some of the songs. I mean where I come from. 'The Lot that Lily Lost in the Lottery'—know that one? Is your skin beginning to tingle, do you feel it on the tip of your tongue yet? That's fine, my lord. I'll sing it to you."

Mr. Pollfax began to sing. He'd give it another minute, he said, when he'd done with Lily; he'd just give me the chorus of "The Night Uncle's Waistcoat Caught Fire."

"Tra la la," sang Mr. Pollfax.

"I bet," said Mr. Pollfax sadistically, "one side of his lordship's face has gone dead and his tongue feels like a pin cushion."

"Blah," I said.

"I think," he said, "we'll begin."

So Mr. Pollfax moved round to the side of me, got a grip on my shoulders, and began to press on the instrument in my mouth. Pressing and drawing firmly, he worked upon the root. Then he paused and increased the pressure. He seemed to be hanging from a crowbar fixed to my jaw. Nothing happened. He withdrew.

"The Great Flood begins," said Mr. Pollfax, putting a tube in my mouth and taking another weapon from the tray.

The operation began again. Mr. Pollfax now seemed to hang and swing on the crowbar. It was not successful.

"Dug himself in, has he?" muttered Mr. Pollfax. He had a look at his instruments. "You can spit, my lord," he said.

Mr. Pollfax now seized me with great determination, hung, swung, pressed, and tugged with increased energy.

"It's no good you thinking you're going to stay in," said Mr. Pollfax

in mid-air, muttering to the root. But the instrument slipped and a
piece of tooth broke off as he spoke.

"So that's the game, is it?" said Mr. Pollfax, withdrawing. "Good
rinse, my lord, while Mr. Pollfax considers the position."

He was breathing hard.

Oh well, he said, there were more ways than one of killing a cat. He'd
get the drill on it. There were two Jews standing outside Buckingham
Palace when a policeman came by, he said, coming at me with the drill,
which made a whistling noise like a fishing line as he drew it through.
The tube gurgled in my mouth. I was looking, as I always did, at Mr.
Pollfax's, at the cowls busily twirling on the chimneys opposite. Wind
or no wind these cowls always seemed to be twirling round. Two metal
cowls on two yellow chimneys. I always remember them.

"Spit, my lord," said Mr. Pollfax, changing to a coarser drill. "Sorry,
old man, if it slipped, but Mr. Pollfax is not to be beaten."

The drill whirred again, skidding and whining; the cowls twirled on
the chimneys, Mr. Pollfax's knuckles were on my nose. What he was
trying to do, he said, was to get a purchase.

Mr. Pollfax's movements got quicker. He hung up the drill, he
tapped impatiently on the tray, looking for something. He came at me
with something like a buttonhook. He got it in. He levered like a signal
man changing points.

"I'm just digging," he said. Another piece of tooth broke off.

Mr. Pollfax started when he heard it go and drew back.

"Mr. Pollfax in a dilemma," he said.

Well, he'd try the other side. Down came the drill again. There were
beads of sweat on his brow. His breath was shorter.

"You see," exclaimed Mr. Pollfax suddenly and loudly, looking angrily up at his clock, "I'm fighting against time. Keep that head this
way, hold the mouth. That's right. Sorry, my lord, I've got to bash you
about, but time's against me.

"Why, damn this root," said Mr. Pollfax, hanging up again. "It's
wearing out my drill. We'll have to saw. Mr. Pollfax *is* up against it."

His face was red now, he was gasping, and his eyes were glittering.
A troubled and emotional look came over Mr. Pollfax's face.

"I've been up against it in my time," exclaimed Mr. Pollfax forcefully between his teeth. "You heard me mention the Œdipus complex
to you?"

"Blah," I managed.

"I started well by ruining my father. I took every penny he had.
That's a good start, isn't it?" he said, speaking very rapidly. "Then I

got married. Perfectly happy marriage, but I went and bust it up. I went off with a French girl, and her husband shot at us out in the car one day. I was with that girl eighteen months and she broke her back in a railway accident and I sat with her six months watching her die. Six ruddy months. I've been through it. Then my mother died and my father was going to marry again, a girl young enough to be his daughter. I went up and took that girl off him, ran off to Hungary with her, married her, and we've got seven children. Perfect happiness at last. I've been through the mill," said Mr. Pollfax, relaxing his chin and shining a torch down my mouth, "but I've come out in the end.

"A good rinse, my noble lord," said Mr. Pollfax.

"The oldest's fourteen," he said, getting the saw. "Clever girl. Very clever with her hands."

He seized me again. Did I feel anything? Well, thank God for that, said Mr. Pollfax. Here we'd been forty minutes with this damned root.

"And I bet you're thinking why didn't Lord Pollfax let sleeping dogs lie, like the telephone operator said. Did I tell you that one about the telephone operator? That gum of yours is going to be sore."

He was standing legs apart, chin trembling, eyes blinking, hacking with the buttonhook, like a wrestler putting on a headlock.

"Mr. Pollfax with his back against the wall," he said, between his teeth.

"Mr. Pollfax making a last-minute stand," he hissed.

"On the burning deck!" he gasped.

"Whence," he added, "all but he had fled.

"Spit," he said. "And now let's have another look." He wiped his brow. "Don't say anything. Keep dead still. For God's sake don't let it hear you. My lords, ladies and gentlemen, pray silence for Mr. Pollfax. It's coming, it isn't. No, it isn't. It is. It is. There," he cried, holding a fragment in his fingers.

He stood gravely to attention.

> "And his chief beside,
> Smiling the boy fell dead,"

said Mr. Pollfax. "A good and final spit, my lord and prince."

1938

The Fly in
the Ointment

It was the dead hour of a November afternoon. Under the ceiling of level mud-coloured cloud, the latest office buildings of the city stood out alarmingly like new tombstones, among the mass of older buildings. And along the streets, the few cars and the few people appeared and disappeared slowly as if they were not following the roadway or the pavement, but some inner, personal route. Along the road to the main station, at intervals of two hundred yards or so, unemployed men and one or two beggars were dribbling slowly past the desert of public buildings to the next patch of shop fronts.

Presently a taxi stopped outside one of the underground stations and a man of thirty-five paid his fare and made off down one of the small streets.

"Better not arrive in a taxi," he was thinking. "The old man will wonder where I got the money."

He was going to see his father. It was his father's last day at his factory, the last day of thirty years' work and life among these streets, building a business out of nothing, and then, after a few years of prosperity, letting it go to pieces in a chaffer of rumour, idleness, quarrels, accusations, and, at last, bankruptcy.

Suddenly all the money quarrels of the family, which nagged in the young man's mind, had been dissolved. His dread of being involved in them vanished. He was overcome by the sadness of his father's situation. "Thirty years of your life come to an end. I must see him. I must help him." All the same, knowing his father, he had paid off the taxi and walked the last quarter of a mile.

It was a shock to see the name of the firm, newly painted too, on the sign outside the factory and on the brass of the office entrance, newly polished. He pressed the bell at the office window inside and it was a long time before he heard footsteps cross the empty room and saw a shadow cloud the frosted glass of the window.

"It's Harold, Father," the young man said. The door was opened.

"Hullo, old chap. This is very nice of you, Harold," said the old man shyly, stepping back from the door to let his son in, and lowering his pleased blue eyes for a second's modesty.

"Naturally I had to come," said the son, shyly also. And then the father filled out with assurance again and, taking his son's arm, walked him across the floor of the empty workroom.

"Hardly recognize it, do you? When were you here last?" said the father.

This had been the machine-room, now the machines had gone. Through another door was what had been the showroom where the son remembered seeing his father, then a dark-haired man, talking in a voice he had never heard before, a quick, bland voice, to his customers. Now there were only dust-lines left by the shelves on the white brick walls, and the marks of the showroom cupboards on the floor. The place looked large and light. There was no throb of machines, no hum of voices, no sound at all, now, but the echo of their steps on the empty floors. Already, though only a month bankrupt, the firm was becoming a ghost.

The two men walked towards the glass door of the office. They were both short. The father was well dressed in an excellent navy-blue suit. He was a vigorous, broad man with a pleased impish smile. The sunburn shone through the clipped white hair of his head and he had the simple, trim, open-air look of a snowman. The son beside him was round-shouldered and shabby, a keen but anxious fellow in need of a haircut and going bald.

"Come in, professor," said the father. This was an old family joke. He despised his son, who was, in fact, not a professor but a poorly paid lecturer at a provincial university.

"Come in," said the father, repeating himself, not with the impatience he used to have, but with the habit of age. "Come inside, into

my office. If you can call it an office now," he apologized. "This used
to be my room, do you remember, it used to be my office? Take a chair.
We've still got a chair. The desk's gone, yes, that's gone, it was sold,
fetched a good price—what was I saying?" he turned a bewildered look
to his son. "The chair. I was saying they have to leave you a table and
a chair. I was just going to have a cup of tea, old boy, but—pardon me,"
he apologized again, "I've only one cup. Things have been sold for the
liquidators and they've cleaned out nearly everything. I found this cup
and teapot upstairs in the foreman's room. Of course he's gone, all the
hands have gone, and when I looked around just now to lock up before
taking the keys to the agent when I hand over today, I saw this cup.
Well, there it is. I've made it. Have a cup?"

"No, thanks," said the son, listening patiently to his father. "I have
had my tea."

"You've had your tea? Go on. Why not have another?"

"No, really, thanks," said the son. "You drink it."

"Well," said the father, pouring out the tea and lifting the cup to
his soft rosy face and blinking his eyes as he drank, "I feel badly about
this. This is terrible. I feel really awful drinking this tea and you
standing there watching me, but you say you've had yours—well, how
are things with you? How are you? And how is Alice? Is she better? And
the children? You know I've been thinking about you—you look worried. Haven't lost sixpence and found a shilling, have you, because I
wouldn't mind doing that?"

"I'm all right," the son said, smiling to hide his irritation. "I'm not
worried about anything, I'm just worried about you. This—" he nodded
with embarrassment to the dismantled showroom, the office from
which even the calendars and wastepaper basket had gone—"this—"
what was the most tactful and sympathetic word to use?—"this is bad
luck," he said.

"Bad luck?" said the old man sternly.

"I mean," stammered his son, "I heard about the creditors' meeting.
I knew it was your last day—I thought I'd come along, I . . . to see how
you were."

"Very sweet of you, old boy," said the old man with zest. "Very
sweet. We've cleared everything up. They got most of the machines
out today. I'm just locking up and handing over. Locking up is quite
a business. There are so many keys. It's tiring, really. How many keys
do you think there are to a place like this? You wouldn't believe it if
I told you."

"It must have been worrying," the son said.

"Worrying? You keep on using that word. I'm not worrying. Things are fine," said the old man, smiling aggressively. "I feel they're fine. I *know* they're fine."

"Well, you always were an optimist," smiled his son.

"Listen to me a moment. I want you to get this idea," said his father, his warm voice going dead and rancorous and his nostrils fidgeting. His eyes went hard, too. A different man was speaking, and even a different face; the son noticed for the first time that like all big-faced men his father had two faces. There was the outer face like a soft, warm and careless daub of innocent sealing wax and inside it, as if thumbed there by a seal, was a much smaller one, babyish, shrewd, scared and hard. Now this little inner face had gone greenish and pale and dozens of little veins were broken on the nose and cheeks. The small, drained, purplish lips of this little face were speaking. The son leaned back instinctively to get just another inch away from this little face.

"Listen to this," the father said, and leaned forward on the table as his son leaned back, holding his right fist up as if he had a hammer in his hand and was auctioning his life. "I am sixty-five. I don't know how long I shall live, but let me make this clear: if I were not an optimist I wouldn't be here. I wouldn't stay another minute." He paused, fixing his son's half-averted eyes to let the full meaning of his words bite home. "I've worked hard," the father went on. "For thirty years I built up this business from nothing. You wouldn't know it, you were a child, but many's the time, coming down from the north, I've slept in this office to be on the job early the next morning." He looked decided and experienced like a man of forty, but now he softened to sixty again. The ring in the hard voice began to soften into a faint whine and his thick nose sniffed. "I don't say I've always done right," he said. "You can't live your life from A to Z like that. And now I haven't a penny in the world. Not a cent. It's not easy at my time of life to begin again. What do you think I've got to live for? There's nothing holding me back. My boy, if I wasn't an optimist I'd go right out. I'd finish it." Suddenly the father smiled and the little face was drowned in a warm flood of triumphant smiles from the bigger face. He rested his hands on his waistcoat and that seemed to be smiling too, his easy coat smiling, his legs smiling, and even winks of light on his shining shoes. Then he frowned.

"Your hair's going thin," he said. "You oughtn't to be losing your hair at your age. I don't want you to think I'm criticizing you, you're old enough to live your own life, but your hair, you know—you ought to do something about it. If you used oil every day and rubbed it in with both hands, the thumbs and forefingers is what you want to use, it would be better. I'm often thinking about you and I don't want you to think I'm lecturing you, because I'm not, so don't get the idea this is a lecture, but I was thinking, what you want, what we all want, I say this for myself as well as you, what we all want is ideas—big ideas. We go worrying along, but you just want bigger and better ideas. You ought to think big. Take your case. You're a lecturer. I wouldn't be satisfied with lecturing to a small batch of people in a university town. I'd lecture the world. You know, you're always doing yourself injustice. We all do. Think big."

"Well," said his son, still smiling, but sharply. He was very angry. "One's enough in the family. You've thought big till you bust."

He didn't mean to say this because he hadn't really the courage, but his pride was touched.

"I mean," said the son, hurriedly covering it up in a panic, "I'm not like you—I—"

"What did you say?" said the old man. "Don't say that." It was the smaller of the two faces speaking in a panic. "Don't say that. Don't use that expression. That's not a right idea. Don't you get a wrong idea about me. We paid sixpence in the pound," said the old man proudly.

The son began again, but his father stopped him.

"Do you know," said the bigger of his two faces, getting bigger as it spoke, "some of the oldest houses in the city are in Queer Street, some of the biggest firms in the country? I came up this morning with Mr. Higgins, you remember Higgins? They're in liquidation. They are. Oh yes. And Moore, he's lost everything. He's got his chauffeur but it's his wife's money. Did you see Beltman in the trade papers? Quarter of a million deficit. And how long are Prestons going to last?"

The big face smiled and overflowed on the smaller one. The whole train, the old man said, was practically packed with bankrupts every morning. Thousands had gone. Thousands? Tens of thousands. Some of the biggest men in the City were broke.

A small man himself, he was proud to be bankrupt with the big ones; it made him feel rich.

"You've got to realize, old boy," he said gravely, "the world's changing. You've got to move with the times."

The son was silent. The November sun put a few strains of light through the frosted window, and the shadow of its bars and panes was weakly placed on the wall behind his father's head. Some of the light caught the tanned scalp that showed between the white hair. So short the hair was that his father's ears protruded and, framed against that reflection of the window bars, the father suddenly took (to his son's fancy) the likeness of a convict in his cell, and the son, startled, found himself asking, "Were they telling the truth when they said the old man was a crook and that his balance sheets were cooked? What about that man they had to shut up at the meeting, the little man from Birmingham, in a mackintosh . . ."

"There's a fly in this room," said the old man suddenly, looking up in the air and getting to his feet. "I'm sorry to interrupt what you were saying, but I can hear a fly. I must get it out."

"A fly?" said his son, listening.

"Yes, can't you hear it? It's peculiar how you can hear everything now the machines have stopped. It took me quite a time to get used to the silence. Can you see it, old chap? I can't stand flies, you never know where they've been. Excuse me one moment."

The old man pulled a duster out of a drawer.

"Forgive this interruption. I can't sit in a room with a fly in it," he said apologetically. They both stood up and listened. Certainly in the office was the small dying fizz of a fly, deceived beyond its strength by the autumn sun.

"Open the door, will you, old boy," said the old man with embarrassment. "I hate them."

The son opened the door and the fly flew into the light. The old man struck at it but it sailed away higher.

"There it is," he said, getting up on the chair. He struck again and the son struck too as the fly came down. The old man got on top of his table. An expression of disgust and fear was curled on his smaller face; and an expression of apology and weakness.

"Excuse me," he said again, looking up at the ceiling.

"If we leave the door open or open the window it will go," said the son.

"It may seem a fad to you," said the old man shyly. "I don't like flies. Ah, here it comes."

They missed it. They stood helplessly gaping up at the ceiling where the fly was buzzing in small circles round the cord of the electric light.

"I don't like them," the old man said.

The table creaked under his weight. The fly went on to the ceiling and stayed there. Unavailingly the old man snapped the duster at it.

"Be careful," said the son. "Don't lose your balance."

The old man looked down. Suddenly he looked tired and old, his body began to sag and a look of weakness came on to his face.

"Give me a hand, old boy," the old man said in a shaky voice. He put a heavy hand on his son's shoulder and the son felt the great helpless weight of his father's body.

"Lean on me."

Very heavily and slowly the old man got cautiously down from the table to the chair. "Just a moment, old boy," said the old man. Then, after getting his breath, he got down from the chair to the floor.

"You all right?" his son asked.

"Yes, yes," said the old man, out of breath. "It was only that fly. Do you know you're actually more bald at the back than I thought. There's a patch there as big as my hand. I saw it just then. It gave me quite a shock. You really must do something about it. How are your teeth? Do you have any trouble with your teeth? That may have something to do with it. Hasn't Alice told you how bald you are?"

"You've been doing too much. You're worried," said the son, soft with repentance and sympathy. "Sit down. You've had a bad time."

"No, nothing," said the old man shyly, breathing rather hard. "A bit. Everyone's been very nice. They came in and shook hands. The staff came in. They all came in just to shake hands. They said: 'We wish you good luck.'"

The old man turned his head away. He actually wiped a tear from his eye. A glow of sympathy transported the younger man. He felt as though a sun had risen.

"You know—" the father said uneasily, flitting a glance at the fly on the ceiling as if he wanted the fly as well as his son to listen to what he was going to say—"you know," he said. "The world's all wrong. I've made my mistakes. I was thinking about it before you came. You know where I went wrong? You know where I made my mistake?"

The son's heart started to a panic of embarrassment. "For heaven's sake," he wanted to shout, "don't! Don't stir up the whole business. Don't humiliate yourself before me. Don't start telling the truth. Don't oblige me to say we know all about it, that we have known for years the mess you've been in, that we've seen through the plausible stories you've spread, that we've known the people you've swindled."

"Money's been my trouble," said the old man. "I thought I needed money. That's one thing it's taught me. I've done with money. Absolutely done and finished with it. I never want to see another penny as long as I live. I don't want to see or hear of it. If you came in now and offered me a thousand pounds I should laugh at you. We deceive ourselves. We don't want the stuff. All I want now is just to go to a nice little cottage by the sea," the old man said. "I feel I need air, sun, life."

The son was appalled.

"You want money even for that," the son said irritably. "You want quite a lot of money to do that."

"Don't say I want money," the old man said vehemently. "Don't say it. When I walk out of this place tonight I'm going to walk into freedom. I am not going to think of money. You never know where it will come from. You may see something. You may meet a man. You never know. Did the children of Israel worry about money? No, they just went out and collected the manna. That's what I want to do."

The son was about to speak. The father stopped him.

"Money," the father said, "isn't necessary at all."

Now like the harvest moon on full glow the father's face shone up at his son.

"What I came round about was this," said the son awkwardly and dryly. "I'm not rich. None of us is. In fact, with things as they are we're all pretty shaky and we can't do anything. I wish I could but I can't. But"—after the assured beginning he began to stammer and to crinkle his eyes timidly—"but the idea of your being—you know, well, short of some immediate necessity, I mean—well, if it is ever a question of —well, to be frank, *cash*, I'd raise it somehow."

He coloured. He hated to admit his own poverty, he hated to offer charity to his father. He hated to sit there knowing the things he knew about him. He was ashamed to think how he, how they all dreaded having the gregarious, optimistic, extravagant, uncontrollable, disin-genuous old man on their hands. The son hated to feel he was being in some peculiar way which he could not understand mean, cowardly, and dishonest.

The father's sailing eyes came down and looked at his son's nervous, frowning face and slowly the dreaming look went from the father's face. Slowly the harvest moon came down from its rosy voyage. The little face suddenly became dominant within the outer folds of skin like a fox looking out of a hole of clay. He leaned forward brusquely on the table and somehow a silver-topped pencil was in his hand preparing to note something briskly on a writing-pad.

"Raise it?" said the old man sharply. "Why didn't you tell me before you could raise money? How can you raise it? Where? By when?"

1936

The Night Worker

A marriage was in the air. In a week the boy's Cousin Gladys was going to be married. The boy sat in a corner of the room out of the way. Uncle Tom and Aunt Annie danced round the girl all day, pushing her this way, pulling her that; only a week to go and now—as the boy watched them in the little dark kitchen, out of the way of people's feet—the dance got fiercer, gayer, rougher. "Do what you like, you're free already," they seemed to say to her. And then: "You dare! You wait! You're still our daughter. Do as you're told." The boy watched them. He was seven. He did not know what a marriage was, and he gazed at them, expecting it to come into the room like a bird, or to be put on the table like a cake.

Aunt Annie stood at one end of the table with her back to the window, making a pie. He watched the mole move on her bony arm as she rolled the pastry.

"Hurry up with that sleeve, my girl. Haven't you taken out the tacking?"

"It's a fiddling job," said Gladys, holding up her needle.

"Here, give it us," said Aunt Annie, wiping the pastry off her fingers and snatching the needle. "Who's taking the Bible class on Sunday, then?"

"Not me," said Gladys.

Aunt Annie flopped the pastry over the pie-dish and the boy saw it hang in curtains over the edge, while his aunt stood straight looking down at the parting in Gladys's thick hair. Aunt Annie's grey hair was screwed back and in her bony face she had bold false teeth, so that she clucked when she talked and had the up-and-down smile of a skull. She had the good nature of a skeleton.

The boy was waiting for her to trim the pastry on the pie-dish. When she had done this she opened the oven door and a smell of hot cake came across the room. In came the boy's Uncle Tom, a sad, cake-eating man. How did a man so short come to marry a woman so tall? It must have been because Uncle Tom looked like a crouching animal who lived by making great jumps. He was a carpenter, whose skin was the colour of chapel harmonium keys; a yellow, Chinese-looking man with split thumbnails and a crinkled black beard and he frightened because he never quite came into the room, but stood in the doorway, neither in nor out, with a hammer or a chisel in his hand.

"I done them stair-rods, my girl," he said. It was like a threat.

"I'll take them round," Gladys said.

"She's going at twelve," said Aunt Annie.

"Jim be there?" asked her father.

"Yes," said Aunt Annie. She seemed to the boy to have the power to make her tall teeth shine on the scowl of Uncle Tom, and to put the idea of springing on us all out of his head. "Jim'll be there. She's taking the boy."

Then Gladys laughed and, leaning down the table, put her soft arm round the boy's waist and rubbed her cheek in his hair.

"I'm taking my young man round. You'll look after me, won't you?" she said. One of their inexplicable fits of laughter started. Aunt Annie's teeth clucked and clicked. Uncle Tom went "Ha, ha, ha," like a saw and lit a pipe.

"Only another week, Glad. It's just because of the neighbours," said Aunt Annie.

"Ay, my girl, neighbours talk," said Uncle Tom, and blew out violet smoke as if he were smoking the neighbours out.

The girl put on a prim, concealing expression. One minute she was a girl and the next a woman, then a girl again.

"Stars above, look at the time. Quick," she cried to the boy, getting up from the table.

They ran upstairs to her room at the back, where he slept too, a room which did not smell of camphor like his aunt's room. He did not like to see Gladys take off her kitchen dress and stand, with bare shoulders and bare arms, in her petticoat, and bare-legged too, because then she became a person he did not know. She was shorter and more powerful. But when her Sunday blue dress was over her head and after she had said "Oh, these blooming things," when the hooks caught in her hair, he liked her again.

"How do I look?" she said, when she had her straw hat on, and, not waiting for an answer, she said: "Now, there's you! Brush your jersey! Quick."

Jim was waiting, she said. They went out of the room like the wind, and the text "Honour Thy Father" swung sideways on the wall. Down those dark stairs they went, two at a time, and were half out of the door when Uncle Tom made his great jump after them.

"Don't forget them stair-rods."

"Goodness," she said, grabbing them, "I'm going dippy."

And then she was going down the street so fast that the boy had to trot.

"Oh!" She breathed more easily when they had got out of her street. "That's better. You ain't seen my new house." But she was talking to the street, not to him, smiling at it. She went along, smiling at the sky and the children playing hopscotch on the pavement, and the green-grocer's cart, as though she were eating the world like an orange and throwing away the skin as she went along. And her breasts and her plump chin jumped in time with her step.

"Which house is it?" the boy said.

"Not yet. Round the corner."

They turned the corner and there was another long street. "In this street?" he said.

"No. Round another corner."

He took her hand. She was walking so fast he was afraid of being lost. And then, down the next street, she calmed down.

Her face became stern. "Look at him, standing like a dummy! He hasn't seen us."

A man in a grey cap and a blue serge suit was standing on the pavement.

"Smoking," she said. "Bold as brass. There's men for you. He promised he'd give it up. Standing there daft and idle."

They were all workers in this family. Everything was work to them. Uncle Tom was always sawing and hammering. He had made the chests of drawers and the tables in his house. Aunt Annie scrubbed and cooked. Cousin Gladys was always sewing and even when she came in from her factory, she had, as they said, "something in her hands"—a brush, a broom, a cleaning cloth, or scissors. Jim was a worker, too. He worked at the post office in the middle of the town. One day Uncle Tom took the boy on top of a tram, and when they came near the post office, he said: "Eh, look out this side and you'll see Gladys's Jim working. He's got a good job. Sometimes he's on nights. He's a night worker. Now, look out for him when the tram slows down." The boy looked into the grey window of the post office as the tram passed by. Inside were dim rows of desks and people and presently he saw Jim in his shirt-sleeves. He was carrying a large waste-paper basket.

"What's he doing?" said the boy.

"Sorting," said Uncle Tom. "Sorting the mail. His father put him into that job when he was fourteen."

The boy saw Jim lift the waste-paper basket and then suddenly empty it over the head of another man who was sitting at a desk. He saw Jim laughing. He saw the man jump down and chase Jim across the office, laughing too.

"Larking about," said Uncle Tom indignantly. "That's government work."

The boy stopped laughing. He was scared of Jim after this. Jim was a tall man with a hungry face, but there was a small grin on his lips, and after seeing him empty the waste-paper basket the boy did not know what to make of him. It made him feel there was something reckless and secretive in the lives of Cousin Gladys and Jim.

Jim stood outside the gate of the house.

"You come to see the house," he said to the boy. The boy murmured.

"Lost his tongue," said Jim.

"I've been in," he said to Gladys.

Gladys took his arm.

"Have you brought the things? I've got the stair-rods."

"I put them inside," he said.

"Oh, let me see," she said eagerly. The three went to the green front door of the house and Jim let them in. It was a small house of grey brick with a bay window.

"There," Jim said, pointing to the things. "I didn't take them upstairs. I waited for you."

On the floor was a washbasin and a jug.

"I must wash them before we go," she said. "Take them to the kitchen."

Jim stood and winked at the boy.

"Orders," said Jim.

"I can't stand dirt," she said, getting up.

"Well," said Jim, "I'm waiting, aren't I?" He put this question to the boy and winked again.

"Oh," Gladys said, "don't be soft."

"Don't look," said Jim to the boy.

And then Gladys and Jim put their arms round each other and kissed. He saw her heels come off the ground and her knees bend. Gladys blushed and stepped back.

"Oh no, you don't, does she?" Jim said to the boy. And he pulled Gladys and gave her another kiss.

"Jim!" she cried. "You'll have me over."

The boy laughed and pulled at her waist from behind and they were all laughing until her shoe kicked the china basin on the floor. That stopped them.

"What'll Ma say when she sees my dress," Gladys said.

"Oh," said Jim. "*He* won't tell." Winking again at the boy. "Here's a penny. Go into the garden and see if you can find some chocolate."

"No," said Gladys, kissing the boy and holding his hand. "He's my young man. He's looking after me."

They walked from room to room in the house. After Uncle Tom's house it was bare and smelled of size and new paint. The curtains were up but there was very little furniture. In the sitting-room there was only a blue carpet and a small settee. Jim and Gladys stood at the door and took deep breaths when they looked at this room. There was a vase on the mantelpiece and Gladys moved the vase from the middle to the end.

"Now I've made it lopsided," she said. "It wants two."

"It wants a picture," said Jim, looking at the bare, lilac-coloured walls. "It looks bare."

"Don't complain," said Gladys, pouting.

"I'm not. I was only thinking," he said, putting his arm round her waist, but she stepped away. Jim gave her a look. The boy had seen her sulk before. He loved her and when she sulked he was frightened.

Jim went out into the hall, and while he was out she stroked the boy's head and pressed him against her leg.

"You like it, don't you?" she said. "You don't think it's bare?"

"No," he said.

"I'll marry you. You don't grouse."

"Here—Glad—what's this here?" called Jim sharply from the hall.
"When you've done spooning. . . ."

Her sulk went at once. She went out. Jim and she were looking at
a small dark spot on the ceiling.

"A leak!" she cried.

"From the bathroom," he said.

"Who left the water on last time?" she said.

"Your mother—washing things," Jim said.

"She never," Gladys said.

They both rushed upstairs. The carpet was not yet down on the
stairs, and their steps and voices echoed. It was a house of echoes. The
boy did not follow. He went to see the painters' pails in the kitchen
and to stir the oily remains of paint in them with a stick. He looked
into the clean sink. He could not understand why Gladys and Jim were
going to live in this house. He wanted to live there with them. He could
not understand the laugh of his aunt and uncle, that peculiar laughter,
so pleased and yet jealous, so free and yet so uneasy, when they talked
about Gladys living in this house. It was a laughter marked by side
glances. The boy couldn't understand why it was important for him to
be there, and he felt lost. He went at last upstairs, and on the landing
he heard them in the bathroom. They were talking. They had forgotten
him. In the evasive way of grown-up people they had gone upstairs to
look at the cause of the water coming through the ceiling and, now they
were there, they were not talking about that at all. They were talking
about people, about some person. The boy stood still and listened.

"They don't want him. *He's* away all the time travelling and she's
having another, that'll be the fifth. Terrible, isn't it? Five, imagine it,"
Gladys was saying.

"Can't someone put her wise?" Jim said.

"I'd throw myself in the river."

The boy saw Gladys falling into the river. He thought: "I wonder
why Gladys wants to get her clothes wet and what will Aunt Annie
say."

"I dunno. Kids are nice. I'd like one like that," Jim said.

"Nobody's kid. That's what he is," Gladys said. When he heard
the word "kid," the boy seemed to himself to swell and to lean and
to topple with importance towards the bathroom door, but some fear
of a woman's hand catching him by the leg or the arm made him
seem to go thin again and lean away, till he crept quickly to the
landing. There were two doors. Quietly he opened one door and went

into a small room. There was nothing in it at all, no curtains to the windows, no linoleum on the floor, no fire-grate either, but only a mousehole. He looked down the mousehole and watched it for a long time but nothing came out of it. There was a smell of mouse which reminded him of his home and he looked out of the window down into three back gardens, but no child was there. He wondered where nobody's kid was, but no child came. So he went to another room, for this was the house he wanted to live in with one room after another, if people would come and live in it and silence the echoes. Quietly he edged out of the room and guiltily looked into the next one. It was in the front of the house and looked on to the street. Each thing in the room seemed to look at him. There was a small carpet on the floor. There was a wardrobe, a dressing-table, and a large bedstead with a mattress on it, but no sheets or blankets. It was like his mother's and father's room, but this one was cold and smelled of the furniture shop. It had the mystery and watchful quietness of an empty bedroom.

"Where are you?" called Gladys. "Where's the boy gone?"

"He's round about," said Jim easily. They were walking towards the room. The boy could not escape. He stood still.

"Ah, there he is," Gladys cried. And they were both in the room with him.

"Who sleeps in this bed?" said the boy. Gladys went red. Jim winked.

"Gladys, who sleeps here?" Jim said.

"I don't know," said Gladys.

"Getcha, she does. She knows," Jim said. "Ask her."

"You do," the boy said, pointing at Gladys. "She does."

"I don't," said Gladys sternly. "Jim does," she said sharply.

"He doesn't," the boy said. He had seen the lies rolling in their glances at each other.

"I do," said Jim.

"You don't," said the boy. "You're a night worker."

"That's a good one," said Jim, who who never laughed but only smiled at the corner of his lips, and now suddenly shouted with laughter. "That's it. That's where I do my work. A night worker, that's where I do my work. Eh, Glad?"

"Jim, shut up," said Gladys primly. "Don't tease."

"I'm not teasing," laughed Jim. "I'm a hell of a night worker." And he made a grab at Gladys, who moved away.

"Jim," she said, "the neighbours. They can hear everything. These walls are like paper."

"You and the neighbours," laughed Jim, and he caught up the boy high in the air and sat on the side of the bed. "One, two, three," he said, and at three he brought the boy down on the bed.

"Come here, Glad," he said, "you have a go. He's ticklish."

The boy called out and kicked.

"Don't," said Gladys, coming to rescue him.

"Ticklish yourself," said Jim, catching her arm and pulling her on the bed. The boy was free.

"Kiss her. Kiss her," cried the excited boy.

"Don't," said Gladys.

"I'll neighbour you," said Jim.

The boy watched them struggling and then he saw Jim was not kissing her but whispering in her ear.

"You are too real, Jim," she said tenderly. And then they were all lying quiet, Jim in the middle of them, with one arm round Gladys's neck and one arm round the boy and the boy wishing he could get away.

"Family already," Jim said. "You must have been on night work, Glad."

"Oh, give it a rest," said Glad. "Remember everything is taken back home. Little pigs have big ears."

"Very nice work too," said Jim.

"Don't be so awful," she pleaded.

"What's awful about it?"

A sigh came from Gladys.

"Very nice, I was saying," said Jim. "Sunday morning. Who's getting up to light the fire?"

"You."

"Me?—No, you."

"Married life," said Jim. "Hear that?"

"Who does sleep here truthfully?" said the boy.

"Nobody does," said Gladys. "But Jim and me are going to when we are married. That satisfy you?"

The boy knew it was true. It was true because it was far beyond his understanding. Jim and Gladys watched him silently, but Jim's arm tightened on her. They nodded to each other, watching the boy.

"And we'll have you for our little boy," said Gladys.

He knew this was not true. He did not want to be their little boy.

They cuddled and kissed and danced about too much; and then people smiled and laughed at them.

"Leave him alone," said Jim. And they all lay there silently, but he was aching to move from Jim's arm and to go. He was thinking of nobody's child and wishing he could find him, see him, watch him, talk to him.

"First question when I get back," Gladys said. "Did you put the stair-rods down? They think it's *their* house."

Yes, the boy wanted to get away from this house that wasn't a house yet, from this bed that was not a bed, and to see Aunt Annie and Uncle Tom, who sat still for hours after they had worked. He was going to ask her who nobody's child was and how big he was, where he lived, to see him, to watch for a long time what he did, to throw something to him to see if he moved, to see if he talked and how his mouth looked when he talked.

"When are we going home?" he said.

1935

The Necklace

"Just checking up on a necklace your wife brought in this afternoon," the older of the two detectives said to me when we got to the police station. He was sucking a peppermint and was short of breath. The younger one kept his hands in his raincoat pockets and didn't say a word, and neither did I. We went into an inner room and sat down. I was afraid of having a smile too big for my face; my mouth was watering. All the time, I could feel the words swelling up in me: "We only did our duty." If you find something in the street, you take it to the police. Of course, if it's valuable you may get a reward. But not necessarily. Anyway, you don't do it for the reward. But all that week I'd kept my eyes open for a notice saying "Reward." Then the young detective pulled the necklace out of his pocket and put it on the table. "Do you recognize this, Mr. Drayton?" he asked.

I recognized it at once. "That's it," I said. "I found it Saturday." Exactly where, they asked, and what time? I told them.

"Do you know who it belongs to?" they asked.

"If I'd known, I would have taken it to them," I said. "I wouldn't have brought it here." It was a silly question, and the next ones were silly, too.

"It doesn't belong to you?" the young one asked.

"Or your wife?" asked the older one.

"Definitely not," I said. "I found it in the street, I told you."

"Do you know a Mrs. Faber?" the young one asked.

"No," I said. "What's she got to do with it?"

"You're a window cleaner, aren't you?" asked the older one. "She lives at seventeen Launceston Road. Do you do a job there?"

"No," I said. "I do twenty-four, fifty-one, and the flats at the end. What's the idea?"

"And you say you found it at the corner of Alston Street and the Promenade on Saturday?"

"That's it. I just told you," I said.

"Just checking up. We have to check up on all lost property," said the older one. And the young one must have had a nod from him, because he got up and left the room. I looked up at the dark-green, glossy walls and the frosted window, and then I heard Nell's voice and her heels on the floor outside in the passage.

I sat there trying to remember everything as her voice came nearer, but there wasn't time. The one thing I could think of was Saturday, January 11: all that rain, and the football match; we beat Hopley Rangers, 3–0. Even when I have been going over it since, my mind gets stuck there. Saturdays, in the season, I used to pack in the job early and go home to my dinner, and when Plushy came round—my mate, Plushy Edwards—we would go off. We'd both been playing for the Rovers a couple of years. Nell sometimes came, too, but she didn't take to Plushy much. Come to that, she must have hated him. It went back to the time when she first met me, and Plushy told her I was a married man with two children and not to break up a happy home. Plushy was always having a lark like that with her. "I don't like men who tell lies," Nell said. It worried her when people made jokes. She really believed them.

But as I say: Saturday, football, I am coming round Alston Street off the Promenade, on my way home, and there it is: a necklace with three strands of big pearls, lying in the gutter. I looked up and down the Promenade. The weather was squally; the rain had browned the pebbles on the beach and had softened the sighing of the sea. The only moving things in sight were the back of a bus that had passed and two or three children running out of the rain a long way off, and the sea gulls. I looked down at the gutter again. It surprised me the necklace was still there. I propped my bike against a lamp and went back and picked the thing up. The pearls were hard and cold, like rice, but wet. I wiped the dirt off them and looked up at the windows of the houses. If there had been someone looking out, I would have shouted: "Anyone lost any-thing?" There was no one. I don't mind admitting that seeing a thing like this upset me. In this job, you see money, watches, and rings left about on desks and dressing tables the whole time. It doesn't worry me, but it annoys me. People miss something, and the next thing they're saying: "It's the window cleaner." I put the necklace into my pocket and I got on my bike. But the rain started coming down hard now, and I thought: "This means no blooming football." Plushy was waiting at my house already, just as fed-up as I was about the weather. The necklace went out of my head.

"Here, lay off. I'm a bachelor," said Plushy when I kissed my wife.

"You're late," she said to me. She always said that. "You two aren't playing football in this, are you? You're wet."

"Yes, look at his hair. That German crop never suited him, did it, Nell?" said Plushy, starting his usual larks, and pretending to dribble a ball round our kitchen as he spoke. "And where have you been? Hill Street? That blonde at twenty-seven, I bet. Look at his face! No, he's not been near Hill Street—oh, no! Dear, oh dear, oh dear!"

"I did Launceston Road this morning," I said.

"I thought you were going up the avenue," my wife said. Her grey eyes looked empty and truthful.

"I did the avenue yesterday," I said.

We had been married two years, and this was her way of loving me —knowing everything I did. Now and then she over-loved me by getting it wrong. When I was out on the job, I would have the idea she was with me, because I was always thinking of her. So when she said she thought I was up the avenue, I felt confused, as if she had been up there and I hadn't spotted her; or as if I ought to say I had been up the avenue, so that she wouldn't have missed me. See what I mean? Sounds silly. I was so soppy about her that I didn't know which was me and which was Nell.

"Coming to the game, Nell?" Plushy asked her, and when she said she had something better to do than stand in the mud and the rain, Plushy left me alone and started on her. "What's she up to, Jim?" he asked me.

"Ironing," she said. "I'm sorry for the poor girl who has to do yours. Have you found her?"

"There'll be no tears at Plushy's wedding," I said. It was one of my mother's sayings.

"It'll be more like a court case," Nell said seriously.

"Jim, she means it," said Plushy.

I changed my clothes, and at two o'clock Plushy and I went off.

I took up window-cleaning when I came out of the army. Plushy persuaded me into it. The money was good. He said he'd heard women all over the country crying out loud in every street to get their windows cleaned. "Just count the windows in this town," he said to me. "More windows than people. Every window a ruddy SOS. Someone's got to do them." But Plushy got fed-up with it after a year. The women got him down. "They're screaming all day for you," he said. "You turn up and it's the wrong time. Women at you all day long—following you round the house, watching to see you don't mark their curtains or spoil their carpets, calling upstairs to someone to lock the drawers: 'It's the window cleaner.' Like they'd got the burglars in." Plushy went off to work in a factory, but I liked being on my own. I stayed on, took over some of his customers. That is how I met Nell.

"Bad luck to see the new moon through glass," Plushy said when I told him about meeting her, and she did look sort of moony. She was in the back bedroom of a house in the avenue, fixing her ear-rings and doing up her face, when I came up the ladder outside. She had reddish hair brushed up so that it was like new copper lit by electric light. Her face was broad, calm, and white. It was my sister who started me using the word "empty" about Nell's grey eyes. It was not the word I would have used myself, but her eyes did make me feel I was going to fall clean through them. When she looked up and saw me (my wash leather had squeaked on the pane), I nearly fell off the ladder. She took her hand from her ear so quickly that she knocked a scent bottle over, and at the same time she shut one of the drawers with her knee.

A man like Plushy, who upset some of the customers by singing non-stop while he worked, would have taken his comb out and run it through his hair and gone on singing. So he made out when I told him. It's a lie. He would have done just what I did. I opened the window and climbed in and said: "Sorry, miss. Let me wipe it up with the leather. If your old lady carries on, say it was the window cleaner."

She stood over me, looking insulted, and watched me wipe the scent off the carpet with the leather. The only thanks I got was: "Close the window when you go out. My Aunt Mary won't mind about the rug." I swear she said "My Aunt Mary," but afterwards she swore she didn't. The woman she worked for was misnamed Mrs. Merry—a gloomy lady in a houseful of books (I never saw so many), with a voice like a high-class ship going out to sea, very snobby—so I might have made a mistake. But it took a bit of time for me to get it into my mind that Nell was not the niece of this rich old bookworm.

Fate is a funny thing. Once it gets going, it never stops. I'd been working at different houses in the avenue for more than a year and I had never set eyes on Nell, but now I seemed to run across her one day after the other. I asked her if her aunt had been angry about the scent.

"No," Nell said. "She didn't mind. That's not my aunt. My aunt's in Manchester. I'm the maid."

I felt a fool trying to puzzle this out. Nell looked up and down the street, as if she were looking for someone. "I told her," she said. "She didn't mind."

"The lady you work for, you mean?" I asked.

"No, my Aunt Mary, in Manchester," she said. "I tell her everything."

I asked her to come out with me, but she changed her mood and said her aunt in Manchester would not like that, and neither would Mrs. Merry.

In those early days, it was always the same. This aunt of Nell's in Manchester wouldn't let her do anything. And to talk to Nell was like talking to two people, for she would turn her head aside when I said anything, as if she were discussing it with this old aunt of hers or someone else before she answered. I couldn't make out what age Nell was, either. To see her—short and solid and with her chin up, marching in slow, long steps down the street—she looked obstinate, like a schoolgirl; other times, when we were talking at a street corner, she had a small, disbelieving smile at the corner of her mouth, like a woman of thirty. She confused me. She was one person one minute and another the next. In the end, she said she would come out to the pictures with me, but I had to ask Mrs. Merry first.

I have said Mrs. Merry was like a ship. She bumped alongside her dining-room table when she came in, and docked at last in an armchair. Not in dry dock: she was rocking a large glass of gin. She asked me a lot of questions about myself, my mother, and my sister, in a hooting sort of voice, and said Nell was a refined, quiet girl and that she didn't like her going out. "She is an orphan, you know," Mrs. Merry said loudly. "I understand her aunt brought her up. Very carefully—you can see. Her aunt in Manchester."

When Nell and I left the house, I could hardly speak for the idea that her Aunt Mary was walking beside us. And later I could pretty well feel her sitting beside us at the pictures. I got fed-up. We went to a milk bar afterwards, and Nell took her coat off. She showed me her bracelet and her wrist watch.

"Aunt Mary, I bet," I said.

"Yes," Nell said, with her nose in the air. "Aunt Mary." Her voice was small and soft, and seemed to me to come very clearly from a long way off.

There was no getting away from this aunt of hers. She lived in a huge house, Nell said, that had an enormous lawn in the shape of an oval, with a gravel path round it and a deodar at one end.

"What's a deodar?" I asked.

"A deodar? A tree," she said. "In the summer, she used to lie in a hammock under it. She taught me French." She was an educated girl; you could see that.

But I expect you're thinking what I was thinking: if Nell's aunt was so rich and classy, why was an educated girl like Nell down in this place working as an ordinary maid? I came straight out with it.

"No," said Nell. She began a lot of remarks with "No" when I asked her things. "There was trouble."

"You got into trouble?" I asked.

"No," she said. "Her husband did."

So Aunt Mary was married. She had got married only two years back, Nell told me. He was an elderly clergyman. I asked Nell what the trouble was. "It's private," she said. She just waved her hands. I had expected her to have broad, flat, strong hands, but they were small and plump; when she saw me looking at them, she put them in her lap and folded her fingers into her palms. But I had seen. She had a bad habit: she bit her nails.

I used to remember this when I got to taking her home to see my mother and sister.

"Class—that's all it is," my sister said. "Loaded down with Aunt Mary's jewellery and lying in bed all day long doing her face." She did not like Nell's lady-like accent.

One Saturday, after football, I told Plushy about Nell's Aunt Mary and the clergyman. "Do you reckon Nell's hiding something?" I asked him. "Has she been in trouble?"

"No," he said. "She just doesn't see the funny side."

"What's funny in it?" I asked.

"Clergyman," Plushy said.

So on Sunday I decided to get at it, and I asked Nell again about the clergyman.

"No," she said, in her usual way. "He was jealous of her giving me things. He had two children of his own. I couldn't stay after that. I can't bear jealousy."

"What was the clergyman's name?" I asked.

"No, you're going to cause trouble."

"How could I do that?"

"I don't know," she said. "You could. If you go and see him and tell him anything, I'll never speak to you again."

"I never want to hear the name of Aunt Mary again," I said. Then I calmed down. "What about you and me—you know—sort of getting fixed up, married?"

Nell was watching me as if I were trying to steal something from her. She sat there—we were sitting in a shelter by the sea—and she was two girls, one of them looking insulted. I oughtn't to have said that about her aunt. She got up and walked off. It was dark, and she didn't speak all the way home and she shook my hand off her arm when I touched it.

The next morning at eight o'clock she was outside our house. I went to the gate, and she ran and banged her head hard against my ribs, nearly knocking the wind out of me, and put her arms round me. She was crying. I took her in at the front door into our sitting room and told the others to keep away.

"She's dead," she said, sitting back from me. "Aunt Mary's dead. I told you a lie. She died last year. I couldn't bear her to be dead. She was going to look after me, and she left all her money—everything— to that clergyman. I didn't want her money, but I couldn't bear it. My father's dead, my mother's dead—I couldn't bear any more."

"There's me," I said. "Forget it."

"I told you a lie," she sobbed in my arms.

It wasn't long before Plushy came in and we were all laughing—my mother, my sister, even Nell.

"Blooming murderer," said Plushy when he heard it. "Look at him. No conscience. Kills a poor girl's auntie just to get his way."

"Shut up, Plushy," said my mother. "The girl's upset."

"It's easy for you, Ma," Plushy said. "But I was getting fond of Aunt Mary."

Nell gaped at him.

"Well, Nell," Plushy said. "He'll have to be your Aunt Mary now."

And so I was, for, except for some worry about where the clergyman had moved to and how he ought to do something for her—but all this

was my mother's argument—Aunt Mary was a back number. Nell and
I got married and we were on our own.

The rain stopped in the afternoon on that Saturday when I found
the necklace. There was a lot of arguing when we got to the ground
about whether we should play, because of the mess the field was in, and
when we did start playing, it was a question of which side could stand
up. Even chaps who were standing still suddenly fell down. The crowd
was killing itself with laughter; you kicked the ball and you were flat
on your back. Plushy and three others slid·for yards into the Hopley
goal and couldn't stop themselves; the Hopley goalie came out at them
and went ahead first at Plushy. Their two heads cracked, wood against
wood; you could hear it across the field. Plushy lost on this deal. It
knocked him out for a few minutes. That is why, after the game, he
went to the doctor's instead of coming home and having his tea with
Nell and me, as he usually did.

I went back home alone. There was a change in Nell. She had done
her ironing and she had put on her blue dress and she had done her
hair. I don't mean that sort of change, though. She didn't often laugh,
but now she came to me nearly laughing. She had the hot look of too
much love. She even had some love left over for Plushy, and was very
upset when I told her about him. She couldn't keep still. She rubbed
against me like a cat when I sat down to tea, and then she leaned
forward to me, pushing her plate nearer, looking at me while I was
telling her about the game. Once or twice she interrupted me. "Sorry,
I love you," she said.

I went on telling her about the game. Presently she sat back and said:
"Haven't you forgotten something?"

She was smiling, but it was a heavy, greedy, large-eyed smile, as if
her own natural smile had been made larger by a reflector.

"Have I left the bike out?" Sometimes I forgot to put the bike away.

"Think," she said. Since we had got married, she liked giving orders.
Slowly the smile went.

"No," she said shortly, and left the room. She really marched out of
it. She went into the bedroom. I waited for her to come back, and when
she didn't I called out: "I want some more tea!"

She did not answer. I pushed back my chair and went into the
bedroom. She was standing at attention, with her back to me, in the
middle of the room, doing nothing, with her hands at her sides. She
did not turn round. Often when I didn't guess what she was thinking,

she used to run off in this way and stand in the next room, stiff and sulking. It would take a long time finding out what was the matter, for the only person she was on speaking terms with was herself. It happened a lot before we were married. But now, when she turned round suddenly, her face was half smiling and appealing. She was wearing the necklace.

When women put on something new, they look high and mighty, as if you had got to get to know them all over again. I don't like it. They also look ten years older. The pearls made Nell's neck look thick. They also made her look as if she weren't married any longer, unless you could afford to pay the extra. I wished I was rich and could have bought pearls for her—well, not bought them myself, but sent her in somewhere to buy them. I don't like those shops.

She came towards me with half a clever tear in one eye. I call it clever; it wasn't real.

"Sorry, sorry," she said. "Don't be cross with me. I couldn't help it. The necklace fell out of your pocket . . . It fell out of your pocket when I was putting your overalls away. I wasn't going through your pockets, I swear, if that's what you think. It fell out on to the bed." And she stepped to the bed and pointed to the place on the green quilt where it had fallen.

Some joke Plushy had once made about his landlady going through his pockets came back to me. For the first time, I knew that Nell had been going through my pockets on and off ever since we were married.

"Nell," I said, "that's not a present for you. I didn't buy it. I found it in the gutter in Alston Street, coming home, dinnertime. You thought it was for you."

"Who is it for?" she asked, all her newness going. "You found it— lying in the street?"

"It isn't for anyone," I said. "I don't know who it belongs to. We'd best take it to the police station."

"Police," she said, frightened.

"Yes," I said. "Some poor kid must have dropped it."

Her face hardened. "You weren't in Alston Street," she said. "You told Plushy you were in Hill Street. I heard you."

"No, I didn't," I said. "Plushy said that."

"No, tell me the truth. You're hiding something," she said. "Where did you find it?"

"Easy on," I said. "I told you. I found it in the gutter in Alston Street."

"Then why didn't you tell me? Hiding it in your pocket!"

"I wasn't hiding it. I just put it there."

"No, tell me the truth," she said again.

"I am," I said. "I'm going to take it round. I forgot it. Some poor kid's mother is carrying on, I bet."

"Her mother!" she said. "Whose mother? Jim, you've bought it for some girl." She put her hands to her neck, took the necklace off, and threw it on the bed. "Oh!" she cried out. "You've bought it for some girl! That's why you were hiding it!" And then she gave a howl and fell sideways on the bed, crying into the pillow, with her blue dress drawn up above her knees, and her legs coming out of it in a way so ugly and awful I could not believe it. I'd seen my mother do this once years ago, and, of course, I'd seen my sister do it often. She was a past master; the whole house stood still when my sister took a dive. But I thought it was the sort of thing that only went on in our family when I was a child. I said to myself: "So this is the girl whose aunt used to lie in a hammock under a deodar, talking French. Class—there's nothing in it!" I wished the time was two hours ago and I was playing football. I wished Plushy would come round.

"My tea's getting cold," I said after a bit. It must have been the way I said it. She sat up at once and came to the kitchen. She poured out the tea and sat down in front of me, and I liked her better with the necklace off, but her round face had become square and her white skin was thickly red down to her neck. Her mouth was as small as a penny. She had picked up the necklace and put it beside her plate.

"I'm waiting," she said.

"Plushy got hurt this afternoon," I said. "He got a crack on the head. You could hear it right across the field."

She did not answer for a long time, and then she said: "You told me that."

I remembered I had.

"How can you tell such lies?" she said. " 'Hear it across the field'! No, I'm sick of Plushy. Who are you married to? Is Plushy dead? I hope so."

"Oh dear, oh dear," I said.

"Stop talking like Plushy," she said. "Who is it for? Who did you buy it for? What's her name? I want the truth!"

"I've told you," I said.

"Aunt Mary warned me about you," she said.

"Your Aunt Mary never saw me," I said. "Aunt Mary's dead, anyway."

"Before she died," she said.

Aunt Mary had come back into our lives. It had been so long since we had even mentioned her or her husband that I could hardly remember who she was for the moment. I realized what a long way we had travelled since Aunt Mary's time, and I thought of what my mother had once said about how quickly the dead drop back into the past. But having her brought back like this from the grave, in this tone, woke up my old jealousy. I admit it; I was jealous of Aunt Mary.

"Please, Jim," Nell said, in a softer, pleading voice. "Who did you buy it for? Why did you do Hill Street this morning?"

So we went over the streets again: Launceston Road, the Promenade, Alston Street, across the High Street . . .

"You bought it at Cleaver's," she said.

"Learn some geography," I said. "I wasn't near Cleaver's."

"Learn it!" she sobbed. "That's all I do. I sit here all day thinking of where you are—one girl after another, just like Plushy."

"You're jealous," I said.

"Of course I'm jealous!" she shouted, in a thick, curdled voice like a man's.

"Now, look—" I said. I put my hand on hers, and she did not take it away. She turned her head from me and then said quietly, as though she were speaking to the necklace: "I know you found it, Jim. I'm sorry, I'm sorry."

I didn't say anything, and after a moment she said softly: "A valuable thing like that."

"It's just Woolworth trash," I said.

"Look at the clip," she said fearfully, handing the necklace to me. "It's worth hundreds."

"Get away!" I said.

"It is. I know it is," she said.

I picked up the necklace. The clip meant nothing to me, but, hearing her soft, truthful voice again, I felt sad. "Put it on again," I said. "You looked nice in it."

"Oh, I couldn't do that," she said. "It isn't ours."

"Go on. You put it on before. Let's see you. Just once more," I said. "It's yours," I said, laughing. I have explained she did not like jokes. She frowned. Then she leaned nearer to me but not looking at me—as if not to see me. "Jim," she said, in a very low voice. "You didn't find it in the street. Truthfully, you didn't, did you? I won't say anything."

"What do you mean?"

"You knocked it off," she said.

The way she said this, as if she were whispering in my ear in the dark, frightened and excited me. Now she was searching my face for some hint or clue. There was a long silence between us.

I reached for the necklace and said: "I'm going round to the police with it now. I'm not a thief." But as I reached, there was a flash in her eyes and she snatched at it, too, as quickly as a cat.

"There'll be a reward!" she said, jumping up and standing away from me. We must have both caught the necklace, because it snapped and all the pearls scattered on to the carpet and over the lino. It was like during the war, when our corporal got his false teeth knocked out in the street. They went everywhere.

We were both down on our hands and knees at once. She was on the carpet. I was on the lino, by the dresser. This was how Plushy found us. There was a big piece of plaster on his forehead, under the curl of his black hair, where the goalie's head had cracked him.

"Don't step on them!" my wife called out.

"There's always something going on here," Plushy said.

"Stand still," we both said, straightening up.

"Let us pray," said Plushy, kneeling down, too. "What is it?"

Nell told him.

"Found it?" said Plushy sarcastically, getting up and standing above us. "What? Finds a necklace in the gutter with no neck in it! Doesn't tell his best friend!"

"Have you got the clip?" my wife asked me.

"Got a clip, too?" said Plushy. "Diamonds, I bet. Proper window cleaner's story. Lost your voice, Jim? Can't you sing?"

Nell reached up from the floor and put some of the pearls into a saucer.

"I bet he only whistles," Plushy said. "Whistling isn't strong enough. Jim, you know that. Whistling doesn't keep it off."

"Help us," said Nell. "Stop talking."

"Temptation," said Plushy, bending down to look. "By rights, I ought to be singing now, in case I slip one into my pocket. Remember old Charlie, Jim? He used to whistle like a canary. He was up someplace —Hill Street, twenty-seven. You know it, Jim—twenty-seven—don't put on that face with me. Charlie started whistling the moment he put the ladder up. Ground floor, he's whistling fine; first floor, O.K.; second floor, getting short of breath, whistle gets weak. What happens? Lady's diamond ring comes clean across from the other side of the room to him. He tries to blow it back. He can't. It comes clean through the glass. He can't get a sound out, leans back and back. Falls off the ladder, three weeks in hospital."

"Get on with the job, mate. Have you got the clip, Nell?" I said.

"I'm looking."

"I reckon singing's better. We always used to sing when we were working together, didn't we, Jim? Remember your lady, Nell, at the avenue?" Plushy put on the high-class hoot of Mrs. Merry. " 'Why doesn't someone stop that man singing?' Well, I did stop. I stopped right in the middle of a bar. Next thing, a five-pound note starts talking to me out of her handbag other side of the room and waving its hands about. Just like I'm talking to you now."

"Her watch, you mean," said Nell, getting up.

"Her watch?" said Plushy.

"Yes," said Nell. "I mean her watch. She missed a watch. I thought I'd never hear the last of it. Nothing funny about that, Plushy. I could have lost my place."

Plushy did not like this.

"What d'you mean, Nell?" I asked.

"It was all right. I found it for her," Nell said.

"Oh," said Plushy sarcastically. "That's something off my mind." Those two hated each other.

"We can't take it round like this," Nell said when we all stood up and looked at the saucer full of pearls. She dropped the clip on top.

"Too true you can't," said Plushy. "Looks too much like a ruddy share-out."

We argued about it for a long time. I was the only one in favour of taking it round and telling the police what happened. I did not want a valuable thing like this in the house, and we couldn't go round to Cleaver's or some place like that and get them restrung until Monday. It would be the end of the week before we could get them to the police.

"But Plushy's a witness," said Nell. "He'll tell them you found it and we broke it by mistake."

"Yes," said Plushy. "And you'll get a reward. What do I get?"

"Ten pounds," said Nell.

"Twenty," said Plushy. "First instalment on a motor bike. Pop up to London for the weekends."

"No. Aunt Mary's was worth hundreds," said Nell.

"Oh," said Plushy. "Got Nell's Aunt Mary back to stay with you?" he said to me. "You never told me. Is she comfortable? A bit cramped in here for her, isn't it?"

Nell put her chin up and looked like the geography teacher at our school when I was a boy. Nell really did hate Plushy, and getting a crack on the head had livened him up even more. He was a lad. We'd made Aunt Mary comfortable in the bath, according to him, or on top of a cupboard, and then he made up a long tale of how she wasn't getting on with the clergyman. His children got on her nerves and she wanted a rest, Plushy said. Nell struggled against it, and then she couldn't hold out any longer. She started to laugh. She laughed as I had never seen her, doubling up over the arm of a chair, and then, suddenly, she got angry. "Stop telling lies, Plushy!" she called out.

On Monday, Nell took the pearls down to Cleaver's to be restrung.

"Sit down, Mrs. Drayton," the older detective said to Nell, and the young one went out and came back in a moment with two cups of tea. When Nell came into any room where I was, the place was changed, and where I was, who I was, and what I was would get mixed up in my mind. It was like beginning to get drunk. Nell pushed the cup of tea away scornfully.

"It's just routine," the older one went on. "We've been asking your husband about the necklace you took round to Cleaver's to be restrung."

"It broke," I said.

"Just a minute, son," the detective said. And to Nell: "Now, you say it is your necklace—your own property? Like you said to Mr. Cleaver: 'It is mine'? Is that correct?"

I had half got up from my chair and had tried to catch her eye when she walked in, but she came in warily, not looking at me but into each corner of the room and then up at the window and back at the door. I might have been a stranger. When she looked in my direction, she didn't see me; at any rate, she quickly turned her head to one side.

"That's correct," she said.

I think my mouth stuck wide open.

"Just a minute!" the young detective said to me sharply, shutting me up.

"But your husband says he found it at the corner of Alston Street and the Promenade," the other one said to her.

She looked at the young detective, then at the older one, then at me. I used to say that she confused me because she was like a couple of girls whispering secrets to each other, but now she was one woman, clear and decisive and firm in voice. There was nothing a long way off in it. It rang, and rang true and harsh.

"That's a bloody lie," said Nell.

"Nell!" I cried. I had never heard Nell use language before in my life.

"It's mine!" Nell shouted at me. "You know it is. Mr. Cleaver knows it is. I asked him what it was worth. He's repaired it for me before. He recognized it. It's been in my family for years. It belonged to my Aunt Mary. I told Mr. Cleaver. He knows. Bring him here. He knows it came to me when she died two years ago. She brought me up. Ask her husband, the Reverend Dickens. He lives in Manchester."

"Nell—" I said.

"What's the address of the Reverend Dickens?" asked the older detective.

"Find out. You're so bloody clever," said Nell. If she was more than one girl, I had never seen this one before—red and square in the face and her eyes moving like knife tips.

"Well," said the dick, "it's exactly like a necklace lost by a Mrs. Faber."

"Is it?" snapped Nell. "Well, it isn't hers. It's mine. It was my Aunt Mary's, I told you. She gave it to me. She gave me everything, all the things I have."

"Oh," said the detective. "Other things. What were they?"

"That's my business," said Nell.

"Mrs. Drayton," said the detective, "you haven't got an aunt, and you never did have, did you? Your father and mother live in London, don't they?"

"They're dead," I said. "Killed in the war. What's that got to do with it? Nell, what's going on?"

Nell suddenly took notice of me, as if she were seeing me for the first time. Her expression went through three changes. It was like seeing three photographs of a person quickly. The first was the square, raging face; the second lost its colour and softened; the third looked pale and sly. This one spoke to me in a low voice across the table, as if we were sharing a secret. "You silly sucker," she half whispered. "You're covering up for Plushy. I won't have Plushy."

And then she shouted at the detective: "Plushy whipped it off Mrs.

Faber! Out with Plushy! Out! Out! My husband knows it." She got up and rushed for the door, but the young one was standing there.

I've left the window-cleaning trade now. I gave it up after the case. I had to. There was too much talk. Nell got three months. She was mad. She must have been: that's the only thing I can think. But she didn't look mad in court. She had just one word for all of us—the police, me, Plushy, old Cleaver, everybody: "Liars." The only straight people in the world were her and her Aunt Mary. It came out in court that she'd worked this Aunt Mary game a couple of times before she met me. Once in Deptford and another time at a place near Bristol. But for that she might have got off—first offence. "Her old auntie got round," Plushy whispered to me when the police were reading her record out to the judge. "Tiring, at her age."

The last I saw of Nell was going downstairs out of the dock with the wardress. She didn't even look at me. I couldn't believe it. I still can't believe it. My mind goes back to the first time I saw her, through the back-bedroom window at Mrs. Merry's, fixing the ear-rings—not hers but Mrs. Merry's—and I say to myself: "January eleventh we beat Hopley, three to nought," and I get stuck there.

1955

The Accompanist

It was the afternoon. Joyce had been with me for nearly two hours when suddenly she leaned over me to look at my watch on the table.

"Half past four," she cried in a panic. "Stop it. I shall be late," and scrambling out of bed, she started getting into her clothes in a rush. She frowned when she caught me watching her. I liked watching her dress: her legs and arms were thin, and as she put up her arms to fasten her bra and leaned forward to pull on her tights she seemed to be playing a game of turning herself into comic triangles. She snatched her pale-blue jersey and pulled it over her head, and when her fair hair came out at the top she was saying, "Don't forget. Half past seven. Don't be difficult. You've got to come, William. Bertie will be upset if you don't. Ivy and Jim will be there and Bertie wants you to tell them about Singapore."

In a love affair, one discovers a gift for saying things with two meanings.

"If they are going to be there, Bertie won't miss *me*," I said. "He used to be mad about Ivy, asked her to marry him once—you told me."

"You are not to say that," Joyce said fiercely as she dragged her jersey down. "Bertie wanted to marry a lot of girls."

So I said yes, I would be there. She put on her coat, which I thought was too thin for a cold day like this, and said, "Look at the time.

Hendrick will be so angry," as she struggled away from my long kiss. Her skin burned and there were two red patches on her cheeks. Then she went.

It was only on her "music days" when she was rehearsing with Hendrick that we were able to meet.

Afterwards I went to the window hoping to see her on the street, but I missed her. I pulled a cover over the bed, walked about and then I came across a shopping bag on the table. Joyce had forgotten it. I looked into the bag and saw it contained eight small apple pies packed in cartons: Joyce was a last-minute shopper and they were obviously meant for the dinner we were all going to eat that evening. Well, there was nothing to be done. I could hardly take them to Bertie's and say, "Your wife left these at my place." Before I left at seven o'clock I ate one. It was cold and dry, but after seeing Joyce, I always felt hungry.

It was a cross-London journey into the decaying district where she and Bertie lived. One had to take one bus, then wait for another. Their flat was on the ground floor of a once respectable Victorian villa. I was glad to arrive at the same time as four other guests, all of us old friends of Bertie's: André, an enormous young Belgian in a fur coat; his toy-like wife, Podge; an unmarried girl who adored Bertie and who rarely said anything; and a sharp dark political girl who worked on a review Bertie sometimes wrote for.

Bertie himself came to the door wearing old-fashioned felt slippers. It was odd to see them on a young man who was even younger than we were—not yet thirty. He had a copy of *Le Monde* in his hand and he waved it in the air as he shouted "Well done!" to all of us in the voice of a housemaster at the School Sports. And as we went in he was jubilant, crowing like a cockerel. "My errant spouse," he said, "is at this moment, I presume, toiling across the metropolis and will be here soon. You see, this is one of Joyce's music days. Hendrick's concert is coming on the week after next and he makes her rehearse the whole time, poor wretch. Of course, it's awfully nice for her."

(Bertie loved things to be "awfully nice.")

"He had discovered," Bertie went on proudly, "that she is the only accompanist he can work with. It's very useful, too"—Bertie looked over his glasses sideways at us—"it brings in the pennies. And it gives me time to catch up on *The Times* and *Le Monde.*"

And he slapped the paper against his leg with something like passion. Then he led us into the bedroom where we were to leave our coats.

Except for André, we were all poor in those days. Flats were hard to find. It had taken Bertie and Joyce a long time to find this one—they had had to make do with Bertie's old room—and they had to wait for Bertie's family furniture to arrive out of storage from the North. As we took off our coats we felt the chill of the large room and I understood Joyce's embarrassed giggles when she spoke of it. It was, in the late-Victorian way, high and large; the mouldings on the ceiling, a thing now admired, looked like a dusty wedding cake with cracks in it. There was a huge marbled and empty fireplace, but—at variance with the period—brutal red tiles were jammed around it and it was like an enormous empty mouth, hungry for coal or the meals served there when the room had been the dining room of earlier generations. In front of it, without curb or fender, a very small electric fire—not turned on—stood like a modern orphan. Bertie was careful with money, and he and Joyce had not been able to afford to redecorate the room. One could detect small faded flowers in the grey wallpaper; in the bay window hung three sets of curtains: net for privacy, then a lighter greenish summer set, and over them heavy, once banana-coloured, curtains, faded at the folds, like the old trailing robes of a dead Edwardian lady.

But it was the enormous bed that, naturally, appalled me. The headboard was of monumental walnut, scrolled at the top, and there were legs murderous to a bare foot. Over the bed was spread a pink satiny coverlet, decorated by love knots and edged by lace from the days of Bertie's parents, even grandparents. It suggested to me a sad Arthurian barge, a washed-out poem from some album of the Love's Garland kind. There was, of course, a dressing table with its many little shelves, and one had the fear of seeing dead heroines in its mirrors and even, in the cold, seeing their breath upon the glass. I caught sight of my own face in it, looking Chinese and sarcastic: I tried to improve my expression. Faded, faded—everything faded. The only human things in the room were our coats thrown on the bed—I dropped mine out of pity on what I hoped was Joyce's side of it—and the hem of one of Joyce's dresses characteristically caught by the doors of a huge wardrobe. The sight of it made me feel the misty air of the room was quivering with Joyce's tempers and her tears.

But I exaggerate—there was one more human thing: Bertie's old desk from his Oxford days against the wall near the inner door, and his long bookcase. This was packed with books on modern history, politics and economics, and here it was that Bertie would sit typing his long articles on foreign politics. We all knew—and Joyce had told me—how she would go to sleep at night to the sound of "poor Bertie's" type-writer. She was a simple girl, but Bertie was charged by a brain that had given him a Double First at Oxford, made him the master of six or seven languages, and kept him floating for years like an eternal student on scholarships, grants and endowments. In the corner stood stacks of *The Times*, *Le Monde* and other periodicals, on the floor.

"Haven't you caught up on these *yet?*" André said.

"You see, they're sometimes useful," Bertie said. And he added with a stubborn laugh, "Joyce, poor wretch, complains, but I tell her I don't *like* throwing things away."

We moved into the other room.

When I was with Bertie I always felt protective of him, but this evening I did feel a jolt when I saw the dining table, which had been pushed into a far corner of the large room. Those apple pies! Moral questions I found had a way of putting out their noses in small ways in these days. But like everyone else I felt affection for Bertie. He loved his friends and we loved him: he was our possession, and in his shrewd collecting way he felt the same about us. His long nose, on which the glasses never sat straight, his pinkness, his jacket stuffed with papers, pens and pencils, his habit of standing with his hands on his hips as if pretending he had a waist, his short legs apart, his feet restless with self-confidence like a schoolboy, were endearing.

His sister-in-law, the only woman to wear a long dress, and her Australian husband were standing in the room.

"And this is William," Bertie said, admiring me. "He's just back from Singapore, idle fellow."

"We have just hopped over from Rome," said Ivy's husband.

Unlike Joyce, Ivy was almost a beauty, the clever businesswoman of the family, and the rest of the evening she seemed to be studying me —so much so that I wondered if Joyce had, in her thoughtless fashion, been talking about us.

We sat around on a deep, frayed sofa or in armchairs in which the cushions had red or green fringes, so that we seemed to be squatting on dyed beards, while Bertie kept us going about people he'd met at the embassy in Brussels, about the rows on the commission—the French delegate walking out in a huff—or a letter in *The Times* in which all the facts were wrong. The dark girl started an argument about French socialism and Bertie stopped it by saying he had got in an afternoon's tennis while he was over there.

He was still delighted with us and swaying on his feet, keen on sending over a volley or smashing a ball over the net. His talk brought back to me the day he had asked Joyce to marry him. It was the only proposal of marriage I had ever heard. All of us, except Ivy and her husband, had been there. We had managed to get one of the public courts in the Park; on the other courts players were smartly dressed in their white shorts and we were a shabby lot. I could see Bertie, who was rolling about like a bundle in old flannels that were slipping down, and sending over one of his ferocious services; I could hear him shouting "Well done!" or "Hard luck, partner!" to Joyce, whose mind strayed if an airplane flew over. I remembered him sitting beside Joyce and Podge and me on the bench when our game was over, with one eye on the next game and the other eye reading a thick political review. It was the time of the year when the spring green is darkening with the London lead. Presently I heard him chatting to Joyce about some man, a cousin of André's who had found an "awfully nice niche" in Luxembourg. At that time Bertie had found no "niche" and was captivated by those who had. Joyce had only a vague idea of what a "niche" was and first of all thought he was talking about churches, but then he was on to his annual dispute with his solicitor, who wanted him to get rid of his family's furniture because storage charges were eating up the trust.

"You see," he said, talking across Joyce and Podge to me, "I shall want it when I get my London base."

Joyce laughed and said, "But you *are* in London."

"Yes," said Bertie, "but not as a *base*. My argument is that I must let the stuff stay where it is until I get married."

André and his wife were playing and she had just skied her ball and, waiting for his moment, André smashed it over. Joyce cried out, "Marvelous!" She had not really been listening to Bertie. And then she turned to him and said, "I'm sorry. I was watching André—Bertie, I meant you—you're getting married! How wonderful. I am so pleased! Who is it? Do tell us."

Bertie gave one of his side glances at Podge and me and then said to Joyce, "You!"

It was really like that: Joyce saying "Don't be silly, Bertie" and "No, I can't. I couldn't . . . I . . ." He got hold of her hand and she pulled it away. "Please, Bertie," she said. She saw, we all saw, he meant it, and she was angry and confused; we saw the other couple coming towards us, their game over. She felt so foolish that she picked up her racket and ran—ran out of the court.

"What's the matter with Joyce?" said André.

Bertie stood up and stared after her and began beating a leg with the review. He appealed to all of us. "I've just asked Joyce to marry me," he said and reported his peculiar approach.

"And she said 'No,' " I said with satisfaction. Love or marriage were far from my own mind; but hearing Bertie and seeing Podge run after Joyce in the Park, I felt a pang of jealousy and loss. In two days I would be far away from my friends, sweating in a job in Singapore. Bertie heard my words, and as always when he was in a jam, he slyly dropped into French. Lightly and confidently he said, *"Souvent femme varie."*

Afterwards it struck me that Bertie's proposal was an appeal: it was the duty of all his friends to get him married. Indeed, Podge said she was afraid he was going to turn to her next. There was even an impression that he had proposed marriage to all of us; but I now see that he was a man with no notion of private life. The team spirit contained his passion, and knowing his exceptional case, he was making us all responsible as witnesses and as friends.

This passed through my mind as we all sat there in his flat listening for the distant ticking of a taxi stopping at the end of the street. Joyce was forbidden to spend money on taxis and would come running in breathlessly saying she had had to "wait hours" for a bus.

Conversation came to a stop. Bertie had at last run down. Suddenly Ivy said, "Bertie, how long was this awful furniture in storage?"

Bertie was not put out. He loved Ivy for calling it awful. He crossed his short, sausage-like legs and sat back with pride in which there was a flash of malice, and flicked his feet up and down.

"Twenty-seven years," he said. "No, let me see. Mother died when I was born, father died the previous year, then my Aunt Pansy moved in for four or five years, that makes twenty-two years. Yes. Twenty-two."

"I like it," said Podge, defending him.

"But it's unbelievable," said Ivy. "It must have cost a fortune to store it."

"That's what my guardian says," said Bertie.

"Why didn't you make him sell it?" said André.

"I wouldn't let him," said Bertie. "You see, I told him it would be useful when I got married."

We used to say that it must have been the thought of having Bertie's furniture hanging over them that had frightened off the many girls he had tried to marry. After all, a girl wants to choose.

Bertie's pink face fattened with delight at the attack. "Joyce hates it," he said comfortably. "She thinks I ought to sell it."

He was wrong; Joyce laughed at his furniture but she dreaded it.

"You'd make a fortune in Australia with furniture like this," said Ivy's husband.

"No," said Bertie. "You see, it was left to me."

He took off his glasses and exposed his naked face to us. I did not believe Joyce when she told me he cried when she had begged him to sell it, but now I did.

If the bedroom had the pathos of an idyll, the furniture in this living room was a hulking manufacture in which historic romance was martial and belligerent. Only in some lost provincial hotel which is putting up a fight against customers do you sometimes find oaken objects of such galumphing fantasy. There was a large armoire with knobs, like breasts, on its pillars, and shields on the doors. Under them, sprays of palm leaves had been carved; the top appeared to be fortified. The breast motif appeared on the lower drawers. The piece belonged to the time when cotton manufacturers liked to fancy they lived in castles.

There was a sideboard which attempted the voluptuous, but oak does not flow: shields appeared on its doors. There were more shields carved on two smaller tables; on the dining table, the curved edges would be dangerous to the knuckles, and its legs might have come from the thighs of a Teutonic giantess. The fireplace itself was a battalion of fire irons, toasting forks, and beside it, among other things, two brass scuttles (also with breasts, coats of arms and legs) that stood on claws. There was a general suggestion of jousting mixed with Masonic dinners and ye olde town criers.

"There ought to be a suit of armour," said André.

The only graceful object was Joyce's piano, which had belonged to her mother. It stood there, defeated.

Bertie nodded stubbornly. "You see," he said, grinning at us, "it's my *dot.*" And gave a naughty kick with his slippers.

Father dead before he was born, mother dead, aunt dead—Bertie was trebly an orphan. He had been brought up by a childless clergyman who was headmaster of a well-known school. There were photos of school and Oxford groups on the mantelpiece. André and I recognized ourselves in the latter: Bertie was an institutional man, his furniture was his only link with common human history. It was the sacred evidence not only of his existence but of the continuity of the bloodstream, the heartbeat and the inextinguishable sexual impulse of his family. He was a rarity, and our rarity too. We were a kind of society for cosseting him. Joyce, who loved him, felt this, and I did too.

But no Joyce came and André cast restless glances at the bottle of sherry, which was now empty. Bertie saw that a distraction was needed. "We can't wait any longer," he said. "Let us eat."

He jumped up, and putting on one of his acts of pantomime, he went to the dining table and picked up a carving knife and fork, and flinging his short arms wide, he pretended to sharpen the knife and then to carve an imaginary roast.

We laughed loudly and Ivy joined him. "Come on!" she said, and pulling *Le Monde* out of his pocket, put it on the dish and said, "Carve this."

Bertie was hurt. "Shame," he said, putting the paper back in his pocket.

Fortunately the front door banged and in came Joyce, breathless, frightened, half laughing, kissing everyone and telling us that Hendrick was giving a lesson when she got there and then would not let her go. And, of course, she had to wait for hours at a bus stop.

"Poor Bertie," she cried and kissed him on the forehead, and shaking her hair, stared back, daring us to say anything that would upset him. She went out to the kitchen and came back to whisper to her sister, "I've got the chops, but I must have left the pud in the taxi. Don't tell him. What shall I do?"

She looked primly at me. She had not changed her clothes, but because she looked prim (and by one of those tricks of the mind) I suddenly saw her standing naked, her long arms freckled, all bones, and standing up to her knees in the water rushing over the rocks of a mountain stream in the North where she and Bertie and I and a climbing party had camped for the night. I was naked too and on the bank, helping her out while Bertie, who refused to go into the river, was standing fully dressed and already, at seven in the morning, with a book he had opened. Bertie was unconcerned.

Yes, I thought this evening as she looked at me—I had one of those revelations that come late to a lover. She stands with the look of a girl who has a strange shame of her bones. She pouts and looks cross as a woman does at an inquisitive, staring child: there is a pause when she does not know what to do, and then she pushes her bones out of her mind and laughs. But that pause has bowled one over. It was because Joyce was so funny to look at that I had become serious about her.

By the time we all sat down to the meal I had advanced to the fantasy that when she laughed, her collarbones laughed. She had quickly changed into a dress that was lower in the neck, so that one saw her long throat. The food was poor; she was no cook, but André had brought wine and soon we were all shouting. Bertie was in full cackle and Joyce was telling us about Hendrick, whom the rest of us had never met, and after dinner Bertie persuaded Joyce to go to the piano and sing one of her French songs.

"Jeune fillette," he called. Quickly, with a flash of nervous intimacy in her glance of obedience, she sat at the piano and began: *"Jeune fillette, profitez du temps . . ."*

Bertie rocked his head as the song came out of her long throat. The voice was small and high, and it seemed to me that she carried it like a crystal inside her. The notes of the accompaniment seemed to come down her arms into her hands—which were really too big—and out of the fingers rather than from the piano. She sang and she played as if she did not exist.

"Her French," André's wife whispered, "is perfect, not like André's awful Belgian accent," and said so again when the song was over.

Joyce had her strange sensual look of having done something wrong.

"She can't speak a word of French," said Bertie enthusiastically. "She was eight months in Paris, staying with Ivy, and couldn't say anything except 'Yes' and 'No.' "

" 'No,' " said André, swelling out to tell one of his long Belgian stories, "is the important word."

"You have Mother's voice," Ivy said to Joyce. And to us: "Mother's was small. And true too—and yet she was deaf for the last twenty years of her life. You won't believe it, but Father would sing the solo in church on Sundays and Mother rehearsed him all the week perfectly and yet she can't have heard a note. When she died, Joyce had to do it. And she hated it, didn't you?"

Joyce swung round on the stool and now we saw—what I had begun to know too well—a fit of defiance.

"I didn't hate *that*, Ivy," she said. *"You* know what I couldn't bear! On Saturdays," Joyce blurted to us all, daring Ivy to stop her, "after lunch before anything was cleared away, he used to make me get the scissors and clip the hair out of his ears, ready for Sunday."

"Joy!" said Ivy, very annoyed. "You exaggerate."

"I don't," said Joyce. "He used to belch and spit into the fireplace too. He was always spitting. It was disgusting."

We knew that the girls were the daughters of a small builder who had worked his way up and was a mixture of religion and rough habits.

"And so," said Bertie to save the situation, "my future spouse began her *Wanderjahre*, abandoned all and ran away to Paris, where Ivy had established herself—and met the Baron!"

Ivy nodded gratefully. "*Your* baron, Joyce!" she laughed.

"Who is the Baron?" the Australian asked.

Now Joyce appealed to Ivy not to speak, but Bertie told them, mentioning he had met the Baron since those days, in Paris and Amsterdam—Bertie kept in touch with everyone he had ever met. It is painful to hear someone amiably destroy one of the inexpressible episodes in one's life and I knew Joyce was about to suffer, for in one of our confiding afternoons she had tried to tell me. It was true that Ivy, the efficient linguist, had started a translation bureau in Paris and the so-called Baron, a Czech exile, used to dictate long political articles to Joyce. In the long waits while he struggled to translate into English, Joyce's mind was far away.

"He always asked for Joyce," Ivy said. "He used to say—"

"You are not to say it!" said Joyce.

But Ivy mimicked him. "I vant ze girl viz ze beautiful ear. One year in Paris she knows no French, no languages—but she understands. How is zat? She does not listen to ze language. She listens to the Pause!"

"Well done!" cried Bertie.

"What the hell is 'the Pause'?" said the Australian.

"Before he started dictating again," I said brusquely.

Bertie looked at me sharply. I realized I had almost given Joyce away. What I think the Baron was trying to say (I told Joyce when she too had asked me what he meant, for she had grown fond of him and sorry for his family too, whom he had to leave in Prague) was that Joyce had the gift of discontinuity. She was in a dream until the voice that was dictating, or some tune, began again. She and I went on talking about this for a long time without getting any clearer about it, and I agree there was some conceit on my part in this theory: I saw myself as the tune she was waiting for.

"André," Joyce called to hide her anger. "Sing us your song. The awful one."

"It's Bertie's song," said André. "It's his tour de force. Play on, Joyce —and put all the Pauses in."

She could always take a joke from André, who looked like a mottled commissionaire. He had all the beer and Burgundy of Brussels in him, all those mussels, eels and oysters, and that venison.

Bertie's song was one more of his pantomime acts to which his long nose, his eyes darting side glances and his sudden assumption of a nasal voice gave a special lubricity. The song was a rapid cabaret piece about a wedding night in which the bride's shoulder is bitten through, her neck twisted and her arm broken and ends with her mother being called in and saying:

> *Ci-gît la seule en France*
> *Qui soit morte de cela.*

Bertie was devilish as Joyce vamped out the insinuating tune. We all joined in at the tops of our voices in the chorus at the end of each verse:

> *Ça ne va guère, ça ne va pas*

—even Joyce, her little blue eyes sparkling at the words she did not understand, though André had once explained them to her. In the last chorus she glanced back at me, sending me a reckless message. I understood it. From her point of view (and Bertie's), wedding nights were an academic subject. Bertie's enjoyment of the song was odd.

"Really, Bertie!" said the dark girl, who had argued with him about French socialism before dinner.

When she got up from the piano, Joyce looked enviously at her sister because her Australian husband had laughed the loudest and had given Ivy a squeeze. Then as Joyce caught my eye again her strange pout of sensual shame appeared and I felt I had been slapped on the face for having thoughts in my mind that matched her own. Her look told me that I could never know how truly she loved Bertie and feared him too, as she would love and fear a child. And she hated me for knowing what I would never have known unless she had mumbled the tale of tears of failure in the grey room next door.

And a glum stare from Podge, Bertie's oldest friend, showed me even more that I was an outsider.

The song had stirred Bertie's memory too, but of something more remote. He planted himself before me and sprang into yet another of his pantomime acts which the sight of me excited. He put on his baby voice: "William and I didn't have our pudding! Poor Bertie didn't have his pudding."

Joyce's face reddened. Their talk of food, money, their daily domestic life, was irritating in my situation. I lived by my desire; *they* had the intimacy of eating. I must have put on a mask, for Ivy said; "William's all right. He's got his well-fed Chinese look."

Even Joyce had once said that about me.

"How awful of me!" Joyce cried to all of us.

I thought we were lost, but she recovered in time.

"Bertie, isn't it terrible? I left it . . ." —she dared not say "in the taxi"—"I left it at Hendrick's."

Bertie's jollity went. He looked as stubborn as stone at Ivy and Joyce. Then with one of his ingenious cackles he dropped into French, which was a sign of resolution in him. *"Tout s'arrange,"* he said. "You can pick it up on Friday when you go there for rehearsal. By the way, what was it?"

"But, Bertie," Ivy said. "It will be stale or covered in mould by then. Apple tarts."

We all saw a glitter of moisture in Bertie's eyes; it might have come from greed or the streak of miserliness in him—it might have been tears.

"We must get them back," said Bertie.

André saved Joyce by coming out with one of his long detailed stories about a Flemish woman who kept a chicken in her refrigerator for two months after her husband left her. It became greener and greener, and when he came back with his tail between his legs she made him eat it. And he died.

André's stories parodied one's life, but this one distracted Bertie while Joyce whispered to her sister, "He means it."

"Tell him Hendrick ate them. He *has* probably eaten them by now. Singers are always eating."

"That would be worse," said Joyce.

After that André bellowed out a song about his military service and the party broke up. We went into the bedroom and picked up our coats while Joyce stood there rubbing her arms and saying, "Bertie, did you know you had turned out the fire?"

I was trying to signal Friday, Friday, Friday to her, but she took no notice. Of course her sister was staying on in London. How long for? What would that mean?

We all left the house. Bertie stood, legs apart, on the step, triumphant. I found myself having to get a taxi for the socialist girl.

"Where on earth are we?" she asked, looking at the black winter trees and the wet, sooty bushes of the gardens in the street. "Have you known them a long time? Do you live in London?"

"No," I said. "I'm on leave. I work in Singapore."

"What was all that extraordinary talk about the Baron?" She sent up a high laugh. "And the Pause?"

I said it was all Greek to me. I was still thinking Friday, Friday, Friday. Joyce would come or she would not come: more and more reluctant as the day drew nearer, with a weight on her ribs, listening for her tune. And if she heard it, the bones in her legs, arms, her fingers, would wake up and she would be out of breath at my door without knowing it.

1974

On the Scent

A big, oblong man, Manningtree gets out of bed in the morning, briskly, straightens up at once, yawns, blows out his chest, then puts on a violet silk dressing gown and is about to shout joyfully:

"Wakey, wakey! Rise and shine! Lash up and . . ." —but no! He looks across to the bed where his gnat of a wife is sleeping under a little fizz of dyed red hair, with her busy mouth wide open, even in sleep, and he stops. Putting on a stealthy look and lifting his knees high, he tiptoes out of the room. Manningtree's face is important. It has a quality that can only be called blatantly public, like a statue's; this is his fortune and his calamity. He is tall. He is handsome. At sixty-two, he still has beautifully polished fair hair, a pink, boyish skin, and still, blue eyes, and, at times, total calm. This is his fortunate side. His stealthy, dramatic look as he tiptoes out of the room is an aspect of the calamitous one; it empties clubs and bars, it empties sofas and corners of rooms at parties, it has emptied messes in two world wars. It is the look of the relentless, booming, whispering story-teller.

Take getting up in the morning.

"I arise," he says—making his blue eyes go very small—"from my humble couch"—pulling down the corners of his mouth to mock pathos—"and poop along"—he is confiding—"to the end of the passage"—he is now secretive—"to get in the milk and the papers." Then he makes a peculiar movement of his lower jaw, which shoots out sideways, at the same time almost closing his mouth, so that he speaks a little grindingly through his teeth and conveys a lurking, better-not-be-caught-red-handed impression. He continues in a tone now sordid, "to see what's going on in the world," and, at this, his face becomes handsome, nearly blank—"to see," he says disparagingly, "if there is anything of interest."

He stares at you when he says this for a long time and most people have to lower their eyes as one does after looking at the blind statue of some soldier or politician. And then the conspiring look comes on again; he leans towards you with his jaw shooting sideways, driving you bit by bit into your corner until you want to put up your hands and surrender, and he goes very mean and nasty about the mouth. "And pick up the post to see if the Manningtree millions have turned up," he adds.

So he describes the first half-hour of the day. His wife, who does not sleep well in spite of doctors and pills of all kinds, is awake, but keeps her eyes closed because she has seen and heard this performance every morning of her married life—except for the war—but she opens them when he brings in her breakfast, keen and singing.

"No luck, old girl! No Manningtree. Boo hoo hoo," he says, collapsing his face.

She could scream.

"Bunny's a fool, an ass, a dolt!" she tells her friends, and all her little bits of jewellery repeat the message in flashes from her neck, her ears, her fingers. "I think I shall go mad. We live in two pokey little rooms. I have nothing to put on. He hasn't even got a pension. Go to London! Go to Paris! My dear, we can't afford the bus fare to go to the cinema. That gas fire is the only comfort I've got in life." She lowers her voice to a dirty whisper. "As for you know what—we gave that up two years after we were married."

And then she tells them the story of this disastrous marriage. There she was, a woman with brains, attractive, too. Men with brains, she never could resist them: Angus, Charles, Duncan, Max— look what they have done. Angus an admiral, Max, governor of somewhere—but just because she was potty about a shifty and brilliant painter who jilted her for an Irish waitress, she had to go and marry Bunny Manningtree on the rebound. He worked for a travel agency and was hopeless at it.

"Of course," she says, pulling herself together, "he is a Manningtree.

Lord Manningtree is his cousin. They are all bankers, shipbuilders, Cabinet ministers, worth millions.

"I always have a look at the *Times* to see if any of them have died," she says, twisting her little face, for she has caught something of his habits after twenty-five years—"but the fool! He even says he doesn't think he's any relation at all, won't even write a letter and here we stick in this hole. And I had talent! We scrape, we sit. I stay in bed half the day and he comes in the evening with his library book, and he reads bits out to me. History! Mexico! That's the latest thing. The Aztecs."

She gives a hysterical laugh.

"D'you know—I asked what he wanted to be when he was a boy. Do you know what he said? An Aztec priest!!!"

She is wrong about this. After breakfast Manningtree walks across the park to earn, as he puts it, "the sordid daily crust." He has an excellent figure, he is presentably dressed, he has the serene, dummy-like expression that would delight any tailor. She is wrong about his wanting to be an Aztec; that was years ago, before the war. He has moved southward since then, across Panama, down the Andes. He is with the Incas, these days. After a few hundred yards, his face attracts attention from passers-by. It has begun to move. It is dramatizing certain arguments about the Virgins of the Sun. He is going over their chief temples, their convents set apart from the Inca towns. He arrives eventually at Macchu Picchu. One hundred female skeletons have been found at that Inca hide-out—were they Virgins of the Sun or were they Manco II's concubines or simply Indians who had fled with him from the Spaniards? Manningtree has doubts. He scents a mystery and his blue eyes go very small. The only way to clear it up is to go back to the sixteenth century. He does this. He has got out of Cuzco unobserved by the Spaniards and although he knows the Inca roads well, the stone causeways six feet wide, scratched on the sides of the Andes or choked by the jungle, he also knows that the only safe, secret way is to go by the Urabamba River. He sets off, with a machete—but back he has to come because the old, old question has arisen. How is he dressed? How is he disguised? At this word, the artfulness of his face is so blatant that children fifty yards away think he is going to eat them.

Alas, Manningtree has now to postpone the answer. He has arrived. He straightens his face and goes into a doorway marked "Staff only," in the Hildegarde Memorial Museum.

This museum had been the white elephant of the city for two generations. The Council would have liked to have sold it or pulled it down; they could not do so. But fashions change. Once deserted except on rainy days, the museum is now visited by thousands of people every year.

It is a fantastic, cream-washed, Neo-Gothic mansion built about 1820 in the park—which was attached to it—by an Austrian archduke for his mistress, the twelfth Duchess of Taxminster. There is a Byron story about her. After the archduke died it was taken over, in the late seventies, by the intellectual son of the steel magnate Rudolf Dabchild and his crippled wife, Hildegarde von Hochfeld-Mannheim, who inherited the Kreutzer fortune. These two beetle-like creatures were compulsive, voracious, indiscriminate collectors. Trainloads, vanloads of remarkable furniture, armour, Spanish choir stalls, icons, Italian ceilings, porcelain, tapestries, pictures, weapons, costumes of all the ages, Chinese, Japanese, and Indian objects, archaeological relics, and the usual cases of Polynesian masks, canoes, poisoned arrows, and stuffed birds and so on, arrived at the mansion and choked it. When Dabchild's wife died, he unloaded it on the appalled city and called it the Hildegarde Memorial Museum. Fortunately a rich trust supported it. It was run by antiquarians originally, but lately, since the dissolution of the British Empire, people who would have been generals or governors of African and Indian provinces in earlier days now dominate the committee. One of these, remembering Manningtree's record in the war, got him his job. Or rather his wife did, by circulating the gossip that he was a connexion of the great Manningtrees.

Even now, Bunny Manningtree won't say what he was doing in the war. He simply says he was sitting on his bottom in the Shetlands, "pooped around" for a few months in the United States, and had something to do with one or two "wheezes." "No initiative," his wife says. "He let them push him into Supply." "Supplying wheezes," he explains. The word "wheeze" comes out with a lingering malicious glee as if he were a schoolboy who has just bought a trick glass of beer at a joke shop or written to another boy in invisible ink. All the same, bits of the war, he says, "had an interest." Up in the Shetlands, for example, he got friendly with the seals and collected moss.

Whatever it was, it was a dead end, as far as his peacetime prospects were concerned. He stands (it must be said that is one thing he can do: stand properly; few people can) about ten yards inside the main entrance of the Hildegarde, looking at the moons of his nails.

Once or twice a year an old acquaintance spots him.

"Good heavens—Manningtree? What are you doing here?"

"On the strength," says Manningtree calmly. And then his other face jostles the calm one away and he narrows his blue eyes, slips his lower jaw sideways, and says in a chewing, secretive, and sordid voice: "Actually—guide. I show the hoi polloi round. Coach parties. It's terrifying." Then his face changes and he straightens to mention the finer aspects of his job.

"V.I.P.'s, too. French mayors, Siamese ambassador, Russians."

He puts his hand to his mouth and coarsely whispers again:

"Minister of Labour last Tuesday."

"There are one or two things worth a look," he says. He leads his friends down the fantastic corridors, passing statues, Japanese paintings, Indian carvings, cases of porcelain. He comes to a door and a sly look comes on.

"Private apartments of the archduke," he says. The friends admire.

"Hoovered three times a week," he says to the ladies. He beckons them on to the centrepiece. It is, of course, the canopied bed of the archduke.

"See the little secret staircase?" he says, nodding to a corner by the bed. He looks noble. His friends grin. He is disappointed by the blatancy of the universal reaction, especially if one of the men lags behind for a second look at the staircase and says: "Very convenient."

Manningtree's sinister face comes on, reprovingly. He nods to the staircase.

"That is why Bismarck tore up the Treaty."

No one has any idea what he is talking about.

Afterwards as the party leaves, Manningtree shakes hands and they go off saying: "Poor old Bunny."

At five o'clock he collects a book or two from the library, goes home, and after dinner he reads. Suddenly he may say to his wife:

"Here's another so-called explorer repeating the same cock-eyed idea. No Inca in his senses would have built a fort there, where it could be dominated by any enemy outside. It wasn't a fort, it was a holy city. The rising sun strikes through the slit on the Intihuatana sundial."

No answer.

"Another howler," he says. "The saddle is not ten thousand feet up. I'd put it nearer eight thousand."

"Perhaps it's grown since you were there," his wife says.

One Monday—Mondays are usually quiet in the winter—a foreigner comes to the Hildegarde Museum. He is a tall, well-built German with clipped grey hair, cold, wide, grey eyes, straight-nosed, straight-lipped, easy in carriage. He buys a guidebook at the counter, walks past Manningtree, and sets off round the museum on his own. As he passes he leaves behind him a worldly smell of cigar, caraway, and some other smell—a scent. The scent disturbs Manningtree. It makes him feel cold. Having nothing to do, he strolls off from room to room, looking for a sunny window. Once or twice he sees the foreigner in the distance. Manningtree's nose twitches. He moves to another room.

"Got it," he says at last. *"Vol de nuit."*

The foreigner can be seen distantly through three doorways. Manningtree dreams.

"Hun. Baron, I suppose. Baltic family. Query, born Lübeck. Staff officer in war. No, not staff officer. Heidelberg, Oxford. Berliner. Villa in Dahlem, pretty district. Take a bus from the Kurfürstendamm. Forget the number."

Manningtree moves on. There is more sun in the south of the buildings. He goes to his favourite room—ancient costumes. His mind travels.

In those days, he recapitulates, the Incas must have held the roads they scratched on the mountains and they certainly had fortified places. They once shelled the Spaniards in Cuzco with white-hot stones. (That, by the way, does not excuse the public rape of several hundred Virgins of the Sun.) Anyone trying to get the gen on Macchu Picchu and to see what Manco II's boys are up to had better take to the jungle following the Urabamba through its gorges. Have to be fit, of course.

Manningtree takes to the jungle. He slips below the fortified line. He has jungle cunning. In the hot depths of the gorges he can keep alive on bananas. He finds a deserted hut and there at night he hangs his shirt over the entrance to keep out the night air of the Andes. After sixty miles on foot, swollen with bites, he is at the base of Macchu Picchu two thousand feet above him. Up he goes; as he gets nearer he sees a sight to shake the spirit of any man. Two bodies come hurtling through the air, pass over him, and crash into the gorge. Aha! The High Priest has caught a couple trying to get to the Virgins of the Sun. Manningtree pauses to consider the old, old problem. How is he dressed? Inca robes? But did the Incas wear Inca robes? Didn't the Spaniards make them wear Spanish costume? And what was Spanish costume in Extremadura in the sixteenth century? An idea comes to Manningtree, a wheeze. Suppose he appears in Macchu Picchu dressed as he is now, in a navy-blue suit with light chalk stripes, white collar, school tie? Why not? Take them by surprise, eh? Probably run away.

That is exactly what happens. Men posted at the main gate make a bolt for it. He walks in and catches a boy—always ask a boy—*Donde está* the High Priest?—always make for a priest. Nasty sight here, by the way: two more men tied by their heels and hanging head down over the precipice—two more cases of trying to get to the Virgins of the Sun. A whole crowd of High Priests come along. They rush him. He is arrested at once. He is tried in the court-house—usual charge, Virgins of the Sun again; and, by the way, archaeologists are wrong: the courtyard described as the residence of Manco II is actually *below* the residence. The military fellers get out their clubs and prepare to beat him to death and then pitch his body into the gorge.

A nasty fix this, but Manningtree has an answer to it. He worked that one out when he was settling the dress problem a few hours ago when he was climbing up the hill. Manningtree's face takes on one of its most public leers of profound cunning, visible (one would guess) but for the Andes, as far away as the Pacific Ocean.

"Oh, High Priest," Manningtree says. "Throttle down a moment. I've been having a peep at your sundial. Art thou not all het up about sunrise and sunset, and what-have-you? Time in short? Am I right? Splendid! well, let me put a little problem to you, something to think over. I come from the future. You're yesterday as far as I am concerned, I'm tomorrow. Tomorrow's sun has already risen before today's has set. D'you follow?"

One of the enclosed Virgins of the Sun stops weaving vicuna and looks out of a window and exclaims:

"Oh thou!"

The fellows put down their clubs and they start a pijaw nineteen to the dozen—not loudly, by the way. At that altitude, the air is thin and voices are soft, a curious point. Manningtree takes his opportunity and talks in signs to the Virgin of the Sun. Where does that road lead to? he signals. She replies, by signs. To the real secret city. Manningtree thought as much. He has always held that Macchu Picchu was an outpost, a decoy. He memorizes her information. Never write anything down! He has always memorized everything.

The German visitor to the Hildegarde has come back to the room where Manningtree has been standing and has been watching him for several minutes. He has noticed that Manningtree is standing in front of a large glass case containing Spanish costumes and at first the German thinks Manningtree is talking to someone. Then he has the idea that since no one is visible the person must be hidden in the glass case. This does not startle him. He is alerted. He has recognized an interesting idea, a possible experience; it has, unfortunately, been used in films. He feels drawn to Manningtree and approaches him.

"Excuse me, sir," he says in rather stiff, good English, "are you by any chance the head director of the museum?"

Manningtree puts on his blank face at once.

"No I'm not, I'm sorry. Can I be of any help?"

"I wonder if you could direct me to the archaeological section?" says the German. "Are you an official?"

Manningtree's nose twitches. He has smelled *Vol de nuit* again. He has a strange cold feeling of being carried into the past.

"Oh no," says Manningtree. "I'm just a sort of chap keeping a sort of an eye." And, in fact, he opens one eye to significant wideness.

"I beg your pardon," says the German. "You are a visitor like myself."

"Oh no," says Manningtree. "For my sins this is where I earn the daily crust. Follow me. I'll show you."

The German stares at him; then he smiles. He remembers. He remembers what the English are like; very soon, as the textbooks say, Manningtree is likely to make a joke. The German prepares himself for this. They walk in a friendly fashion across the room together, and nodding to the cases, Manningtree says in his sinister voice: "This is where we keep the *disguises.*"

"The disguises?" the German repeats politely. Somewhere here, at any moment, will come the joke.

"The costumes," says Manningtree with wonderful coolness.

"Ah!" The German is relieved. The joke has been accomplished. Manningtree becomes friendly.

"Have you seen the Private Apartments?"

"Yes. Of little interest," says the German. "Just the little incident of Bismarck and the Treaty."

Manningtree is delighted. One does not often meet the man with inside knowledge. But he is still worried by the smell of *Vol de nuit.*

"Here," he says, "this is what you want. Archaeology. There are two rooms. Early British village?" Manningtree offers. "The Western lake culture?"

"Africa?" He hesitates shyly. "Inca?"

The German shrugs his shoulders and walks brusquely forward.

"This is what I want." He opens his catalogue. "The Mayas."

Vol de nuit! Maya! Manningtree suddenly knows something. His face closes. He had been right first go.

"You speak English very well. You were up at Oxford?" he asks.

"Yes. I had been at Heidelberg. My family comes from Lübeck, but I live in Berlin now."

"Dahlem," says Manningtree.

"Yes," says the German warmly.

"Lovely trees. You can get a bus, I seem to remember, from the Kurfürstendamm, I forget the number—was it eighty-six?"

"Interesting," says the startled German. "When were you there last?"

"Never," says Manningtree. "Not actually, ever."

"This is extraordinary," says the German.

Manningtree puts on his most asinine, blushing, apologizing face.

"Always interested in places, local buses, trains. I collected time tables at school. I used to play at running goods trains all over Europe —the world actually. Fun. Something of interest."

The German is puzzled and takes a long look at Manningtree. He is weighing up the question of madness, for Manningtree looks very childish, stupid, his chin dropping, his mouth open. Manningtree changes the subject.

"I'm not a Maya man," he says. "I'm afraid I'll be no good to you," Manningtree apologizes. "I moved on to the Incas.

"The Incas, now, that's another thing," he goes on. "I mean I'm not a scholar. I just potter. The priesthood, the roads. Clever people. Time, for example. They understood it."

The German edges away.

Manningtree follows him closer.

"And another thing—how they got the information through the Andes. Two thousand miles, three more like it. No writing, no letters, no telephone—memorized it." He pauses. "What was their secret?"

His face is blameless.

"No radio," he concludes.

The German gives a sharp turn of his head. He is uncertain. Is Manningtree mad? Manningtree is now studying the cases of Mayan objects.

"Mayas are interesting too. You know them well?" says Manningtree humbly.

"Yes," said the German.

"I tried it, before the war. There were too many problems," says

Manningtree. "I moved out of Mexico on to the Incas. For instance, here's a thing, I bet you can tell me, the sort of detail that I get stuck in, I mean, fed up with. The palace at Mitla—you know the palace at Mitla? I mean the second Incan palace."

"But you *do* know the Mayas!" says the German suspiciously.

"Nothing," says Manningtree. "I mean the High Priest had put the wind up the kings and all that and the kings got very cunning."

Manningtree begins his well-known jaw-sliding and significant eye-rollings.

"They cut three back doors so that they could nip out fast before the old boy could spot them—rather neat? The snag is—and this is where I stick—if you go to Mitla today there are no back doors. And, what's more, if you look up your Father Bourgoa you'll see he says there were six rooms. Actually there are only four. What d'you make of that?"

"Bourgoa's sources were unreliable," says the German affably. "He was repeating hearsay. What year were you there?"

"Alas and lackaday, never," says Manningtree. "Never had the wherewithal. I just go pooping around old books."

"Pooping!" exclaims the German.

"Just pooping and pottering," says Manningtree.

" 'Pooping'—I don't understand that English word," says the German. "I have heard it . . . yes . . ."

The German, who up to now has had simply a sharp, intelligent German face, like thousands of others one sees along the Baltic, suddenly has a memory and *his* face changes. He seems to put on weight as if he had just eaten too much. His cheeks swell over his jaw, which fattens; tears like juices come into his eyes, which nearly close and look sly. At the sight of this, Manningtree's pink face blushes, his eyes begin watering too. He also fattens. The two men stand melting in front of each other like blushing snowmen as though the temperature of the room has shot up twenty degrees.

"I envy you going to Mexico," says Manningtree.

"Oh I haven't been there either," says the German.

The German goes on and, for the first time, his English syntax is clumsy:

"But it is always historical that makes for you the interest? I don't think so. When we met on the night train from New York to Chicago in December 1940, was that pooping, Captain Manningtree? You were interested in the Virgins of the Sun."

Manningtree stares at him.

"I was a pooper, too!" exclaims the German with delight, extending his hand. "Hochstadt."

"Hochstadt!" Manningtree nods. And then he winks at the German.

"Vol de nuit, a great mistake, old boy. Terrible give-away. We followed you all over the States. It clings. No offence. What are you up to now?"

The German looks humble.

"I have a small cinema," he says sadly. "Not Dahlem any more."

"Hoi polloi, eh? Well, I suppose," says Manningtree, "it brings in the daily crust."

And, in sympathy, he looks over the floors, walls, and ceilings of the Hildegarde Memorial Museum with disgust.

"By the way, I always wondered," says Manningtree, "how did you manage after we got your radio?"

"Like the Incas," says the German. He has got his revenge. He has made a joke.

The Hildegarde Museum closes. Manningtree walks home across the park. He tells his wife about the encounter.

"I recognized him the moment he came in," he says. "Smelt him. I didn't let on. I didn't say anything. 'Aha!' I thought. 'Baron von Trondheim,' I says to meself! I just lay low"—he crouches. "I shammed dead"—he closes his eyes. "Memory got busy. He recognized me too. I don't know how, deep fellow."

"I wonder!" says his wife.

"Ah," says Manningtree, screwing up one eye and rubbing a finger joint on a thoughtful tooth. "Still an agent, I think. He gave the name Hochstadt."

Manningtree's pleasure fades. He looks gloomy.

"Manningtree millions not arrived, I suppose? No. Ah well. Have to wait for another war, but I'll be past it. My memory's going. I couldn't remember the number of the Dahlem bus. Bad show."

1960

Double Divan

Two workmen were carrying a double divan bed, slung on ropes from their shoulders, down the busy streets in the warm fume of a London dusk. The man behind was ginger-haired. He had a moustache of sweat, a hard, factory mouth, and blue, unwilling eyes. The weight of the bed kept his head down, and the pace of the big-potato-bummed man in front was dragging him along on the tips of his toes almost at a trot. They were travelling fast.

Presently the traffic lights were against them and they stood still.

"How much farther?" said the man in front. He could not turn his head.

"You're bloody right," said the man behind.

The lights changed, the traffic gave a loud swallow and moved forward, and the two men were driven over the crossing. On they raced, not daring to stop. They came to a wide road-junction and then the lights went red again. The man behind felt the warm radiator of a lorry toasting his backside.

"Gone deaf or something; how much farther?" called back the man in front.

"What d'you mean, how much farther? You got the paper," said the man behind.

"What bleeding paper?" said the man in front.

"The address she give you," said the man behind.

"Who?" said the man in front.

"The paper she give you," said the man behind.

"I haven't got no bleeding paper," said the man in front.

The man behind rolled his eyes and wagged his knees about. The bed swayed with him and the man in front went as pink as a sausage in the neck as he steadied it.

"Call the keeper, lock me up, I'm barmy," said the man behind.

Motor horns started blowing, the lorry radiator pressed closely on the trousers of the man behind. A bus driver put his head out and shouted: the lights had changed. The two heaved at the bed and rushed over the crossing. They advanced to the next side-turning and the leader swung round there, put his end of the bed down and they faced each other.

"She spoke to you. You was the last to see her," said the leader. "She didn't give me no address."

"You fixed the job. All she said to me was, 'Be careful. Be careful,' she said, 'and mind the casters,' " said the man behind.

The man in front was large and dazed. He wiped his forehead and felt in his jacket pockets. A pigeon came down in the dusk and he looked at the bird enquiringly. He felt in his waistcoat pocket and looked up to the rows of windows for help. All knowledge of where he had been told to take the bed had gone. The man behind took the rope off his aching shoulders and threw it on the bed.

"What name was it?" said the man behind.

"Ida or Mary or like that," said the man in front.

"Ida or Mary, very tasty, very sweet," jeered the man behind. "Ida what?"

"I'm trying to think," said the man in front.

"You'd better stop thinking and go back and find her," said the man behind.

"She's left. Moved out," said the man in front.

The man behind sat down on the bed and took his cap off. "Is she waiting there—where we're going, this woman, this Ida, this party?"

"I got it!" exclaimed the man in front. "Robinson—that's the name. Mrs. Robinson. There was two of them."

The man behind got up and rolled his eyes and put his tongue out. "Open the door," he cried. "Open the door and let me out."

The large man stood searching his mind.

"She came over to the yard in the morning," the man in front said.

" 'The name is Robinson, Mrs. Robinson,' she says. 'My sister is moving her flat and I want you to get a bed out for her, a big one.' Married woman, see, giving orders, doesn't tell you anything and expects you to know the lot. 'I can't do that,' I says, 'I work all day.' 'I don't want it moved in the daylight,' she says. 'It's not my bed, it's my sister's.' 'I don't want to know your business,' I says. 'I'll move what you like, but I can't do it till the evening.' 'What are we arguing about?' she says. 'That's what I want you to do.' "

"Get on," said the man. "I don't half sweat."

"She give me the address. Next thing, after work, I go up to the flat. Number twenty-six. Top floor. She comes out with glasses on. The carpets are gone, all the furniture, just the bed in the back room. 'I'll tell my sister,' she says. 'Ida,' she calls out. 'Here's the man.' Ida—that's the sister, see—comes out of the kitchen. 'What man, Mary?' says the sister. 'The man about the bed,' says this Mrs. Robinson."

"Step on it," said the man behind.

"I can't," said the man in front, "or you won't follow. This Ida wasn't like the other. She had a fur coat on and first of all I thought she was sweating, her face was red and steamy, only a girl. She had a handkerchief in her hand and she dropped it. 'Excuse me,' I said, and picked it up. It was wet. She was crying. She gives one look at me and then the waterworks start up again and she goes off to the kitchen, leaving me, see, with the other one. 'Wait here,' Mrs. Robinson says. 'I must go to my sister. She's not very well. She's upset.' 'Oh,' I says, 'having trouble . . . ?' "

"Here," said the man behind. "Pack it in. Here's a van coming. We got trouble here."

The two men put the ropes round their necks and moved on to the entrance to a public-house yard. The dray horses struck with bearded hoofs at the cobbles as they strained past.

"Put her here," said the man behind, lowering his end. "I'm going to have a beer."

The two men stood the striped bed on end against the side wall of the public-house. They looked at the bed, silently telling it not to move while they were gone, and they went into the public-house. The shadow of the bed could be seen against the frosted glass of the bar window.

"Know anyone of the name of Robinson round here?" said the man behind. "Number twenty-six, The Terrace?"

"You see hundreds of faces, you never know the names," the barman said, picking up his cigarette from the bar.

"We're moving a bed," said the man behind, "for a Mrs. Ida something."

"Miss, not Mrs.," said the man in front. "She wasn't married."

"Mrs., must be," said the man behind. "Double bed."

"That don't follow," said the barman, winking at the customers.

"It'd be a funny thing for a single woman to have a double bed," a man said.

"What's funny in that?" the barman said.

"When his old woman rolls on him," the customer said. "I sleep with myself."

"I lay you do, Jim," said the barman.

Two squeaks of laughter went up from two old women sitting on a bench.

"She is a young woman and she isn't married," said the man in front.

"It must be," said the man behind, "some tart."

"Oh dear," said one of the women on the bench, hiding her face in the top of her glass. "Language, now we hear it."

"Ginger," said the leader, taking his beer to a table, "you're right. That Mrs. Robinson must have given me the paper and it has dropped out. She wrote it down on the mantelpiece, and while she was writing her sister called out from the kitchen and Mrs. Robinson put the pencil down and says, 'I'll be back. My sister wants to talk to me.' "

He sat down, the man in front said, and he waited in the flat. He sat on the bed; it was the only thing in the room to sit on. "The only furniture they hadn't moved," he said, "was a brass coal-scuttle with some fire-irons and an electric kettle in it." He knew about that because he had had an eye on the electric kettle, and Mrs. Robinson knew he had because she said to him, "Don't you touch those. They are mine." The flat was a pretty place; to give an example, the paint was green, but not the common green, and the walls were pink, but not what you would call right out pink: a lady's place. You could tell that by Ida's voice.

"Perhaps," said the man behind, going up to the bar for two more pints and speaking over his shoulder as though he were spitting, "she couldn't pay the rent. Was it a shop? Did she give you the address of a shop?"

"No," said the man in front, "it wasn't a shop. I had a look out of the window. You could see the canal through the tops of the trees. And that's what messed me up. They were having an argument next door. I could hear them carrying on. The next thing the door bangs. Mrs.

Robinson shouts out in a temper, 'I'll tell him to go.' There's a sort of free-for-all in the door and in comes the sister, Ida, still crying. She marches up to me and she says, very sharp, 'Give me a pencil. I want you to take this bed to Mrs. Robinson's house.' Of course, I hadn't got a pencil. But before I could tell her this, Mrs. Robinson comes in. She was shouting. 'No, Ida,' she says, 'I won't have it. Not after what you said. You're a pig. Keep your beastly bed.' Your beastly bed, oh dear, that's what she said. She says, 'I am only trying to help you. If you haven't got any reputation to think of,' she says, 'the rest of the family have. What would the neighbours say if they saw a double bed go out of a single girl's flat into the van with the rest in broad daylight? There,' she says, 'Ida, I've told you the plain truth. Someone's got to tell you.' "

"Oh dear, oh dear, oh dear," said the man behind. "Sisters, you say."

"Taking no notice of me," said the man in front. "I'm the wall. 'Now which of you ladies is having it?' I says. 'I'm having these,' says Mrs. Robinson, picking up the scuttle and things in both arms like someone was robbing her. 'My sister's having it,' says Ida, opening her bag and looking for a pen. 'No,' says Mrs. Robinson, putting down the scuttle and snatching her pen from her. 'Not after what you said. We've slept in a single bed all the time we've been married and we can carry on.' A regular ding-dong. And then Mrs. Robinson says, 'What are you going to sleep on to-night, Ida?' "

"Ah!" said the man behind.

"Oh dear," said the man in front. "You ought to have seen Ida's face. She stops talking, her mouth stays open. She gives a hoot as if she had struck a mine. 'Ooh! Oooh!' she goes. There's a flood again. 'Oooh,' she hoots, 'what shall I do, what shall I do? I don't care where I sleep. I don't care what happens to me.' And then she goes over to the window and cries out, 'I shall throw myself in the canal. I shall kill myself. I don't want to live. I told him I would, he's broken my heart.'

"Mrs. Robinson says, 'The number of times you've hanged yourself, drowned yourself, and put your head in the gas oven, Ida, you'd fill a cemetery. He was a married man and you knew it. You said the same after Arthur and after Len. Please excuse me,' she says to me.

"And, Ida answers back: 'You're married, Mary. You've got a husband and children. Won't anyone marry me? I came home from the office and I cooked him a meal every night.'

" 'That was Philip, not this one,' Mrs. Robinson calls out. 'Because of his stomach.'

"Ida looks at her sister and stops crying at this. Annoyed. 'There were two with bad stomachs,' Ida says sharp. 'You're always unfair to me. They said it was because of their wives.'

"That's what she said," said the man in front, looking at his untouched beer with indignation, indignant with himself. He took a long swallow of it.

"Straight," he said, watching the beads of froth float on the dark current towards his lips. He put the glass down; he had finished it. "Two married men with bad stomachs."

"And then," he said, "Ida, the single girl, began to laugh, not a laugh in the ordinary way . . ."

"Hysterics," said the man behind. "My wife's sister does it."

"No," said the man in front. "Too dry. More like a bark than a laugh. She laughed at Mrs. Robinson, she laughed at me. 'Oh dear,' she laughed. She couldn't stop. 'It's all because I had a double bed,' she says, 'I ought to have kept to singles.'

"You ought to have seen the married one's face when she said this. Didn't like it. In front of me, see. I couldn't help it, could I? 'Oooh, Ida,' she says, 'how can you?' Very classy. 'Don't mind me,' I says. Ida gives me a wink. 'Oh yes it is,' Ida says. 'Ask this gentleman. I'll never get married till I get a single, will I?' she says. 'Ida, shut up!' says Mrs. Robinson. 'It's no good rushing things, miss,' I says. 'There you are!' says Ida.

"She comes up to me," said the man in front, "this Ida, and she says, 'Take this bed and the coal-scuttle and things to my sister's address. She's a respectable married woman.' And then she turns on her sister and says, 'You had the fender when Arthur left me and the armchair, Mary. I'm keeping the rest till next time. You've furnished your flat bit by bit out of my broken heart.' You ought to have seen the look she gave her sister; sarcastic, it wiped the floor up with a wet rag all round her. If looks could kill."

"I know what I'd do," said the man behind, "with a girl like that Ida if she was my daughter. I'd take her knickers down and I'd paste her. What's class? A tart's a tart anywhere. My wife's sister is one— talk of love, it's turned on like a tap."

"There was the best electric kettle in that scuttle that I ever see," said the man in front.

The two men studied the shadow of the bed on the window. It did not seem to them like the bed they had been talking about and they bought two more drinks in order to be able to look it in the face. They went outside and they were astonished to find the dusk had gone—the

London night was in full bud and blossom. They swayed down the yard entrance and considered the bed with many renewed attempts at impartiality. With its very wide stripes it was an object now hard to focus.

"Better lift it into the yard," said the man in front, "so's no one will touch it while we go back to the house."

They lifted the bed and lowered it again in the yard at the back of the public-house.

"A bed like that's worth a bit of money," said the man behind. "It's worth fifteen quid."

"Twenty," from the man in front.

"Seven years ago, before the war, you'd have given ten pounds for it," said the man behind.

"Talk sense," said the man in front, suddenly lighting with rage. "The war didn't last seven years."

A quarrel broke out between the two men. Their shouts banged about up and down the yard until the dogs barked at them.

"Where's the money for this job?" shouted the man behind. "I don't let go of this bed till I get my money."

The man in front suddenly sat down.

"You'll get your money," he said.

"Too true I will," said the man behind. "I'm going back to the house to see if they're there."

And he went. The man in front watched him go without surprise. When he was out of sight the man in front began to feel the springs, and then gently to bounce up and down. He smiled as he bounced and then the smile grew to a laugh. "Oh dear, what a disappointment for Mrs. Robinson," he said. And to spite her he put his feet up on the bed and lay down. "I wonder," he said, "what that other poor girl is doing now?"

He was asleep when Mrs. Robinson, Ida, and the man behind returned. They found the bed in the darkness by his snores.

"Mary," cried out Ida, clapping her hands, "there's a man in it."

1946

A Story of
Don Juan

One night of his life Don Juan slept alone. Returning to Seville in the spring, he was held up, some hours' ride from the city, by the floods of the Quadalquivir, a river as dirty as an old lion after the rains, and was obliged to stay at the finca of the Quintero family. The doorway, the walls, the windows of the house were hung with the black and violet draperies of mourning when he arrived there. Quintero's wife was dead. She had been dead a year. The young Quintero took him in and even smiled to see Don Juan spattered and drooping in the rain like a sodden cockerel. There was malice in his smile: Quintero was mad with loneliness and grief. The man who had possessed and discarded all women was received by a man demented because he had lost only one.

"My house is yours," said Quintero, speaking the formula. There was bewilderment in his eyes; those who grieve do not find the world and its people either real or believable. Irony inflects the voices of mourners, and there was malice, too, in Quintero's further greetings; he could receive Don Juan now without that fear, that terror which he brought to the husbands of Seville. It was perfect, Quintero thought, that for once in his life Don Juan should have arrived at an empty house.

There was not even (as Don Juan quickly found out) a maid, for Quintero was served only by a manservant, being unable any longer to bear the sight of women. This servant dried the guest's clothes and in an hour or two brought in a bad dinner, food which stamped up and down in the stomach, like people waiting for a coach in the cold. Quintero was torturing his body as well as his mind, and as the familiar pains arrived they agonized him and set him off about his wife. Grief had also made Quintero an actor. His eyes had the hollow, taper-haunted dusk of the theatre as he spoke of the beautiful girl. He dwelled upon their courtship, on details of her beauty and temperament, and how he had rushed her from the church to the marriage bed like a man racing a tray of diamonds through the streets into the safety of a bank vault. The presence of Don Juan turned every man into an artist when he was telling his own love-story—one had to tantalize and surpass the great seducer—and Quintero, rolling it all off in the grand manner, could not resist telling that his bride had died on her marriage night.

"Man!" cried Don Juan. He started straight off on stories of his own. But Quintero hardly listened; he had returned to the state of exhaustion and emptiness which is natural to grief. As Don Juan talked, the madman followed his own thoughts like an actor preparing and mumbling his next entrance; and the thought he had had, when Don Juan first appeared at the door, returned to him: a man must be a monster to make a man feel triumphant that his own wife was dead. Half-listening, and indigestion aiding, Quintero felt within himself the total hatred of all the husbands of Seville for this diabolical man. And as Quintero brooded upon this it occurred to him that it was probably not by chance that he had a vengeance in his power.

The decision was made. The wine being finished, Quintero called for his manservant and gave orders to change Don Juan's room.

"For," said Quintero dryly, "His Excellency's visit is an honour and I cannot allow one who has slept in the most delicately scented rooms in Spain to pass the night in a chamber which stinks to heaven of goat."

"The closed room?" said the manservant, astonished that the room which still held the great dynastic marriage bed and which had not been used more than half a dozen times by his master since the lady's death was to be given to a stranger.

Yet to this room Quintero led his guest and there parted from him with eyes so sparking with ill-intention that Don Juan, who was sensitive to this kind of point, understood perfectly that the cat was being let into the cage only because the bird had long ago flown out. The humiliation was unpleasant. Don Juan saw the night stretching before him like a desert.

What a bed to lie in: so wide, so unutterably vacant, so malignantly inopportune! He took off his clothes, snuffed the lamp wick. He lay down knowing that on either side of him lay wastes of sheet, draughty and uninhabited except by bugs. A desert. To move an arm one inch to the side, to push out a leg, however cautiously, was to enter desolation. For miles and miles the foot might probe, the fingers or the knee explore a friendless Antarctica. Yet to lie rigid and still was to have a foretaste of the grave. And here, too, he was frustrated; for though the wine kept him yawning, that awful food romped in his stomach, jolting him back from the edge of sleep the moment he got there.

There is an art in sleeping alone in a double bed, but this art was unknown to Don Juan. The difficulty is easily solved. If one cannot sleep on one side of the bed, one moves over and tries the other. Two hours or more must have passed before this occurred to him. Sullen-headed, he advanced into the desert, and the night air lying chill between the sheets flapped and made him shiver. He stretched out his arm and crawled towards the opposite pillow. The coldness, the more than virgin frigidity of linen! He put down his head and, drawing up his knees, he shivered. Soon, he supposed, he would be warm again, but, in the meantime, ice could not have been colder. It was unbelievable.

Ice was the word for that pillow and those sheets. Ice. Was he ill? Had the rain chilled him that his teeth must chatter like this and his legs tremble? Far from getting warmer, he found the cold growing. Now it was on his forehead and his cheeks, like arms of ice on his body, like legs of ice upon his legs. Suddenly in superstition he got up on his hands and stared down at the pillow in the darkness, threw back the bedclothes and looked down upon the sheet; his breath was hot, yet blowing against his cheeks was a breath colder than the grave, his shoulders and body were hot, yet limbs of snow were drawing him down; and just as he would have shouted his appalled suspicion, lips like wet ice unfolded upon his own and he sank down to a kiss, unmistakably a kiss, which froze him like a winter.

In his own room Quintero lay listening. His mad eyes were exalted and his ears were waiting. He was waiting for the scream of horror. He knew the apparition. There would be a scream, a tumble, hands fighting for the light, fists knocking at the door. And Quintero had locked the door. But when no scream came, Quintero lay talking to himself, remembering the night the apparition had first come to him and had made him speechless and left him choked and stiff. It would

be even better if there were no scream! Quintero lay awake through the
night, building castle after castle of triumphant revenge and receiving,
as he did so, the ovations of the husbands of Seville. "The stallion is
gelded!" At an early hour Quintero unlocked the door and waited
downstairs impatiently. He was a wreck after a night like that.

Don Juan came down at last. He was (Quintero observed) pale. Or
was he pale?

"Did you sleep well?" Quintero asked furtively.

"Very well," Don Juan replied.

"I do not sleep well in strange beds myself," Quintero insinuated.
Don Juan smiled and replied that he was more used to strange beds
than his own. Quintero scowled.

"I reproach myself; the bed was large," he said.

But the large, Don Juan said, were necessarily as familiar to him as
the strange. Quintero bit his nails. Some noise had been heard in the
night—something like a scream, a disturbance. The manservant had
noticed it also. Don Juan answered him that disturbances in the night
had indeed bothered him at the beginning of his career, but now he
took them in his stride. Quintero dug his nails into the palms of his
hands. He brought out the trump.

"I am afraid," Quintero said, "it was a cold bed. You must have
frozen."

"I am never cold for long," Don Juan said, and, unconsciously
anticipating the manner of a poem that was to be written in his
memory two centuries later, declaimed: "The blood of Don Juan is hot,
for the sun is the blood of Don Juan."

Quintero watched. His eyes jumped like flies to every movement of
his guest. He watched him drink his coffee. He watched him tighten
the stirrups of his horse. He watched Don Juan vault into the saddle.
Don Juan was humming, and when he went off was singing, was singing
in that intolerable tenor of his which was like a cock-crow in the olive
groves.

Quintero went into the house and rubbed his unshaven chin. Then
he went out again to the road where the figure of Don Juan was now
only a small smoke of dust between the eucalyptus trees. Quintero went
up to the room where Don Juan had slept and stared at it with accusations and suspicions. He called the manservant.

"I shall sleep here to-night," Quintero said.

The manservant answered carefully. Quintero was mad again and the
moon was still only in its first quarter. The man watched his master

during the day looking towards Seville. It was too warm after the rains, the country steamed like a laundry.

And then, when the night came, Quintero laughed at his doubts. He went up to the room and as he undressed he thought of the assurance of those ice-cold lips, those icicle fingers and those icy arms. She had not come last night; oh, what fidelity! To think, he would say in his remorse to the ghost, that malice had so disordered him that he had been base and credulous enough to use the dead for a trick.

Tears were in his eyes as he lay down and for some time he dared not turn on his side and stretch out his hand to touch what, in his disorder, he had been willing to betray. He loathed his heart. He craved —yet how could he hope for it now?—that miracle of recognition and forgiveness. It was this craving which moved him at last. His hands went out. And they were met.

The hands, the arms, the lips moved out of their invisibility and soundlessness towards him. They touched him, they clasped him, they drew him down, but—what was this? He gave a shout, he fought to get away, kicked out and swore; and so the manservant found him wrestling with the sheets, striking out with fists and knees, roaring that he was in hell. Those hands, those lips, those limbs, he screamed, were *burning* him. They were of ice no more. They were of fire.

1950

Passing the Ball

Two years ago, when I had finished at the hospital and was waiting for a grant to come through, I put in a month as a locum for a country doctor.

When I first went to see him the doctor switched on his desk lamp, turned it to shine full in my face, and said in a rough voice, as if he were finishing a mouthful of hay:

"How old are you?" he said. "If I may ask? Married? Do you hunt? I mean where were you at school?"

He began pulling out the drawers of his desk one by one and, shutting them recklessly with a number of bangs, rang for his dispenser and said something to her about a horse. After this he leaned forward and fell to tapping the side of his tin wastepaper basket with a riding-crop in slow, trotting time. His look was uninterested.

"Yes, yes, yes," he said lazily from the saddle. "We don't want a lot of your new-fangled ideas here. This isn't the usual kind of practice. The man I have here has got to be a gentleman. You can hand out your penicillin and your M. & B. You can put the whole parish in an iron lung, fill them with American drugs—I know that's the modern idea —but it's my experience of forty years of doctoring that a gentleman's worth the lot. Have a drink? Do you know the Fobhams?"

I could see up the doctor's meaty nose and underneath his chin when he raised it to utter this name in the voice of one who had suddenly put on court dress. By nature Dr. Ray was a man of disguises, and a new one with every sentence. Two whiskies stabilized him. A heavy, guilty blush came down from the middle of his head, enlarged his ears, and went below his collar. His hands became confidential; one of them was put on my shoulder; his voice lowered and, if shrewdness was in one blue eye as sharp as a pellet, the other became watery with anxiety.

"What it boils down to, old man, is this," he said, sneering at himself. "Half the village at the surgery door thinking they're going to die because they've cut their fingers, and threatening to write to the Ministry of Health because you won't issue free crutches and corsets. The usual thing. The day's work, eh? All in it. Forget it. The important thing is this."

"Yes?" I said.

"I'm telling you." He sharpened. "The only people who count here are fifteen families: the private patients. That's where the living is. I've been here most of my life and I've made quite a nice thing out of it. I don't want it spoiled. They're the people to watch. I get a call from them—I go at once. I don't want anyone coming in here and ruining it with a lot of new-fangled stuff."

"Frankly," he added, "I can't afford it."

The doctor stepped back, opened his mouth wide and felt his face in several places.

"I think you're the right sort of chap," he said. "Have another drink? There are only three illnesses in this place—bridge, horses, and marriage—you're not married? Glad to hear it. And there's only one medicine: tact. In any case," he said, "it's August. Everyone's away."

In that month the woods in the small estates seemed to lie under glass. The cottages fluffed like hens in the sun; the large houses had a sedate and waxen gleam. The air seemed to hang, brocaded, from the enormous trees. I drove on my rounds from one tropical garden to the next. Men like cock pheasants drove out of Georgian houses in their shooting brakes; their women's voices went off like the alarm call of game. In the rivers, large, clever trout, living like *rentiers* on their capital, put themselves at the disposal of the highly taxed fishermen on the banks of the beautiful river. There was the warm bread smell of the harvest in the fields and of tweed, roses, and tobacco in the bars. In their houses, most of them built in the eighteenth century, the fifteen families were hidden. There Mrs. Gluck ordered more honeysuckle so that next year it would climb into *every* bedroom; there the Admiral did his jigsaw puzzle and the young Hookhams came down from the week's climb towards the Cabinet in London; two miles off, Lord Fobham, wearing plimsolls, let off a wing of his house at a tremendous rent and spent his evenings stiffening himself with gin in the company of Mr. Calverley, a cultivated alcoholic who often—I was to discover —lost his clothes and had slept, against the will of their owners, in most of the houses round about. Mrs. Luke sat moustached and quietly chewing on her fortune in a house famous for its monkey puzzles. At Upley was the financier Hicks, who had shot the head off the stone pelican on the gate of his drive; in the mill house near the water meadows was Mrs. Scarborough ("Pansy") Flynn, three times divorced, nesting like a moorhen and listening for the voices of men. And then there were the Bassilleros, who brought into the country an odour of Claridges; indeed, his violet complexion gave "Jock" Bassillero's face the surprised appearance of one cut out of a hotel carpet and seen in fluorescent light.

I have conveyed an impression of tropical luxury in my account of this August, but in fact it was the coldest August for many years. We had influenza in the village. The tropical quality came from the fifteen families; at a certain stage, portions of civilization reach a Tahitian condition and are hot enough to be moved to a climate less mild than the English one; indeed, there was a good deal of talk among the fifteen families of emigrating to Jamaica. I found this tropical tendency almost at once. A few days after I had taken over from the doctor, there was a party at the Hickses'.

I heard there had been a party when Mr. Calverley was brought into the surgery. He had a cut on top of his head and was supported by a few friends. Mrs. Bassillero was among them.

"What have you been up to?" I said as I dressed the wound.

Mr. Calverley was wearing no collar and no jacket and smelled strongly of ivy. He had curling black hair and looked gentle, savage, and appealing.

"The gutter fell on him," said one of the women. "Is it deep? Is it all right? Poor Tommy. He was climbing after Pansy Flynn."

The sympathy annoyed Calverley. He knocked the dressing out of my hand, jumped up, and drove his friends back to the door.

"I'll kill you all," he said.

Hicks, the financier, a man who illustrated the Theory of Conspicuous Waste, by the habit of dropping the first letter of many of his

words, said: " 'hut up, Tommy. 'it down. 'ook at Ray, he's making 'ight
of it."

"That's not Ray," someone said. "Ray's on holiday."

" 'ood 'od," said Hicks. " 'an't have quacks here."

I had got Calverley back in the chair.

" 'ight poison us. State 'octor? No?"

Calverley looked up at me with a quiet, intimate, head-hunting
smile.

"I'll kill you," he said to me in a soft and cultivated voice.

Mrs. Bassillero started talking loudly to someone on the other side
of the surgery about the sexual life of a couple called Pip and Dottie.

I found Calverley's tie on my carpet the next morning.

In the next two or three days I heard odds and ends about the
Hickses' party. Calverley had got half-way up the ivy at the side of the
house. Hicks had put his foot through his drawing-room window. One
or two cars were having their wings straightened at the garage and Lady
Fobham, to whom I was called, had been in the lily pond.

And then there was a telephone call from the Bassilleros. I was out
on my rounds and the message followed me from house to house. It
was half past twelve before I got to the Bassilleros'. Mr. Bassillero (the
message said) had had "one of his attacks."

The Bassilleros lived in a house built in 1740. I noticed, as I went
in, paintings of several famous dead horses, a great many medals. With
its white and its gold, the house was a pretty example of the architec-
ture of the period. A Spanish servant let me into a wide hall where a
large naval battle was going on in a gilt frame on the wall opposite the
door. It was a picture filled with impudent little waves, clouds, and sails,
like Mrs. Bassillero's blue-grey curls. She came to me wearing a smart,
sand-coloured version of the county's tweed uniform. She walked with
the artificial jerk of the hips taught to débutantes in her time. One
eyelid was lowered in a little, trained, quarter-wink. She was five feet
high, broad-chinned, thin-limbed, and narrow like a boy.

"I had a message at the surgery . . ." I began. Mrs. Bassillero had
a pretty voice and the seductive, abrupt, bad manners of her generation
which set it off.

"I rang for Ray."

"He's on holiday," I said.

"That's a body blow," she said. "We always have Ray." She stood
there, her violet eyes picking me over, preparing to haggle with me, do
a deal, or ask me what I bet her that she could not get Ray back at once

from the other end of the earth if she wished to.

"You're using Ray's car," she accused me. "He said he'd lend it to me." Mrs. Bassillero put her head on one side to see if this "try on" would succeed.

"It belongs to the practice," I said.

Mrs. Bassillero gave the faintest jerk to her head and one eyebrow moved, as if she were shaking off a very close bullet.

"Hard luck on me," she said.

"I am sorry about Mr. Bassillero," I said. "May I see him? What is the trouble?"

Mrs. Bassillero considered me and hummed. Then again came that jerk of the head, shaking off the bad news: the bad news was myself.

"I rang up to ask Ray to luncheon," she said. "I forgot he's away." And then, doing a deal again: "Will you stay?"

"I was told Mr. Bassillero had had an attack," I said.

"He has," she said. "He's lost his voice again."

"He can't speak," she said. Her direct eyes now were made to mist with skilful appeal.

"I had better look at his throat," I said.

Mrs. Bassillero suddenly laughed like a man.

"If you really want to," she said. "You don't understand. What a bore Ray isn't here! When I say he can't speak, I mean he *won't* speak. We're not on speaking terms. We had a row after the party at the Hickses'. You must stay to luncheon. There's no one to pass the ball. Everyone's away. We always get Ray when my husband's voice goes. You'll stay? Now I will take you to my husband."

She trod out of the room slowly like a cat and I followed her to the door of her husband's study.

"Look at his throat, doctor," she said loudly as she opened the door.

Mr. Bassillero was a short person, too. He was considering his fishing rods and did not look up at once when I came into the room.

"Damn glad you're here, doctor," he said. "Trouble."

"I'm sorry to hear that," I said.

Then Mr. Bassillero looked up and said: "Who are you?"

Tact, I remembered, was the thing. I did not say Mrs. Bassillero had sent for me. Mr. Bassillero had that kind of dark handsomeness which is fixed like a pain to one aspect of a luxurious head. He was only about forty-five, but he seemed to have receded into the loud pattern of his clothes. He was wearing a plum-coloured tweed suit with green lines squared on it, a design that made him nearly invisible in any well-

furnished room. His violet cheeks had been embossed on him twenty-
five years ago. Mr. Bassillero, I was to find out, had undergone a severe
cure for drinking. His cure had left him stupefied. His main occupation
during the day, I soon gathered, was to consider whether he would
change his clothes. He was a man who knew he was dressed for something—but for what escaped his mind.

"I think I shall go in and change," was one of his frequent sentences.
Or "I shall put on my other boots and go down to the village."

Mr. Bassillero was looking at my worn grey suit.

"Mrs. Bassillero has very kindly asked me to luncheon," I said.

"We usually have Ray," said Bassillero. "Always passes the ball.
Understands women. Can cap anything. She," Mr. Bassillero pointed
a neutral finger at the door, "better warn you—has lost her voice. Can't
speak."

"It is damp weather for August," I said.

"Yes, put on a Burberry this morning," Mr. Bassillero agreed. "Cold
enough for a coat. Difficult speaking to someone who doesn't answer,
difficult to keep it up. We've got Spanish servants—never stop."

Mr. Bassillero had talked a lot, but now his supply of words went.
We stared at a silver dog on his desk. We were saved by one of the
Spaniards calling us to luncheon.

We went into a room so high and large that the Bassilleros were like
a pair of mere anemones at the bottom of a tank. I, on the contrary,
had the sensation of growing uncomfortably tall; one of my difficulties
during the meal was a dread that I would shoot up and hit the ceiling.

"If you will ask my husband he will, I am sure, give you something
to drink," Mrs. Bassillero said as we sat down.

"I wonder if I could get you to trouble *her* to pass us down the bread.
Spanish servants always forget something," said Mr. Bassillero.

I had become wired in as a telephone for Mr. and Mrs. Bassillero.
I found myself bobbing in my chair from right to left, collecting one
set of remarks, passing them on, and then collecting and disposing
again. I found myself very soon telling Mr. Bassillero that his wife was
going to London on the evening train, I found myself telling her that
Mr. Bassillero was going to Scotland. Mr. Bassillero told me he had
found "some damn Spanish thing" in his cutlets; Mrs. Bassillero asked
if I had just bought a new motor mower, *would* I allow it to be left
out in the rain, considering the price of things now. I sat trying to make
myself shorter. We had arrived, I thought, at last at a safe topic: the
weather. As I have said, it was a cold August. The Bassilleros had put

on their heating. Mr. Bassillero eased now that we had returned to his favourite, indeed his only, subject.

"Thought of changing my shirt this morning," he said. "Putting on a warmer one. Not a single warm shirt in my drawer."

If the Bassilleros could not speak they could, of course, hear.

"I imagine, doctor, when you can't find a shirt where you are lodging, you go to the linen room or you go to Mrs. Thing?" said Mrs. Bassillero.

Mr. Bassillero asked me if I did not agree that in a properly run house, as my lodgings probably were, there was a place for everything and you did not have to turn the house upside down to get it. Not only that, he said, my Mrs. Thing probably spoke English.

Mr. Bassillero spoke mainly to the salt at his end of the table; Mrs. Bassillero looked at a large picture of a horse called Bendigo, which had won the Jubilee Stakes in the eighties.

Mrs. Bassillero said: "I'm sure you, doctor, speak foreign languages well."

A group of Cupids above my head seemed to be beckoning me up. I fought my way down to the subject of the weather.

"It is clouding over again," I said.

The attempt did not help us.

"In any case," said Mrs. Bassillero, "I'm sure you never change into warm shirts at this time of the year. You wear a light summer overcoat."

"I haven't got one," I said.

"What?" said Mr. Bassillero.

I repeated the sentence to his end of the table.

"Good God," he said.

"Did you lose it?" said Mrs. Bassillero with sharp interest.

"Some fellow pinch it?" asked Mr. Bassillero.

For a moment they were almost united. They even looked at each other for a second, then their glances skidded away.

"No, I just haven't got one," I said.

Mr. Bassillero sank back, like an invalid, into his handsomeness. He looked at me with total unbelief.

"I thought you were going to say," he said bitterly, "some fellow took it. Tom Calverley took mine at the Hickses' on Saturday. I took his. Only thing to do."

"Men are too extraordinary, doctor," said Mrs. Bassillero. "You are no taller than my husband, but I'm sure you wouldn't be such a fool as to come home in Tommy Calverley's overcoat. He's six foot three.

I mean right down to your boots. Polar. I mean, surely you'd pick one your own size. Even after a party."

"Calverley took mine. I took his. Fair's fair," said Bassillero, speaking to me.

"On a cold night," I said.

"Two in the morning," said Bassillero.

"I see you are not on my side, doctor," said Mrs. Bassillero, giving the shake to her grey curls.

"After a party I might come away in mink," I said. I risked a lie: "I once did," I said. I looked hopefully at both of them to see if we were happier now.

Mrs. Bassillero had a gay but humourless manner; a joke about mink was unacceptable.

"What an *odd* thing to do," she said coldly.

I had offended Mr. Bassillero too; he looked at me with distaste. In mixing up men's and women's clothes, I had been sartorially disagreeable. He rang off, so to say, and spoke to himself.

Mrs. Bassillero said to me in her short, crushing style: "I hope you returned the coat."

"Of course," I said.

"Because I do think if one wilfully takes someone else's coat one ought to return it, don't you? Or not? I don't know about men. I mean, there's Tommy Calverley's ridiculous coat hanging up in the cloakroom still. I expect you saw it?"

I don't like being snubbed. "I thought of selling it," I said.

Mr. Bassillero looked up. His colour had become a darker violet.

"Sold it!" exclaimed Mr. Bassilero.

"No," I calmed him. "I was speaking to Mrs. Bassillero about a coat I took."

"Oh," said Mr. Bassillero, "if Tom Calverley's sold my coat . . ."

Mr. Bassillero was unable to go on with this idea. He looked at me suspiciously: it appeared to him I was trying to get him away from the ground on which he was making his stand.

"Took my coat and hadn't the grace to bring it back," he said to me.

Mr. Bassillero became magnetic.

"Daren't," he said. "Daren't bring it back."

There was a long silence at the table. At either end of it the Bassilleros had receded into the events of the Hickses' party. Mr. Bassillero was the first to speak, and his voice seemed to come from three days away.

"Wouldn't pay him either," he said.

He glanced at the window and the sky, looked at his jacket wondering if he would change again.

"Knows what he left in his pocket," he said.

Mrs. Bassillero's head made a small dodge. She got up.

"Shall we have coffee next door?" she said. She walked ahead and opened the door. Bassillero held me back.

"You a married man, doctor?" he said.

"No," I said.

"Neither is Ray," he said.

Mr. Bassillero looked lost, as if by some misfortune he was the only married man in the world.

"Are you coming?" called Mrs. Bassillero.

"Engaged?" said Bassillero, recovering hope.

"No," I said.

Mr. Bassillero thought this over.

"It makes no odds," said Mr. Bassillero. "A fellow takes your coat, eh? You take his? All right. You find your wife's gloves in his pocket. Now what do you do? Where are you, I mean to say—what? You've got a scientific brain—explain it. Eh? See what I mean?"

I passed into the drawing-room, where Mrs. Bassillero's thin legs looked like scissors, and one cutting and racketing knee appeared from under her skirt as she sat pouring the coffee.

"Do sit down, you look so unsteady," said Mrs. Bassillero as I took my coffee. She poured out a cup for her husband and turned her back to him when he took it.

"I *do* think," she said in a gush, turning to me. "I *do* think it's too extraordinary about men. I mean the way they have become humble in the last two hundred years. I mean they used to dress up to please women and to be admired by them; hours doing their hair and their faces. Now it's the other way on. I do think it's sweet of you to give it all up. So self-effacing. I mean you all dress alike, and take each other's clothes."

She paused. Not only her face, but the hard-headed knee seemed to be advancing at me. The dealer's voice in her suddenly came out.

"After a couple of martinis, when you've got one eye on the man who is making a pass at you and the other ripping around for somewhere to put your gloves, one has no idea which coat is which. You stick them anywhere. They all look alike. One might be married to anybody."

When she said this, Mrs. Bassillero's pleasant violet eye gave its trained quarter-wink.

"That, at any rate, is the story you've got to sell for me to Mr. Bassillero," she appeared to be signalling.

I saw that this was the crisis; this was where Ray, having "passed the ball" for half an hour, would now rise to the occasion and administer his medicine. What would he do? Would he distract Mr. Bassillero with some anecdote about a tailor, a horse, or a fish; or entangle Mrs. Bassillero in some social crossword puzzle about the first Fobham marriage? To show how unsuited my mind was to the situation—I tried, as they say, to get at the facts and to reconstruct the incident. I got back to the scene in my surgery on the night of the Hickses' party. Who was there? What were they wearing? I went over the people one by one and then I saw Calverley sitting in my chair.

"Good heavens," I said. "I've just remembered something. You know when Calverley came to my surgery that night, he wasn't wearing an overcoat. Actually, he hadn't even got a jacket on."

I didn't know what Mrs. Bassillero's relations with Mr. Calverley were; but Mrs. Bassillero's startled eyes suddenly stared into a scene that neither Mr. Bassillero nor I knew about; she was too taken aback to wink.

"I see," she said. "You mean he hadn't taken my husband's coat at all?"

"Or," I said, making it worse, "he'd probably left it somewhere."

She looked at me scientifically in a way that suggested that I was the kind of man who couldn't keep his mouth shut even if it were stitched. Then she gave the small flick of her head and, turning to her husband, she spoke to him directly for the first time.

"That is why he hasn't brought it back," she said. "It's at Pansy Flynn's. . . ."

Into that name Mrs. Bassillero might have been pouring machine-gun fire.

"Not the first time your coat has been there, my dear," she followed up. "It probably walked there by itself, it knows the way."

The astonishment in Mr. Bassillero's face was chiefly that of a man who finds himself, through no fault of his own, suddenly on speaking terms with his wife again. He could not believe it. Then he slowly saw the innuendo. He appeared to be about to shoot back at his wife— indeed, his arms moved nervously; I suppose he felt he was not dressed in the right clothes for uttering a domestic sarcasm, for all he did was suddenly to pull down his two waistcoat ends with a force that made his collar stand out.

And then I had the only sensible idea that occurred to me during the luncheon party.

"I'm passing there"—I did not say where—"on my way to the surgery. I will pick up your coat for you, Mr. Bassillero. In fact, if you like to give me Mr. Calverley's, I will make the exchange. I'll drop yours in for you this evening."

I looked from one Bassillero to the other and I saw that, having done my worst, I was beginning to triumph. I saw the embarrassment of two people who are about to lose the object of a very satisfying quarrel. Reluctantly Mr. Bassillero saw his grievance go; suspiciously Mrs. Bassillero considered the peace. Presently they fell into an argument about who was going to London and who to Scotland and when. It ended where so many of the discussions of the Bassilleros' must have done on the central situation of their marriage; that Mr. Bassillero couldn't go to Scotland—indeed, anywhere else—until he could freely decide which coat to wear, and that Mrs. Bassillero never made up her mind until she saw what he was doing first.

It is pleasant to do good to people. As I put Calverley's coat in the car and drove off from the Bassilleros', I felt that Dr. Ray would congratulate me. I had been a telephone for the Bassilleros, I had been the catalyst, I had administered "the only medicine." Calverley's coat, like Calverley disembodied, sagged beside me on the seat. Long, a dim, grey herringbone cloth, it was not in fresh condition. The collar was greasy, there were the spots of Calverley's personal life on it; it was worn at the pockets and the second button hung loose. It had been left in so many places; it had been returned by so many hands; it had hung on so many alien hooks. It probably smelled of whisky. As it lounged there in its creases, I could imagine Calverley's head sticking out of the collar, the face with the gentle eyes, the violent mouth, and the head-hunting smile. An ordinary stretch of herringbone tweed, with its tradition of decorum, can never before have conveyed such sensations of rampage and free will, though now it lay sly, slothful—conceivably, I fancied, in remorse.

I drove for a couple of miles through the long settled greenery of this part of the country. It was the time of the year when the chestnut leaves are dark and drying. I had no intention of stirring up a mare's nest at Mrs. Flynn's, but went to Calverley's house. He lived in a small white lodge, a pretty, even arty place with a peacock cut out of the yew hedge.

I got out, picked up the coat, and knocked at the door and listened to the bees humming under the windows as I waited. A cottage woman who said she came in to clean and cook for Mr. Calverley opened to me.

"I have brought back Mr. Calverley's coat," I said. "I believe he and Mr. Bassillero took the wrong ones the other day."

The cottage woman took the coat in the guarded way of one who had been taking in the discarded clothes of Mr. Calverley from all kinds of undesirable people for many years.

"Where is the jacket?" she said. "He had a jacket."

"I don't think they swapped jackets," I said. "Perhaps I could take Mr. Bassillero's coat back, if you know where it is."

The cottage woman became a defender of private property.

"Mr. Calverley's gone to London," she said.

She had stepped back to hang the coat up in the little hall of the house and I followed her in.

"He didn't say anything to me about a coat," the woman said.

"Isn't it hanging up there?" I said.

"There's nothing there," she said, pointing to the mackintoshes and jackets hanging on the pegs. There was, I saw at once, a short grey herringbone coat hanging among them.

"I think I *see* Mr. Bassillero's coat behind the mackintosh," I said, advancing eagerly.

The woman backed towards the peg, made herself swell, and barred the way.

"Oh no," she said, "that is Mr. Calverley's coat."

"Oh—I mean the one behind the mackintosh . . ."

The cottage woman folded her hands on her apron and stuck her elbows out.

"That's his best one," she said. "He only got it three days ago."

"Three days—but that's extraordinary. Are you quite sure?"

"I look after all Mr. Calverley's things. I'm mending it. It's the one," she said, playing her trump card with dignity, "that had the accident."

The woman's cheeks puffed with offence.

"You can see for yourself," she said, stepping scornfully out of the way.

I went to the peg and got the coat off the peg. As I did so, a peculiar thing happened. It divided into two pieces. It had been ripped almost in two from tail to collar. Half of one pocket was hanging off. The woman's face swelled with a purple blush.

"Mr. Calverley had a few friends in and it got torn," she said.

"No buttons either," I said.

The woman did not like my grin.

"Mr. Calverley," she said, "often buys new things and gets dissatisfied. He is very particular about his clothes. He said it was too short on him."

Naturally, Bassillero was the name on the tape.

At the end of the month Dr. Ray came back. My last interview was in some respects like the first. He had a new disguise; he was sunburned. He put his hands in the pockets of his navy-blue jacket, tightening it at the waist; on his head was an imaginary yachting cap; and he swung from side to side in his swivel chair. After hunting, he said, yachting was the finest training for any profession. It taught you not to cross the line before the gun goes off.

"Which is what you did," he said; "you weren't very bright when you let Calverley have his coat back before you got Bassillero's."

"But how could I take that back?" I said. "It was ripped to pieces."

"Did you ever notice Calverley's hands?" said the doctor. "Ever see him on a horse? Or pick up a head waiter by the collar?"

Dr. Ray buzzed for his dispenser, and when the girl came in he asked her to find out whether Mr. Bassillero was still in Scotland. Then, as it were, swinging the tiller over and coming round into the wind, Dr. Ray looked me in the face.

"I think you've made the right decision. Keep out of general practice. Now did you have any other trouble? The Fobhams—all quiet there? No heavy weather? Very odd—perhaps they're away too."

1950

The Landlord

It was due to the boldness of Mrs. Seugar, who always got what she wanted, that they came to live in the semi-detached house called East Wind. They were driving through that part of the town one Sunday. Mrs. Seugar was bouncing on the seat and sighing: "Snobby district. I like it snobby, refined, a bit of class." And her little eyes, like caterpillars' heads, began eating up everything they passed until she saw East Wind. The adjoining house was called West Wind. "Oh stop!" she called out. "Look—posh! That's the house I want. You could live in a house like that. I mean, be one of the toffs and look down your nose at everyone. I don't mean anything nasty. Get out and see if they'll sell it."

Wherever Mrs. Seugar moved, a spotlight played on her; but Mr. Seugar lived in a deep, damp-eyed shade of shame, the shame of always obliging someone. Unable to step out of it, he had shuffled a lot of money out of his shop into his pocket and piled it on to Mrs. Seugar, who stood out in the spotlight seeing that she was taken notice of. Mr. and Mrs. Seugar left the car, went to the house, and were asked in by the man who was to be their landlord. He was having tea in a shabby room, with pictures and books, a very tall man with nothing to remark about him except that as the Seugars advanced he retreated, slipped back like a fish with eyes like lamps and with a coarse little open mouth.

Mrs. Seugar sat herself down and let her legs fall open like a pair of doors.

"I have set my heart on your house. Oh, it's posh, cute," she said. "Isn't it? Haven't I?" Mr. Seugar with his knees together confirmed it.

"Would you sell it to us?" Mrs. Seugar said.

The landlord poured them out two cups of tea and slipped back into the corner watching them as if he were having a dream of being robbed. (In the end, it was he who robbed them. A scholar and gentleman, he asked a tremendous price: Mrs. Seugar was knobbed with jewellery.) But first of all he put them off. They could have, not this house, but the one next door, he said.

"I own both."

"Who lives next door?" said Mrs. Seugar. "Ask him who lives next door. Why should *I* talk—oh, it's so posh," she said, elbowing her husband. "You make me wear out my voice."

"Who . . ." began Mr. Seugar.

"No one," said the landlord.

"Then you can move in next door and we can move in here," cried Mrs. Seugar. "What did I say? Would you believe it—I said to my husband: 'That's the house I want, go and ask,' but he wouldn't. He makes objections to everything—well, I call it daft to make objections all the time. It makes people look down on me for marrying him. I don't mean anything nasty."

The shadow of shame came down like a dark shop blind over Mr. Seugar, and indeed that is where his mind was—in his shop. In half an hour the landlord was showing them round the house, Mr. Seugar following them like a sin, giving a glance into every room after the other two had gone on, being called forward for lagging behind. When the visit was done, Mr. Seugar bought the house, wiping his feet up and down on the carpet as he did so, crying inside himself at the tremendous price, and bewildered because, in buying something that could not be wrapped up in paper and slipped into his overcoat pocket, he felt exposed.

When they got home and shut their door, Mrs. Seugar began to shout everything she said. He was snobby (the landlord); it was a pleasure to hear him talk the way the snobs talk, la-di-da. It was lovely; but if you haven't the cash it doesn't help you being a snob. She felt at ease having someone to look down on straight away.

"He's a recluse," said Mr. Seugar.

"He isn't," shouted Mrs. Seugar, grabbing him back from her husband. "He never stopped staring at me. I could have died," shouted Mrs. Seugar. "Fancy him letting us have the house like that, no questions. It's barmy. Funny thing him living in that house all his life—he must have got pig-sick of it—and me killing myself to have it, it shows what I say, you never know. You say I'm mad."

At the end of the month Mrs. Seugar led her furniture into East Wind, and when it was all in, Mr. Seugar followed it like a mourner. They settled in and Mrs. Seugar sat there with her legs wide open and her shoes kicked off, going through the names of all the people she was going to look down her nose at. "Listen," said Mr. Seugar from the shade. No shop bell to call them, no one popping in from down the street; they were hearing the only sound in their lives: the landlord poking his fire in the house next door.

"Talk!" said his wife to him. "But for me you wouldn't be here, say something. Not business. Talk. Talk snobby. Oh," sighed Mrs. Seugar, "I bet you talk in the shop. I've got everything on," she said, having a look at her gold watch, her diamond brooch, and so on, "and I feel a fool, you sitting with your trap closed. A snob would talk."

At that moment they both started. The front door was being opened, shoes were being wiped on the mat, there were steps in the hall.

"What's that?" said Mr. Seugar.

"Burglars, I'd welcome it," said Mrs. Seugar.

Mr. Seugar went out and met their landlord walking down the hall. He was just putting a key into his pocket. He was surprised by Mr. Seugar, murmured something, walked on, and then was stopped by the sight of their stair carpet. Murmuring again, he flicked like a fish sideways into the sitting-room, looked at Mrs. Seugar in a lost way, and then sat down.

"I've been for a walk," he said.

"A constitootional," said Mr. Seugar.

"Shut up, Henry," said Mrs. Seugar, "until remarks are addressed to you."

The landlord looked round the room where his pictures and his books had been and then glanced at the Seugars.

"Dreadfully late," he said suddenly, went to the window, which was a low one, opened it, and stepped over the sill. Once over, he walked down the garden into his own garden next door.

"Dreadfully, awfully, frightfully—late," Mrs. Seugar was repeating in ecstasy.

Mr. Seugar came out of his shame. "Blimey. See that? Forgot he's moved! He's still got the key."

A terrible quarrel broke out between the Seugars. That was a call, Mrs. Seugar said. No, it wasn't, said Mr. Seugar, it was a mistake. Mr. Seugar was so ill-bred he hadn't realized it was a call, but must pass remarks. If a visitor says "walk" you don't say "constitootional" afterwards, correcting him. Why repeat? It's daft. Not only that, he came to see her, not Mr. Seugar. A man, Mrs. Seugar said, was what she wanted, her ideal, who talked soft and gave you a good time, a lovely man, not the fairy prince and all that twaddle, but a recluse who could fascinate you and give you things.

"Out of mean spite you gave him the bird," she said to Mr. Seugar. Mr. Seugar did not know what to do. At last he got a spade and went out to the garden to dig.

The next day just as lunch was put on the table, in came the landlord, walked straight into the dining-room, ahead of Mr. Seugar, sat down in Mr. Seugar's place before the joint, and started to carve.

"Henry!" Mrs. Seugar warned her husband.

Mr. Seugar said nothing. Their landlord handed them their plates and then rang the bell for an extra one. Mrs. Seugar talked about her summer holiday. People were stand-offish there, she said, and she couldn't get a corset.

"I apologize for the beef," said the landlord.

Mrs. Seugar kicked Mr. Seugar under the table.

"D'you believe millions now living will never die?" asked Mrs. Seugar to keep conversation going. "I mean they'll live, not pass out. It sounds daft. We had a circular. We put up a notice saying: No Hawkers. No Circulars; but that doesn't stop some people. Not never die, they must be fools to think that, what some people's minds get on, they must be empty. I want a bit of life. I'm not morbid."

"Millions now living?" said the landlord. "Will never die?"

"I'm surprised," said Mrs. Seugar, "they are allowed to give out circulars like that in a neighbourhood like this."

"I am sorry, I do apologize for the sweet," said the landlord. "It is my fault. I am awfully thoughtless. I will make a confession."

"A confession. Oh!" cried Mrs. Seugar, clapping her hands.

"It is terrible," said the landlord. It was one of his longest speeches. "I forgot I asked you to lunch."

"Henry," said Mrs. Seugar. "Close your mouth, we don't want to see what you've eaten."

Presently the landlord looked at the pattern on the plates, then at the table, then at the walls. He got up and, murmuring, went suddenly out.

"You can see what has happened," said Mrs. Seugar.

"What I said yes'day, day before," said Mr. Seugar.

They sat there dwindling at the table, terrified.

"He's barmy," said Mr. Seugar humbly—the customer is always right. "He's forgot he's moved. Like people who order the same groceries twice."

"Father," said Mrs. Seugar—she always called him Father when she was accusing him: he had failed in this respect. "Ever since we've been up here you've shown you're not used to it. Why didn't you tell me you asked him in for a bite?"

"Who carved the joint? Am I barmy or is he?" said Mr. Seugar.

"I was glad for him to carve. It used to be his house. I have manners if some people haven't," said Mrs. Seugar.

Mr. Seugar began one of his long, low, ashamed laughs, a laugh so common that Mrs. Seugar said he could keep that for the next time. Mr. Seugar stopped suddenly and kept it for that. He had kept so many things for the next time in his life that they got stale.

"If any person calls to be laughed at, it's you, Father," said Mrs. Seugar. Mr. Seugar waited till she went out of the room and then did a small dance, which he stopped in alarm when he caught sight of himself in the mirror. A blush darkened his face and he went out to dig in the garden. Later his wife brought out a cap for him to wear; she didn't, she said, like to see a man digging without his cap.

If they had had a cat or a dog, Mrs. Seugar said, it would have been just the same; why make a difference when it was a human being who came in at the front door, said a word or two in the sitting-room, and went out by the window? For all the time she was left alone, Mrs. Seugar said, it was company.

"It's a man," said Mrs. Seugar.

"What's he say?" said Mr. Seugar.

"It isn't what he says," Mrs. Seugar said. "With those snobby ones it is the way they say it, it's what d'you call it, that pansy drawl. I love it. He likes to hear me talk."

"Oh," said Mr. Seugar.

"Yes," said Mrs. Seugar. "Why?"

"I just said 'Oh,' " said Mr. Seugar. "I'll try the window myself."

And copying the landlord, Mr. Seugar himself stepped over the sill into the garden to his digging.

"That isn't funny, it's vulgar," called Mrs. Seugar after him.

Mr. Seugar said: "Oh, sorry. No harm," and came back over the sill into the room and went out the proper way to put things right.

One evening the following week he met their landlord coming downstairs fast in his slippers.

Mr. Seugar went into his store-room at the shop on early closing day and sat on a sack of lentils. He was trying to get a few things clear in his mind. "He sold me the house. I bought it. But I hadn't the right to buy it, there was no notice up." Suddenly the truth was clear to him. "I bought *him* as well. He was thrown in. It's like sand in the sugar."

And then the cure occurred to him. Mr. Seugar went home to his wife and said:

"We must arst him in. We've never arst him in. If we arst him he'd see his mistake."

"He never wanted us to have this house," said Mrs. Seugar. Once a month she suffered from remorse. "We oughtn't to have done it. It's a judgement."

"Arst him."

They laid out a table of ham and cake and tea and put a bottle of port wine on the sideboard. Mr. Seugar lit a whiff to make the hall smell and went all over the house to be sure the landlord wasn't there already and then walked up and down there until he arrived. He came at last and gave a long hand to Mr. Seugar.

"I hope you are comfortably settled. I ought to have come before but I have been very busy. I must go and present my apologies to Mrs. S.," said the landlord.

"We have been meaning to ask you a long time," said Mrs. Seugar.

"I go away so often," said the landlord.

"You live next door to people all your life and never see them," said Mrs. Seugar, "yet someone from the other end of the earth you keep running into. How long is it since you've spoken a word to the people in the fish shop next door, Henry?"

"This morning," said Mr. Seugar.

"Don't tell lies," Mrs. Seugar said. "Ten years more like it."

Mrs. Seugar drank a glass of port and went red. An evening of pleasure succeeded. They were celebrating the normality of their landlord.

"Is a woman's life what you call over at forty-five?" asked Mrs.

Seugar. "You work and what is there? You can't settle, you wish you could, but no, you must be up looking out of the window. *You* have settled. You've got your books, you can read. I can't, it's daft, I can't lose myself in something. If I could *lose* myself!"

Their landlord looked at Mr. and Mrs. Seugar and they could see he was appreciating them. Mrs. Seugar's voice went like a lawn-mower running over the same strip of grass, up and down, up and down, catching Mr. Seugar like a stone in the cutters every now and then, and then running on again. They had a long conversation about boiler coke. It turned out that their landlord used anthracite, which did not affect the lungs, and Mr. Seugar said they had paraffin at the shop in his father's time.

There was a pause in the conversation. The landlord looked at the clock and yawned. Presently he knelt down and they thought he was tying his bootlaces; he was untying them. He took his shoes off, then his collar and tie, unbuttoned his waistcoat.

"If you will forgive me," he said, "I'll go to bed now. Don't let me break up the party. I'll just slip off. You know your rooms."

"Sssh," said Mrs. Seugar when he had gone. "Say nothing. Listen."

Mr. and Mrs. Seugar sat like the condemned in their chairs. They heard their landlord go upstairs. They heard him walking in their rooms above. Then evidently he discovered his mistake, for they heard him rush downstairs and out of the house, banging the door after him. The following night Mr. Seugar went up to their bedroom at nine o'clock to get some matches and found their landlord fast asleep, in their bed.

Service was always Mr. Seugar's motto. He bent slightly over the bed, rubbing his hands. "And the next pleasure?" he appeared to say.

Mrs. Seugar came in. When she saw their landlord lying in his shirt, half out of the bedclothes, she made one of her sudden strides forward, squared her chins and her cheeks, and made a grab at her husband's pyjamas, which had been thrown on the bed. At the same time she gave him a punch that sent him through the doorway and threw the pyjamas after him. "Take those things away," she said.

Mr. Seugar was an inhuman man; he was not sorry for himself, but he was sorry for his pyjamas. He picked them up. As he did this, he saw Mrs. Seugar settling into an attitude of repose and heaving her breath into position. From Mr. Seugar's point of view, on the fourth stair outside and on an eye level with his wife's ankles, never had Mrs. Seugar seemed more beautiful; it was as if she were eating something that agreed with her and that other people could not get.

"Where are yours?" whispered Mr. Seugar emotionally.

Mrs. Seugar never answered questions. Now she came out of the room and quietly closed the door. "So refined!" she said. "His mouth was shut."

Mr. Seugar opened his mouth at once. He and Mrs. Seugar had not slept apart for twenty-eight years and, in a voice irrigated by what with him passed for feeling, Mr. Seugar mentioned this fact.

A new contralto voice came from Mrs. Seugar's bosom. "There are times," she said, "when a woman wants to be alone. I'll take the spare room."

And what Mrs. Seugar said she would take, she always took. In the spare room she lay awake half the night going over the past twenty-eight years of her life with a tooth comb. You make your circumstances or they make you, she thought. Which is it?

By "circumstances," she meant, of course, Mr. Seugar, who lay on the living-room sofa frivolously listening to the varying notes of the springs. An extraordinary dream came to him that night. He dreamed that thieves had removed the ham-and-bacon counter from his shop. At six o'clock he woke up, put on an overcoat, and went up to what was, after all, his bedroom. The landlord had gone. Mr. Seugar put his hand under one of the pillows and pulled out his wife's nightdress and threw it into the corner with his pyjamas when he had taken them off. Unfairness was what he hated.

"If I had had a different life," said Mrs. Seugar to her friends, "things would have been different for me. I sacrificed myself, but when you're young you don't know what you're doing. I don't mean anything nasty against Father, he's done what he could, it's wonderful, considering . . ."

Mr. Seugar went out and played bowls when the shop was closed. He pitched the ball down the green, watching it as it rolled, and when it stopped he called out: "How does that smell?"

The fishmonger at the other end called back: "Strong."

But what Mr. Seugar was really thinking as he pitched the ball was: "I lay he's in the kitchen making tea." Or "I lay a pound he's having a bath." Or "What you bet he's gone to bed?" Mr. Seugar was a betting man by nature. He would bet anyone anything, only they did not know he was doing so. "It's a mug's game," Mr. Seugar said, knowing that he was a mug. He did not bet only on the bowling green; he betted while he was digging in the garden, turning round suddenly and looking at the windows of both houses to see if anything had happened while

his back was turned. A starling on the chimney would give him a start
and he would stick the spade in the ground and go inside to see what
had happened. One day when he thought he had betted on everything
his landlord could possibly do, he met him upstairs on the landing of
the house.

"Are you looking for someone?" said Mr. Seugar, leaning forward
over an imaginary counter as he spoke.

"Yes," said the landlord and walked on, disregarding Mr. Seugar as
he always did, like a customer moving on to the next counter.

"My wife," said Mr. Seugar, always one to oblige, "is in the sitting-
room."

The landlord stopped and considered Mr. Seugar with astonishment.

"*Your* wife!" he said.

"Oh," screamed Mr. Seugar—the scream was inside him, in his soul,
and was not audible. "Oh," he screamed. "The deception. I never
thought of that."

He saw how he had been diddled. He went out into the garden and
dug, dug, dug. Worm after worm turned in the damp soil. "I am mad,"
said Mr. Seugar. Mr. Seugar dropped his spade and, pulling out his key,
he opened his mouth, put on a fish-like expression, and went round to
his landlord's house. He let himself in. Out of the study came the
landlord.

"Good morning," said the landlord.

Mr. Seugar did not answer, but marched up the stairs and had a bath.
After that he came down to the study. His landlord had gone, but Mr.
Seugar sat there in front of the fire. Then, in order to annoy them next
door, poked the fire.

1948

The Ladder

"We had the builders in at the time," my father says in his accurate way, if he ever mentions his second marriage, the one that so quickly went wrong. "And," he says, clearing a small apology from his throat as though preparing to say something immodest, "we happened to be without stairs."

It is true. I remember that summer. I was fifteen years old. I came home from school at the end of the term, and when I got to our place not only had my mother gone but the stairs had gone too. There was no staircase in the house.

We lived in an old crab-coloured cottage, with long windows under the eaves that looked like eyes half-closed against the sun. Now when I got out of the car I saw scaffolding over the front door and two heaps of sand and mortar on the crazy paving, which my father asked me not to tread in because it would "make work for Janey." (This was the name of his second wife.) I went inside. Imagine my astonishment. The little hall had vanished, the ceiling had gone; you could see up to the roof; the wall on one side had been stripped to the brick, and on the other hung a long curtain of builder's sheets. "Where are the stairs?" I said. "What have you done with the stairs?" I was at the laughing age.

A mild, trim voice spoke above our heads.

"Ah, I know that laugh," the voice said sweetly and archly. There was Miss Richards, or I should say my father's second wife, standing behind a builder's rope on what used to be the landing, which now stuck out precariously without banisters, like the portion of a ship's deck. The floor appeared to have been sawn off. She used to be my father's secretary and I had often seen her in my father's office; but now she had changed. Her fair hair was fluffed out and she wore a fussed and shiny brown dress that was quite unsuitable for the country.

I remember how odd they both looked, she up above and my father down below, and both apologizing to me. The builders had taken the old staircase out two days before, they said, and had promised to put the new one in against the far wall of the room behind the dust sheets before I got back from school. But they had not kept their promise.

"We go up," said my father, cutting his wife short, for she was apologizing too much, "by the ladder."

He pointed. At that moment his wife was stepping to the end of the landing where a short ladder, with a post to hold on to at the top as one stepped on the first rung, sloped eight or nine feet to the ground.

"It's horrible," called my step-mother.

My father and I watched her come down. She came to the post and turned round, not sure whether she ought to come down the ladder frontwards or backwards.

"Back," called my father.

"No, the other hand on the post," he said.

My step-mother blushed fondly and gave him a look of fear. She put one foot on the step and then took her foot back and put the other one there and then pouted. It was only eight feet from the ground: at school we climbed half-way up the gym walls on the bars. I remembered her as a quick and practical woman at the office; she was now, I was sure, playing at being weak and dependent.

"My hands," she said, looking at the dust on her fingers as she grasped the top step.

My father and I stopped where we were and watched her. She put one leg out too high, as if, artlessly, to show the leg first. She was a plain woman and her legs (she used to say) were her "nicest thing." This was the only coquetry she had. She looked like one of those insects that try the air around them with their feelers before they move. I was surprised that my father (who had always been so polite and grave-mannered to my mother, and had almost bowed to me when he had met me at the station and helped me in and out of the car) did not go to help her. I saw an expression of obstinacy on his face.

"You're at the bottom," he said. "Only two more steps."

"Oh dear," said my step-mother, at last getting off the last step on to the floor; and she turned with her small chin raised, offering us her helplessness for admiration. She came to me and kissed me and said:

"Doesn't she look lovely? You are growing into a woman."

"Nonsense," said my father. And, in fear of being a woman and yet pleased by what she said, I took my father's arm.

"Is that what we have to do? Is that how we get to bed?" I said.

"It's only until Monday," my father said again.

They both of them looked ashamed, as though by having the stairs removed they had done something foolish. My father tried to conceal this by an air of modest importance. They seemed a very modest couple. Both of them looked shorter to me since their marriage: I was very shocked by this. *She* seemed to have made him shorter. I had always thought of my father as a dark, vain, terse man, very logical and never giving in to anyone. He seemed much less important now his secretary was in the house.

"It is easy," I said, and I went to the ladder and was up it in a moment.

"Mind," called my step-mother.

But in a moment I was down again, laughing. When I was coming down I heard my step-mother say quietly to my father, "What legs! She is growing."

My legs and my laugh: I did not think that my father's secretary had the right to say anything about me. She was not my mother.

After this my father took me round the house. I looked behind me once or twice as I walked. On one of my shoes was some of the sand he had warned me about. I don't know how it got on my shoes. It was funny seeing this one sandy footmark making work for Janey wherever I went.

My father took me through the dust curtains into the dining-room and then to the far wall where the staircase was going to be.

"Why have you done it?" I said.

He and I were alone.

"The house has wanted it for years," he said. "It ought to have been done years ago."

I did not say anything. When my mother was here, she was always complaining about the house, saying it was poky, barbarous—I can hear her voice now saying "barbarous" as if it were the name of some terrifying and savage Queen—and my father had always refused to alter anything. Barbarous: I used to think of that word as my mother's name.

"Does Janey like it?" I said.

My father hardened at this question. He seemed to be saying, "What has it got to do with Janey?" But what he said was—and he spoke with amusement, with a look of quiet scorn:

"She liked it as it was."

"I did too," I said.

I then saw—but no, I did not really understand this at the time; it is something I understand now I am older—that my father was not altering the house for Janey's sake. She hated the whole place because my mother had been there, but was too tired by her earlier life in his office, fifteen years of it, too unsure of herself, to say anything. My father was making an act of amends to my mother. He was punishing Janey by "getting in builders" and making everyone uncomfortable and miserable; he was making an emotional scene with himself. He was annoying Janey with what my mother had so maddeningly wanted and which he would not give her.

After he had shown me the house, I said I would go and see Janey getting lunch ready.

"I shouldn't do that," said my father. "It will delay her. Lunch is just ready.

"Or should be," he said, looking at his watch.

We went to the sitting-room, and while we waited I sat in the green chair and he asked me questions about school and we went on to talk about the holidays. But when I answered I could see he was not listening to me but trying to catch sounds of Janey moving in the kitchen. Occasionally there were sounds: something gave an explosive fizz in a hot pan, and a saucepan lid fell. This made a loud noise and the lid spun a long time on the stone floor. The sound stopped our talk.

"Janey is not used to the kitchen," said my father.

I smiled very close to my lips, I did not want my father to see it, but he looked at me and he smiled by accident too. There was understanding between us.

"I will go and see," I said.

He raised his hand to stop me, but I went.

It was natural. For fifteen years Janey had been my father's secretary. She had worked in an office. I remember when I went there when I was young she used to come into the room with an earnest air, leaning her head a little sideways and turning three-quarter-face to my father at his desk, leaning forward to guess at what he wanted. I admired the great knowledge she had of his affairs, the way she carried letters, how quickly she picked up the telephone if it rang, the authority of her voice. Her strength was that she had been impersonal. She had lost that strength in her marriage. As his wife, she had no behaviour. When we were talking she raised her low bosom, which had become round and duck-like, with a sigh and smiled at my father with a tentative, expectant fondness. After fifteen years, a life had ended: she was resting.

But Janey had not lost her office behaviour: that she now kept for the kitchen. The moment I went to the kitchen, I saw her walking to the stove where the saucepans were throbbing too hard. She was walking exactly as she had walked towards my father at his desk. The stove had taken my father's place. She went up to it with impersonal enquiry, as if to anticipate what it wanted, she appeared to be offering a pile of plates to be warmed as if they were a pile of letters. She seemed baffled because the stove could not speak. When one of the saucepans boiled over she ran to it and lifted it off, suddenly and too high, with her telephone movement: the water spilled at once. On the table beside the stove were basins and pans she was using, and she had them all spread out in an orderly way like typing; she went from one to the other with the careful look of enquiry she used to give to the things she was filing. It was not a method suitable to work in a kitchen.

When I came in, she put down the pan she was holding and stopped everything—as she would have done in the office—to talk to me about what she was doing. She was very nice about my hair, which I had had cut last term; it made me look older and I liked it better. But blue smoke rose behind her as we talked. She did not notice it.

I went back to my father.

"I didn't want to be in the way," I said.

"Extraordinary," he said, looking at his watch. "I must just go and hurry Janey up."

He was astonished that a woman so brisk in an office should be languid and dependent in a house.

"She is just bringing it in," I said. "The potatoes are ready. They are on the table. I saw them."

"On the table?" he said. "Getting cold?"

"On the kitchen table," I said.

"That doesn't prevent them being cold," he said. My father was a sarcastic man.

I walked about the room humming. My father's exasperation did not last; it gave way to a new thing in his voice. Resignation.

"We will wait if you do not mind," he said to me. "Janey is slow. And by the way," he said, lowering his voice a little, "I shouldn't mention we passed the Leonards in the road when I brought you up from the station."

I was surprised.

"Not the Leonards?" I said.

"They were friends of your mother's," he said. "You are old enough to understand. One has to be sometimes a little tactful. Janey sometimes feels . . ."

I looked at my father. He had altered in many ways. When he gave me this secret his small, brown eyes gave a brilliant flash and I opened my blue eyes very wide to receive it. He had changed. His rough black hair was clipped closer at the ears and he had that too young look which middle-aged men sometimes have, for by certain lines it can be seen that they are not as young as their faces. Marks like the minutes on the face of a clock showed at the corners of his eyes, his nose, his mouth; he was much thinner; his face had hardened. He had often been angry and sarcastic, sulking and abrupt, when my mother was with us; I had never seen him before, as he was now, blank-faced, ironical and set in impatient boredom. After he spoke, he had actually been hissing a tune privately through his teeth at the corner of his mouth. At this moment Janey came in with a smile but without dishes, and said lunch was ready.

"Oh," I laughed when we got into the dining-room. "It is like . . . it is like France."

"France?" they both said together, smiling at me.

"Like when we all went to France before the war and you took the car," I said. I had chosen France because that seemed as far as I could get from the Leonards.

"What on earth are you talking about?" said my father, looking embarrassed. "You were only five before the war."

"I remember every bit of it. You and Mummy on the boat."

"Yes, yes," said my step-mother with melancholy importance. "I got the tickets for you all."

My father looked as though he was going to hit me. Then he gave a tolerant laugh across the table to my step-mother.

"I remember perfectly well," she said. "I'm afraid I couldn't get the peas to boil. Oh, I've forgotten the potatoes."

"Fetch them," my father said to me.

I thought she was going to cry. When I came back, I could see she *had* been crying. She was one of those very fair women in whom even three or four tears bring pink to the nose. My father had said something sharply to her, for his face was shut and hard and she was leaning over the dishes, a spoon in her hand, to conceal a wound.

After lunch I took my case and went up the ladder. It was not easy to go up carrying a suitcase, but I enjoyed it. I wished we could always have a ladder in the house. It was like being on a ship. I stood at the top thinking of my mother leaning on the rail of the ship with her new husband, going to America. I was glad she had gone because, sometimes, she sent me lovely things.

Then I went to my room and I unpacked my case. At the bottom, when I took my pyjamas out—they were the last thing—there was the photograph of my mother face downwards where it had been lying all the term. I forgot to say that I had been in trouble the last week at school. I don't know why. I was longing to be home. I felt I had to *do* something. One afternoon I went into the rooms in our passage when no one was there, and I put the snap of Kitty's father into Mary's room—I took it out of the frame—and I put Mary's brother into Olga's, and I took Maeve's mother and put her into the silver frame where Jessie's mother was: that photograph was too big and I bent the mount all the way down to get it in. Maeve cried and reported me to Miss Compton. "It was only a joke," I said. "A joke in very poor taste," Miss Compton said to me in *her* voice. "How would you like it if anyone took the photograph of your mother?" "I haven't got one," I said. Well, it was not a lie. Everyone wanted to know why I had an empty frame on my chest of drawers. I had punished my mother by leaving her photograph in my trunk.

But now the punishment was over. I took out her picture and put it in the frame on my chest, and every time I bent up from the drawers I looked at her, then at myself in the mirror. In the middle of this my step-mother came in to ask if she could help me.

"You are getting very pretty," she said. I hated her for admiring me.

I do not deny it: I hated her. She was a foolish woman. She either behaved as if the house, my father and myself were too much hers, or as if she were an outsider. Most of the time she sat there like a visitor, waiting for attention.

I thought to myself: There is my mother, thousands of miles away, leaving us to this and treating us like dirt, and we are left with Miss Richards, of all people.

That night after I had gone to bed I heard my father and my

step-mother having a quarrel. "It is perfectly natural," I heard my father say, "for the child to have a photograph of her mother."

A door closed. Someone was wandering about in the passage. When they had gone I opened my door and crept out barefoot to listen. Every step I made seemed to start a loud creak in the boards and I was so concerned with this that I did not notice I had walked to the edge of the landing. The rope was there, but in the dark I could not see it. I knew I was on the edge of the drop into the hall and that with one more step I would have gone through. I went back to my room, feeling sick. And then the thought struck me—and I could not get it out of my head all night; I dreamed it, I tried not to dream it, I turned on the light, but I dreamed it again—that Miss Richards fell over the edge of the landing. I was very glad when the morning came.

The moment I was downstairs I laughed at myself. The drop was only eight or nine feet. Anyone could jump it. I worked out how I would land on my feet if I were to jump there. I moved the ladder, it was not heavy to lift, to see what you would feel like if there were no ladder there and the house was on fire and you had to jump. To make amends for my wicked dreams in the night I saw myself rescuing Miss Richards (I should say my step-mother) as flames teased her to the edge.

My father came out of his room and saw me standing there.

"What are you pulling such faces for?" he said. And he imitated my expressions.

"I was thinking," I said, "of Miss Compton at our school."

He had not foreseen the change in Miss Richards; how she would sit in the house in her best clothes, like a visitor, expectant, forgetful, stunned by leisure, watchful, wronged and jealous to the point of tears.

Perhaps if the builders had come, as they had promised, on the Monday, my step-mother's story would have been different.

"I am so sorry we are in such a mess," she said to me many times, as if she thought I regarded the ladder as her failure.

"It's fun," I said. "It's like being on a ship."

"You keep on saying that," my step-mother said, looking at me in a very worried way, as if trying to work out the hidden meaning of my remark. "You've never been on a ship."

"To France," I said. "When I was a child."

"Oh yes, you told me," said my step-mother.

Life had become so dull for my father that he liked having the ladder in the house.

"I hate it," said my step-mother to both of us, getting up. It is always surprising when a prosaic person becomes angry.

"Do leave us alone," my father said.

There was a small scene after this. My father did not mean by "us" himself and me, as she chose to think; he was simply speaking of himself, and he had spoken very mildly. My step-mother marched out of the room. Presently we heard her upstairs. She must have been very upset to have faced going up the ladder.

"Come on," said my father. "I suppose there's nothing for it. I'll get the car out. We will go to the builder's."

He called up to her that we were going.

Oh, it was a terrible holiday. When I grew up and was myself married, my father said: "It was a very difficult summer. You didn't realize. You were only a schoolgirl. It was a mistake." And then he corrected himself. I mean that: my father was always making himself more correct: it was his chief vanity that he understood his own behaviour.

"I happened," he said—this was the correction—"to make a very foolish mistake." Whenever he used the phrase "I happened" my father's face seemed to dry up and become distant: he was congratulating himself. Not on the mistake, of course, but on being the first to put his finger on it. "I happen to know . . . I happen to have seen . . ."—it was this incidental rightness, the footnote of inside knowledge on innumerable minor issues, and his fatal wrongness in a large, obstinate, principled way about anything important, which, I think, made my beautiful and dishonest mother leave him. She was a tall woman, taller than he, with the eyes of a cat, shrugging her shoulders, curving her long graceful back to be stroked and with a wide, champagne laugh. My father had a clipped-back monkeyish appearance and that faint grin of the bounder one sees in the harder-looking monkeys that are without melancholy or sensibility; this had attracted my mother, but very soon his youthful bounce gave place to a kind of meddling honesty, and she found him dull. And, of course, ruthless. The promptness of his second marriage, perhaps, was to teach her a lesson. I imagine him putting his divorce papers away one evening at his office and realizing, when Miss Richards came in to ask if "there is anything more to-night," that there was a woman who was reliable, trained and, like himself, "happened" to have a lot of inside knowledge.

To get out of the house with my father, to be alone with him: my heart came alive. It seemed to me that this house was not my home any more. If only we could go away, he and I; the country outside seemed to me far more like home than this grotesque divorced house. I stood longing for my step-mother not to answer, dreading that she would come down.

My father was not a man to beg a woman to change her mind. He went out to the garage. My fear of her coming made me stay for a moment. And then (I do not know how the thought came into my head) I went to the ladder and I lifted it away. It was easy to move a short distance, but it began to swing when I tried to put it down. I was afraid it would crash, so I turned it over and over against the other wall, out of reach. Breathlessly, I left the house.

"You have got white on your tunic," said my father as we drove off. "What have you been doing?"

"I rubbed against something," I said.

"Oh, how I love motoring," I laughed beside my father.

"Oh, look at those lovely little rabbits," I said.

"Their little white tails," I laughed.

We passed some hurdles in a field.

"Jumps," I laughed. "I wish I had a pony."

And then my terrible dreams came back to me. I was frightened. I tried to think of something else, but I could not. I could only see my step-mother on the edge of the landing. I could only hear her giving a scream and going over head first. We got into the town and I felt sick. We arrived at the builder's and my father stopped there. Only a girl was in the office, and I heard my father say in his coldest voice, "I happen to have an appointment . . ."

My father came out, and we drove off. He was cross.

"Where are we going?" I said, when I saw we were not going home.

"To Longwood," he said. "They're working over there." I thought I would faint.

"I—I . . ." I began.

"What?" my father said.

I could not speak. I began to get red and hot. And then I remembered. "I can pray."

It is seven miles to Longwood. My father was a man who enjoyed talking to builders; he planned and replanned with them, built imaginary houses, talked about people. Builders have a large acquaintance with the way people live; my father liked inside knowledge, as I have said. Well, I thought, she is over. She is dead by now. I saw visits to the hospital. I saw my trial.

"She is like you," said the builder, nodding to me. All my life I shall remember his moustache.

"She is like my wife," said my father. "My first wife. I happen to have married again."

(He liked puzzling and embarrassing people.)

"Do you happen to know a tea place near here?" he said.

"Oh no," I said. "I don't feel hungry."

But we had tea at Gilling. The river is across the road from the tea-shop and we stood afterwards on the bridge. I surprised my father by climbing the parapet.

"If you jumped," I said to my father, "would you hurt?"

"You'd break your legs," said my father.

Her "nicest thing"!

I shall not describe our drive back to the house, but my father did say, "Janey will be worried. We've been nearly three hours. I'll put the car in afterwards."

When we got back, he got out quickly and went down the path. I got out slowly. It is a long path leading across a small lawn, then between two lime trees; there are a few steps down where the roses are, and across another piece of grass you are at the door. I stopped to listen to the bees in the limes, but I could not wait any longer. I went into the house.

There was my step-mother standing on the landing above the hall. Her face was dark red, her eyes were long and violent, her dress was dirty and her hands were black with dust. She had just finished screaming something at my father and her mouth had stayed open after her scream. I thought I could *smell* her anger and her fear the moment I came into the house, but it was really the smell of a burned-out saucepan coming from the kitchen.

"You moved the ladder! Six hours I've been up here. The telephone has been ringing, something has burned on the stove. I might have burned to death. Get me down, get me down. I might have killed myself. Get me down," she cried, and she came to the gap where the ladder ought to have been.

"Don't be silly, Janey," said my father. "I didn't move the ladder. Don't be such a fool. You're still alive."

"Get me down," Janey cried out. "You liar, you liar, you liar. You did move it."

My father lifted the ladder, and as he did so he said:

"The builder must have been."

"No one has been," screamed my step-mother. "I've been alone. Up here!"

"Daddy isn't a liar," I said, taking my father's arm.

"Come down," said my father when he had got the ladder in place. "I'm holding it."

And he went up a step or two towards her.

"No," shrieked Janey, coming to the edge.

"Now, come on. Calm yourself," said my father.

"No, no, I tell you," said Janey.

"All right, you must stay," said my father, and stepped down.

That brought her, of course.

"*I* moved the ladder," I said when she came down.

"Oh," said Janey, swinging her arm to hit me, but she fainted instead.

That night my father came to my room when I was in bed. I had moved my mother's photograph to the bedside table. He was not angry. He was tired out.

"Why did you do it?" he asked.

I did not answer.

"Did you know she was upstairs?" he said.

I did not reply.

"Stop playing with the sheet," he said. "Look at me. Did you know she was upstairs?"

"Yes," I said.

"You little cat," he said.

I smiled.

"It was very wrong," he said.

I smiled. Presently he smiled. I laughed.

"It is nothing to laugh at," he said. And suddenly he could not stop himself: he laughed. The door opened and my step-mother looked in while we were both shaking with laughter. My father laughed as if he were laughing for the first time for many years; his bounderish look, sly and bumptious and so delicious, came back to him. The door closed.

He stopped laughing.

"She might have been killed," he said, severely again.

"No, no, no," I cried, and tears came to my eyes.

He put his arm round me.

My mother was a cat, they said, a wicked woman, leaving us like that. I longed for my mother.

Three days later, I went camping. I apologized to my step-mother and she forgave me. I never saw her again.

The Spanish Bed

Out of the stream of cars with boats on their trailers that drive out from Colchester towards the giddy light of the sea, only one or two will turn off at a fingerpost marked To VILLAS. The drivers find themselves at a small house that until some twenty years ago was the home of John Osorio Grant, the novelist. It is a small place, painted in a fresh grey that gleams in the sun, rather like the silvery mud banks of the estuary when the tide is low, and is really three little villas with pinched bay windows, which Grant knocked into one somewhere about 1912 while living there for forty years with his sister. The house then passed to an enterprising man in the oyster trade who made money in a fashionable restaurant in London and was admired in the village for taking the mean little bays out of the house and putting in two long landscape windows in their place, a man greedy for views. But he tired of the country, as Londoners do, and sold the house to the present occupier, a Dr. Billiter, a retired mining engineer and mineralogist from the North who has lived a wandering working life in Chile, Bolivia and for a long time in Mexico.

The doctor is a big man, overweight, as soft as an elephant, his jacket and trousers hanging on him like a hide. He walks in a creeping way, stooping as very tall men do, as if he were following a scent, often nibbling a biscuit. In the village it is felt to be unnatural for a man of his size to be living alone. "Pure accident" he says has brought him to the village and he waves a heavy arm to give himself the careless, even frivolous air of a balloon that has slipped its mooring and taken off into the sky. What he means is that there are "pure" accidents and "vulgar" accidents; the pure accidents occur only to a scientific mind which has been long-headedly prepared for them.

He had been reading the novels of John Osorio Grant over and over again as a recreation in the lonely evenings of a life on mining sites where one gets sick of the company around one. A good detective story is like the detective work of mineralogy in a brisker, more relaxing form. His revered, though very trying mother had often kept house for him during long spells of his career and it was on the last of his exasperating trips with her to the silver mines at Guanajuato—where her mania for buying unwanted, picturesque rubbish in Mexican markets was getting on his nerves—that she redeemed herself by an astonishing discovery.

In a pile of rotting paperbacks she spotted a book called *A Visit to the Osorio Mines*. Printed in Mexico City in 1902 and full of misspellings, it was Grant's first book, written when he was nineteen and had been sent out to learn Spanish by his family, who were Osorio's agents in England. A juvenile book of fifty pages, it had never been published anywhere else and was unknown in Grant's list of works. The doctor became, in that instant, a potential bibliophile: he had a treasure.

A second accident occurred—it must be an example of the "impure," for it could happen to any of us—about a year before his retirement, when he was planning to return to England and live in the country with his mother, in one of those English villages that are the scene of Grant's novels: places equipped with a squire, a clergyman, spinsters, a dubious City man, a vigilant postmistress and a house with a panelled library, gleaming with the knowledge and the corpses it had seen. But his dear mother died. Mexico became suddenly empty: he packed and went to comfort himself in his dreamed-of England, but there the emptiness of his dream made him fretful. It was at one of his lowest moments, when he was cheering himself with a dozen oysters in a London restaurant, that he found himself talking to the oysterman who owned Villas. The ghost of Grant suddenly came in to occupy the empty stool beside the doctor at the bar. In the course of a few weeks he ate dozens of oysters and found himself buying Villas, and Grant's ghost came down with him.

The doctor was lonely no more. From that time he talked and hummed to himself, throbbing with the sensation that he was a miracle. It cannot be said that he "heard" Grant telling him to put the place back into the state it had been in *his* time, for there was nothing mystical in the doctor; despite his slothful look, he was a restless, practical man. He was certainly "impelled" to tear out the blatant landscape windows the oysterman had put in, to put back the narrow bay windows so as to darken the house, and to uncover the stone floor that lay under the oysterman's chic parquet, as a beginning. He had always been called "the Doctor" in Mexico because of his distinction in his science; now he felt an exuberant desire for distinction in a new field. He had no friends, but he boldly created the at first imaginary Friends of John Osorio Grant Society. After a year or so they numbered about seven. They wrote to him and one or two called and he slowly got together material for a pamphlet saying that Grant was a shamefully neglected figure in the history of the detective novel, the creator of the famous Detective Inspector Coffin.

As he wrote and rewrote his sentences, a pencil drawing of Grant, which he had found at a bookseller's in Colchester, looked down and seemed to say, "Enough of Inspector Coffin. What about me?" Grant had been eclipsed by his sister, the marvellous gardener and Queen of Flower Shows in local memory, just as the doctor had been dominated by his mother.

In the bluster of a spring morning another example of "pure accident" occurred. The doctor was working in the room he called his "office," which used to be Grant's study, when he heard a loud jangling noise in the bedroom above. Slates blown off? A gutter gone? Water coming through? Burglars? (On this, particularly, he was sensitive. Villas had been burgled after Grant had died.) In the manner of Inspector Coffin, the doctor went up the uncarpeted stairs to his bedroom and caught the village girl who came in to clean, bouncing saucily on the high iron bed, a decorative Spanish object with a tin panel, lacquered in black and yellow triangles at the head, and very loose, which had belonged to Grant and which the doctor had found rusting in a garden shed. Caught out, red as puberty in the face, the girl got off the jangling bed, picked up a broom and pretended to sweep the tiled floor. Shy as he was large, the doctor jerked a big thumb at the room in a general apologetic way, and went away humming.

He wished that the girl's mother still worked for him and had not pushed this impertinent daughter into the job, for she always gaped at his size, which put her into a state of swallowed giggles. But this incident changed her. From that morning she became timorous and propitiating—she was frightened that he would tell her mother. Nervously she watched him. She was all "Yes, Doctor" and "No, Doctor." She brought him apples, she brought him biscuits—he liked nibbling biscuits, for he was a hungry hypochondriac who thought that with the exception of oysters, a square meal made him put on weight. In a week or two she came in with a Christmas card in an envelope with a long-out-of-date stamp on it.

"Very pretty," he said.

"See what it says," she said. "It was in Gran's cardboard box." Gran was long ago dead.

The doctor opened the card and then looked at the girl, who seemed to him suddenly rooted in genius or complicity. Villagers often showed him useless antiques in the hope of turning a penny or merely to show that they knew more about the place than he would ever know. Did the girl know the importance of what she had pilfered? He hoped not. But she had done what no publisher, no library, no Record Office or correspondent had been able to do. The faded ink on the card said: "Love to you, Gran dear, and all your family. Clarissa Ward." And, thank God, there was an address. He had discovered what people in the village either did not know or had forgotten, a detail which he had longed to know ever since he took the house: the address of Grant's widow.

Apart from that boyish visit to Mexico there was only one odd incident in Grant's life. As the doctor used to say lightly to any member of the Society who came to the house, "We know that he returned to England. We know that he settled here with his sister. Then there are two missing years during which, as the records show, he married a Miss Ward. Who she was, what happened to her, no one knows. The marriage lasted two years. She vanished and his sister returned. No one in the village remembers Miss Ward. It looks as though—" he would add roguishly, "as if the two ladies did not get on. Anyway, Miss Ward seems to have been unimportant."

The word "unimportant" was slurred over. As a mineralogist the doctor believes that no fact, however small, is unimportant. Put all the facts together and one gets the whole: think of the hundreds of now precisely known facts about the formation of crystals that explain the unanswerable existence of metals. It irked him as it would have irked Inspector Coffin, that a small fact about Grant eluded him and, as he looked at the card, he already felt the itch for an erotic secret that comes even to amateur biographers.

The doctor did nothing about the card at first, for the picture of Grant rebuked him. On the other hand, Inspector Coffin egged him on. Eventually the inspector won and the doctor sat at his typewriter, writing and rewriting a letter to Miss Ward. With a tact that seemed to him enormous and painful he said nothing about Grant. He simply wrote that he was the owner of Villas and was writing an account of the house because of its unique historic interest. He understood that she had once lived there and he would be grateful if she would consent to see him. When the letter was done, he fell into melancholy. The woman was probably dead. No reply came. After a few weeks he wrote a second letter, enclosing a copy of the first. Still no reply. Hope died. Then it occurred to him to write in his own naked hand: the clumsy personal hand, he had found, often achieved what the machine could not. He came out into the open: he said that in Mexico he had come across a little book written by John Osorio Grant which had never been published in England. He would be delighted to show it to her. This brought a reply at once from a Miss Carter saying that Miss Ward, who was seriously ill, asked her to thank him and to say she received no visitors.

Dr. Billiter rushed from his house and walked down the short rough path to the village, down the street and then up again, his face shining like the face of a euphoric but silent town crier, waving an arm boastfully. "Miss Ward, once the wife of John Osorio Grant, is alive! She exists! No one but myself knows it. You've been hiding this from me but I've found out for myself."

The only question was: Did the child know what she had done? No doubt she had eavesdropped and heard him mention the name to visitors. Still, to be certain, he bought her some sweets in the village shop. She was a hungry child.

More important was the question of the race with death. Miss Ward was old; she was ill. By the end of the week he could stand his torment no more. He set out on the drive across the middle of England to Nottingham and stood on Miss Ward's doorstep.

The house was small and trim—not in the mining or lace-making districts. He rang the bell and a small woman with grey hair pulled back painfully from a bony forehead opened the door. He jerked a thumb at the traffic and people passing in the street as if throwing them and himself away and becoming nothing.

"My name is Billiter—Dr. Billiter," he began. "I have been in correspondence with a Miss Carter . . ."

The woman looked back into the hall of the house and then gazed at him, taking in his size very much in the stupefied way of the village girl at Villas. Then she tried to enlarge herself, and in a grand voice with a tremor in it she said, "We always have Dr. Gates. Why did he send *you*? It's too late. I was telephoning all day yesterday to the hospital and in the end I had to get the ambulance myself. It is a scandal. Miss Carter is in hospital. I am Miss Ward and I shall report the matter to the authorities." At that word the small woman's neck quivered.

"Miss Ward!" cried the doctor. His thick lips parted, his mouth was wet with wonder. For a moment he wanted to pick her up and carry her off, the treasure, ten times more precious than all the silver in Mexico. "But it is *you* I wanted to see," he marvelled.

She pushed her head back and looked up at him with suspicion. He saw this and spoke in his natural voice, which was as soft and polite as the buzzing of a large bee. "Miss Carter wrote to say *you* were ill and I feared—"

Miss Ward addressed the street. "I am not ill," she said. "I'm in very good health."

"I apologize for the intrusion," he said. "I happened to be passing. I am sorry to hear Miss Carter is in hospital. I really came about our correspondence. By the way, I am not a doctor."

"Then why do you call yourself one?" she said.

"Not a medical doctor. I am a mineralogist." He began to fiddle with the zipper of his briefcase. "It's about Villas," he said, appealing to her.

"What villas?" said Miss Ward. "Miss Carter is my secretary. I am not interested in buying villas or anything—"

"No," he said. "Let me explain. It's the name of my house. I am a great admirer of the work of John Osorio Grant and I am working on . . ."

He had by now got his pamphlet and the letters out of his case.

Miss Ward had bold, grey-greenish, salty eyes, and at the name of Grant the lid of her right eye slowly drooped and closed until it looked like a small ivory ball, and the left one like the tip of a pistol. "There's no one of that name here. I do not let rooms," she said. And with that she closed the door in his face. Just before it was completely closed, he heard her say loudly to someone he supposed to be in the hall, "Damn you."

The doctor stared at the red brick of the house. "Glazed midland clay," he muttered, "probably a hundred years old; it never weathers."

It was as implacable as the woman had been. He got back into his car, wagging his head, jerking his thumb at passing cars, humming to himself, "Poor John. Poor John." Privately he always called Grant by his Christian name when he thought of him. John had become part of himself, like a brother.

When he saw the village girl next day he lied to her, unnecessarily. He said, "Yesterday I had to go to London."

One of the small annoyances of receiving visitors at Villas, even members of the Society and especially their wives, is that they are far more interested in the garden than in the house when the summer comes. He is obliged to listen to their botanical comments and hear them say, "She was a wonderful gardener."

The garden has little interest for him: it had meant nothing to John. It was the sister's empire. The doctor is proud of having filled in the oysterman's tiled swimming pool and shows you that the old pond reappeared afterwards from the spring which had fed the vulgar pool That proves a point.

"You remember the pond in *Death Among the Lilies?*" he says.

He leads you back along a brick path. The ladies say it is a pity that the place has "been let go so wild" and crowd around some unusual rose or lily or shrub they have detected. At the end of a brick path they notice two statues—or rather, there are two plinths. On one, a goddess-like figure in graceful robes is placed, rather blotched by lichen in the face and looking ill-used and sulky. On the other plinth there is only a pair of feet. The figure was knocked down by the motor mower of the oysterman's gardener. The odd thing is that visitors often tactfully avert their eyes from the feet and replace the missing statue in their minds.

"Are *they* anyone in particular?" visitors often ask.

This annoys the doctor. He dismisses the figures. No, he says, they are only ornamental. Grant's sister picked up a taste for garden statues in Italy and she bought a pair from Stillbury Manor when the Electricity Board took over the big house. She got them for a pound apiece. It is a small satisfaction to him that here he can refer to a document; he nods to the house and says, "I can show you the receipt inside." Often as he walks around he picks up a stone and throws it into a flower bed. One has the impression that he is throwing it at someone—possibly Grant's sister.

Once he gets people back into the house his eager pride comes back.

He looks down, confiding, into the face of anyone who asks a question. "The last man put parquet floors down in the rooms downstairs," he says. "This is the original stone floor." He has ripped out the modern fireplaces, of course. Furniture, he says, was a difficulty. Grant's sister, they say, had one or two valuable family things—two or three of the smaller pieces had been stolen by burglars who had broken in after John's death. But Grant's taste was for the plain and useful. Chic modern wallpaper has been scraped off. Whitewash returned, good clean whitewash.

You follow the doctor's pachydermic figure. It darkens the passages or the stairs, fussing over what relics he has found and what he is going to find. He jerks a thumb as you pass a chair, a table, a rug or a picture and says "Chair" or "Table" or "Rug," and so on. He is all modesty in his passion for the obvious. Looking out of a window he may say "Garden" or "Bird in apple tree" or "Field" or "Boy kicking football." Outside of his science he has a kind of compassion for facts, hoping they may divulge something privately to him one day.

His most apologetic moment is in Grant's study—no original furniture, but it is redeemed by his collection of Grant's novels and the files and the pencil portrait. Lately he has found out that the dealer has lied to him: the portrait is not of Grant. So the doctor says "Probably Grant" and likes to think that it will somehow turn into Grant's likeness if it is kept long enough. He gets the visitors out of this room quickly to Grant's severe bedroom. This has been perfectly reconstructed. Spanish- or Mexican-looking tiles are back on the floor and there is the Spanish bed—the one the village girl was caught lying on.

After the defeat at Nottingham and when the year climbed into the summer, the doctor took to going to the sailing club, the only place where Grant had not been effaced by his sister, but the sole interest of the raconteurs of that place was how much any figure of the past had drunk or what sort of boat he had had. About this there were arguments: none could remember. To one story he did listen carefully. The tale was that Grant had gone out one afternoon and, in classic fashion, had got stuck in the mud in a falling tide and had had to sit there half the night. They added that a girl was in the boat: this is a common myth in English estuaries. Still—you never know.

Then one day—late in August—the doctor was seen skipping fast to the post office to send a telegram.

Another example of "pure" accident had occurred. He had received a letter with a Nottingham postmark. He studied the envelope and postmark several times before he opened it. It was addressed in a large hand that rushed downhill almost off the envelope. The letter was from Miss Ward. He raced through it, missing most of what it said the first time, and then he read it slowly again. The striking thing was that all the *t*'s were crossed with long lines so that a squall of sleet seemed to be blowing across the page.

"Dear Dr. Billiter," the letter began, "I do not know if you recollect our meeting, the other day . . ."

The other day! It was five months ago!

". . . but I do apologize for the confusion, due to the sad circumstances of my friend's sudden illness."

She went on to say that she would so much like to see the pamphlet about Villas he had mentioned and thought there were many things she remembered about the place, although it was years since she had been there. Would he send her a copy? Or if he were over in Nottingham, she hoped he would call.

Going over the letter once more, the doctor saw it was dated three weeks before the postmark on the envelope. There was a postscript squeezed on to the bottom of the page and the last word had been crowded out:

"I am grieved to say that poor Miss Carter has d—"

Two days after his telegram, not waiting for a reply, the doctor drove to Nottingham yawning with appetite. He finished a packet of biscuits and had to stop to buy a cake before he got once more to Miss Ward's doorstep.

For a few seconds he could not believe he was looking at the same woman. The grey hair was not drawn back but was now loose and blond. She was wearing a violet jacket and bright-pink trousers which showed she had a droll little belly and was plumper and younger. He remembered meagre eyelashes; now they were long. Only the drooping of the right eyelid convinced him she was the same woman. Her shoes had high heels and she had a prowling step as she led him into a pretty room at the back of the little house, and when they sat down he noticed the high-arch shoe. She gazed at him with a doll-like satisfaction and did not listen at all to his explanations and politenesses, waving them away in a chatting fashion. But when he said how sorry he was to hear about her poor friend, her voice changed and she gave a short shake of her head. "Don't speak of it," she said in a reciting voice and choosing her words sadly and carefully: "It was a stroke."

Suddenly she stopped reciting. "So you live at Villas? How extraordinary. How time passes. And you knew *dear* Ossy? Where did you meet? In Mexico?"

"Dear Ossy!" The pet name shocked him. Obviously she had not taken in what he had just told her. "Dear Ossy"—how lightly a husband is thrown away.

"John," he said, staking his claim to the man. "No. I never met him. I found his book—or rather my mother did—as I told you. I was in Mexico long after his time. I've brought the book to show you."

She merely glanced at it and put it on the table. "It's a paperback," she said. "I thought you said it was in leather—valuable."

"Oh, but it *is* valuable: a rarity. These things are often worth a great deal."

"How much?" she said. "Thousands?"

"Oh no, not thousands—perhaps fifty or a hundred. I wasn't thinking of the money."

"You should," she said and began to wag her foot up and down. Afterwards he remembered the sudden small frenzy of her foot and, once more, that drooping eyelid that gave him the impression he was talking to two women at once.

"Anyway," she said and the eye opened, "you live in that awful house, those mean miserly little windows! And those stone floors! It was so damp! It was ruining his books—he'd lived there for years. The chimney smoked too. Poor Ossy, he ought to have been a priest. But I heard some rich man bought the place and made a lot of improvements, made it fit to live in. Ossy was very—you know—close."

The doctor was annoyed to hear his dream attacked. "I've put the bay windows back. They give the place its date—1820— its character. And the stone floors too; of course, I put in a damp course. I wanted it to be as it was in John's time," he said stoutly. And he went on to describe all the things he had done, room by room, until he saw again that she was not listening to him but studying him in detail, with a pleased ironical flirtatious smile on her face. She interrupted him.

"Does your wife like it?" she said. "Are you married?"

"Oh no, not actually," said the doctor, finding himself to his surprise apologizing.

"Why do you say 'not actually'?" She laughed. "I mean, it's not my business," said Miss Ward.

The biographer did not like being questioned. He jerked a thumb at his life as he did at things. He explained about his mother.

"Those mothers!" she said. "Was she an invalid?"

He decided to stop her questions and to get *his* life out of the way as quickly as possible by a comic exaggeration. "She had enormous, one might almost say preposterous, good health. Her death was a shock." For he himself still felt an emptiness he was fighting to fill.

"It's so unfair. It leaves guilt. One is always a prisoner," she said and her little mouth—a spoiled mouth, he thought—slipped at the corners. Then she brightened.

"You know, Ossy and I were only married two years," she said invitingly. "I do not use his name."

"Yes, I gathered . . . I was going to ask you . . ."

"The traffic is terrible in this street. Can't you hear it, even at the back?" she said to the walls of the room.

"I can't say I do."

"Humming?" she said.

This worried her, but defying the traffic, she burst out with: "Two years! When I heard he was dying—I used to keep in touch with old Granny Blake in the village, I always sent a card every Christmas, she was really the only friend I had there—I felt I had to go and see him. Even after all those years one has a picture of people in one's head. I made Miss Carter drive me there. She tried to stop me, but I just had to go. Isn't that strange? After all, he had been my husband, in spite of everything, but leave that alone. It was really shocking—big gaps in the shelves in his library where I waited. Those stone floors. His sister wouldn't let me go up at first. She told Miss Carter I was drunk. I had to force my way upstairs. Miss Carter made her let me go. That room, that horrible bed—you know he had a terrible Spanish bed?—it was the bed that shocked me and the bedclothes had not been changed. He had died two hours before and, you won't believe it, they hadn't closed his eyes. Ossy was a big man, like you, and now his body was like   insect's. His teeth! He couldn't have minded if I was drunk,   e?"

     illiter murmured. The stern Miss Ward he had met the first   ared and the enamelled face cracked at the mouth into the ask her about the house if only she would let him direct the conversation.

"I'll show you something," she said and went to an album which was lying on a table and put it on his knee. There was an old picture of a boat lying on the hard and John, a big man with a heavy moustache and wearing a yachting cap, was standing with his arm around a young girl—herself. He had a rudder in his free hand.

"His sister," she said, "wouldn't go near the water. Not after he got stuck on a mud bank all night with her once."

"Ah now," said the doctor. "I remember hearing—"

"He didn't love her. He loved me," she said.

This is embarrassing but better, thought the doctor nervously.

"I can prove it," she said. "Come here." And she made him come to the French window that looked out on to a small paved garden with ferns planted against the walls and a pool with lilies in it. In the centre of the pool stood a stone figure.

"Ossy got Sidney McLaughlin to do it. Do you know his work?"

"I'm afraid I don't. You mean he did the statue?"

"Of course," she said. "It's me—soon after we were married."

"Very nice. Very pretty," he said politely.

"When I left his poor body in that room I walked up the path—you know the path, you must do—and there it was. He hadn't moved it. He'd kept it. After everything—bad things! That is love, isn't it?"

"You mean at Villas?" said Dr. Billiter, so embarrassed by this talk of love that he had not been looking at the figure but at the paving, noting that it was sandstone. And then the meaning of her words hit him.

"At Villas. Of course," she said.

Dr. Billiter looked closely at the figure and became flabby with unbelief. He studied the figure in every detail. With scarcely any doubt the figure was the one missing from the plinth in his garden and he fingered the catch on the window. Or was it a copy? Perhaps these ornamental figures were manufactured by the score. He could not speak. He glanced at Miss Ward and saw she was watching him with a look, half complacent, half cunning, a look that brought the village girl who worked for him to his mind. He had to struggle against his whole training and nature, against years of looking at rock and automatically naming it. Miss Ward was a deluded woman. He could not say to her, "I'm afraid you're mistaken or someone has taken you in. That figure is not you, it's one of a pair of ordinary ornamental figures that came from the garden at Stillbury Park. John's sister bought them. I've got the invoice in my papers."

"Of course I was young," she was now reciting calmly. "Long dresses had just come in for the evenings and one wore one's hair long and tied like that."

The doctor was helpless. Painfully he allowed himself to split in two. He allowed himself to drift away with her into fantasy. "You must feel very happy to be remembered. It's charming."

"And so *like*," she insisted. "You can see." And she fetched the photograph and made him look again at it.

There was not the slightest resemblance between the face and body of the statue and the fat girl with short black hair and wearing a heavy jersey and clumsy gumboots.

She must be mad, he thought. There was only one truth he could tell. "You have solved a mystery for me," he said. "I've often wondered what happened to the statue—you know, there is only the plinth there now, only the feet . . ."

"What feet? It's got feet," she said indignantly.

"I've asked everyone in the village what happened to it. No one knew."

"Who did you ask?" she said sharply.

"Everyone. Gardeners. Builders," he said. "The pair must have looked rather nice together."

"The pair?" she said. "There was only me. No one else."

Oh God, thought the doctor. I suppose people see only what they want to see.

"Anyway," he said, "it's the best piece of news I've had for a long time. To know it's safe. It's wonderful it came to you."

"He left nothing to me." ·

"Or perhaps his sister . . . ?" he suggested.

"His sister!" She laughed at that. "*You* didn't know her."

The doctor made a last attempt. "In the sale after he died?" he asked.

Miss Ward now laughed victoriously. Her fingers nipped his jacket by the sleeve and she drew him from the window. As he moved towards his chair she pulled his cuff tight and her fingers pinched as she made him flop beside her on the sofa. She leaned closely to him. "I stole it," she whispered.

"I don't believe you!" said Dr. Billiter as playfully as he could in his heavy way.

"I did. I stole it."

"A heavy thing like that," he teased. "You couldn't."

"I have *friends*," she said. And then she became querulous, talking to herself rather than to him; this talking, as if to someone else in the room, was one of the irritations in listening to her. She was saying, "Ossy's family said, 'Who are her people? Who are her friends?' " And then openly to him: "Who wants people? I have *friends*, very good friends, very close friends.

"Oh, it would make a wonderful story for your book! His sister shut up the house but she forgot one thing—you can't shut up a garden! It was screamingly funny. I won't tell you *who* they were, but they were *friends!* They got into the garden at night by the back lane and pulled it out—into their car, of course. I can't go on calling you Doctor—what do *your* friends call you?"

"James," he said, hating to give it to her.

"I shall call you Jimmy," she said. "Jimmy. It's such a thrill—stealing, don't you think? I bet you like stealing things?"

"I suppose the nearest I've come to it is forgetting to return a book. Sweets, of course, when I was a boy," he said.

"There you are!" she said. "You must call me Clarissa. When you were in the mines in Mexico, didn't you steal silver?"

"Of course not, Clarissa"—another surrender there—"it's just lumps of crystal."

"I would have!" she cried.

He was on the point of giving her a small lecture on the crystalline origin of ores, of striation, the seeping of water, the dead pressure of rock for hundreds of thousands of years—the knowledge was at his fingertips, but the faculty for uttering facts had left him. He was adrift in her imagination. There was a vacancy in his mind, and out of it, as her fingers pinched him, his mouth spouted one of the rare and reckless inspirations of his life. "You were not *stealing*," he said. "You were only taking what was your own."

"Yes," she said firmly.

"You were," he said, "taking yourself."

The moment he said this he couldn't believe that he had been capable of saying a thing so nonsensical and so cruelly untrue.

Miss Ward let go of his sleeve and moved away to look at him with wonder, a pretty wonder in which there was a tinge of morbid seductive gloom, like a shadow setting off a brilliant light. "You are a very clever man, Jimmy," she mumbled gravely. "I'm so grateful to you. It's a long

time, so long, long and long since I have been able to open my heart
to someone who understands. I can *talk* to you. I'm so glad you've
come." She jumped up. "We must drink to it! What will you drink?
Champagne? Yes, let us have champagne—but you'll have to open the
bottle. I can't stand noise." She put her hands to her ears.

"It's rather early," said Dr. Billiter.

"It isn't! Don't move. I'll get it."

He watched her walk out of the room and feared the prowl of her
arching feet. He went to the French windows and once more his
fingers went to the catch. Secretively he opened the door and stepped
into the little flagged garden and looked closely at the figure. Now
there was absolutely no doubt: the figure was not a copy, it *had* certainly come from Villas. The feet—left behind—had been replaced
and were awkwardly held to the figure by a rusting iron band. The
"friends" had been in a hurry and careless, if what she said was true:
there was a repaired crack across the waist. Very likely they had had
to carry the statue in two pieces. His mind was wandering into the
sadness of a hopeless lust and his hands itched. Morally the thing
belonged to Villas and to him. He felt ashamed, now that he was
alone, that he had not spoken out. Why should the delusions of others paralyze one's own desires? Why does one give in? A fantasy of
his own jumped into his mind. He saw himself telling her the truth,
bringing her to her senses. She gave in and begged him to take the
thing, generously he offered her money—she refused—he wrapped
the statue in sacking with his own hands, roped it, cased it, carted it
into his car and saw the amazement of the village as, in a self-dis-
paraging way and not to injure her—mustn't do that—he would say
that he had managed to find the figure in some garden shop or stone
mason's. In some way, John applauded . . .

The dream exhausted him. He heard Miss Ward's steps. He went
back to the room. At least now, he hoped, they would settle down and
he could ask her more questions.

"I was having another look at *you*," he said, nodding to the garden,
astounded to hear himself giving in to her once more as, carefully
putting a napkin over his hand, he removed the wire from the cork of
the bottle.

She put her hands to her ears. "I don't think you were a miner or
whatever you call it, Jimmy," she said. "I think you've been a waiter.
Is it over?"

"There," he said. And slowly poured out a glass.

"You're so attentive," she said. "I'm sure your real name is Charles. You were at the old Café Royal!"

"That's right!" He laughed. "And you ordered *quenelles de brochet.* I remember it like yesterday."

"Now you are making fun of me," she said severely.

Oh dear, she was beginning again.

"I am not. To the two goddesses," he said, raising his glass to her and to the figure.

"Whew!" she said when she drank and held out her glass for more. "You are a strange man," she said and her eyelid drooped. "Tell me truthfully"—she spoke of truth-telling as an abnormality—"why are you writing about Ossy, the house and everything? Changing it. Digging out that old Spanish bed?"

"I like doing things," he said. "That bed was a find."

"Not for Ossy," she said. "Not for me." She made a prudish horrified face. "It clattered! The noise!" she said. "I wasn't in love with him. He took me from my friends. I told you I had friends, a lot. He was years older than me and his sister watched me. If I was on the telephone, she always listened behind the door."

The doctor was not sure that *he* ought to listen to her. And he wished she had not brought in the champagne.

"*I* know why you took the house. Why do you want to be Ossy? Why do you want to be someone else? Did you do something"—she pouted —"*wrong* in Mexico? I mean—police?"

"Indeed not!" he said shortly.

"I did," she said proudly. "Ossy went off to Holland on the boat and I didn't want to go. I sold all his books, his father's books, while he was away—the valuable ones, I mean."

"I don't believe you," he said.

"Don't pretend to be stupid," she said. "Four thousand pounds. Well, he didn't give me any money. And other things too."

"I still don't believe you," he said.

"So I know why you have come here. You want to take my statue away. Someone told you I'd got it. You want to put it back on those horrible feet in your garden. I saw it when you were looking at it. That is why you kept writing letters, isn't it? Why do you keep on humming?" Her voice was becoming a shout.

He had never seen suspicion, despair and anger so suddenly splinter a face so that she turned into the old woman he had seen on the step the first time. Her face was cracking like stone and then, to his eyes, there was the mica-like glister of tears on it.

She dropped her glance to the floor and put her hands to her ears. "Stamp, stamp, stamp," she shouted like a soldier.

"Clarissa," he said. "Please. I've not come for your statue. I told you I did not know it was here."

She took her hands from her ears. "What did you say? Feet are stamping," she appealed to him.

"I said I haven't come for your statue."

"Yes you have. Why don't you take *me*, not that thing. Take me back to Villas with you. I'm in prison here." The eyelid did not droop: both eyes stared at him. "But you won't take me, will you? Oh no, you're frightened," she said slyly.

He was indeed frightened and appalled when she got up, thinking she was going to rush at him, but instead she went pathetically to the door and her hand struggled with the handle. Outside in the hall she called out, "Miss Carter. Miss Carter."

"She is mad," the doctor said aloud; "she is calling to the dead. She had got my book in her hand."

He lumbered after her. What does one do with mad women? Shake them? Startle them? Shock them by an enormous shout? She was going up the stairs, holding on to the banister. One shoe had fallen off and, out of politeness, he picked it up.

"Clarissa!" he bellowed. "You've got my book."

And following her cautiously, fearing he might have to grapple with her, he heard a door open above and saw a frail old woman in a dressing gown looking over the banister. She was carrying a stick.

"What is it, darling?" the old woman said in a voice like a man's. "Why are you dressed up like that? You know it's forbidden." And dropping her stick, gripping the rail and in pain, one arm useless, the woman he had been told was dead grunted down the stairs.

"The police have come," Miss Ward sobbed. "Help me."

The old woman stopped and called out, "You are Dr. Billiter. I told you not to come here. Look what you've done. Stay where you are."

Miss Ward reached the old woman, who put her arm around her and said, "There, darling. It's all right."

"Let me help," said Dr. Billiter. "I understood—"

"Go away," called the old lady. "She needs me. You don't understand. Please go. Go at once."

"She said . . ." the doctor began. "She has my book . . ."

"I know what she said," the old woman said. "You're a naughty girl, darling, dressing up like that. You know that as long as I am alive I'll look after you."

"He's trying to take me away," Miss Ward whispered. "Make him go. I haven't done anything." She let the book drop from her hand.

"You can do one thing," the old woman called over Miss Ward's head to Dr. Billiter. "You can ring Dr. Gates. The number's in the red book in the front room. He knows."

And the old woman sat on the stairs holding Miss Ward as Dr. Billiter crawled up after the book and put the shoe down. "Shoe," he said out of habit and went down to the telephone.

When he came back and stood on the linoleum in the hall, he saw there was no one on the stairs. The house was silent. He waited and then he tiptoed to the door and went out into the street and stood still, breathless, not knowing where he was, until he saw his car. It was a long time before he could recall how to drive it and where he was going, and when the cars raced past him, heading for God knows where, and as the fields and trees and towns lurched at him as if they were going to vomit over him, he could only think: Carter alive! Carter alive! He rustled the biscuit bag in his pocket, but could not eat. Three hours on the road! Turned sixty as he was, he wished his mother were fulminating beside him. When at last he got to Villas, its windows catching the sea-light of the evening, the sight calmed him, but once he was inside he was scared by the speechless doors in the rooms. He could not rid himself of the feeling that they were closed against him, that the place was not his and that Clarissa Ward would open them and even John himself would be in his study, laughing at his notes and files.

That night he did not sleep in the Spanish bed. In the morning, looking out of the spare-room window at the back he saw the empty plinth. Pointlessly he waved an arm at it, and then, at nine o'clock, the village girl came.

"When I come yes'day," she said, accusing him, "you wasn't there."

She had uttered, it seemed to him, a profound truth.

A month or so later there was a letter from Miss Carter enclosing a cutting from a Nottingham paper: "Sept. 17th, Clarissa Ward, *tragically* . . ." He knew what the word meant. She had wanted that tragedy to occur at Villas!

The Satisfactory

"When one says that what one is still inclined to call civilization is passing through a crisis," Mr. Plymbell used to say during the last war and after it when food was hard to get, and standing in his very expensive antique shop, raising a white and more than Roman nose and watching the words go off one by one in the air and circle the foreign customer, "one is tempted to ask oneself whether or not a few possibly idle phrases that one let fall to one's old friend Lady Hackthorpe at a moment of national distress in 1940 are not, in fact, still pertinent. One recalls observing, rightly or wrongly, at that time that one was probably witnessing not the surrender of an heroic ally but the defeat of sauces. Béarnaise, hollandaise, madère—one saw them overrun. One can conceive of the future historian's enquiring whether the wars of the last ten years, and indeed what one calls 'the peace,' have not been essentially an attack on gastronomy, on the stomach and palate of the human race. One could offer the modest example of one's daily luncheon . . ."

Mr. Plymbell can talk like *The Times* forever. Not all the campaigns of our time have been fought on the battlefield. His lunch in those bad days was a study.

At two minutes before half past twelve every day, Plymbell was first in the queue in the foyer outside the locked glass doors of Polli's

Restaurant, a few yards from his shop. On one side of the glass Plymbell floated—handsome, Roman, silver-haired, as white-skinned and consequent as a turbot of fifty; on the other side of the glass, in the next aquarium, stood Polli with the key in his hand waiting for the clock to strike the half hour—a man liverish and suspended in misanthropy like a tench in the weed of a canal. Plymbell stared clean through Polli to the sixty empty tables beyond; Polli stared clean through the middle of Plymbell into the miasma of the restaurant-keeper's life. Two fish gazed with the indifference of creatures who have accepted the fact that neither of them is edible. What they wanted, what the whole of England was crying for, was not fish but red meat, and to get meat at Polli's one had to be there at half past twelve, on the dot.

First customer in was Plymbell. He had his table, in the middle of this chipped Edwardian place, with his back to one of those white pillars that gave it the appearance of a shop-soiled wedding cake mounted on a red carpet, and he faced the serving hatch. Putting up a monocle to his more annoyed eye, he watched the chef standing over his pans, and while he watched he tapped the table with lightly frantic fingers. Polli's waiters were old men, and the one who served Plymbell had the dejected smirk of a convict.

Plymbell used hardly to glance at the farcical menu and never looked at the waiter when he coldly gave his order. "Two soups," said Plymbell. "Two roast beefs . . . Cheese and biscuits," he added. "Bring me mine now and you can bring the second order in a quarter of an hour, when my secretary arrives."

It was a daily scene. Plymbell's waiter came forward with his dishes like one hurrying a funeral in a hot country, feebly averting his nose from the mess he was carrying on his dish. He scraped his serving spoons and, at the end, eyed his customer with criminal scorn. Plymbell's jaws moved over this stuff with a slow social agony. In fifteen minutes he had eaten his last biscuit and was wetting his finger to pick up the small heap of crumbs he had worked to one side of his plate. Plymbell looked at his watch.

Exactly at this moment Plymbell's assistant used to come in. Shabby, thin, with wrinkled cotton stockings and dressed in black, a woman of forty-five, Miss Tell scraped on poor shoes to the table. She carried newspapers in a bundle under an arm and a basket in her hand. He would look carefully away from her as she alighted like some dingy fly at the other side of the table. It was astonishing to see a man so well dressed lunching with a woman so bowed and faded. But presently she would do a conjuring trick. Opening her bundle, Miss Tell put a newspaper down on the roll of bread on her side plate and then she picked it up again. The roll of bread had gone. She had slipped it into her lap. A minute passed while she wriggled to and fro like a laying hen, and then she would drop the roll into the basket by the leg of her chair.

Plymbell would be looking away from her while she did this and, his lips hardly moving, he would speak one word.

"What?" was the word.

She replied also with one word—the word naturally varied—cringing toward him, looking with fear, trying to get him to look at her.

"Sausages," she might whisper.

"How many?" Plymbell would ask. He still did not look at her.

"Half pound," she said. On some fortunate days: "A pound."

Plymbell studied the domed skylight in the ceiling of the restaurant. The glass was still out in those days; the boards put there during the war when a bomb blew out the glass had not been replaced. Meanwhile the waiter brought a plate of soup to Miss Tell. She would stare at the soup without interest. When the waiter went, she lifted the plate across the table and put it in Plymbell's place and then lowered her head in case other customers had seen. Plymbell had not seen, because he had been gazing at the ceiling, but, as if absent-mindedly, he picked up a spoon and began to drink Miss Tell's soup, and when he had finished, put her plate back on her side of the table, and the waiter took it away.

Plymbell had been lunching at Polli's for years. He used to lunch there before the war with Lady Hackthorpe. She was a handsome woman—well-cut clothes, well-cut diamonds, brilliantly cut eyes, and sharply cut losses. Plymbell bought and sold for her, decorated her house.

Miss Tell used to go home to her parents in the evenings and say: "I don't understand it. I make out her bill every month and he says: 'Miss Tell, give me Lady Hackthorpe's bill,' and tears it up."

Miss Tell lived by what she did not understand. It was an appetite.

After 1940, no more Lady Hackthorpe. A bomb cut down half of her house and left a Hepplewhite bed full of broken glass and ceiling plaster on the first floor, and a servant's washstand on the floor above. Lady Hackthorpe went to Ireland.

Plymbell got the bed and a lot of other things out of the house into his shop. Here again there was something Miss Tell did not understand. She was supposed to "keep the books straight." Were Lady Hackthorpe's things being "stored" or were they being "returned to stock"?

"I mean," Miss Tell said, "if anyone was killed when a thing is left open it's unsatisfactory."

Plymbell listened and did not answer. He was thinking of other things. The war on the stomach and the palate had begun. Not only had Lady Hackthorpe gone. Plymbell's business was a function of Lady Hackthorpe's luncheons and dinners, and other people's, too. He was left with his mouth open in astonishment and hunger.

"Trade has stopped now," Miss Tell said one night when she ducked into the air-raid shelter with her parents. "Poor Mr. Plymbell never goes out."

"Why doesn't he close the business, Kitty?" Miss Tell's mother said.

"And leave all that valuable stock?" said Mr. Tell. "Where's your brain?"

"I never could fathom business," said Mrs. Tell.

"It's the time to pick up things," said Mr. Tell.

"That's a way to talk when we may all be dead in a minute," said Mrs. Tell.

Mr. Tell said something about prices being bound to go up, but a huge explosion occurred and he stopped.

"And this Lady Hackthorpe—is she *friendly* with this Plymbell?" said old Mrs. Tell when the explosion settled in as part of the furniture of their lives.

"*Mr.* Plymbell," Miss Tell corrected her mother. Miss Tell had a poor, fog-coloured London skin and blushed in a patch across her forehead. "I don't *query* his private life."

"He's a man," sighed Mrs. Tell. "To hear you talk he might be the Fairy Prince or Lord Muck himself. Listen to those guns. You've been there fifteen years."

"It takes two to be friendly," said Miss Tell, who sometimes spoke like a poem. "When one goes away, it may be left open one way or another, I mean, and that—" Miss Tell searched for a new word but returned to the old one, the only one that ever, for her, met the human case. "And that," she said, "is unsatisfactory."

"You're neurotic," her mother said. "You never have any news."

And then Miss Tell had a terrible thought. "Mum!" she cried, dropping the poetic accent she brought back from the West End every night; "where's Tiger? We've left him in the house."

Her mother became swollen with shame.

"You left him," accused Miss Tell. "You left him in the kitchen." She got up. "No one's got any heart. I'm going to get him."

"You stay here, my girl," said Mr. Tell.

"Come back, Kitty," said Mrs. Tell.

But Miss Tell (followed across the garden, as it seemed to her, by an aeroplane) went to the house. In her panic Mrs. Tell had left not only the cat; she had left her handbag and her ration books on the kitchen table. Miss Tell picked up the bag and then kneeled under the table looking for Tiger. "Tiger, dear! Tiger!" she called. He was not there. It was at this instant that the aeroplane outside seemed to have followed her into the house. When Miss Tell was dug out alive and unhurt, black with dust, six hours later, Mr. and Mrs. Tell were dead in the garden.

When Plymbell talks of that time now, he says there were moments when one was inclined to ask oneself whether the computed odds of something like eight hundred and ninety-seven thousand to one in favour of one's nightly survival were not, perhaps, an evasion of a private estimate one had arrived at without any special statistical apparatus—that it was fifty-fifty, and even providential. It was a point, he said, one recollected making to one's assistant at the time, when she came back.

Miss Tell came back to Plymbell's at lunch-time one day a fortnight after she had been dug out. She was singular: she had been saved by looking for her cat. Mr. Plymbell was not at the shop or in his rooms above it. In the vainglory of her escape she went round to Polli's. Plymbell was more than half-way through his meal when he saw her come in. She was wearing no hat on her dusty black hair, and under her black coat, which so often had ends of cotton on it, she was wearing navy-blue trousers. Plymbell winced: it was the human aspect of war that was so lowering; he saw at once that Miss Tell had become a personality. Watching the wag of her narrow shoulders as she walked, he saw she had caught the general immodesty of the "bombed out."

Without being invited, she sat down at his table and put herself sideways, at her ease, crossing her legs to show her trousers. Her face had filled out into two little puffs of vanity on either side of her mouth, as if she were eating or were containing a yawn. The two rings of age on her neck looked like a cheap necklace. Lipstick was for the first time on her lips. It looked like blood.

"One enquired in vain," said Plymbell with condescension. "I am glad to see you back."

"I thought I might as well pop round," said Miss Tell.

Mr. Plymbell was alarmed; her note was breezy. "Aren't you coming back?"

"I haven't found Tiger," said Miss Tell.

"Tiger?"

Miss Tell told him her story.

Plymbell saw that he must try to put himself for a moment in his employee's situation and think of her grief. "One recalls the thought that passed through one's mind when one's own mother died," he said.

"They had had their life," said Miss Tell.

A connoisseur by trade, Plymbell was disappointed by the banality of Miss Tell's remark. What was grief? It was a hunger. Not merely personal, emotional, and spiritual; it was physical. Plymbell had been forty-two when his mother died, and he, her only child, had always lived with her. Her skill with money, her jackdaw eye had made the business. The morning she died in hospital he had felt that a cave had been opened inside his body under the ribs, a cave getting larger and colder and emptier. He went out and ate one of the largest meals of his life.

While Miss Tell, a little fleshed already in her tragedy, was still talking, the waiter came to the table with Plymbell's allowance of cheese and biscuits.

Plymbell remembered his grief. "Bring me another portion for my secretary," he said.

"Oh no, not for me," said Miss Tell. She was too dazed by the importance of loss to eat. "I couldn't."

But Polli's waiter had a tired, deaf head. He came back with biscuits for Miss Tell.

Miss Tell looked about the restaurant until the waiter left and then coquettishly she passed her plate to Plymbell. "For you," she said. "I couldn't."

Plymbell thought Miss Tell ill-bred to suggest that he would eat what she did not want. He affected not to notice and gazed over her head, but his white hand had already taken the plate, and in a moment, still looking disparagingly beyond her, in order not to catch her eye, Mr. Plymbell bit into one of Miss Tell's biscuits. Miss Tell was smiling slyly.

After he had eaten her food, Mr. Plymbell looked at Miss Tell with a warmer interest. She had come to work for him in his mother's time, more than fifteen years before. Her hair was still black, her skin was now grey and yellow with a lilac streak on the jaw, there were sharp stains like poor coffee under her eyes. These were brown with a circle of gold in the pupils, and they seemed to burn as if there were a fever in their shadows. Her black coat, her trousers, her cotton blouse were cheap, and even her body seemed to be thin with cheapness. Her speech was awkward, for part of her throat was trying to speak in a refined accent and the effect was half arrogant, half disheartened. Now, as he swallowed the last piece of biscuit, she seemed to him to change. Her eyes were brilliant. She had become quietly a human being.

What is a human being? The chef, whom he could see through the hatch, was one; Polli, who was looking at the menu by the cash desk, was another; his mother, who had made remarkable ravioli; people like Lady Hackthorpe, who had given such wonderful dinner parties before the war—that circle which the war had scattered and where he had moved from one lunch to the next in a life that rippled to the sound of changing plates that tasted of sauces now never made. These people had been human beings. One knew a human being when the juices flowed over one's teeth. A human being was a creature who fed one. Plymbell moved his jaws. Miss Tell's sly smile went. He looked as though he was going to eat *her*.

"You had better take the top room at the shop," he said. "Take the top room if you have nowhere to live."

"But I haven't found Tiger," Miss Tell said. "He must be starving."

"You won't be alone," said Plymbell. "I sleep at the shop."

Miss Tell considered him. Plymbell could see she was weighing him against Tiger in her mind. He had offered her the room because she had fed him.

"You have had your lunch, I presume," said Plymbell as they walked back to the shop.

"No—I mean yes. Yes, no," said Miss Tell secretively, and again there was the blush like a birthmark on her forehead.

"Where do you go?" said Plymbell, making a shameful enquiry.

"Oh," said Miss Tell defensively, as if it were a question of chastity. "Anywhere. I manage. I vary." And when she said she varied, Miss Tell looked with a virginal importance first one way and then the other.

"That place starves one," said Plymbell indignantly. "One comes out of there some days and one is weak with hunger."

Miss Tell's flush went. She was taken by one of those rages that shake the voices and the bones of unmarried women, as if they were going to shake the nation by the scruff of its neck. "It's wrong, Mr. Plymbell. The government ought to give men more rations. A man needs food. Myself, it never worries me. I never eat. Poor mother used to say: 'Eat, girl, eat.' " A tear came to Miss Tell's right eye, enlarged it, and made it liquid, burning, beautiful. "It was funny, I didn't seem to fancy anything. I just picked things over and left them."

"I never heard of anyone who found the rations too much," said Mr. Plymbell with horror.

"I hardly touch mine since I was bombed out," said Miss Tell, and she straightened her thin, once humble body, raised her small bosom, which was ribbed like a wicker basket, gave her hair a touch or two, and looked with delicate resolution at Plymbell. "I sometimes think of giving my ration books away," she said in an offhand way.

Plymbell gaped at the human being in front of him. "Give them away!" he exclaimed. "Them? Have you got more than one?"

"I've got father's and mother's, too."

"But one had gathered that the law required one to surrender the official documents of the deceased," said Plymbell, narrowing his eyes suggestively. His heart had livened, his mouth was watering.

Miss Tell moved her erring shoulders, her eyes became larger, her lips drooped. "It's wicked of me," she said.

Plymbell took her thin elbow in his hand and contained his anxiety. "I should be very careful about those ration books. I shouldn't mention it. There was a case in the paper the other day."

They had reached the door of the shop. "How is Lady Hackthorpe?" Miss Tell asked. "Is she still away?"

Miss Tell had gone too far; she was being familiar. Plymbell put up his monocle and did not reply.

A time of torture began for Plymbell when Miss Tell moved in. He invited her to the cellar on the bad nights, but Miss Tell had become light-headed with fatalism and would not move from her bed on the top floor. In decency Plymbell had to remain in his bed and take shelter no more. Above him slept the rarest of human beings, a creature who had three ration books, a woman who was technically three people. He feared for her at every explosion. His mouth watered when he saw her: the woman with three books who did not eat and who thought only of how hungry Tiger must be. If he could have turned himself into a cat!

At one point Plymbell decided that Miss Tell was like Lady Hackthorpe with her furniture; Miss Tell wanted money. He went to the dark corner behind a screen between his own office and the shop, where sometimes she sewed. When he stood by the screen he was nearly on top of her. "If," he said in a high, breaking voice that was strange even to himself, "if you are ever thinking of *selling* your books . . ."

He had made a mistake. Miss Tell was mending and the needle was pointing at him as she stood up. "I couldn't do that," she said. "It is forbidden by the law." And she looked at him strictly.

Plymbell gaped before her hypocrisy. Miss Tell's eyes became larger, deeper, and liquid in the dusk of the corner where she worked. Her chin moved up in a number of amused, resentful movements; her lips moved. "Good God," thought Plymbell, "is she eating?" Her thin arms were slack, her body was inert. She continued to move her dry lips. She leaned her head sideways and raised one eye. Plymbell could not believe what he saw. Miss Tell was plainly telling him: "Yes, I *have* got something in my mouth. It is the desire to be kissed."

Or was he wrong? Plymbell was not a kissing man. His white, demanding face was indeed white with passion, and his lips were shaped for sensuality, but the passion of the gourmet, the libidinousness of the palate, gave him his pallor. He had felt desire, in his way, for Lady Hackthorpe, but it had been consummated in bisques, in *crêpes*, in *flambées*, in *langouste* done in many manners, in *ailloli*, in bouillabaisse and vintage wines. That passion had been starved, and he was perturbed by Miss Tell's signal. One asks oneself (he reflected, going to his office and considering reproachfully his mother's photograph, which stood on his desk)—one asks oneself whether or not a familiar adage about Nature's abhorrence of a vacuum had not a certain relevance, and indeed whether one would not be justified in coining a vulgar phrase to the effect that when one shuts the front door on Nature, she comes in at the back. Miss Tell was certainly the back; one might call her the scullery of the emotions.

Plymbell lowered his pale eyelids in a flutter of infidelity, unable honestly to face his mother's stare. Her elderly aquiline nose, her close-curled silver hair tipped with a touch of fashionable idiocy off the forehead, her too-jewelled, hawking, grabbing, slapdash face derided him for the languor of the male symptom, and at the same time, with the ratty double-facedness of her sex, spoke sharply about flirtations with employees. Plymbell's eyes lied to her image. All the same, he tried to calm himself by taking a piece of violet notepaper and dashing off a letter to Lady Hackthorpe. Avocado pear, he wrote, whitebait (did she think?), *bœuf bourguignon*, or what about *dindonneau* in those Italian pastes? It was a letter of lust. He addressed the envelope, and, telling Miss Tell to post it, Plymbell pulled down the points of his slack waistcoat and felt saved.

So saved that when Miss Tell came back and stood close to his desk, narrow and flat in her horrible trousers, and with her head turned to the window, showing him her profile, Plymbell felt she was satirically flirting with his hunger. Indignantly he got up and, before he knew what he was doing, he put his hand under her shoulder blade and kissed her on the lips.

A small frown came between Miss Tell's eyebrows. Her lips were tight and set. She did not move. "Was that a bill you sent to Lady Hackthorpe?" she asked.

"No," said Plymbell. "A personal letter."

Miss Tell left his office.

Mr. Plymbell wiped his mouth on his handkerchief. He was shocked by himself; even more by the set lips, the closed teeth, the hard chin of Miss Tell; most of all by her impertinence. He had committed a folly for nothing and he had been insulted.

The following morning Plymbell went out on his weekly search for food, but he was too presumptuous for the game. In the coarse world of provisions and the black market, the monocle was too fine. Plymbell lacked the touch; in a long day all he managed to get were four fancy cakes. Miss Tell came out of her dark corner and looked impersonally at him. He was worn out.

"No offal," he said in an appalled, hoarse voice. "No offal in the whole of London."

"Ooh," said Miss Tell, quick as a sparrow. "I got some. Look." And she showed him her disgusting, blood-stained triumph on its piece of newspaper.

Never had Miss Tell seemed so common, so flagrant, so lacking in sensibility, but also never had she seemed so desirable. And then, as before, she became limp and neutral and she raised her chin. There were the unmistakable crumb-licking movements of her lips. Plymbell saw her look sideways at him as she turned. Was she inviting him to wipe out the error of the previous day? With one eye on the meat, Plymbell made a step towards her, and in a moment Miss Tell was on him, kissing him, open-mouthed and with frenzy, her fingernails in his arms, and pressing herself to him to the bone.

"Sweetbreads," she said. "For you. I never eat them. Let me cook them for you."

An hour later she was knocking at the door of his room, and carrying a loaded tray. It was laid, he was glad to notice, for one person only. Plymbell said: "One had forgotten what sweetbreads were."

"It was nothing. I have enjoyed your confidence for fifteen years," said Miss Tell in her poetic style. And the enlarged eyes looked at him with an intimate hunger.

That night, as usual, Plymbell changed into a brilliant dressing gown, and, standing before the mirror, he did his hair, massaging with the fingers, brushing first with the hard ivory brush and then with the soft one. As he looked into the glass, Miss Tell's enquiring face kept floating into it, displacing his own.

"Enjoyed my confidence!" said Plymbell.

In her bedroom Miss Tell turned out the light, drew back the curtains, and looked into the London black and at the inane triangles of the searchlights. She stood there listening. "Tiger, Tiger," she murmured. "Where are you? Why did you go away from me? I miss you in my bed. Are you hungry? I had a lovely dinner ready for you— sweetbreads. I had to give it to him because you didn't come."

In answer, the hungry siren went like the wail of some monstrous, disembodied Tiger, like all the dead cats of London restless beyond the grave.

Miss Tell drew the curtains and lay down on her bed. "Tiger," she said crossly, "if you don't come tomorrow, I shall give everything to him. He needs it. Not that he deserves it. Filling up the shop with that woman's furniture, storing it free of charge, writing her letters, ruining himself for her. I hate her. I always have. I don't understand him and her, how she gets away with it, owing money all round. She's got a hold—"

The guns broke out. They were declaring war upon Lady Hackthorpe.

Tiger did not come back, and rabbit was dished up for Plymbell. He kissed Miss Tell a third time. It gave him the agreeable sensation that he was doing something for the war. After the fourth kiss Plymbell became worried. Miss Tell had mentioned stuffed veal. She had spoken of mushrooms. He had thoughtlessly exceeded in his embrace. He had felt for the first time in his life—voluptuousness; he had discovered how close to eating kissing is, and as he allowed his arm to rest on Miss Tell's lower-class waist, he had had the inadvertent impression of picking up a cutlet in his fingers. Plymbell felt he had done enough for the vanity of Miss Tell. He was in the middle of this alarmed condition when Miss Tell came into his office and turned his alarm to consternation.

"I've come to give my notice," she said.

Plymbell was appalled. "What is wrong, Miss Tell?" he said.

"Nothing's wrong," said Miss Tell. "I feel I am not needed."

"Have I offended you?" said Plymbell suspiciously. "Is it money?"

Miss Tell looked sharply. She was insulted. "No," she said. "Money is of no interest to me. I've got nothing to do. Trade's stopped."

Plymbell made a speech about trade.

"I think I must have got—" Miss Tell searched for a word and lost her poetic touch—"browned off," she said, and blushed. "I'll get a job in a canteen. I like cooking."

Plymbell in a panic saw not one woman but three women leaving him. "But you are cooking for me," he said.

Miss Tell shrugged.

"Oh, yes, you are. Miss Tell—be my housekeeper."

"Good God," thought Plymbell afterwards, "so that was all she wanted. I needn't have kissed her at all."

How slowly one learns about human nature, he thought. Here was a woman with one simple desire; to serve him—to slave for him, to stand in queues, to cook, to run his business, do everything. And who did not eat.

"I shall certainly not kiss her again," he said.

At this period of his life, with roofs leaving their buildings and servants leaving their places all round him, Plymbell often reflected guardedly upon his situation. There was, he had often hinted, an art in keeping servants. He appeared, he noted, to have this art. But would he keep it? What was it? Words of his mother's came back to him: "Miss Tell left a better job and higher wages to come to me. This job is more flattering to her self-importance." "Never consider them, never promise; they will despise you. The only way to keep servants is to treat them like hell. Look at Lady Hackthorpe's couple. They'd die for her. They probably will."

Two thousand years of civilization lay in those remarks.

"And never be familiar." Guiltily, he could imagine Lady Hackthorpe putting in her word. As the year passed, as his nourishment improved, the imaginary Lady Hackthorpe rather harped on the point.

There was no doubt about it, Plymbell admitted, he *had* been familiar. But only four times, he protested. And what is a kiss, in an office? At this he could almost hear Lady Hackthorpe laughing, in an insinuating way, that she hardly imagined there could be any question of his going any farther.

Plymbell, now full of food, blew up into a temper with the accusing voices. He pitched into Miss Tell. He worked out a plan of timely dissatisfaction. His first attack upon her was made in the shop in the presence of one of the rare customers of those days.

"Why no extra liver this week, Miss Tell? My friend here has got some," he said.

Miss Tell started, then blushed on the forehead. It was, he saw, a blush of pleasure. Public humiliation seemed to delight Miss Tell. He made it harder. "Why no eggs?" he shouted down the stairs, and on another day, as if he had a whip in his hand: "Anyone can get olive oil." Miss Tell smiled and looked a little sideways at him.

Seeing he had not hurt her in public, Plymbell then made a false move. He called her to his room above the shop and decided to "blow her up" privately.

"I can't *live* on fish," he began. But whereas, delighted to be noticed, she listened to his public complaints in the shop, she did not listen in his room. By his second sentence, she had turned her back and wandered to the sofa. From there she went to his writing-table, trailing a finger on it. She was certainly not listening. In the middle of his speech and as his astounded, colourless eyes followed her, she stopped and pointed through the double doors where his bedroom was and she pointed to the Hepplewhite bed.

"Is that Lady Hackthorpe's, too?" she said.

"Yes," said Plymbell.

"Why do you have it up here?" she said rudely.

"Because I like it," said Plymbell, snubbing her.

"I think four-posters are unhealthy," said Miss Tell, and circled with meandering impertinence to the window and looked out on the street. "That old man," she said, admitting the vulgar world into the room, "is always going by."

Miss Tell shrugged at the window and considered the bed again across the space of two rooms. Then, impersonally, she made a speech. "I never married," she said. "I have been friendly but not married. One great friend went away. There was no agreement, nothing said, he didn't write and I didn't write. In those cases I sympathize with the wife, but I wondered when he didn't communicate. I didn't know whether it was over or not over, and when you don't know, it isn't satisfactory. I don't say it was anything, but I would have liked to know whether it was or not. I never mention it to anyone."

"Oh," said Plymbell.

"It upset Dad," said Miss Tell, and of that she was proud.

"I don't follow," said Plymbell. He wanted to open the window and let Miss Tell's private life out.

"It's hard to describe something unsatisfactory," said Miss Tell. And then: "Dad was conventional."

Mr. Plymbell shuddered.

"Are you interested?" asked Miss Tell.

"Please, please go on," said Plymbell.

"I have been 'the other woman' three times," said Miss Tell primly.

Plymbell put up his monocle, but as far as he could judge, all Miss Tell had done was make a public statement. He could think of no reply. His mind drifted. Suddenly he heard the voice of Miss Tell again, trembling, passionate, raging as it had been once before, at Polli's, attacking him.

"She uses you," Miss Tell was saying. "She puts all her rubbish into your shop, she fills up your flat. She won't let you sell it. She hasn't paid you. Storage is the dearest thing in London. You could make a profit, you would turn over your stock. Now is the time to buy, Dad said. . . ."

Plymbell picked up his paper.

"Lady Hackthorpe," explained Miss Tell, and he saw her face, small-mouthed and sick and shaking with jealousy.

"Lady Hackthorpe has gone to America," Plymbell said, in his snubbing voice.

Miss Tell's rage had spent itself. "If you were not so horrible to me, I would tell you an idea," she said.

"Horrible? My dear Miss Tell," said Mr. Plymbell, leaning back as far as he could in his chair.

"It doesn't matter," said Miss Tell, and she walked away. "When is Lady Hackthorpe coming back?" she said.

"After the war, I suppose," said Plymbell.

"Oh," said Miss Tell, without belief.

"What is your idea?"

"Oh no. It was about lunch. At Polli's. It is nothing," said Miss Tell.

"Lunch," said Plymbell with a start, dropping his eyeglass. "What about lunch?" And his mouth stayed open.

Miss Tell turned about and approached him. "No, it's unsatisfactory," said Miss Tell. She gave a small laugh and then made the crumb movements with her chin.

"Come here," commanded Plymbell. "What idea about lunch?"

Miss Tell did not move, and so he got up, in a panic now. A suspicion came to him that Polli's had been bombed, that someone—perhaps Miss Tell herself—was going to take his lunch away from him. Miss Tell did not move. Mr. Plymbell did not move. Feeling weak, Mr. Plymbell decided to sit down again. Miss Tell came and sat on the arm of his chair.

"Nothing," she said, looking into his eyes for a long time and then turning away. "You have been horrible to me for ten months and thirteen days. You know you have." Her back was to him.

Slices of pork, he saw, mutton, beef. He went through a nightmare that he arrived at Polli's late, all the customers were inside, and the glass doors were locked. The headwaiter was standing there refusing to open. Miss Tell's unnourished back made him think of this. He did no more than put his hand on her shoulder, as slight as a chicken bone, and as he did so, he seemed to hear a sharp warning snap from Lady Hackthorpe. "Gus," Lady Hackthorpe seemed to say, "what are you doing? Are you mad? Don't you know why Miss Tell had to leave her last place?" But Lady Hackthorpe's words were smothered. A mere touch —without intention on Plymbell's part—had impelled Miss Tell to slide backward on to his lap.

"How have I been horrid to you?" said Plymbell, forgetting to put inverted commas round the word "horrid."

"You know," said Miss Tell.

"What was this idea of yours," he said quietly, and he kissed her neck. "No, no," she said, and moved her head to the other side of his neck. There was suddenly a sound that checked them both. Her shoe fell off. And then an extraordinary thing happened to Plymbell. The sight of Miss Tell's foot without its shoe did it. At fifty, he felt the first indubitable symptom. A scream went off inside his head—Lady Hackthorpe nagging him about some man she had known who had gone to bed with his housekeeper. "Ruin," Lady Hackthorpe was saying.

"About lunch—it was a good idea," Miss Tell said tenderly into his collar.

But it was not until three in the morning that Miss Tell told Plymbell what the idea was.

And so, every weekday, there was the modest example of Mr. Plymbell's daily luncheon. The waiter used to take the empty soup plate away from Miss Tell and presently came forward with the meat and vegetables. He scraped them off his serving dish on to her plate. She would keep her head lowered for a while, and then, with a glance to see if other customers were looking, she would lift the plate over to Mr. Plymbell's place. He, of course, did not notice. Then, absently, he settled down to eat her food. While he did this, he muttered, "What did you get?" She nodded at her stuffed basket and answered. Mr. Plymbell ate two lunches. While this went on, Miss Tell looked at him. She was in a strong position now. Hunger is the basis of life and, for her, a great change had taken place. The satisfactory had occurred.

But now, of course, French cookery has come back.

1955

About the Author

V. S. PRITCHETT was born in 1900. In addition to being a short-story writer, he is a critic, autobiographer, biographer, novelist, and travel writer. Sir Victor is a foreign honorary member of the American Academy of Arts and Letters and of the Academy of Arts and Sciences. He is a vice-president of the Royal Society of Literature. In 1975 he received a knighthood. He lives in London with his wife.